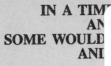

Joanne

IN A TIME ~~OF BITTER TRAGEDY~~
AN~~D ...~~
SOME WOULD ~~LIVE, SOME WOULD~~ **DIE,**
AND ~~...~~

Michou Valet ~~te: The war that~~ made
her a woman, she ~~held fast to a land she could~~ not
lose—and a man she would not, dared not love . . .

Guy Chalmers: An American winebroker and secret agent of the Resistance, he discovered with
Michou a hunger he'd buried long ago. Now he would
fight by her side—for her precious vineyards and her
proud heart . . .

Lucien Desroches: The war made him rich; the
past made him powerful. Now an insatiable lust for
Michou would make him reckless—and deadly . . .

Erich Mueller: The Nazi lieutenant knew his desire
for Michou was forbidden and dangerous—but he
would risk everything for a fleeting moment of her
love . . .

Alexandre Valette: Michou's father lived for his
child, his land, his country—and nothing would take
them from him. Nothing . . .

Sylvie de Bacqueville: Michou's cousin, her de-
ceptive charm and alluring beauty concealed an insatiable hunger that would shock any woman—and
seduce any man . . .

**IT WAS A TIME
OF TREACHERY AND BLAZING
PASSION . . . A TIME OF**

BLOOD AND WINE

Penny Colvin

POCKET BOOKS

New York   London   Toronto   Sydney   Tokyo

An *Original* Publication of POCKET BOOKS

 POCKET BOOKS, a division of Simon & Schuster Inc.
1230 Avenue of the Americas, New York, NY 10020

ISBN: 0-671-63391-0

First Pocket Books printing January 1989

10 9 8 7 6 5 4 3 2 1

POCKET and colophon are trademarks of
Simon & Schuster Inc.

Printed in the U.S.A.

For Jay,
for his patience and support;
and for Alexander and Catherine,
whose naps made this book possible.
Many thanks to Con Sellers,
mentor and generous friend.

1

Damn the sunshine. Why couldn't it rain as it did in any normal spring? Michou Valette snapped another bud off the vine. The grapes at least were doing well—the weather was perfect for them.

But it was also perfect for the German panzers grinding across France. Michou toed the dry soil. No rain, no mud. Nothing to slow them down. Nothing to keep them from reaching Marc, stationed near the Somme River in the north.

Straightening, she pressed her hands against the small of her back. Pinching the tiny buds wasn't her favorite chore, even if it did give the wine more character. It didn't do much to keep her mind off Marc, the war, and the fear knotting her insides, souring her mouth like the tannin of a wine not ready.

Shading her eyes with one hand, Michou waved at her father as he moved to the next row in the adjoining vineyard. She wished she could talk to him, but she knew this was one thing he just wouldn't understand. His beautiful, blond, nineteen-year-old daughter no longer a virgin? His violet-eyed *petit chou* pregnant? *Impossible!* She could hear him shout the denial.

No, she couldn't tell Papa, and Maman would just look at her sadly and say nothing. That would be worse than Papa's anger. And she couldn't tell Marc because he was off fighting the Germans. If only her grandmother weren't so sick—she'd understand. She was the only one who ever did.

Michou bent again over the vine. The baby flowers stuck to her fingers, flowers that would never become grapes. She dismissed the thought as quickly as it came. She hadn't any notion of how to go about it, and besides, even if she did, she

1

wouldn't want to. If there really were a baby, it was Marc's, and it might be all of him she'd ever have again. No, she could never do anything to harm their child, no matter how difficult it was going to be for her.

Brushing the damp hair off her forehead with the back of her hand, Michou moved to the next plant. She wished the fluttering in her stomach would go away; the fresh green scent of the crushed buds, usually soothing, was almost unpleasant today. And not even the May sun could warm her hands—they'd been as cold and damp as the bottle cellar since she first suspected.

Even knowing she was pregnant would be better than this; then she could make some decisions, some plans. Now all she could do was wait, and she hated waiting. That was one reason why she'd seduced Marc when he was home on leave. She'd always planned on saving herself for their wedding night, and Marc—mature, loyal, dutiful Marc—had never pressured her; but they both knew the end of the *drôle de guerre,* the phony war, couldn't be far away. The beginning of real war would change everything.

It certainly hadn't taken much to make him see things her way. She smiled at the thought. Even Marc, with all his responsibility and wisdom, had just groaned when she slid her fingers under the waistband of his pants that night six weeks ago. Six weeks—it was hard to believe. Sometimes it seemed like years; other times, like minutes.

She shivered as she remembered Marc's excitement—and her own. She hadn't really known exactly what to do; her mother had never spoken of sex, only love, and the whispered information from her friends at school hardly seemed reliable. But she had remembered one particularly vivid story her cousin Sylvie told and the respectful silence that greeted it. Perhaps it was worth a try.

And it had worked. Marc had hardened under her fingers, his breath coming in little gasps, and she relaxed her body against his chest and parted her lips. His kiss probed deeper, and his hand moved up from her waist to caress her breast.

"Michou?" Marc whispered, gently grasping her shoulders and looking into her eyes.

She had smiled back at him and nodded. This was exactly what she wanted, and she wasn't going to do anything to stop him.

His fingers ran rapidly down the front of her dress, and almost magically it was unbuttoned to her hips. He pushed the dress off her shoulders, and as it fell to the floor, he scooped her into his arms and carried her to the bed.

Her insides melted as Marc ran his hands up from her knees to the inside of her thighs with light, feathery strokes. Arching her back, she raised herself up to meet him and with a single fluid motion Marc entered her.

They'd found a new place to make love every day of his leave, and it had been the best week of her life. The possibility of war ceased to exist when they were together; the only thing that had ever mattered more than Marc was the château, and she could see no reason why she shouldn't have both.

Boots crunched on the gravel drive, and Michou lifted her head. Her father smiled at her, his bushy gray eyebrows raised high above his brown eyes. He rested one hand on his hip and the other on a large stake at the end of the row.

"Time for lunch?" she asked.

Alexandre Valette nodded. "I just don't understand why you like it out here so much."

"Yes, you do, Papa. And don't tell me again I should want to learn painting from Maman instead of winemaking from you." Michou put her hands on her hips and narrowed her eyes but couldn't keep from smiling. She knew her father was secretly pleased with her ambition to be a winemaker but about as likely to admit it as he would be to praise a new wine.

Papa just laughed, smoothing his large gray moustache with his thumb. "Little good it ever does to tell you anything. Almost as bad as your younger brother, you are."

Michou rolled her eyes. *"Peste.* I wish he'd stop talking about running away to fight the *Boches.* It makes Maman so unhappy."

His smile faded. "If this war goes on long, he may get his wish."

"Lucien says it's going to be over quickly." She couldn't keep the sarcasm out of her voice.

"Lucien!" Her father spat. "That's what I'm even more

afraid of. I don't care if he is Henri's son. It's people like him who'll do their best to make sure—" He flicked his hand to finish his sentence.

Michou had grown up listening to her father's stories about the Germans. He'd fought in the last war and still resented them enough to refuse to ship his wine to Germany even though Saint-Émilions sold better there than in England. His heart always won any contest with his pocketbook.

"But we can't lose!" Michou said, twisting off a final bud. She ran a few steps to catch up with Papa.

"Just don't talk about it in front of your mother, *hein?*"

"I know." Michou sighed. Papa always tried so hard to protect Maman from everything unpleasant. She thought it was silly, but that was just how he was. She hated it when people treated her like that.

As they approached the graceful white stone château, Michou looked up to her grandmother's second-story window. She wasn't there again today. That meant either she felt well enough to join the family for lunch downstairs or she was in bed, not even up to watching by the window for Michou and Papa.

Michou's throat tightened. She knew her grandmother was old, but she couldn't stand to think about the château without her. Everything was going wrong at once. She swallowed hard and thrust her chin up. There was no point in feeling sorry for herself.

Instead, she forced herself to smile at her father as he rocked back on his heels and commented as he always did: "Nice place, *hein?*"

"Pas mal," Michou said. Somehow their little ritual made her feel more cheerful. Papa was right: Château Bourdet *was* nice, and she was the fourth generation of Valettes to think so. She loved the arched windows and mansard roof, and the tall round towers on each end had always been part of the fairy stories her grandmother used to tell her and her brothers. It was more formal than most of the châteaux in Saint-Émilion, many of which were just glorified farmhouses, but even so, it wasn't pretentious. Her mother's roses and Mémé Laure's herb garden were friendlier than the carefully shaped hedges they'd replaced.

Michou was proud of Château Bourdet; no matter what else happened, it and the vineyards and the wine would always be there. Nothing could change that.

Except maybe the Germans.

But what good did it do to worry about them now? No more good than it did to worry about being pregnant or about Marc. One problem at a time, and the most immediate concerns first—her grandmother, her hotheaded brother, the vines. Michou took a deep breath and pressed her shoulders back as she and her father entered his office through a side door of the château.

Three days later, Michou climbed the spiraling stairs to her bedroom on the top floor of the tower. At least Mémé Laure had improved enough to come down for dinner three nights running, and she and Papa had finally finished grooming the vines.

She skipped up the last steps. All the other bedrooms were on the second floor of the main building, but her mother had redecorated the old tower as a surprise for Michou's sixteenth birthday.

She smiled as she remembered the look on her mother's face when she'd flung open the door—Maman had been so afraid she wouldn't like it. There was little danger of that, though; Maman's taste was exquisite, and the mauve- and cream-colored room delighted her. The delicate curved lines of the Louis XV furniture Maman had chosen suited her perfectly. But what she liked best of all was the watercolor Maman had painted for her of Château Bourdet and the vineyards. For the first time, it had almost seemed as if her mother accepted her ambition to be a winemaker.

The clattering of hard-soled shoes on the stone stairs behind her interrupted her thoughts, and she paused outside her bedroom door. Her brother's head, with its curly light brown hair brushed back from his high forehead, emerged first, followed by his tall, lanky body. Although he was four years younger, Philippe was already half a foot taller than she was.

"Wait up!" Philippe's breath came in little spurts. He leaned against the wall.

"Why weren't you at dinner?"

"The Germans. They attacked the Somme!"

The knot in Michou's stomach became a fist pounding upward, knocking the air from her lungs. "What?" She cleared her throat and repeated herself. "What did you say?"

"The Somme. The Germans attacked it today."

"Oh, no," Michou whispered. Marc's regiment was still garrisoned at Dury, on the Somme. Her head felt like a balloon, and her heart thudded in her ears. She braced herself against the door; she would not faint again, no matter how bad it was.

"How do you know?" she asked. Maybe he was teasing—Philippe loved to plague her.

"On the radio. At Édouard's. You know, the one he and I built." He was still panting.

"Did Marc's parents hear, too?" It had to be the truth; Édouard was Marc's little brother.

"Yes. I ran all the way home. Thought you'd want to—"

"Thanks." Michou closed her eyes tightly and bit her lower lip.

"You all right?" Philippe stepped forward.

"Yes." Michou could hear the concern in his voice. She opened her eyes and breathed deeply. I'm fine. You should apologize to Maman for missing dinner, though. She was worried."

Philippe shrugged. "I can take care of myself."

"That's not the point. But I don't want to argue with you now. Just go apologize. And don't tell either Maman or Papa what you just told me."

"But they'll—"

"Please, Philippe." She tried to smile. He was so eager, too eager, and never understood why anyone got upset with him. "I know you can take care of yourself. But think of Maman and Papa."

He shrugged again and turned to leave.

"Thanks for the news."

Philippe waved his hand and disappeared down the stairs.

Michou sagged against the doorway. Just because there was fighting on the Somme, it didn't mean Marc was hurt or even involved. The thought made her feel a little better, and she pushed open the door.

But as soon as she saw the huge mahogany bed where she and Marc had dared to make love on his last night home, the tears came. She flung herself on the violet-sprigged coverlet and buried her face in the pillow scented with her grandmother's lavender water. At least Mémé Laure had improved enough to talk to her last week, and now she knew.

Marc *had* to be all right. Nothing could happen to him, not when she was carrying his baby.

When she'd told her grandmother, Mémé Laure hadn't been either surprised or shocked. She'd just said that war sometimes did that to people and they couldn't be blamed, and she'd asked lots of questions about how Michou had been feeling.

She sat up and pressed her wrists against her breasts, swollen and tender for three weeks now. And there's been no bleeding again this month. Mémé Laure had told her that was one of the signs.

There'd been other indications, too. Yesterday she'd fainted while she was helping her father rack the new wines. The cloyingly sweet aroma had been too much. Papa had been concerned, but she'd just let him think she'd been working too hard. She didn't like doing that, but it was better than telling him the truth now.

That would just have to wait. She rubbed her hand across her smooth, flat stomach. Mémé Laure had told her she wouldn't really begin to show for another two or three months, and a lot could happen before then. Maybe the war would be over, and she and Marc could get married. People would count on their fingers and whisper when the baby came early, but that happened to lots of girls.

She didn't want to think about the other possibilities, but she couldn't help it: Marc might die; the Germans might win; she might have to leave the château, maybe go live in Paris; her parents might never speak to her again. But she couldn't give up Château Bourdet for the baby or the baby for the château. She just couldn't.

And she wouldn't.

The door connecting the tower to the second floor of the main building squeaked open, and Michou jumped up from the bed. After she poured cold water from the pitcher into the washbasin, she hurriedly splashed her face and blotted it dry,

then peered into the ornately framed old mirror that hung
over the tulip-wood commode. She looked terrible; her eyes
stared back at her, huge and so dark they looked almost black
against her pale skin, and her full lips were puffy and
chapped.

A soft tap sounded at the door, followed by her mother's
voice. "Michou? May I come in?"

Michou moved slowly to the bureau next to the commode before answering. "Of course." She picked up the
antique *tastevin* Papa had given her for her seventeenth birthday and stroked its smooth surface, then replaced it among
the other pieces of her collection.

The door swished open and Michou turned to face her
mother. As always, she couldn't help thinking how regal and
beautiful Maman was. No one—except Papa—treated
Catherine Valette like a crystal angel. If only she'd inherited
her mother's height along with her coloring—that was what
made the difference. It was much harder to be condescending
to someone you had to look up at.

Then she noticed Maman's frown. Had Mémé Laure told
her about the baby? Of course not—Mémé Laure would
never interfere like that.

"Philippe told us," her mother said. "I'm so sorry. But
I'm sure Marc is fine." Her eyebrows made a straight line
over her slender nose.

"I told him not to say anything!" Michou crossed her
arms, digging clenched fists into her ribs.

"Listen to me." Maman sat on the edge of the bed.
"You've been doing too much. Your father told me about
yesterday. We both think you should rest for a couple of
days."

"But that'll just make it worse. At least when I'm helping Papa, I don't think about Marc all the time." She relaxed
her hands and cupped her elbows in them.

"Well, maybe some lighter work, then. I could use some
help."

Michou looked up at her mother.

"Word came from my parents today." She tapped her
long fingernails lightly on the marble-topped console table
next to the bed. "They're leaving Paris. Everyone is leaving
Paris. They're coming here."

"But—"

"I know. They don't like your father. Well, it can't be helped. War makes things different. Besides, they'll only stay here for a few days. They plan to go on to the summer house in the Pyrénées."

Michou forced her mouth shut. Her grandparents had so disapproved of her mother's marriage to a "farmer," they had never once in twenty-five years come to visit their daughter and grandchildren at the château. Michou just couldn't imagine her tall, stern silver-haired grandmother trying to make amends to her father now.

"They're really coming here."

Maman nodded. "And I'd like your help."

"What does Papa say?"

"He agrees with me."

"All right." Michou sighed. She knew how important it was to Maman to prove that Papa was not just a farmer and that the château was much more than a farm. If she could help, she would.

But she wasn't looking forward to her grandparents' arrival. She knew from experience how difficult they could be, especially her grandmother. And her cousin, Maman hadn't mentioned anything about her.

"What about Sylvie?"

"She refuses to leave Paris. Claims the Germans don't scare her. Your grandmother is quite displeased with her."

Michou choked back a laugh. That was a change—it was usually Sylvie who could do nothing wrong and Michou who aroused her grandmother's displeasure.

Maman stood up. "Listen to me. Everything will be fine." She walked to the door and turned. "Get some sleep, now."

Michou crossed the room to her mother and kissed her on both cheeks, inhaling the soft rose perfume that was Maman's signature. "I will. And don't worry about me."

Her mother shook her head and laughed. "Just wait until you have children. Then you'll know how impossible that is."

After her mother closed the door, Michou sank down onto her bed. She already knew how right Maman was.

2

When she reached the landing, Michou hesitated. She could hear her mother's clear soprano underscored by the low chuckle of her grandfather. Grandpère would be happy to see her, she knew, but Grandmère would be stately and cold, and that was something she'd never gotten used to. She'd tried so hard to please her when she lived with them in Paris, but Grandmère seemed to find fault with everything she did.

Holding her shoulders back, she descended the stairs smoothly, her head up, one foot in front of the other, as Grandmère had shown her. She was halfway down before she caught her grandfather's attention.

He smiled and held out his hands. "And here's my little Michou! I'm so pleased to see you!"

Forgetting the lessons, Michou flew down the remaining stairs. "Grandpère! You're really here!" She hugged him and kissed his cheeks. He'd always done what he could to protect her from Grandmère and Sylvie, and she loved him for it even if it hadn't always worked.

She turned to her grandmother, a taller, more severe version of Maman, and took her hand. "Good day, Grandmère." She brushed her lips against the powdered cheek. Her grandmother's lilac perfume seemed even stronger than usual—it made her a little queasy. "It's nice to see you again."

"And it's a pleasure to see you again, Michèle." Her grandmother released Michou's hand and stepped back. "You've changed very little, I see."

Michou forced her lips into a smile. "Neither have you, Grandmère," she said. Why did it have to be like this? Why

10

couldn't her grandmother just accept her? She knew why, though—she was just too much like her father.

Grandmère turned to Maman. "I expect Alexandre and Philippe are working in the fields?"

"Vineyards," Michou said. She couldn't help it.

Her grandmother frowned, and the creases in her forehead deepened.

The door rattled, and Papa and Philippe stepped into the entry. Papa strode forward and shook hands with Grandpère and Grandmère. "We saw the car. Hope you didn't have any difficulty finding us."

"None at all. Getting here from Bordeaux was the easiest part of the trip," Grandpère said. He kissed Philippe.

Maman nudged Michou. "Better tell Cécile there'll be two more for—"

"I'll go," Philippe said. He sprinted down the hall before anyone could stop him.

Grandmère cleared her throat. "Perhaps it would be wise to discuss our plans now." She looked at Maman. "Your father and I would like to take you and Michou with us to the summer house. We don't think it will be safe here."

"But—" Michou's throat tightened. She couldn't leave now. Papa needed her help. And what if Marc came home? There'd been reports that hundreds of soldiers overrun on the Somme had been pouring into Paris. He might be on his way.

Maman and Papa looked at each other. "Let's discuss this in the salon," Maman said. She shook her head at Michou.

Michou crossed her arms tightly and gnawed on her lower lip as she followed. She didn't care what they decided—she would not desert Château Bourdet.

Finally alone for a few minutes, Michou strolled in Mémé Laure's herb garden behind the château. It had been two days since her grandparents' arrival, and now things were as normal as possible. There was an uneasy truce on at the château and a war on in the rest of France. She hadn't told anyone except Mémé Laure that she had no intention of going to the summer house, no matter what her parents decided. She hoped she wouldn't have to.

She brushed her hand along the tops of the lavender buds. In another two or three weeks, the low silvery-green bushes would be in fragrant bloom and so full of bees she'd have to be careful when she cut them for Mémé Laure's sachets and potpourris. She grimaced. In two or three weeks, France might be full of Germans.

A door clicked softly, and she looked up. Cécile, the family's cook since her parents' marriage, stood outlined against the bright light from the kitchen. "Michou?" she called.

"Over here."

"Your maman says to tell you there's a visitor in the small drawing room."

"Who is it?"

Cécile paused for a moment. "Lucien."

Michou spun around on her heel. "What does *he* want?" She hoped he didn't think dating Marc's sister gave him special privileges.

Cécile shrugged.

Michou snapped off a few stems of lavender and stuck them in her pocket. She'd take them to Mémé Laure later. "I'll be there in a minute." She had no intention of hurrying; Lucien certainly hadn't been invited, and this was the first free time she'd had all day.

Cécile nodded and stepped back into the kitchen, and the garden was silent again. As she picked her way through the herbs, Michou ran her finger over the scar in her eyebrow. When she was thirteen, she'd tried to stop Lucien from beating up Philippe, and he'd thrown her onto the gravel. If only Alain had been there. But—

She let herself in the back door. There was no point in thinking about Alain. He was gone, and wishing wouldn't bring him back.

Finger-combing her fine curls, she glanced at the hazy reflection in the glass covering one of her mother's water-colors. Her silver-blond hair hung to her shoulders, a halo of snarls. But too bad. It was only Lucien, after all. She pushed open the paneled double doors.

Lucien Desroches lounged in front of the fireplace, his elbow resting on the mantelpiece. After he nodded at Michou, he removed the cigar from his mouth, flicked it onto the clean grate, and tucked the ebony cigar holder into his jacket pocket.

She crossed her arms and lifted her chin. "You wanted to see me?"

"Yes. I've got some news for you. About Marc." He stepped forward, putting his hands on his hips.

"About Marc? What's happened?" Michou's throat constricted, and her mouth went dry. *Mon Dieu,* maybe he was dead. But why would Lucien be the one to tell her that? Wouldn't they send someone official? Probably not. She wasn't Marc's wife. And now maybe she would never be.

"Oh, he's still alive. I was visiting his sister when the call came," he said.

"But what, then?" Damn him! Why was he playing with her like this?

"He's wounded. Took one in the chest when the Germans made the push across the Somme."

Michou backed away. "Oh, no." Her legs became vines, unable to support her weight. But she could not collapse. Not in front of Lucien. "Is it bad? Where is he?"

"Some buddies managed to get him as far south as Poitiers. One of them called the Laurents. He's in a hospital there. Just thought you might want to know. I'm really sorry." He put a finger across his thin lips and glanced away briefly before advancing toward her. "Let me know if there's anything I can do."

Michou sidestepped behind an armchair and gripped its back, her arms stiff. Shivering suddenly even though the evening was warm, she clenched her teeth to keep them from chattering. She knew Lucien wasn't a bit sorry. He'd chased after her since she was sixteen, but Marc had always been there. It would suit him just fine if Marc didn't live. The only thing that would make him happier would be to watch Marc die, just as he had watched Alain.

Michou shook her head to get rid of the buzzing in her ears. "Please go."

"I understand," Lucien said. "You're probably upset. I'll come back again when there's more news."

"I'd rather call Marc's parents."

"Have it your way." He shrugged. "By the way, the wound is pretty serious."

She didn't turn to watch him go, but she listened for the doors to bang shut. Her jaw ached and her eyes burned, but she would not let herself cry until he was gone.

The thud didn't come. Her spine prickled, and she shuddered.

Lucien grabbed her shoulders, pulling her around. His long nails dug into her skin through the light blouse. "As I said, anything I can do—" He raised his eyebrows. "Anything at all." His smile didn't reach his pale blue eyes.

Michou jerked away. "You can leave. Now." If he touched her again, she'd hit him. Not that it would do much good—he'd probably just laugh. But she wouldn't be able to help it, not when protecting her baby had already become instinctive.

She didn't look around until she heard the door close. This time he was gone. She could cry now, but the tears wouldn't come.

She flung herself into the chair next to the fireplace and put her head in her hands. Lucien's cigar smoke hung in the air, and bile rose in her throat.

The doors clattered again, and she looked up quickly. But it was only her father standing in front of her, his head lowered.

"Your mother told me Lucien was here. Did he tell you about Marc?" He raised his eyes to hers.

"How did you know?"

"Marc's mother called. She wanted us to tell you." He pulled his ear and shifted his weight to his other foot. "Everything all right?"

Michou nodded. "Did she say it was serious?"

"Pretty bad."

She closed her eyes and leaned her head back on the chair. It was true. "He's in Poitiers?" she asked. Then she opened her eyes and sat up straight.

"That's what she said."

Michou stood up and kissed her father on both cheeks. "Thanks, Papa. I'll be fine. I just want to be alone for a while."

"I'm truly sorry, *chérie*. This may seem hard, but it's war, *hein?* If we don't win, it'll be much worse." He shook his head. "Much worse." He put his arm around her shoulders as they walked to the door. "Would you like me to tell your mother you won't be down for dinner?"

"Please. And"—Michou ducked from under his arm and ran to the stairs—"tell Grandmère and Grandpère I'm sorry."

Alexandre watched his daughter race up the stairs. *Nom de Dieu,* he ached for her. But he was proud of her courage. She'd never been a whiner, never complained when she hurt herself. She'd weather this, too. And what she put up with from Catherine's mother! The woman was a harpy, and she picked at Michou constantly. Why he'd let Catherine talk him into sending Michou to school in Paris he'd never know.

He ran his thumb over his mustache. He'd missed Michou's help these last few days. Made him think even more about Alain than usual—she sort of took his place. Much better than Philippe. That boy would never be a winemaker. More interested in his wires and tubes, he was.

Alexandre moved slowly toward the family room. Catherine would be waiting. Must be patient with her. This visit was as hard on her as on everyone else. Damn her mother and her damnable plans. Still trying to run Catherine's life. And his.

He threw open the door. Catherine sat at the piano, clasped hands resting in her lap and head bowed. The room was dark, and he turned on a lamp before putting his hands on her shoulders.

"How is she?" She pressed her cheek against his hand.

"Seems fine. Lucien told her, the vulture."

She turned. "Does this change anything?"

"Not for me. Germans get this far, they'll get to Bayonne, too. I want you and Michou here."

"Good." She stood and kissed him. "I'm still glad I married you."

Michou tapped softly on Mémé Laure's door, not wanting to disturb her grandmother if she was asleep. Although she was feeling much better, she hadn't yet recovered completely from last month's attack of bronchitis.

"Come in." Mémé Laure's voice was still lower than usual.

Michou opened the door and smiled. Her grandmother was sitting in her armchair by the fireplace, her crocheting in her lap. She held out the lavender. "See? It won't be long before it blooms." She put the stems in Mémé Laure's little hand.

Mémé Laure sniffed the lavender, then laid it on the armrest. "Thank you, dear." She waved at the chair on the other side of the fireplace. "Sit down and tell me what's happening downstairs. I don't know whether to go down for dinner tonight." She looked at Michou over her glasses, the corners of her warm brown eyes crinkling.

Michou sat down. "I'm not."

"What did they do now?" Mémé Laure's smile faded. She put her crocheting into the basket at her feet.

"It's not them," Michou said, and tears stung her eyes. She got up and ran to her grandmother, hiding her face in Mémé Laure's lap. "It's Marc. He's wounded."

Mémé Laure stroked Michou's hair. "All you can do is pray, *n'est-ce pas?*"

Michou lifted her head and shook it. "I'm going to the hospital."

"But do you think that's wise? How are you going to get there? And what about the baby?"

"I *have* to go!" Michou bit her lower lip, salty from tears. Wiping her eyes, she stood up and walked to the window. She readjusted the blackout curtain and then turned back to her grandmother. "If Marc knows we're going to have a baby, maybe he won't—" She couldn't say it.

"I understand," Mémé Laure said. "I would have done the same thing for your grandfather. Now, tell me what you're going to do." She leaned back and rested her cheek on her hand.

Michou crossed her arms and stood in front of her grandmother. "He's in Poitiers. I'm going to ride my bicycle there."

"That's a long way to ride." Mémé Laure rubbed her chin.

"I know. But the trains are a mess, and I can't think of any other way." Michou paced back to the window.

"Perhaps Marc's parents are going."

Michou faced her grandmother. She hadn't even thought of that. Maybe she could go with them. Then she remembered her grandparents' descriptions of the roads choked with refugees fleeing the Germans. "But Grandpère says the roads are impossible. A bicycle would be faster. They'd be going the wrong way—everyone is headed south."

"But, dear, I'm sure it can't be safe for you. Or the baby," Mémé Laure said.

"I'll be careful. I'm sure I could be there in two days." That part worried her the least. She'd often ridden to Libourne and back in a day and not been at all tired. She knew she could make it to Poitiers.

Mémé Laure leaned forward and gestured toward the bureau. "Bring me the porcelain box."

Michou sighed with relief as she handed her grandmother the box. She hadn't raised another objection.

Mémé Laure opened the box and took out some money. "Here," she said. "I want you to find someplace nice to stay. And eat right. If you're set on doing this, you must take good care of yourself and the baby, n'est-ce pas?"

Michou hugged her grandmother. "Thank you," she whispered.

"And I suppose you want me to say nothing of this to your parents?" She peered over her glasses, her gray eyebrows arched high.

Michou shook her head. "Not until dinner tomorrow. I don't want them trying to find me." She should be in Angoulême by then. And the day after that, she'd be with Marc in Poitiers.

Jesus, he wanted her. A tight smile pulled at Lucien''s lips as he pulled into the drive leading to Château LeClair-Figeac. When his father died, this second-rate château would be his and it wouldn't be second-rate for long. Château Bourdet was right next door. He'd have it and Michou, too.

His smile stretched wider at the thought. After she got over Marc, she'd be sorry she'd waited so long. He braked the red Mercedes-Benz sharply in front of the château and dust filtered into the car. He'd screwed most of the available local girls who interested him, and some of the unavailable ones as well. They liked him fine, thought he was good-looking, good in bed. Why the hell should she be so different?

Merde! He slammed the car door. She wouldn't be different for long. The Germans were going to win, and Marc was going to die. She'd be glad to have him.

He scowled as he looked at the building in front of him. A château—hah! It was a cottage compared to Château Bourdet, and the wines weren't much better than *vin ordinaire*. But running it was better than being shot at, and he'd certainly be in the army now if he hadn't had the foresight to persuade his father to let him manage it on a trial basis. At least he didn't have to live here all the time.

And after he got Michou, he wouldn't live here at all. He'd turn the farmhouse over to his winemaker and live at the real château on the hill. He'd show his father he could make good on his own, that he was every bit as good as Alain Valette had ever been. The old man had harped at him for years: "Why can't you be more like Alain? He never causes Alexandre this kind of grief." Blah, blah, blah. Well, he was going to show Father just how much he could be like Alain—Château Bourdet was going to be his.

Lucien pushed open the door. The entry was dark. He hadn't told Jacques he'd be back this evening—he'd half expected Madame Valette to ask him to dinner. After all, the Valettes and the Desroches had been business associates and friends for years. For generations, actually—his grandfather had shipped the wines of Château Bourdet for old man Valette long before Alexandre had taken control, and Alexandre and his father had grown up best friends. It was only natural that the relationship should continue.

He turned on the light and walked down the narrow hall to the kitchen. It was too bad things had changed after Alain died. Oh, the families were still friendly enough, but somehow the friendliness didn't include him. Nobody except Michou, though, made a point of being nasty, and she was the only one he really cared about. It was almost as if she blamed him for her brother's drowning. But she couldn't know—

The clatter of pans was followed by a hoarse curse, and Lucien spun on his heel and retraced his steps. Eating in the kitchen with Jacques and his fat old wife was not what he had in mind tonight. Perhaps if he stopped by the Laurents'—but no, Gabrielle was a bigger bore than her brother, Marc, that stuffy bastard. He only bothered with her because somehow she made him feel closer to Michou. Jesus, he wanted her, ached for her.

Ducking his head, he eased into the car and slumped in the leather seat. Then he pulled a cigar from his jacket pocket and fitted it into the holder. Screw them all. He'd just drive into Libourne and spend the evening at Le Chat Noir.

He lit the cigar and blew the smoke out his nostrils. Nice—those little Davidoff Havanas were worth every cent. He leaned back in the seat. Maybe he'd make up for what he had lost at the tables last week. It was about time for a change of luck.

3

෨

Michou started awake. It was still dark. She rolled onto her back and kicked the damp covers to the foot of the bed. She'd awakened so many times it had to be almost morning. She couldn't go back to sleep. The dream would just come again. Better to stay awake and wait for dawn.

She wiped the sweat from her forehead. It was the same dream, the one that had started after Alain drowned. It always began with the river.

Green and cold. And big. Too big to swim across. "Don't get in the water," Papa orders. The white building swallows him. Then the green-and-black turtle head, dull eye blinking. The water rises around her. She can't move. "Papa, Papa!" Lucien's face, huge, eyes shining blue ice, lips pulled thin against teeth. "Lucien!" The river swallows her. The turtle paddles by. Looking up, she sees its belly, shimmery. Her hair floats across her eyes. Cold. She's cold. Papa will be mad.

Then the coffin. She wonders who is dead. The turtle sits on top. It stares at her before it swallows itself. She looks in the coffin. It's Alain. He stares at her, dull eyes blinking. Then the coffin swallows him. Alain is dead. Alain dead. Alain—

But it had been Marc in the coffin this time, a black hole in his chest. She shivered, reached down for the covers, and pulled them over her shoulders. She'd opened her curtains after turning her light out last night and now, straining her eyes, she could make out the bicycle paniers on the chair under the window. At last. It was getting light.

She sat up and hugged her knees to her chest. Her

20

breasts still felt tender, but not so much as last month. She had to get out of bed slowly, though, or she'd be sick. And this morning especially she couldn't afford that.

She'd left a piece of Cécile's heavy country bread on the console table—sometimes eating a little before getting up helped keep her stomach where it belonged—and she chewed it slowly. Papa was going to be angry, but perhaps he'd understand after Mémé Laure explained. She hoped so. She hated making him mad.

But this time she couldn't avoid it.

She swung her legs over the edge of the bed and paused. Her stomach stayed put. So far, so good. The real test was standing. She eased her body up.

Her stomach bounced. Damn! If she didn't throw up now, she'd be nauseated all day. She bent over the washbasin and willed herself to vomit, to get it over with.

Nothing happened. Giving up, she straightened and grabbed her clothes off the chair. She wasn't going to feel perfect—so what? Marc had a lot more to complain about.

She dressed quickly in a pair of Philippe's old pants rolled almost to her knees and a light blouse topped with a blue sweater. The mornings were still cool, but by lunch she'd have to knot the sweater around her waist.

Last night she'd sewn a pocket in her cap for Mémé Laure's money. After she stuffed her hair into the cap, she hoisted the paniers over her shoulder. Had she forgotten anything?

The bed—she always made it. Balancing the baskets with one hand, she pulled the coverlet up with the other. Now everything looked normal. She'd told Maman she planned to bicycle to Gabrielle's for the day, so no one would miss her until dinner. And even then they might think she was staying over. Until she didn't call.

She descended the stairs quietly and let herself out the door at the bottom of the tower. As she made her way to the barn to get her bicycle, sunlight sliced through the plane trees in front of the château.

She pedaled out the front gate, breathing deeply, the cool, flower-scented air calming her jittery nerves. Neat rows of vines spiraled out from the deserted gravel road, gradually giving way to rose-colored stone buildings when she reached the outskirts of Libourne.

After she turned off for Poitiers, the traffic steadily increased. Horns blared, babies cried, and her lungs burned from the exhaust fumes. Before yesterday, the war had seemed far away and unreal; now she was in the middle of it.

She swerved sharply and bounced onto the shoulder as an impatient refugee passed the slow-moving truck in front of him. Gripping the handlebars tightly, she eased the bicycle back onto the roadway.

Her heart pounded in her ears. She'd have to keep a sharper watch—she didn't want to fall and maybe hurt the baby. As long as that didn't happen, she didn't care if she had to pedal all the way there in a ditch. Nothing could stop her from getting to Marc now.

Guy Chalmers leaned back in the chair as he tamped the tobacco in his pipe. Even with a war on, French food was excellent, much better than the English fare he'd survived on in his digs at Cambridge or even the American food his mother had served.

He lit the pipe and signaled the waiter. Too bad he'd had to wolf his lunch down. But the Germans had reached Rouen yesterday, and he had to get to Paris before they did. Damn Dad anyway for being such a bloody stubborn old ass.

When the waiter approached, he paid the check and stood up. How Dad ever got the notion to stick it out in France he'd never know. It had taken both him and Jacob Schweiger to convince him that a British subject would not be welcome in a France occupied by Nazis.

Guy shook his head as he remembered Jake's story. He'd heard rumors about Hitler's treatment of the German Jews, but they were nothing compared to the nightmare Jake had lived. He'd managed to escape to France. And now it looked as if even France wasn't going to be safe much longer.

Because it would be a miracle if the Germans didn't win. At this point only a fool could believe otherwise. And even though Dad was stubborn as hell, a fool he wasn't. As soon as he'd heard that Italy had declared war on France, he'd given in, and Guy had left an hour later to make the financial arrangements in Paris.

He smiled and nodded at the *patron* as he opened the door. *"Au revoir,* monsieur. A wonderful meal."

The plump Frenchman raised his glass. "And good luck to you, monsieur."

Ducking his head, Guy stepped through the door and onto the sidewalk. It had got even warmer, and the diesel fumes overpowered the pipe smoke. He laid the pipe on the dash and stripped off his sweater before he slid into the seat of the green Citroën. He should make better time now that he was out of Bordeaux. He'd be satisfied if he got to Angoulême by dark.

He bumped the car off the curb. After nosing it into the heavy traffic, he turned at the first intersection. Cutting across the horde so he could head north was the hard part. The village streets were so narrow there wasn't much room to maneuver.

He rubbed the back of his neck as he waited for an opening. Jake was right—France had already lost. He'd been so busy helping Dad with the wine-shipping business, he hadn't thought much about the war. Until a couple of months ago, no one really had.

Now that was all changed. It was too late to fight for France. But Britain hadn't given up yet. Maybe they'd take him even though he was American and almost thirty-two.

He spotted a hole in the traffic and stepped on the gas. Once he was out there, they'd just have to stop for him. Brakes squealed, and a man behind the wheel of a little car topped with a large mattress shook his fist and shouted, *"Pauvre con!"*

Guy shrugged and held out his hands, palms up. The poor fool undoubtedly thought the mattress would protect him from the bombs that had probably destroyed his home. Guy continued cautiously. When he reached the road toward Paris he turned onto it and sighed. Finally.

He reached for his pipe and lit it again, cupping his hand against the breeze from the open window while he steered with his elbow. Once out of town, he concentrated on the countryside. It might be a long time before he came back to France again. God, he hated to leave, and he'd only lived here since he was sixteen. It must be killing his father—he'd been in Bordeaux for forty years.

Suddenly traffic picked up again. He put the pipe back on the dash and gripped the wheel with both hands. No one paid any attention to the center line, and northbound cars frequently ended up in the ditch when impatient refugees tried to pass. A wreck he couldn't afford.

By the time he reached Angoulême, his back ached and his head throbbed. "Enough," he muttered. It wasn't quite dusk, but there was no point in pushing any farther tonight. He'd stop at the first hotel. Dinner, some sleep, then on the road again at dawn.

Michou clambered off her bicycle and hefted it onto the sidewalk. Her legs quivered, and she stumbled. She leaned against the bicycle for a minute. Then she guided it with one hand along the sidewalk. She *had* to find a place to stay tonight.

She rubbed her arm, and it tingled. Too much sun. Grandmère would have a nasty comment about that. Her lips twitched. Grandmère would have so much to complain about, she probably wouldn't know where to begin. *If* she was still there when Michou got back.

She walked her bicycle past five hotels before she found one with a room. After she propped the bicycle against the building, she locked it and slid the paniers off the fender.

The proprietor stood at the door, letting down the blackout curtain, and he waved her inside. "Got one room left," he said. "You planning on eating here." It wasn't a question.

She nodded.

He handed her the key. "Up the stairs and third door to your right. Bathroom's at the end of the hall."

When Michou reached the room, she rattled the key into the lock and kneed open the door. She dumped the paniers onto the only chair. The room was dismal: the floor was slanted, the ceiling low, the wallpaper dirty and torn. Michou sank onto the bed, and the springs creaked. She stretched out. Maybe it was lumpy, but at least it wasn't a bicycle seat.

A few minutes later she caught herself drifting into sleep. She rubbed her eyes and stood up. If she fell asleep now, she'd miss dinner and then wake starving in the middle of the night. She changed into the blue dress she'd carefully packed so she'd look nice for Marc. Oh, God, please let him be alive when she got there.

Her stomach squeezed into a knot. Maybe some dinner would help. She let herself out of the room. The hall reeked of garlic, rancid oil, and urine, and she held her breath until she reached the stairs.

In the dining room, the proprietor waved her toward the only seat left. The small table was next to the kitchen door, and a man with gold-streaked brown hair sat on the side opposite it, his elbows resting on either side of his plate.

He looked up when she pulled out the chair. "Good evening," he said, and smiled.

She nodded and sat down, scooting forward until her feet rested on the floor. She hoped he didn't expect her to make conversation.

"I don't recommend the lamb." He poked at a dark cube on his plate. "It seems to have grown up into a sheep while I've been sitting here."

A smile tugged at the corner of her lips, and her eyes met his. She lowered her gaze quickly. He looked pleasant enough, but she didn't really feel like being friendly tonight.

"On your way to Bordeaux?"

She shook her head, keeping her eyes on the menu. "Poitiers."

"Well, we're both going in the wrong direction, it seems. I'm headed for Paris." He swirled the wine in his glass before he took a swig. His upper lip curled. "Forgot what I was drinking for a minute. Not much of a wine list here."

"Not much of anything here." She put down the menu.

He scanned the wine list. "Here's something that doesn't sound too bad. If I order it, would you drink a glass?"

The waitress, a thin, sour-faced woman, stomped to the table. "Ready?"

Michou ordered *poulet rôti* and *pommes frites*, and the woman headed toward the kitchen door.

"Wait a minute." Her dinner partner motioned the waitress back. "And a bottle of the 1934 Château Bourdet."

Michou smiled.

"You know the wine?"

"My father makes it."

He laughed, his teeth gleaming ivory against his tanned face. "Well, it's a damn good wine, and I'm glad to meet you. My name's Guy Chalmers."

She introduced herself and offered her hand.

"Then I take it you'll drink a glass with me?" He shook her hand.

"One." Even as she said it, she felt disloyal. She blushed and bit her lip. Here she was agreeing to have a glass of wine with another man while Marc lay in a hospital bed.

"Good year, thirty-four. Especially in Saint-Émilion. Not as much tannin as the Médocs."

"You know wine, then?"

He leaned back and laced his fingers behind his neck. "Should. I'm a shipper."

The waitress dropped a large plate in front of Michou and then returned in a minute with the bottle of wine and another glass. She smacked them down on Guy's side of the table.

He poured Michou a glass. "Is the chicken okay?"

Michou shrugged. "A little dry, but not bad." She took a sip of the wine. "What do you think?"

He lifted his thick eyebrows. "Surprisingly good. Better than I remembered."

"Why surprisingly?" She jabbed at the chicken. His condescending tone irritated her.

"Well, I ship out of Bordeaux, so I don't do much with Saint-Émilions. They just don't have the popularity with the British. Too bad." He looked at the label. "Desroches et Fils. Say, wasn't there a scandal—"

She grimaced. She'd told Papa that Lucien's scheme would hurt their reputation, but he refused to consider changing shippers. "It didn't involve our wine." The chicken turned to paste in her mouth.

"I remember now. Something about the *fils* putting fancy names on wines from the Midi—passing them off as Pomerols and Saint-Émilions. Whatever happened to him?"

"His father bought him out of it." She kept her voice flat and laid her knife and fork across the plate. She wasn't hungry anymore. She stood up. "Thank you for the wine."

His chair scraped against the wood floor as he rose. "Thank you, too. Perhaps I'll see you at breakfast?"

"I doubt it. I'm leaving very early." No matter how attractive he was, she had no desire to talk to him again. She shook his outstretched hand and moved away. When she reached the door, she impulsively looked back over her shoulder.

He raised his glass to her and grinned. "Good luck."

Squaring her shoulders, she stepped into the lobby. *Mon Dieu,* it wasn't right for her to forget Marc, even for a minute. She twisted a strand of hair around her finger. It was as if her thoughts were Marc's breath, his blood, his lifeline, and she'd let it fall slack while talking to Guy. "Please forgive me, *mon cher,*" she murmured.

She climbed the stairs slowly. Her knees were stiff, and her face stung from the sun and the wine. She yawned. She hoped she'd be too tired to dream tonight.

Michou paused on the hotel steps to take off her sweater. Even though it was early, the air was already warm. She hummed to herself as she tucked the sweater into the basket. In just a few hours she'd be with Marc.

When she reached the sidewalk, she froze. Her bicycle wasn't where she'd left it. She smashed her fist against the wall. It couldn't be gone! Blinking back the tears that blurred her sight, she ran her fingers gingerly over her bruised knuckles.

Slowly, she sank down on the steps, resting her forehead on her knees and gripping her ankles tightly. Now she'd have to walk, and it would take her three times as long. Oh God, what if she didn't make it in time?

The door slammed behind her, and she looked up. Guy Chalmers stood next to her, his eyebrows raised. He wore tan slacks and a navy-blue sweater and held a small suitcase in one hand.

"Something wrong?"

"Someone stole my bicycle."

"You're riding a bicycle to Poitiers?" His eyebrows arched higher above his dark brown eyes.

She nodded. "I thought it would be faster than a car."

"I'm inclined to agree with you, after yesterday." He laughed. "But driving is still faster than walking. May I offer you a ride? I'm going right through Poitiers."

She stood up and brushed off the back of her pants. She didn't know him, really, but what he said was true and Marc was hurt, so—

"Yes," she blurted. Now she had to, no second thoughts.

"Fine." He bent down and picked up the paniers in his free hand. "This your luggage? My car's around the corner. Let's hope *it's* still there."

She followed him down the narrow sidewalk. When they reached the car, he unlocked the trunk and set the paniers and his suitcase in it and then opened the door for her.

"Thanks." She leaned across the seat and unlocked his door. "Really. I have to get there today."

"No problem. I'm glad for the company."

Her stomach jolted bile into her throat as the car bounced onto the street. She clapped her hand over her mouth and stared straight ahead. She'd forgotten to take bread to her room last night, and she hadn't wanted to wait for breakfast. Now her stomach was getting even.

She slid her hand back down onto her lap and looked sideways at Guy. His eyes were on the road—maybe he hadn't seen.

He glanced at her. "You hungry? We can stop at the *boulangerie* on the next block."

"All right. If you let me buy." She didn't like owing people favors.

He stopped the car in front of the bakery, and she jumped out. She dashed into the shop and asked for a *baguette* and three *croissants*. In two minutes, she was back in the car again.

After she handed Guy a *croissant,* she pulled a small piece from hers and chewed it slowly.

"What are you going to Poitiers for anyway?" He bit off a quarter of the *croissant.*

She swallowed.

"Sorry. Probably none of my—"

"No. My fiancé was wounded. He's there." She took another bite and tried to chew, but the pastry expanded, filling her mouth. She rolled down the window and stuck her head out. Vomit flew out of her mouth, and tears stung her eyes.

The car stopped, and a hand patted her back between

her shoulders. She wiped her mouth and pulled her head in. Her cheeks burned.

"You okay?"

She nodded and pressed her hands against her cheeks. Her palms felt icy.

"Well, I'll take it easy, anyway."

She leaned back and crossed her arms tightly over her stomach. "I'm fine now. Guess it was just nerves—Marc, my bicycle, everything going wrong."

"He's wounded pretty badly, huh?"

"In the chest."

"Maybe you should try eating again." He turned his head. "Try the bread."

She tore off a chunk and gnawed at the hard crust. Her nausea was gone, thank God. Maybe everything was going to be all right after all. She glanced at Guy, and he shifted his eyes back to the road.

"Feeling better?"

"Much." She smiled. He was a nice man. If he was shocked by what she was doing, he certainly didn't show it.

She propped her arm on the windowsill. Traffic seemed lighter today. Maybe they'd make it to Poitiers by afternoon.

4

The sunlight preceded Michou, slanting across the empty expanse, shortening and finally disappearing as the door swung back into place. Her shoes clicked a snappy rhythm on the gray marble floor—*Marc is here, Marc is here*—as she strode to the reception counter at the base of the stairs. Her stomach quivered—with excitement this time, not nausea.

She cleared her throat, and the white-wimpled nun looked up, her dark eyes swimming behind thick glasses. "Yes?" She pursed her lips and tapped a pencil on the desk.

Michou smiled. No starched nun was going to daunt her now, not when she'd come this far. "I'm here to see Marc Laurent. Can you tell me where he is?"

The nun ran the pencil down a list and then turned the page. She scanned it slowly and shook her head. "I don't see his name."

"But he has to be here." Michou crossed her arms over her stomach and took a deep breath, inhaling the stench of decaying flesh overlaid by disinfectant. She released it slowly. "Please look again"—she peered at the nun's name tag—"Sister Jeanne."

Sister Jeanne shrugged and glanced back at the list. "There is no one by that name on our patient roster." She clapped the book shut.

There had to be a mistake. Sister Jeanne looked efficient, but she had to be wrong. What if she wasn't, though? Michou pounded her fist on the counter. Her throat tightened. "Look again! I know he's here!" Her voice sounded shrill, and it vibrated in her ears.

Sister Jeanne pinched her mouth shut and pushed the ledger toward her. "Why don't you look?"

Standing on her toes so she could see the list, Michou read every name silently. Her finger touched each one as she repeated it inside her head, inside her heart. On the next page, her finger traveled much more slowly, and her heart cried, *Slower still,* be certain, be certain.

No Marc. Old Pinchface was right. Michou pushed the book back across the counter.

"Perhaps he left already," Sister Jeanne said. She flipped back a few pages and mouthed a smile. "Here he is— he arrived on June ninth. Let me see if I can find when he was discharged." She thumbed through a few more pages before she stopped, her forehead creasing in a frown.

"What is it?"

"This Marc Laurent, he is a relative, your brother?"

Michou shook her head. What difference could that make? "My fiancé."

The nun tucked the book under her arm and marched around the counter. "Just a minute, please." Before she entered the door marked *Défense d'entrer,* she swiveled her head and peered at Michou, her lips set in a thin line.

Michou shuddered. The large foyer suddenly seemed much cooler, as if the warm summer day had slipped into autumn. She pulled her sweater out of the pannier and tugged it over her head.

She paced to the large open stairway. Damn, but the sour old nun seemed to be taking a long time—something must be wrong. She clamped her teeth together. No. Nothing was wrong. It was just a mix-up. Marc was up those stairs. Marc was all right. In only a few more minutes they'd be together, she'd be holding him in her arms, telling him about their baby.

The clank of the closing door and tapping footsteps echoed loudly throughout the foyer, and Michou spun around. An older nun leaning on a cane limped toward her while Pinchface returned to the desk.

The older nun gestured toward a bench by the door. "Shall we sit?"

Michou followed her to the bench, waiting while the nun lowered herself slowly. Why were they taking so long to tell her where Marc was? Didn't they understand he'd need her?

And she needed him. Once he was well, he'd take care of her, of the baby. Everything would be the way it was supposed to be.

The nun leaned the cane against the wall and patted the bench. "Sit down, child. I'm Sister Hélène. You're Marc Laurent's fiancée?"

Michou nodded as she sat. Perhaps they thought Marc was hurt too badly to have a visitor—that was it. She twisted a strand of hair tightly around her finger. Well, they'd just have to change their minds. Or if they wouldn't, she'd find some way to see him even if she had to sneak up those stairs and search every room.

Sister Hélène rested her hand on top of Michou's. "I'm so sorry."

Michou sucked in her breath and stared at the nun.

Sister Hélène put her hands on Michou's shoulders and looked in her eyes. "We called his family. He died yesterday."

"No!" Michou's scream reverberated from the vaulted ceiling and inside her head. "No!" She shook the nun's hands off and jumped up. "I don't believe you!"

The light faded, and pain knifed through her chest. A voice buzzed dimly, "The poor child's fainted. Get—"

What was she doing on the floor? The smooth marble chilled her through the sweater and the thin dress, the dress she'd changed into before coming to the hospital, the dress in Marc's favorite shade of blue, iris blue he called it, to match her eyes. Marc. No—no—

She pushed away the hand pressing a damp cloth to her forehead. It couldn't be true. Not Marc—solid, wise, dependable Marc. Not Marc—she couldn't remember a time without him, couldn't imagine it now. *Mon Dieu*, she'd loved him for half her life. How could he be dead?

She lifted her head. Sister Hélène knelt in front of her, a white cloth gripped in her hand. Michou pushed herself on her elbows, and the nun helped her sit.

"Are you feeling better?"

Michou nodded, and the movement made whooshing sounds inside her head.

The nun rose slowly, bracing herself with her cane. "I'm terribly sorry. We have a chapel here. Perhaps you'd like to pray there."

Pray for what? Pray for whom? What kind of god would kill her lover? Allow the father of her baby to die? God could go to hell. If he existed at all. If there was a hell other than this one. She shook her head.

"God be with you then, child."

Michou thrust her chin out and straightened her shoulders. "I'm fine now." She picked up the paniers and moved slowly toward the door.

When she stepped outside, the warm air pressed against her, and she gasped, clinging to the railing for support. She collapsed onto the stone stairs and hunched forward, her face buried in her hands.

Marc was dead.

She had to accept it. For his baby's sake, for her sake. Marc would never be there to make things right—she'd just have to do it herself. But how? She felt a twinge in her abdomen, like a piece of thread snapping, and she leaned back against the step, rubbing her flat stomach.

Even though the sun was hot on her shoulders, she shivered. What was she going to do now?

Clamping his jaw, Guy slammed on the brakes of the Citroën. Both lanes were filled with cars heading toward him. Christ, what bloody fools the refugees were! As if driving a few hundred miles farther south would save them from the Jerries. At this rate he wouldn't even make it out of Poitiers before the Germans swarmed all over it, let alone get to Paris. He banged his fist down on the horn. The loud blare satisfied him even though it didn't produce any results.

He stuck his head out the window and yelled. "Hey, get over." Diesel fumes burned his eyes.

The bushy-moustached man in the car facing him waved his arm impatiently. "Back up! Back up!"

Guy pulled his head in and looked over his shoulder. It seemed to be the only way out. He put the car in reverse and backed slowly to the corner. The street was still clear behind him, so he stepped on the gas and swung the car around. At least he'd be the first in the parade even if he was going the wrong way.

He tapped his fingers on the steering wheel as he inched the car back along the crowded streets. Maybe a little delay wouldn't be such a bad idea. If he waited until dusk and then drove all night, he'd probably make better time. Then he could swing by the hospital and see if Michou had found her boyfriend. Poor kid. Didn't look more than sixteen and her boyfriend—fiancé—all shot up. Damn the Nazis and their goddamn *Führer*.

He'd been sorry to leave her, afraid of what she might find. She had tried so hard to be strong, and her natural dignity combined with those violet eyes and that unruly platinum hair appealed to him in a way he hadn't experienced in a long time.

A smile pulled at the corner of his lips. *Hah!* He never could fool himself for long. He'd hated leaving her alone in front of that big gray hospital, and his bad temper and impatience were as much because of that as because of the clogged streets.

He snorted. He was certainly much too old for her, at least twice her age, anyway. Besides, she had a boyfriend—a lover, if his guess was right about the reason for her illness this morning. And after Lydia—

He cranked the wheel sharply to avoid a bicyclist. Well, even if it didn't make any sense, he was going back to that hospital.

As he pulled up in front of the hospital, a lone figure crouched on the steps caught his attention. Sunlight glinted on the mass of tangled blond curls. Could that be Michou? She had been wearing a blue dress, too. No, it was just a child. He let out his breath.

He was halfway up the stairs before he realized the child *was* Michou. He ran up the remaining steps, but she didn't look up, not even when he stood in front of her, his shadow falling across her shoulders. Her tiny body shuddered, and a lump settled in his stomach.

"Michou?" he said softly. He wanted to stroke her hair, but he stopped himself.

She drew in a long, sobbing breath before she looked up. Her face was white, and a splotch of blood stained her lower lip. Her eyes looked filmed, but there were no tears in them.

"They said he's dead." She bit her lip, and more blood welled up.

Guy pulled out his handkerchief and sat down beside

her. Holding her chin in his hand, he gently dabbed at the blood. A faint odor of medicine clung to her hair. "What are you going to do?"

She laid her head back on her knees. "They said I could pray." Her muffled voice sounded bitter.

Guy hesitated. He had to get to Paris, and if he took her back to Château Bourdet, he'd never make it there before the Germans. Still, he had to do something. She wasn't in any condition to be left alone.

He put his arm around her shoulders. She didn't relax against him, but she didn't pull away either. He patted her arm. "Why don't you come with me to Paris? I can take you home afterward." Damn, what a sucker he was. Just what he needed—dragging a grieving, probably pregnant teenager to a city that would be overrun by Germans any day.

But it didn't matter—he couldn't make himself leave her alone here.

Michou didn't answer for a minute. Then she looked up and shrugged. "I have to go somewhere," she said. Her voice was scratchy and toneless, like a bad telephone connection from someplace far away.

5

❧

Grasping the rail, Michou pulled herself up. Her joints, even her bones, ached. It was as if she'd aged years since she'd learned of Marc's death. And she didn't know how long ago that had been. The nun's words echoing in her head were a roar in the distance. *He died yesterday . . . he died yesterday . . . he died . . .*

She covered her ears with her hands. What had she just said? When Guy asked her to go to Paris, had she agreed?

She dropped her hands and clenched her fists. Well, why not? She didn't have the strength to walk home, the courage to face her parents, to see their pity, to hear their anger when they found out about the baby. Not yet, anyway.

Guy's hand cupped her elbow, and she leaned against him for a minute before stiffening and pulling away. "Where's your car?" she asked.

Guy pointed to the bottom of the stairs. "The streets are a mess. How about some lunch and a walk before we leave?"

"No," Michou said. The thought of food disgusted her. She just wanted to get away from this place, from its odor of death. She wanted to be far away from the place where Marc had died. "Let's go now."

Guy's eyebrows lifted. "All right." He gripped her arm tightly with one hand and picked up her panniers with the other. "We'll give it a try."

She started down the stairs. Her legs were glass, ready to shatter into a million splinters at each step. Suddenly the heat pressed against her. She stopped and pulled off her sweater.

"Let me take that." Guy plucked the sweater from her hands before he opened the car door.

Michou eased into the seat. She took a deep breath as Guy started the car. As it edged into the traffic, the buzzing in her head faded. Not long ago she'd been happy riding in this car with Guy, counting the miles until she'd see Marc.

She sat stiffly, holding her face rigid while the tears rolled down her cheeks and dropped onto her hands. Blinking hard, she wiped her face with the back of her hand. She couldn't give in now. She had to think of Marc as he had been, not as a corpse in a casket. Not like Alain.

After Alain's funeral, she'd vowed she'd never again watch the dirt falling on someone she loved. She'd only been ten when Alain had drowned, but she'd never forgotten.

When she and her family arrived at the church, everyone turned to watch them walk to the front. She wore her new blue dress, the one she'd been saving for a school party, and it rustled against her legs. Was everyone looking at her because of the noisy dress? She pressed the skirt against her legs and walked without bending her knees. She tried to hold her breath. Carnations smelled bad, like the horrid candy Sylvie's maman and papa, Uncle Julien and Aunt Yvonne, used to send before their car wreck. When she died, nobody had better send carnations.

She stared at Maman's straight back as she climbed the steps to the casket and forced her legs up the stairs behind her. Don't cry now. "Grief is private," Maman had said. But if that was true, why were there funerals? She hated funerals. She'd never go to another one, even if Maman got mad.

The casket gleamed at her, and she couldn't make herself close her eyes, even though she'd sworn she wouldn't look. They wouldn't shut, just like the time she kept them open to see if the shampoo would really sting.

Alain lay there, his hands folded across his chest. His eyes were closed and his skin was white and he looked and smelled dead. She gasped, and Maman glared at her over her shoulder. She had bitten her lip until she could taste the blood, and she squeezed her eyelids together. Don't cry. Don't cry now.

God, she still hated funerals. Leaning her head against the car window, she shut her eyes. She'd say good-bye to Marc her own way. Grief was a private thing; so was love.

It was dark when a movement of the car jolted her awake. She jerked herself upright and yawned. She must have slept for hours. Her throat was scratchy and her eyes burned. Trying to ignore the rumbling in her stomach, she rubbed her eyes.

"Awake?" Guy glanced at her.

"I think so," she said. "Where are we?"

"Not too far from Paris. Are you hungry?"

"No."

Keeping his head facing the road, Guy tossed a sack from the seat into her lap. "You have to eat."

When she opened the sack, the aroma of bread and meat drifted out. She stuck her hand into the sack and grabbed something cold and slimy. She dropped it and closed the bag. "I'm not hungry."

"Eat." Guy didn't look at her. "You need it. And your baby needs it, too."

Michou grimaced. She supposed it was a fairly obvious conclusion to reach after the way she'd thrown up all over his car this morning. Had her parents figured it out as well? *Mon Dieu,* she hoped not.

She reached back into the sack, pulled out the remnants of a *baguette,* and ripped off a piece. Crunching the crusty bread, she leaned back in the seat. As soon as she swallowed, her stomach stopped rolling.

She had just finished eating when they reached the outskirts of Paris. Despite the dark and the blackout, traffic was even heavier than it had been in Poitiers. Partially covered headlights glowed softly like an army of fireflies, and the rumble of many motors crept through the closed windows.

Guy jerked the wheel. "Sorry," he said. "It's so damn hard to see the holes with these blinders over the lights. Just hope I don't get run off the road again." He was silent for a minute. "Have you been to Paris before?"

Michou twisted the top of the sack into a cylinder. "I lived here with my grandparents for three years. They have a house near the Parc de Monceau."

"Did you like it?"

She crumpled the sack into a ball. She'd been so angry when her parents had sent her away. And hurt. "Paris, yes."

"But not your grandparents?"

"Grandmère has never liked *me*." And still didn't, she thought.

He tapped his fingers on the steering wheel. "So you probably don't want to stay there with them. I can get you a room at the Victoire if you'd like. That's what I'd been planning to do."

"They're on their way to the Pyrénées. Why don't you stay at the house instead? Sylvie will be there, but she'll be very nice to you." Michou rolled down the window. The air felt cool against her warm cheeks.

"Sylvie?"

"My cousin." She tried to keep her tone impartial. No sense trying to explain about Sylvie. Besides, he'd never believe it after he met her. No man would.

Sylvie switched on the bedside lamp. God, what a racket! Would the Germans just start pounding on doors in the middle of the night? She glanced at the clock on her nightstand. Three. This was ridiculous. She just wouldn't answer the door.

She lay back down, drawing the pale blue coverlet up to her chin. The knocking continued. She exhaled sharply. *Merde*. She might as well get up. Whoever it was apparently wasn't going to stop.

Sighing, she grabbed her white satin robe from the foot of the four-poster bed. Breathing in the faint scent of Chanel No. 5 that still clung to it, she slipped it on as she descended the stairs. "I'm coming," she shouted, turning on the light. The pounding stopped.

She pulled aside the blackout curtain covering the small window at the top of the door and peered out. The light from the entry hall illuminated two figures, one tall and the other quite short. Probably not Germans, anyway. Not unless they were invading with an army of children.

"Who are you?" she said loudly.

The smaller person stepped forward. "It's Michou. Open the door."

Quickly, Sylvie unlocked the door. "What are you doing here? Are you crazy? Everybody else is leaving!" She yanked Michou into the entry, and the man followed. "Get in here before you get me arrested for a blackout violation."

While she kissed her, Sylvie glanced over Michou's head at the handsome man standing behind her. She smiled at him and patted her hair, smoothing the curve of the long pageboy into place on her shoulders. Thank God she'd had her hair and nails done yesterday.

"I'm Sylvie de Bacqueville," she said, and held out her hand.

"Guy Chalmers." Guy stepped forward to grip her hand.

Sylvie lowered her eyes. She was glad she hadn't bothered to sash her peignoir. He was certainly very good-looking. Just what was he doing with Michou? She'd been in love with Marc Laurent forever. Besides, Guy looked much too sophisticated for the silly child.

When she looked up, Guy had turned to Michou. "She needs to rest," he said without taking his eyes off Michou. The concern in his voice was sincere.

Sylvie sniffed and tied the sash. "Of course. She knows where her room is." She nodded toward the stairs.

Michou stepped forward. "Guy is staying here, too. He can't check into a hotel at this hour. And it's all my fault."

"Well, certainly. He can have the Directoire room, next to mine. Grandmère always keeps it ready." Sylvie tilted her head so her strawberry-blond hair fell sleekly across one eye, and she looked up at Guy. "You don't need to bother with your luggage tonight. There are nightclothes in the bedroom—if you want them."

"Thanks, but it's no problem." He leaned toward Michou. "Go to bed. Now," he said, squeezing her shoulder.

"Yes, sir," Michou said. She stooped to pick up the paniers Guy had leaned against the door, but he snatched them away.

"Would you mind?" he asked, handing them to Sylvie.

She forced her lips into a smile. "Of course not." Anything for her dear little cousin. What could he possibly see in Michou? Did he know about Marc? Well, if Michou was keeping two men dangling, she had to give her some credit.

"Thanks. I'll just be a second." Stepping onto the porch, he shut the door quickly behind him.

Sylvie started up the stairs, bouncing the paniers after her. "Well, come on," she hissed at Michou. What in hell was wrong with her? She looked like an Edvard Munch portrait, all white skin and huge dark eyes.

Michou didn't move.

"Are you all right?"

Michou nodded and shuffled toward her.

Sylvie reached the top and waited for Michou, tapping her long red nails on the banister. Something was definitely wrong. Grandmère was forever yelling at Michou for running up the stairs.

She shrugged. Maybe Michou was tired. Or maybe she was just growing up. She opened the bedroom door and tossed the paniers on the green bedspread. "See? Nothing's changed." She stepped out of Michou's way and smirked. She knew Michou had always hated the green bedroom, but she'd never told Grandmère. Not that Grandmère would have done anything about it anyway.

Michou turned to face her. "Thank you. Good night." She closed the door.

Sylvie hurried across the hall and into her room. Peering into the mirror over her dressing table, she grabbed up her brush, then ran it through her hair. She tossed her head so her hair swung about her shoulders and laid the brush back down. After she stroked red lipstick onto her mouth, she dabbed some more Chanel No. 5 behind her ears.

The door clicked downstairs, and she smiled at her reflection before turning and racing down the stairs. Guy was the most fascinating-looking man she'd seen in ages. She'd soon put an end to his interest in Michou. A casual mention of Marc ought to do it.

When she reached the bottom, Guy stood in the entry hall. "Beautiful house," he said.

"Would you like to see more?"

Guy shook his head. "I need to get some sleep. I've got a lot of business to attend to tomorrow." He picked up his suitcase and moved toward the stairs.

Sylvie put her hand on his arm. "You must be starved. What about something to eat?"

"Really, I'm fine. Thanks, though."

Frowning, she pulled her hand back and followed him up the stairs. This was going to be harder than she'd thought.

Perhaps Michou was the key. She touched her finger to her lips and glanced down at the Aubusson runner stretching down the hall. "Is Michou all right? I mean, she looks simply awful. I'm terribly worried about her. And I promised Marc I'd watch out for her. You know Marc? Her fiancé?"

"Didn't she tell you?" He stared at her.

"Tell me what?"

"Marc is dead."

"Oh." She twisted her sash around her hand. Damn it! That ploy had certainly backfired. Now she looked like an idiot, pretending to be close when it was obvious Michou didn't trust her enough to reveal something that important. "Poor Michou! She must be taking it awfully hard—she didn't say a word. What happened?" Wrinkling her forehead, she looked up at Guy.

He told her about taking Michou to the hospital, how excited she'd been about seeing Marc, and then returning to find her sitting in shock on the steps. "I'll take her home on my way back. Would you watch her tomorrow? She's like a sleepwalker." His eyes narrowed. "Damn Nazis."

Sylvie looked at him and sighed heavily. "Poor Michou," she repeated. "Of course I'll take care of her." She pointed to the door next to hers. "This is your room."

"Thanks. I probably won't see you in the morning." He rested his hand on the doorknob.

"Do plan on staying here until you leave." She tossed her hair out of her eyes and smiled. "We'll have dinner waiting for you."

"Great. I'm already looking forward to it." He nodded at her and shut the door.

Sylvie grinned at his door. She'd covered up pretty well—he hadn't suspected a thing. Men were so easy to fool. So he was looking forward to tomorrow. Perfect. She was, too.

6

❧

A taxi at last. Michou climbed into the back seat and rolled down the window to clear out the musty odor of sweat and Gauloises. Thank God neither Guy nor Sylvie had been up. She didn't mind Guy's concern, but she didn't want to explain anything to anyone this morning.

Especially Sylvie—Guy had probably told her about Marc. Her phony pity would be nauseating. She folded her arms across her chest. Besides, she wanted to visit Rachel alone. She hadn't seen her for two years, and Sylvie—and Grandmère—had never approved of her friendship with a Jewish girl, no matter how wealthy her parents.

But she didn't care what they thought. Leaning back, she ran her fingers along a rip in the coarse brown seat cover. Rachel would understand about the baby—her little boy must be about a year old now. And she wouldn't say anything stupid about Marc.

The wheels screeched as the taxi careened around a corner. She glanced up as she slid across the seat. The taxi sped the wrong way down a one-way street. No cars charged toward them, no horns honked, no pedestrians stared. Where was everyone? She shuddered. "What—"

The driver shrugged. "Why not? It's shorter. And no *flics* left to catch me." He swiveled his bald head and stared at her, a cigarette dangling from the corner of his lip. "You're lucky, mam'selle. You see the notices? Paris is an open city. You're my last ride. Picking up the family and heading south, I am." Banging his fist on the wheel, he turned back to face the deserted street. "The *Boches* will be here in a day."

Michou leaned forward. "That soon?" She shook her head. Suddenly the fog surrounding her since she'd learned

43

of Marc's death cleared, replaced by newsreel flashes of grim
Nazi storm troopers crushing Vienna, Prague, Warsaw. She
must have been insane to come here, to expose her baby to
this danger.

"Allez! Government ran to Tours almost a week ago. Did
it in secret, though. After they promised to fight house to
house if they had to. Begged us to stay." He pulled at the
collar of his black turtleneck. *"Tiens,* I should've known
better and got out last week. Might be too late now." He
pulled the taxi next to the curb. "Rue Gautier."

Michou handed him the fare and got out. Paris was lost,
and the street was as barren as her heart. The stillness was
eerie, as if even the bricks and trees awaited the Germans.
There wasn't another car in sight, and iron gratings barred the
windows of the *épicerie* across the street. She picked her way
along the sidewalk through rotting garbage and broken pieces
of furniture and abandoned baggage.

She stopped with a jolt. What if Rachel had gone, too?
She rolled her eyes and started up the steps to the apartment
Rachel and Joseph had lived in since their marriage two years
ago. Nothing to do but find out.

The stench of tobacco and garlic made her stomach turn
as she climbed the creaky stairs to the third floor. This place
was certainly different from the Isaacs' house. It was just like
Rachel to refuse her parents' help.

Michou knocked on the door, and the sound echoed
down the empty hallway. She held her breath and listened for
footsteps.

She sighed when she heard a muffled thud followed by
an exasperated, "David! Stop that!" Rapping again on the
door, she called "Rachel! It's me, Michou."

Locks snapped, and the door flew open. Rachel stood in
the doorway, her arms outstretched and her straight hair
framing her face like a blackout curtain. "I don't believe it!"
she said. She pulled Michou close and hugged her before she
kissed her cheeks. "But it's just like you to come to Paris
when everyone else is running away."

Michou tried to smile, to say something light, to pretend
to be strong, but all her resolve was gone. Tears stung her
eyes, and she grabbed Rachel's hand.

Rachel's grin faded, and her dark eyebrows pulled together. She squeezed Michou's hand. *"Mignonne,* what's wrong? Are you in trouble?"

Michou nodded and gulped hard. She let Rachel lead her to the couch. Between sobs, she told Rachel about Marc and the baby.

Rachel listened without saying anything. When Michou finished, she put her arm around her shoulders. "Do you want to stay here with us?" she asked.

"N-no," Michou hiccupped. "I mean, I can't. Papa needs help in the vineyards. And Mémé Laure just isn't well."

"What will they do when—"

"I don't know." Michou twisted her hair around her finger. "But if they make me leave, I'll come to you. If you're still here. Aren't you scared?"

A crash sounded from the next room. Rachel sighed and stood up. "To death. Joseph tried to make me go with my parents, but I couldn't leave him. You know." Her smile looked tired. "But I'm so worried about David. Just a minute. I'll get him before he destroys his crib." She disappeared behind the brown curtain hanging in the doorway.

Michou closed her eyes and rested her head against the back of the couch. Crying helped, but now the tension bracing her had gone. She felt as limp as a new vine in the hot sun.

Rachel returned carrying a brown-eyed little boy on her hip. "Here he is." She grinned, and the tightness in her face relaxed. "Cute little monkey, isn't he?"

David smiled and reached out toward Michou.

"Oh! He's wonderful! May I hold him?" Michou held out her arms.

Rachel swung him onto Michou's lap. "He's heavy."

David snuggled against Michou's breasts, and the thudding in her chest receded. "Good morning," she said. She brushed her face against his soft black hair. He smelled like soap.

"Goom," David said. He wiggled away and, turning to face her, ran his fingers across her wet cheeks. Tilting his head, he looked up at her and said, "Wah."

Michou hugged him. In a few months she'd have a child just like this one, maybe even a boy with Marc's dark hair and eyes. A child who'd never know his father, who'd grow up in a

country occupied by his father's murderers. New tears
burned her eyes, but she blinked them away. "Can he walk
yet?"

"Almost. He takes steps. Want to see?" Rachel picked
David up and stood him on the floor. She pointed toward the
window. "You stand over there. He seems taken with you.
Maybe he'll come to you."

Michou walked to the window, then squatted on her
heels. Stretching out her arms, she said, "Come here, David.
Walk to me."

David took a tottering step, stopped, and looked back at
his mother. He turned his head around carefully and stared at
Michou, as if deciding whether he could trust her. Suddenly
he yelled and charged toward her, swaying back and forth but
managing to keep his balance.

When he reached her, Michou scooped him up and
kissed his warm cheeks. "What a special boy!" she said.

Rachel clapped. "Hooray! David walked! Won't Papa be
excited?"

Michou tightened her arms around David. Marc would
never see his baby walk.

As Rachel took her baby from Michou, she frowned.
"What's that?" she said, pointing out the window.

Michou turned and pulled aside the lace curtain. She
sucked in her breath. The horizon was orange, and hug
billows of dark smoke smothered the morning's clear sky.
"Mon Dieu! They must be attacking already!"

"Joseph!" Squeezing David to her, Rachel sat down
slowly in the chair by the window. "The army called up all
the war-plant workers three days ago. He's out there." She
rested her chin on David's head and stared out the window.

Michou shivered. "You and David come with me. We've
got to get out of here. You can stay at Château Bourdet until
Joseph comes home."

"No." Rachel's voice was muffled. "I have to wait for
him. We'll be all right. You go."

"Will you at least promise to come after Joseph returns?
It just isn't safe for you here." Michou patted Rachel's shoulder. Damn Joseph for putting his politics before his family.

"I can't." Rachel's lips twisted in an effort to smile.
"You know Joseph—it's a matter of conscience, he says."

Michou put her hands on her hips. "And I know you. And *your* conscience. But if you change your mind—"

"I won't." Holding David in her arms, Rachel stood up. "I want you to stay, *mignonne,* but I'm worried. Let's go find you a taxi."

Michou kissed David and then Rachel. "You're right. But I'll never find another taxi. I doubt there's one left in all of Paris. It's only a mile or two. I can walk."

"Call me when you get there."

As she stepped into the dingy hallway, Michou forced her lips into a smile. "Be resolute," she said. How many times had they bolstered each other's courage during those horrible times at school with that charge? Oh, how small those troubles looked now!

"Be resolute." Rachel smiled and shut the door.

Michou ran down the stairs and onto the sidewalk. The sky was gray and the air bitter. Swinging her arms, she strode in the direction of the eighth arrondissement. Before long, smoke clogged her nostrils and she gasped. Her stomach tensed with slow cramping waves, and she clasped her arms across her middle and moaned.

Still she walked, glancing up occasionally at the terrifying sky. One foot in front of the other, one step at a time. She stumbled but kept moving. One foot in front of the other, one foot—

She didn't know how long it had been since she left Rachel's apartment. The trees along Avenue de Valois cast dim shadows across the sidewalk when she opened the gate in front of her grandparents' house. Guy's green car wasn't parked in front.

She let herself in quietly and was halfway up the stairs when Sylvie called after her.

"Where have you been? I've been frantic!"

Michou turned slowly. "I went to see Rachel."

"You might have told me. Guy asked me to take care of you. He seemed to think you needed it." Sylvie sneered.

"Did he say when he'd be back?"

"In time for dinner."

"Dinner! Have you seen the sky? The *Boches* are burning Paris!" Michou clenched her teeth.

"You silly!" Sylvie stuck out her tongue. "That's us.

They're just burning the depots before the Germans get there."

"Oh." Michou put out a hand to brace herself against the wall.

Sylvie started up. "Are you feeling all right? You look feverish."

Michou stared at her for a moment, then pushed herself away from the wall. "I'm fine. Just tired, that's all. I walked back."

"Will you want dinner?"

Michou nodded. Sylvie'd love it if she could have Guy all to herself. Well, she'd be damned before she'd please her.

Sylvie furrowed her brow. "You should rest, Michou. I can bring your dinner to your room. I wouldn't mind. Really."

"Just wake me if I don't come down in time." She banged her door shut.

After she stripped back the covers, she climbed into the bed. The lavender-scented sheets cooled her hot skin. Was the lavender at home blooming yet? But no, she'd only been gone three days. Only three days, and it was a different world. Only three days, and now Marc was dead and the Germans were on their way to Paris. If she couldn't leave right now, all she wanted to do was sleep and forget.

The fist gripping at her bowels awoke her at the same time as the pounding on the door. For a minute she didn't remember where she was. She'd dreamed of the river again, but this time the water had been warm and it had gushed up between her legs.

She rolled to her side and pulled her knees to her chest. *Mon Dieu,* the pain! The knocking continued, and she opened her eyes. The damp sheets stuck to her skin.

"Michou?" Sylvie rattled the doorknob. "Michou, are you awake?" She opened the door, and the light from the hall fell across the bed.

Michou raised her head and looked first at Sylvie and then at the sheets. They were stained dark red. The cloying smell of blood made her gag. Just like the hospital. What was—

Oh, God! No! Not the baby! She moaned as a fist wrenched at her insides again.

Sylvie gasped. "What's happening!" She turned on the light. "You've ruined Grandmère's sheets!" She put her hands on her hips. "It's just your monthlies, *non?*"

"No." Michou panted, grabbing her middle. "My baby. Something wrong. Not the baby, too! Get help! The blood— my baby—"

"What!" Sylvie's mouth dropped open. "Your baby?" She stepped closer and stared at Michou. "Are you sure? Is Marc the father?"

Michou groaned. "Call Rachel. Hurry!"

Sylvie ran to the door and said, "I'll be right back."

Michou curled in on herself, pressing her legs together. "Stay where you are, little one," she gasped aloud. "Please don't die."

Sylvie returned with towels and a basin of water. "I called Rachel," she said. "Guy has gone for her. She's going to try to bring the midwife who delivered her baby." She pulled the covers back over Michou. "She said to keep you warm."

Michou nodded, her teeth chattering. She'd do anything to keep this baby, Marc's baby. Cramps wrenched her insides for what seemed like hours, and she rolled back and forth. When they eased, she gulped down the water Sylvie offered.

Footsteps thudded on the stairs. Sylvie put down the glass. "They're here," she said.

Rachel rushed into the bedroom. "We found the midwife." She stepped aside. "This is Michou. It's her third month."

The midwife pulled back the covers. "Get up," she ordered.

Michou cringed against the bed. Maybe there was still a chance to save the baby if she did the right thing. The wrinkled midwife looked stern and efficient, her steel-gray hair pulled back in a bun and her lips set in a thin line. But what if she really didn't know what to do? Getting up couldn't be right. It would only make the blood come faster.

The midwife tugged on her arm. "You must get up. It will be easier to pass the tissue that way."

"No!" Michou jerked her arm away. "It isn't tissue! It's my baby. I don't want to lose my baby."

The midwife pointed to the bloody sheets. "It's too late, *ma petite*. You need to get rid of it or the bleeding will not stop." She put her hands on her hips.

"There's no way to stop it?" Michou wiped the tears from her face.

"Not now," the midwife said. "And it's best not to. You must accept it."

Michou grated her teeth as another spasm gripped her middle. She panted, sweat mixing with the tears running down her cheeks. She rocked her head back and forth on the pillow as the cramps pulsed through her body.

Must accept.
Marc dead.
Baby dying.
Must accept.
Baby dying.

"No!" she shrieked. This baby had to live. She willed it to live. It must not die.

7

The midwife patted her hand. "You can have another. You're very young, and it's easy to make a baby, *non?*" She smiled. "Your husband will be glad to help."

"He's dead." Michou squeezed her eyes shut and gasped as another cramp sliced her abdomen. Marc's baby was dying, and she could never have another. Hot tears flooded her eyes again as she felt hands stripping off her underwear and pulling her legs to the side of the bed.

"She's passed it!" The midwife sounded triumphant.

Michou opened her eyes. The midwife pointed to brownish lump on the sheet. Could that be her baby? She swung her head back and forth slowly. It was over.

She allowed Rachel and the midwife to pull her from the bed and stood shivering, so numb she didn't feel any embarrassment while the midwife sponged her belly and thighs with cold water.

Grumbling, Sylvie changed the bed, and the midwife ordered Michou back into it and then packed old towels between her legs.

"You should stop bleeding soon," she said, pulling the covers over Michou. "Keep still and stay warm."

Sylvie leaned over Michou. "I'm sorry about your *husband,*" she whispered.

The midwife smoothed back Michou's hair. "You'll be all right now. Do you want me to stay with you?"

Michou shook her head. "Thank you for helping me," she said. She closed her eyes. What was Sylvie going to do? Would she tell everyone? Well, it didn't matter now. Nothing mattered now. Nothing at all. Nothing . . .

51

The knock at the door awakened her. "Michou? It's Guy. May I come in?" He strode across the room and opened the curtains.

The harsh light made Michou blink. She sat up, drawing the covers up to her chin. The smell of old blood still lingered in the room. She waited for her stomach to heave but nothing happened. Of course it wouldn't. She drew a deep breath. She wasn't pregnant anymore.

"I've come to say good-bye." Guy turned to face her. A muscle in his jaw twitched.

"What?"

"I've talked to Sylvie and Rachel. They'll take care of you," he said. He paused, holding out open hands. "The Germans are here. I've got to get—"

"But I can't stay here. I won't. I'm fine now. You *have* to take me with you!" Michou gripped the covers.

"Are you sure?"

She nodded vigorously. "I'll be ready in ten minutes." She'd be ready in two if it meant getting out of this room, this house, this city. Still holding the covers around herself, she swung her legs over the edge of the bed.

"All right. I *will* feel better if I can get you home. Especially now. I'll wait downstairs." He let himself out.

When Michou stood up, the room turned black. She hung on to the bedpost until the dizziness passed. She splashed cold water on her face and, peering into the mirror, tugged a comb through her snarled hair. Except for the purplish circles under her eyes, she didn't look any different, didn't look as if her whole life had changed in two days.

She remembered thinking the same thing when Alain died. Why didn't death show on her face? How could the outside stay the same when the inside was shattered like the mirror she smashed the day he drowned?

She put down the comb. Breaking the mirror hadn't helped. Nothing had. Nothing would.

After she dressed quickly in the old brown pants and a light blouse, she tossed the paniers on the bed. She gathered her dress and sweater from the chair where they still lay. Smoothing out the blue dress, Marc's favorite dress, she squeezed her eyes shut against the stinging tears. She'd had so much hope when she'd put it on before going to the hospital. Now she'd never wear it again. She folded it and put it on top of the sweater.

Downstairs, when Michou reached the entryway, Sylvie glanced at her and then turned back to Guy. "I still don't see why you have to leave right now," she said, pouting. "If only you knew all the trouble I had finding something decent for dinner. And Aimée has been cooking for—"

"Sorry," Guy said. "Can't be helped." He took the paniers from Michou. "Are you sure you're going to be all right?"

Sylvie sniffed and flicked her hand in the air, her red nails gleaming. "Oh, she'll be fine. Don't be fooled—she may look as fragile as a Degas ballerina, but really she's as strong as a peasant." She laid her hand on Guy's arm and looked up at him. "You positively won't reconsider?"

"Positively," Guy said. "I've got to return to Bordeaux. My father's there, and I have to get him out of France before the Germans get there. He's British."

"Oh," Sylvie said. She dropped her hand and faced Michou. "Give your parents my love." She raised her eyebrows and put her hands on her hips. "And my sympathy for their loss."

Michou opened the door and escaped onto the porch before Sylvie could kiss her. Damn her! She'd always loved using Michou's follies against her, blackmailing her practically into slavery with promises not to tell Grandmère of her latest escapade. Well, this time it wouldn't work. She'd tell Maman and Papa herself before she'd let Sylvie intimidate her again.

She eased herself into the car, staring at the intricate iron gateway in front of the mansion across the street so she wouldn't have to watch Sylvie gushing over Guy. At least he didn't act as stupid as most men did about her. Marc had never been fooled, either.

Guy climbed into the seat beside her and slammed the door. "Quite a girl, your cousin," he said. "I take it you've never been close."

Michou shook her head.

"Well, at least she was thoughtful enough to have the cook pack us something to eat." He patted the package resting between them. "It's going to be a long trip."

* * *

Guy put the car in gear and tapped lightly on the gas pedal as the wall of cars jarred forward a few feet. At this rate, the Nazis would be running over them all before nightfall. Horns blaring, cars on both sides tried to edge into the tiny space in front of him. He pinched the bridge of his nose. Just what he needed—another damn headache.

He glanced sideways at Michou. Her face was pale, but she wasn't showing any of the signs of fever the midwife had warned them to look for—no flushes or sudden chills. She hadn't spoken since they left the house on the Avenue de Valois five hours ago, and he hadn't tried to talk, either.

He braked again. The riot of cars, trucks, wagons, bicycles—anything that could move—crowding out of the fallen city demanded all his attention. Getting to Paris had been easy compared to this. Soldiers and refugees on foot moved faster than the vehicles.

The Citroën topped a rise, and Michou moaned, "Oh, no!" Cars stretched bumper to bumper across both lanes for miles ahead. "We'll never get home."

"Not if we stay on this road." Guy flipped open the glove compartment. "Check the map. Maybe we can find some other way."

Michou spread the Michelin road map out in her lap as the car lurched a few more feet. "Here." She pointed to a tiny line. "It's probably nothing more than a path, but it might be faster than this."

He leaned over and ran his finger along the map. "It joins the highway about—let's see—" He checked the scale. "About three miles further. Let's give it a try."

Ignoring curses and raised fists, Guy fought the car toward the left shoulder. As it finally bumped onto the rutted dirt road, he wiped the sweat from his forehead.

"Thank God." Michou relaxed her grip on the door handle.

Guy shifted into third for the first time since turning onto the Boulevard Raspail that morning. "Let's just hope it keeps heading south."

He stuck his pipe in his mouth and gnawed on the stem. Damn, he wished he could do something more for Michou.

Poor kid. So upset about losing that baby, even though it was probably for the best.

He scooped the pipe into the pouch of Virginia tobacco. If only he could tell her she'd get over it more quickly if she didn't keep it all inside—just like a champagne bottle with the cork ready to explode against the ceiling. He knew about that.

Keeping his eye on the narrow road, he fumbled for the matches, lit the pipe, and inhaled the spicy-sweet smoke. Too bad it was so damn hard to help someone. Dad might as well have been speaking to that champagne bottle when he'd urged him to talk about Mother, about coming to live with a parent he hardly knew in a country where no one else spoke English.

Guy shifted down into second as the car bounced into a large pothole. Well, Dad had tried, but it hadn't done any good at all. He'd suffered over his mother's death, blaming and pitying himself, but he'd refused to talk about it.

He rubbed his forehead. He'd paid for his silence. And so had Dad. It took months for that cork to work itself out, but Christ, when it did—

He shook his head. He had to try. "What was Marc like?" Staring at the curve ahead, he lit the pipe again. Smoke curled up into his eyes.

Michou crossed her arms. "He was only twenty-four."

"Had you known him for long?"

"All my life." She ducked her head forward so her hair curtained her face.

"Oh." He was making about as much progress as they had on Route Nationale No. 20.

"He was my brother's best friend."

Guy glanced at her. Maybe this would go somewhere. "Were they in the army together?"

"Alain's dead."

He bit the pipe stem as he braked for the sharp turn. "Germans?"

She shook her head, and her hair swept across her cheeks. "He drowned when he was fifteen." Her voice sounded flat, like a schoolgirl reciting multiplication tables.

Guy raised his eyebrows. Where did he go from here?

Condolences would sound inane; anything else would sound callous.

"He was trying to save Lucien Desroches's little brother."

"Of the Desroches wine scandal?"

Michou nodded and turned her head toward the passenger window.

"This Lucien one of Marc's friends, too?"

"Marc hated him." She paused. "Are we still going south?"

Another dead end. Guy laid the pipe on the dash. "I don't think so." The car reached a straight stretch, and he stepped on the gas. Wheat fields on either side rushed by as the needle jumped up to forty miles an hour. Maybe the curve at the end would put them back on course.

Michou gasped as he shifted down. "Look!"

Cars surging toward them filled the road ahead. The driver of the first car stuck his head out the window and shouted, "Turn back! Turn back! The *Boches* are behind us!"

Guy slammed on the brakes and jerked the car into a field. "Let me see that map again," he said. He coughed as dust rolled into the car.

Michou handed it to him, her hand shaking. "There was another road a little way back. Right after the bridge."

He draped the map over the steering wheel. Christ, they must have come fifty miles since the turnoff. The damn map wasn't any help at all. He tossed it onto the back seat. "We'll give it a try," he said.

After he backed the car around, he followed the swarm of refugees to the crossroad. "No signpost." He sighed as he swung the car onto an even narrower road. "Let's hope this doesn't end at some farmer's doorstep."

"Or the German army's," Michou said, her voice low and her lips barely moving. Her hands tensed into tight fists in her lap.

"I should have left you in Paris. Goddamn stupid of me. Should have realized—"

"Don't," she said. "If you hadn't, I would've found another way."

Guy relaxed his grip slightly on the steering wheel. "I believe you." What a fighter she was. Sylvie was right. She was like a dandelion puff—deceptively fragile and amazingly hardy at the same time. Not at all like Lydia.

He frowned. His ex-wife's courage was only for public display, like a new hairdo or a pair of fancy shoes. When she didn't get exactly what she wanted, she didn't struggle for it— she just left. But even that wouldn't bother him now if it weren't for Tessie. It was her he hated losing, not her mother.

He sighed and ran his fingers through his hair. Well, at least he'd be seeing his daughter soon. That is, if the damn road led anywhere except back to Paris. He leaned forward and pulled his shirt away from his sticky back.

"It's getting dark," Michou said. "We've been driving for hours and where are we? Nowhere." She unwrapped the food parcel, and the pungent smell of overripe Camembert filled the car. She spread some on a piece of bread and offered it to him.

"Thanks." He held his breath as he took a bite. "Anything else besides cheese in there?" Although he wouldn't admit it to a Frenchman, he'd never learned to like their strong-smelling cheeses.

"Some cold chicken."

He shoved the rest of the bread into his mouth and held out his hand. "Sounds great." Steering with one hand, he chewed on the leg. "You eat, too." He drew his eyebrows together and glared at her as if she were his four-year-old daughter.

Michou nodded, her mouth full. She swallowed. "Don't worry about me," she snapped. She ducked her head and fumbled with the package.

"I didn't mean to sound patronizing," he said. He tossed the chicken bone out the window and then glanced at her. "But I am worried about you. And it's not because I think you can't take care of yourself."

She tilted her head and stared intently ahead as if she hadn't heard. "Listen. What's that noise?"

Shaking his head, he rolled his eyes. "Horns. Goddamn horns." He stopped the car and peered into the dusk. A shadowy stream of vehicles bobbed slowly alongside them. "Look over there. Isn't that the route nationale?" he said, slumping against the seat and pointing. "It looks as if this road runs into it in about half a mile."

Michou crossed her arms tightly against her belly and bent forward. "They're going to kill us all," she whispered. She turned to him, her eyes shimmering in the dim light. "And I don't care."

He stepped on the gas, and the car lurched ahead. God, he wanted to put his arms around her, to comfort her, but he was afraid she'd only crawl deeper into herself, maybe shut him out entirely. But bitterness was better than hopelessness, and he could hear the hatred in her voice despite her words. His eyes watering from staring into the darness, he guided the car toward the incessant honking.

"Right back where we started from," Michou said as the car approached the intersection.

A faint vibrating hum crescendoed suddenly into a roar. Thrusting his arm in front of her, Guy stomped on the brakes. "Get out!" he shouted. He opened her door and shouldered her onto the ground.

A black hulk, flames spurting from gun nozzles, swept over the crowded road.

8

Guy flung himself on top of Michou, and she stiffened and gasped but didn't cry out. "Bastards!" he shouted as staccato bursts of machine-gun fire hammered the roof of the car.

After the rattle of the guns faded, he eased himself off her and rolled to his side. "You okay?" He hoped he hadn't landed on her too heavily, broken a rib or something. All he'd been thinking of was protecting her from the sons of bitches.

He grimaced. Such nobility—and a lot of good it would have done. They both could have been killed by the same bullet.

"Yes." Michou raised her head.

"Keep down!" he hissed into her ear. "They might come back." Goddamn stinking Nazis. Pushing himself up onto his elbows, he squinted into the darkness. Except for a few dark shapes, the highway was empty, the way cleared for German tanks.

He slowly turned his head. Dozens of cars, many of them on their sides or upside down, littered the fields and ditches. He'd been afraid something like this would happen, had been listening for the sound of planes almost without realizing it.

He sniffed. Smoke and gas fumes filled the air. Risky as it was, they needed to move away from the overturned car in front of them. He hoped Michou hadn't seen the motionless figures inside.

"I think we'd be safer in that ditch," he whispered. "Keep low and follow me." His voice echoed dully in the sudden quiet. There had to be hundreds of refugees out there, not one making a sound.

Michou shivered and gulped. "All right."

59

He patted her on the shoulder. She seemed shaken but not even close to hysteria, thank God. She was braver than a lot of men he knew.

"Now," he said, creeping forward. Gravel bit into his forearms and thighs as he pulled himself toward the ditch. He crawled into it and jerked his head around.

A buzzing drone cut the eerie silence, and Michou was still several feet away.

He threw himself out of the ditch, grabbed her hands, and heaved her toward him. Wrapping his arms around her, he rolled them down the slope just as several planes swooped low over the road.

He held her tightly against him until the roar of the planes receded into a distant rumble. "Not much for them to shoot at this time," he said. "Maybe they won't come back."

Michou drew a long shuddering breath. "How can they do it? How can they shoot at people who can't shoot back? Babies and children and women and old men." Her voice cracked. "You saw them—all those dead people in their cars. What did they do to the *Boches?*"

Guy pressed her head against his chest. Not a word about fear, about how close she'd come to dying. Just sorrow for the innocent dead and anger at the senseless cruelty. Maybe the anger would lead to healing. But, Christ, he wished this hadn't happened, not on top of everything else. All he wanted to do was get her home to her parents. He smoothed her hair with his free hand. He felt so responsible—he'd insisted on taking her with him to Paris, he'd let her talk him into taking her back. The only reason they weren't dead was luck, blind luck.

Finally, Michou stopped sobbing. "Could you do it? Could you kill women and children?" She swiped at the tears on her face, her hand clenched into a fist.

He paused before he answered, thinking of Tessie. He'd never killed anyone. He hadn't thought of fighting the Nazis as killing other human beings, but there it was. Soldiers killed—that was what they did, from the general who gave the orders to the flier who dropped the bomb to the infantryman who pulled the trigger. And he was going to England to be a part of it.

"I wouldn't want to," he said. "I don't like the idea of

killing anyone. But I'd do it if they threatened the people I care about—my daughter, my father." And Michou, he added to himself. "That's just what Hitler is doing."

She nodded. "I think I could kill Nazis. I think I might even want to. For Marc. For my baby. For those people out there." Hiccuping, she flicked her hand toward the highway. "But I could never do something like that."

"I hope I never have to."

"The airplanes haven't come back." The quiver was gone from her voice. "It's so quiet. Is anyone else out there?"

He sat up, cautiously poking his head above the rim of the ditch and scanning first the sky and then the fields. "A few people wandering around. No planes. Probably figure their job is done." He cocked his head in the direction the airplanes had come from. "Wait a minute."

"I hear it, too," Michou said. She grabbed his arm. "Get down!"

He peered into the darkness, trying to see what made the husky whirring noise. "It's not planes."

Michou pulled herself up beside him. "What is it?"

"Motorcycles, hundreds of goddamn motorcycles. We have front-row seats for the parade. The bastards are on their way to Bordeaux."

Michou coughed and lifted her head from Guy's shoulder. Her throat ached from the the effort of holding back her tears as the German army rolled down the highway in front of her. First the motorcycles, then the armored cars, then the tanks. At last the rear guard, mounted on big blue-gray motorcycles, ordering them all back to Paris.

Guy stood up and held out his hands to her. "Guess we'd better see about the car. Hope it still runs."

She let him pull her up. "What are we going to do?"

He winked at her and jerked his thumb toward the German soldier watching them from his motorcycle. "Pretend to go back. Pull off on the first side road we can find. Pray like hell it doesn't lead us to Paris."

"Or back to the Route Nationale."

"Or into more Germans."

She shrugged. Praying wasn't going to help. And besides, it didn't really make much difference. The *Boches* in

Paris, the *Boches* in Saint-Émilion, maybe even at Château Bourdet by the time she got there. *Merde,* the *Boches* stinking up the whole world.

She bit her lip and glanced up at Guy. It mattered to him. What had he said? His father was British. But then he must be—

"You're only half French?" she asked.

He shook his head. "Father's British, Mother's American."

"But you speak French perfectly."

"I've lived here since I was sixteen." He checked the tires. "No flats, at least. Let's see if it'll start." He got into the car and turned the key. The engine sputtered and then started.

Michou slid in next to him. "But then you're in danger, too. What if they stop us?" Even if she didn't care what happened to her, it just didn't seem right not to care about him. He'd already risked a lot for her, staying in Paris longer than he would have if it hadn't been for her. And he'd probably saved her life, shoving her out of the car like that.

"You thought I was French—why wouldn't a German think the same?" His face expressionless, he stared at the Nazi and steered the car back onto the highway.

"Tête de cochon," she muttered as the soldier motioned them forward.

Guy kept his eyes on the road. "Smile when you say that next time," he said, "and he'll probably think it's a compliment."

"You'll never see me smile at a Nazi swine."

"There might come a time when you find it more useful than a curse." He glanced at her, his face serious now. "Safer and smarter not to let them know what you think."

Michou twisted in her seat. "You mean collaborate? As Sylvie plans to do?" She couldn't believe he'd suggest that. She hoped all her teeth would drop out if she ever smiled at a German.

He shook his head. "We both know why Sylvie stayed in Paris. That's not what I mean. Just don't antagonize them if you can help it."

"It's hard not to antagonize someone you'd like to kill. I'm not like Sylvie. She never got in any trouble because she was always so sweet and charming no one would ever believe anything bad about her. Especially Grandmère." She snorted. "Sylvie the perfect. Perfect liar, that's what. I can't be like that."

Guy sighed. "I suspected as much. But please—at least don't be stupid." He turned the car toward the ditch as a motorcycle soldier waved them off the road.

Another column of armored cars roared past. Michou rested her chin in her hand and stared at the floor. How many more could there be? Too many, there were just too many. They were going to trample France, change it forever.

"Look." Guy touched her shoulder and nodded ahead. "See that inn? I'm pretty hungry." He winked and grinned. "Shall we give it a try?"

Behind the inn, a narrow road disappeared into a stand of poplars. She knew what he really meant, and it had nothing to do with breakfast. Her lips twitched, the closest she'd come to smiling since she'd found out about Marc. Maybe the Germans wouldn't notice a single car driving away from a country inn. "I'm starving," she said.

They'd certainly been lucky. Michou stretched and yawned. Not only had they escaped unnoticed from the inn, but the road had actually taken them in the right direction. More or less. They'd wound around on tiny rutted lanes for a whole day until they'd finally ended up in Bourges, and from there it had taken another full day to Bergerac. Only a few more miles now to Saint-Émilion.

Even though the road was deserted, those miles through familiar countryside seemed to take longer than all the rest of the trip, longer even than her bicycle ride a week ago. Then she'd had hope—for Marc, for the baby, for France.

Now nothing remained. People along the way had been optimistic when they'd heard that Marshal Pétain had taken charge, but Michou didn't believe it would make any difference. The rest of France was going to fall, just as Paris had. Michou didn't believe in hope anymore; she didn't believe in God anymore; she didn't believe in anything at all. And she didn't feel anything anymore except hatred for the *Boches*, the murderers of her lover and child.

She frowned as Guy shifted down for the curve in front

of Château LeClair-Figeac. Lucien's red roadster was parked in front of the old farmhouse. As soon as he found out she was home, he'd be knocking on the door, offering his condolences, pretending compassion, sympathy, concern. Well, he could go to hell. She'd tell Maman she didn't want to see anyone, especially Lucien.

Sensing Guy's eyes on her, she focused on his pipe lying on the dashboard. Usually she didn't like the smell of tobacco, but there was something comforting about Guy's pipe smoke. Just as there was something comforting about him. He hadn't tried to tell her what to do or offer her advice. And he hadn't even been fooled by Sylvie.

Michou rested her chin on her hand and stared out the window. She hoped Guy got his father and made it safely to England. His wife and daughter had to be worried about him. He'd told her a little more about them during the long drive, mostly stories about Tessie. She could tell from the way he talked about her how much he adored her and how sad it made him to be away from her. He hadn't said much about his wife, though. In fact, he'd seemed almost reluctant to talk about her. She wondered why.

"Almost there?" he asked.

"Next turn."

Gravel crunched under the tires as the car slowed and turned in the gate. Michou lifted her eyes. The arched windows of Château Bourdet gleamed red with the setting sun's reflection, and the white stone glowed warm pink.

As soon as Guy came to a stop, she jumped out of the car and ran toward the vineyard. She breathed deeply. The air was clean—no diesel fumes, no sickroom odors. Just the fresh smells of cut grass and worked earth.

When she reached the vineyard, she bent over the vines and fingered the young grapes. They'd survived. The Germans might have killed Marc and her baby, but the grapes were still there.

Straightening, she looked out over the vineyards and then turned back toward the Château. Maman and Papa stood on the steps.

Maybe there was something to believe in, after all. And something to fight for.

9

❧

Lucien took a last drag on the Havana cigar and flipped the butt onto the road. Turning, he sneered at Berthe, crammed into the rumble seat and frantically clutching her frumpy brown hat to keep it from blowing off. Not much of a loss if it did. How in hell a sister of his could be so fat and plain he'd never know. And she dressed like an old woman. Didn't even try. Stupid cow ought to be married by now, but she had never even had a boyfriend.

He shook his head. Well, at least she was useful—did the cooking, ran the house for Dad, didn't bitch too much. Best of all, Berthe's long friendship with Michou gave him a good excuse to visit Château Bourdet without too much risk of arousing her bad temper. Michou was the only person in the world whose contempt bothered him. He tightened his grip on the steering wheel. Except for Father, she was the only one who ever sneered at him. The only two people who mattered, and they both—

"Does Michou know I'm coming with you and Gabrielle?" he asked. Squinting, he brushed his hair out of his eyes. Good thing he'd hidden away enough gasoline to last for a while—he loved driving his roadster with the top down, loved the wind and the speed, loved the envious glances. It had been the first thing he'd bought when money from the wine scam started rolling in. The old man had tried to make him sell it when the bastards caught him, but he'd refused.

"I mentioned you might drive us," Berthe said. She bent her purse handle back and forth with her free hand.

"She say anything?"

Gabrielle giggled. "She asked me if you'd joined the German army yet. You know, since you were so sure about

65

everything and all." She twisted in her seat toward him, the
giggle dying and her brown eyes glassy with tears from the
wind. "She said it was people like you who killed Marc. Just
as much as the Germans. I tried to tell her it wasn't so, she
was mixed up, but she wouldn't listen."

Lucien snorted and handed Gabrielle a cigar. "Here,
light this for me," he said. He liked that—Marc's own sister
defending him to Michou. He wondered if Gabrielle would
defend him when she found out his plans didn't include her
for much longer.

Berthe leaned forward. "She doesn't want to see you.
She said you should just drop us off and come back later."
She lowered her eyes and sat back in the seat. "I told her you
wouldn't stay."

"Made a liar out of yourself again, didn't you?" he said,
taking the cigar from Gabrielle. He drew in the pungent
smoke and let it roll around in his mouth before he inhaled.
"When are you going to learn not to make promises for me?"

"Please, Lucien," Gabrielle whined. "Don't upset
Michou. You know how much she loved Marc. She's just not
herself yet."

He rolled his eyes and took another drag on the cigar.
Gabrielle was even more of a fool than he'd thought. Just like
her brother. Another honorable idiot killed by his own
honor—and stupidity. Marc had tried to convince Gabrielle
to stop seeing him, said he was a coward and a traitor, but the
silly little *putain* believed that since they'd slept together, he
was going to marry her.

Maybe he should humor the two of them this once,
though. After all, he still had plenty of time. "All right," he
said. "I'll leave. But only after I tell her the news." He'd
certainly made the right decision when he'd sat down by the
fat German sergeant at Le Chat Noir last week. His quick
friendship with Wolf Kohler had already proved useful. There
was no way he'd go without seeing Michou's reaction—it was
the only reason he'd endured chauffeuring his sister and
Gabrielle. That and the opportunity it gave him to show off
his Mercedes-Benz.

He turned the red roadster into the long drive leading to
Château Bourdet. It felt natural pulling up in front of the
broad steps, as if he belonged. Someday he really would.

He followed Berthe and Gabrielle into the entry and waited with them while Cécile fetched Michou. He supposed it was too much to hope the old slut didn't tell Michou he was waiting with her friends. He pulled out his silver corkscrew, flipped open the blade, and edged it under his fingernails, one by one. When he finished, he clicked it shut and rubbed it between his palms. It had been Michou's once, a present from her father for her sixteenth birthday. But he'd taken it from the gift table when no one had been looking. It had been the beginning of his collection. He slipped it back into his pocket.

He heard voices on the stairs and turned from studying an insipid watercolor of the vineyards during harvest. Michou stood at the top of the curved stairway, seeming even tinier and more fragile than usual. Her dark violet eyes narrowed when she saw him and, her arms stiff at her sides, she gripped her white skirt. Jesus, he wanted her, he'd always wanted her, and he didn't care what it took—he'd *make* her want him.

His lips trembled, but he forced them into a smile. Maybe with Marc dead he finally stood a chance. Maybe he'd let someone else tell her about the German decree. It was worth a try. "How are you, Michou?"

"Fine," she said, glaring at him as she descended the stairs.

"I can't stay," he said, "but I wanted to tell you how sorry I am about Marc." At least he *sounded* sincere, he told himself.

"That's nice of you," Michou said sarcastically. Turning away without offering her hand, she kissed Gabrielle and Berthe on both cheeks. "Why don't we go out back? Even though Maman had to plant turnips and potatoes in the flower garden, what's left of her roses is lovely. I'll have Cécile bring the three of us some *citronnade*." She spun around and headed down the entry hall toward the back foyer.

"Just a minute," Lucien said, his smile fading. He cracked his knuckles. Damn her! Why did she always have to treat him like shit? His hands shook, and he clenched them into fists.

Michou glanced over her shoulder at him. "Yes?" she

said, and pressed her full lips into a thin line. "I thought you had to go."

Gabrielle tittered and gave him a little push toward the door. "Go on, Lucien. You aren't interested in our talk."

He stared at Gabrielle. She looked like a stork, all long skinny legs and angles. He didn't know how he'd endured her this long—he'd never cared much for her mousy-brown hair and thin lips. And he didn't like a woman who could look straight into his eyes. Much better when she had to look up at him.

Gabrielle dropped her hand and giggled again.

"I have some news I thought you might be interested in," he said to Michou.

"It must be bad," she said. "You always manage to find it out before anyone else."

"Half good and half bad." He grinned. "You heard yesterday the Germans are dividing France into two sections—occupied and unoccupied."

She nodded. "Well?"

"Well," he said, "the line runs right through the middle of Château Bourdet."

Alexandre leaned the shovel against the post and wiped the sweat from his forehead. The family heirlooms didn't amount to much—a sapphire-and-diamond necklace-and-earring set that had belonged to his grandmother, Elisabeth Olivier, the ruby and emerald sets Catherine had brought with her, and some miscellaneous rings and bracelets—but he'd be damned if he'd watch some German carry them off. Let them rot in the soil first.

He stomped the dirt down and poured a bucket of water into the depression. After it drained, he added more dirt and tamped it down again. It was best not to underestimate the Nazis. He headed back toward the *cuvier* to get another bucketful.

He smiled as he pushed open the door to the vat room and breathed in the perfume of oak and wine. He might be an occupied Frenchman when he ate and slept, but, by God, he was free when he made his wines. The line of demarcation put the château, *caves,* and the upper vineyards in occupied

France and the *cuvier, chais,* and lower vineyards in the unoccupied sector.

Alexandre filled the bucket and returned to his new vault in the upper vineyard. He'd considered burying the jewelry in the lower vineyard but reasoned that would be where the *Boches* would expect it to be. Anyway, he didn't have much faith in German decrees. If the Nazis didn't get driven from France damn soon, all of her would be occupied.

Before he dumped the water, he paused. Not that there were that many Germans around yet—so far just a few patrols and the sleepy-eyed sergeant billeted with them, whose responsibility it was to guard the border, and not making a thorough job of it, at that. But he didn't want to chance it. Shielding his eyes with his hand, he scanned the vineyards and the road.

Something moved behind the trees lining the drive. The Nazi sergeant? No. The movement had been furtive, and Sergeant Kohler loved to strut about in his shiny black boots, making a show of his importance. Alexandre grinned as he thought of Michou's comment. "A jackbooted jackass" she'd called him when she'd first seen him patrolling their vineyards two weeks ago. And she was right. He'd had no problem bribing Kohler to look the other way while he escorted two English fliers into the unoccupied portion of the vineyards. Only thing worse than a *Boche* was a *Boche* who was a traitor, too.

The figure in the shadows ran to the next tree. Perhaps another English soldier stranded after Dunkirk had found his way to Château Bourdet, sent by the same priest in Libourne who'd brought the fliers. Well, playing hide-and-seek with a Nazi, even a crooked one like Kohler, just wasn't smart. You could never trust a traitor, really. Especially if he thought *he* was being cheated.

Alexandre toted the bucket to the next row and left it there. Anyone asked him about it, he'd just say he was watering some new cuttings. Stupid Nazi *cochons* wouldn't know they were always planted in the spring, not in August.

He ambled toward the drive. As he approached the trees, a man dressed in workers' clothes stepped forward.

"Bonjour," the man said in heavily accented French. "I look for Monsieur Valette."

"Oui," Alexandre said, offering his hand. "I am Alexandre Valette." He studied the young man. Slender, blond, obviously English. Damn Father Francis—he shouldn't have let this one come unescorted. He barely spoke the language, and looked as if he'd stolen what he was wearing from someone's clothesline.

"Monsieur Tissier sends me," the man said. "I am English. Can you help me?"

"Monsieur Tissier?" Alexandre said. How did Georges know he'd been helping the English? Had he heard rumors at his café in Saint-Émilion? Alexandre smoothed his moustache with his thumb. "What did he say?"

"Father Francis is his confessor. He said tell you this."

"Nom de Dieu!" Alexandre muttered. He'd tell Father Francis a thing or two when he saw him again. He hadn't hesitated a minute when the priest had asked for his help, but Father Francis had to be more careful. Alexandre trusted Georges Tissier—they'd been friends for years—but he wondered whom else Father Francis had told. And whom Georges had told. This was not the way to fight a war. Because that's what they were doing. And if they didn't use their heads, they'd all end up losing them.

"Come with me." Alexandre motioned the young man to follow. "And don't talk. Not to anyone. *Compris?*" He'd just keep him in the *cuvier* until he could contact an escort. It was safer for everyone if he was the only one involved, and he knew his children well enough to know they'd want to help. But Philippe was such a young hothead he'd probably do something stupid, and Michou, well, even though she was cooler, almost too cool since she'd come back, she had a lot of healing to do.

As Alexandre led the Englishman toward the circular drive in front of the château, Sergeant Kohler emerged from the front door. Alexandre glanced sideways at the young English soldier. "Keep walking," he said.

Kohler approached, one of Cécile's plum tarts in his hand. Catching a glimpse of the Englishman, he narrowed his small eyes.

Alexandre nodded. "Got another worker to replace the two who didn't work out."

"Same pay?" Kohler asked, and took a bite of the tart. Some of the purple filling dribbled onto his uniform, and he swiped it off with the back of his hand.

"Same pay." *Nom de Dieu,* what a pig the Nazi was. Even when he sucked in his belly in an effort to impress Michou, it hung over his belt. The way he preened and pranced around her disgusted Alexandre. Obviously the fool thought himself quite the ladies' man. Michou's refusal to speak a single word to him hadn't daunted him at all.

"Fine," Kohler said with his mouth full. He eyed the Englishman. "Good-bye," he said in English.

The young man opened his mouth, then closed it firmly.

Alexandre pointed toward the *cuvier.* "Come on," he said. "You can start by cleaning the vats." He was determined to keep up the pretense for his family's sake even if Kohler didn't bother. The last thing he wanted was for Michou to discover an English soldier hiding in the *cuvier.* Even though she hadn't been in the vineyards or vat room since she'd come back from Paris, he'd play it safe just in case. Besides, he needed the help—all the casks and *cuves* had to be washed before the vintage. And it was only fair that the Englishmen earn their keep: it cost fifty francs a head to persuade the fat sergeant to turn his the other way.

After he led the young soldier into the vat room, Alexandre smiled at him. "You are now in Free France," he said.

10

ॐ

Michou tucked the napkin more securely into the top of the picnic basket as she hurried toward the *cuvier*. She hoped her visit and Cécile's fresh plum tarts would please Papa—he'd seemed so tired and distant for the last couple of weeks. He was working too hard, and it was her fault. She should have realized before this that he'd never ask for her help. She shouldn't have needed Mémé Laure's reminder that even during war, grapes kept growing and wine kept fermenting.

When she saw the Nazi sergeant, she gripped the basket handle tightly and cursed under her breath.

Kohler's slouch turned into a strut as soon as he spotted her. "Good day, mademoiselle," he said.

Michou lifted her chin. She'd almost rather listen to German than to his awful French. It was as if stealing her country and killing her lover weren't enough for the Nazis— this one had to mutilate her language, too. She kept her eyes focused straight ahead.

"Good day," he said again, raising his voice.

She glanced at him and kept walking toward the *cuvier*. He might keep her from crossing the line, but she'd be damned if she'd speak to him.

He strode alongside her. "Your father hired another new worker," he said. "Probably won't need your help."

She shrugged and quickened her pace. This was the third one this week. What was Papa up to? Even without her assistance, he shouldn't need that much outside help in August.

When she reached the border, Kohler stopped. She pushed open the door to the *cuvier* without looking behind her and paused for a minute to savor the wine-scented coolness. Maybe Papa thought she'd never want to make wine again. It wasn't that she'd lost interest, though. She'd just been so caught up in her own unhappiness she hadn't thought about anything else.

She heard a low murmur coming from the first-year *chai*. "Papa?" she called. "I've got a surprise for you."

"Just a minute," Papa shouted. "I'll be right out. Just finishing topping up some of the barrels. You don't need to come back."

"I don't mind," she said. The first-year *chai* was one of her favorite places. Philippe had never understood why she liked it so much, but then he'd never liked much of anything that had to do with winemaking, especially if it involved work. He particularly hated the tedium of transferring the new wines from one barrel to another. She smiled. Philippe the Rash—if the results weren't immediate, he didn't want to bother. Racking the wine was just one step in an interminable series as far as he was concerned.

She headed toward the *chai* entrance. Besides, she was curious about the new worker. Ever since the mobilization, outside help had been hard to find. Perhaps Papa had taken him on now to ensure he'd have some extra help with the vintage, only a few weeks away.

Just as she reached the door, Papa stepped out and shut it quickly behind him. He kissed her cheek. *"Eh bien!* You've come to help again?" he said. "Good. I've missed you. The wine has missed you." He pulled her hand through his arm and patted it. "Let's go up front. I'll put you to work cleaning the crusher." He took the basket and winked at her. "After we check out the contents of this."

She leaned her head against his shoulder. His shirt felt rough against her cheek, but it was a comforting roughness, like his smell of earth, wood, and wine. She'd been wrong to stay away so long. The *cuvier* was a sanctuary, and Papa was its guardian.

"The Nazi said you hired someone," she said. She lifted her head and looked at him. "Is he going to help, too?"

Papa cleared his throat. "I decided he wouldn't do," he said. "He's gone." He avoided her eyes.

"But I heard voices," she said.

"I must have been talking to myself," he said, staring at his shoes. His gray hair fell into his eyes.

"Just a minute," she said. "I just want to take a peek and make sure nothing has changed." She marched in and scanned the dark room. Three rows of large oak barrels filled the *chai*. The hose Papa used for topping the wine lay on the floor, as if he'd dropped it there when she called. She frowned. He'd said he was finished. It wasn't like him to leave the hose out.

As she turned to go, a muffled cough came from the other end of the *chai*. She spun around. "Who's there?" she said. "Come out now!"

"It's all right," Papa said quickly from behind her. "You can come out."

A tall figure unfolded itself from behind the barrel and stood up, cap in hand.

Michou took one look at him and suddenly knew what Papa was up to. "You're English, aren't you?" she said.

If only she could tell someone else. But Papa had said it was too dangerous, and he was right. Still, it would have made her feel better to be able to talk to Mémé Laure about it. Michou wasn't used to keeping secrets from her. She hoped she was better at it than Papa had been.

She pulled the navy-blue and white shirtwaist over her head and buttoned it slowly. She had to put out of her mind what she and Papa had been doing for the last week. Today was his fiftieth birthday, and Maman had invited several guests for tonight. Papa deserved a nice evening, free from worry, and she was going to make sure nothing disturbed him.

Michou paused in front of her dressing table. The bottle of jasmine perfume Marc had given her for her birthday sat in front of the mirror. Sometimes the little reminders hurt the most, especially when they were unexpected. She had finally put his picture in her dresser drawer because even a casual glance at it brought back the tears, the heart-twisting pain of the day she had learned he was dead. Later, when she was stronger, she'd promised herself, she'd put it back. She still wasn't ready for that step, but perhaps—

Tentatively, she picked up the crystal flask and removed the stopper. The scent drifted up, bringing with it memories as clear and sweet as the perfume. Perhaps she should wear it tonight for Marc—and for Papa, who, unlike some wine-makers, enjoyed the smell of perfume. "A woman and a wine should both have a *bouquet*." he always said. She inhaled deeply, then dabbed some behind her ears and on her wrists.

Looking in the mirror, Michou patted her silver-blond hair back into place and tried out a smile. Almost normal, she decided. The dark circles had disappeared from under her eyes, and her lips no longer seemed thin with tension.

She adjusted her collar. The white made her look even more tanned than she was. Good thing Grandmère had gone back to Paris after the Nazis ordered the refugees back home. What reprimands Michou would have had to listen to about being in the sun without her hat and gloves.

This time Michou's smile was almost genuine. Grand-mère would be absolutely horrified if she knew Michou had actually helped English soldiers to freedom. A lady certainly wouldn't behave like that either—war was a man's job and risk-taking a man's responsibility.

After she checked to make sure the seams in her stock-ings were straight, Michou put on her new navy pumps and tottered over to the window. The silly shoes pinched her feet. Well, she'd just have to suffer for a while. Maybe she could take them off during dinner—no one would notice then.

A cloud of dust on the road caught her attention. Surely no one would dare to arrive this early. Maman would be furious. She turned to run downstairs and tell her but stopped at her door. Lucien was still living at Château LeClair-Figeac. Perhaps Berthe and Henri Desroches were going to see him before coming to Château Bourdet. She hoped not. It would be just like Lucien to invite himself along. She returned to the window.

A large black touring car drove past the entrance to the château, stopped, backed up, then swung into the driveway.

Michou pressed her forehead against the window and peered down as the car came to a halt in front of the steps. Three German soldiers got out.

She gasped and backed away from the window. What

were they doing here? Had they found out about the Englishmen? She had to warn Papa.

Her stomach churning, she kicked off her shoes, grabbed them, and raced down the stairs to the second floor. She sprinted down the hall to Papa's bedroom and tapped on the door.

"Papa!" she hissed.

No answer. She opened the door. He wasn't there.

She ran lightly to the top of the stairs and crept down a few steps until she could see the entryway.

Dressed in their evening clothes, Maman and Papa stood arm in arm in front of the Germans. Papa nodded at the tallest one, an officer with a soft chin and gray-streaked blond hair. "*Oui*, I understand," Papa said.

Michou let out her breath. Surely the Germans didn't bother explaining the situation to someone they were arresting. They must want something else. She slipped her feet back into her shoes and walked slowly down the stairs.

When she reached Maman and Papa, the other two soldiers took off their caps. The tall officer who had been speaking to Papa bowed and clicked his heels.

"My daughter, Michou," Papa said. "Major Stecher."

"*Enchanté*," he said, and bowed again. He turned to Papa. "Please see to it that our rooms are ready at once." His French was fluent but heavily accented.

Michou stiffened. More Nazis in her home? Well, she didn't intend to speak to them either. This Stecher didn't look as if he'd be interested in fifty-franc bribes, though, and she doubted if he'd be easy to fool. His blue eyes seemed to take in everything at once.

She thought of Guy's advice and frowned. How could she possibly be polite to a Nazi after what had happened to Marc and her baby? No, she wouldn't give in. *Alors*, let Guy have a pack of Nazis billeted on him and see how he'd act.

Major Stecher pivoted on his heel and spoke in German to his men. They were returning to the black car when another car roared up the drive.

"You are expecting company?" Stecher asked, raising one eyebrow.

Maman's face remained impassive. "We are having

guests for dinner. It is my husband's birthday," she said quietly.

"I will be most pleased to join you," Stecher said. His smile did not reveal his teeth.

Georges Tissier pulled his battered old Citroën up behind the German staff car. Biting her lip, Michou glanced at Papa. What if Monsieur Tissier had another Englishman with him?

Papa put his hand on her arm and shook his head slightly as the major followed his men to the car. "Wait here with your mother," he whispered. He trotted down the steps after the Germans.

Drops of perspiration trickled between Michou's breasts. She walked to the doorway and waved at Georges, forcing herself to smile. If he'd brought an Englishman, at least he hadn't let him sit in the front seat this time. Maybe he'd learned his lesson. Papa had exploded at him last time because of his carelessness with the soldiers.

Papa introduced Georges to Major Stecher while the soldiers unloaded a large trunk and several suitcases from the big car. Smiling, Georges shook hands with each of the Germans and then offered to carry one of the suitcases into the château. Papa stared at him for several seconds before he picked up another suitcase and followed him up the steps.

Winking at Michou, Georges set the suitcase at the foot of the sweeping stairway. He kissed Maman's cheek. "I see you've some unexpected guests for Alexandre's party," he said, his brown eyes twinkling with amusement.

Michou's cheeks burned. He was actually enjoying himself, she thought. They were risking their lives, and he acted as if it were a terrific game. As the Germans lugged the trunks into the entry, she forced herself to take a deep breath. Stay calm, she told herself.

Alexandre dropped the suitcase he was carrying next to the one Georges had brought in. "Catherine, would you please show Major Stecher and his men their rooms upstairs? Michou and I will entertain Georges while we wait for the other guests." He nodded at the major. "We have a guest suite on the third floor. I hope you find it comfortable."

Stecher bowed. "*Merci*, Monsieur Valette, for your ex-

cellent hospitality." His smile shaded into a sneer before he
turned and followed Maman and his men up the stairs.

Papa rolled his eyes and motioned Michou and Georges
into the salon. He shut the door and turned to Georges.
"Well?" he demanded. "Did you bring one?"

Georges grinned. "Of course. I put him in the trunk, just
like you said to."

"You're going to have to take him back with you," Papa
said. "We can't chance it tonight. Not with Stecher and his
men here. And Stecher invited himself to dinner. I won't be
able to leave the party." He slumped into a chair by the
fireplace.

"But what am I going to do with him?" Georges said.
He rubbed his bald head. "There are more Nazis in Saint-
Émilion than here. And he can't stay in my trunk—"

"Let me do it, Papa," Michou said. "It's probably safer
tonight—Stecher will be with you, and the other two don't
know their way around yet. I can slip out after dinner and
take him to the *chai*." She turned to Georges and held out
her hand. "Give me your key."

Georges shrugged, raised his eyebrows, and looked at
Papa. "Well?" he said.

Papa sighed. "Give it to her. Otherwise we'll have to
listen to her arguments until the Nazi comes back. And I've
already heard them all." He stood up and shook his finger at
Georges. "But no more—not until things calm down around
here. *Compris?*"

Georges nodded and dropped the key into Michou's
hand as another car crunched into the graveled drive. She
smiled at Papa as she put the key in her pocket. "Don't
worry," she said. "I know what to do."

"Just be careful," Papa said. "Don't be a fool—like
Georges here." He took her arm. "Let's greet our guests."

Several friends arrived in quick succession, and even
though she didn't forget about the key in her pocket, Michou
was too busy to worry about it for a while. During dinner,
though, she found it hard to concentrate on Henri's account
of Lucien's latest follies or Philippe's explanation of the newest contraption he and Édouard Laurent had built. No matter
how much she tried to avoid looking at Major Stecher, she

kept glancing at him and fingering the key to the Citroën's trunk.

Dessert finally arrived, and she forced herself to eat every bite of Cécile's special *dacquoise* even though it tasted like paper to her. She drained her glass of Château d'Yquem as Berthe and her father rose from the table.

"We have to drive back to Libourne tonight," Henri said. "Curfew, you know." He shook hands with Papa. "Wonderful dinner," he said, turning to Maman. "As always." He kissed her on both cheeks. "And you look beautiful. As always."

"And you're such an old flatterer," Maman said. "As always." Smiling, she followed him to the dining-room door.

"Stay with your guests," Henri said to her. "We can see ourselves out."

Michou stood. "I'll walk you to your car," she said. She linked arms with Berthe and followed Henri out of the dining room. When she reached the entry, she laughed and rolled her eyes. "Thank God that's over," she whispered to Berthe. "I hope I never have to eat with another Nazi again."

Henri shook her hand before he got into his car. "Thank your mother again for me," he said. "And tell your father he's a lucky man."

After Berthe and her father drove away, Michou walked casually to Georges' Citroën. Cursing the full moon, she glanced up at the Nazis' windows on the third floor, but the blackout curtains made it impossible to tell if anyone was still awake. She held her breath, stuck the key into the lock, and eased the trunk lid up.

The sound of slow, deep breathing came from the trunk. The English soldier was asleep! She shook his shoulder gently until he stirred. "Quiet," she hissed. "Get out." While he climbed out, she waited, gripping the key so tightly her nails cut into her palm.

At least he wasn't in uniform, she thought. He was tall and slender, and his straight black hair hung in his eyes. There seemed to be something familiar about him. Then she realized what it was—except for his two-day growth of beard and scruffy clothes, he looked a bit like Lucien. "Follow me," she whispered. She grabbed his arm and led him toward her tower.

Suddenly the front door opened and a stream of light shot out before it was quickly closed.

"Halt!" The voice was guttural, deep.

Michou stopped, and the English soldier bumped into her. Her throat was tight, but this time she had to speak to a German. "What do you want?" she asked.

The German stepped into the moonlight. "Mademoiselle Valette?" he said.

"Yes," she said, and tittered. *Mon Dieu,* she was glad it wasn't Stecher. Her idea would never work with him. She slipped her arm around the Englishman's waist and leaned against him. She hiccupped and clamped her free hand over her mouth. "Pardon me." She giggled again. "Beautiful moon, isn't it?"

The German stared first at her and then at the Englishman. "Who is he?" he asked.

"Lucien Desroches," she said. "He lives nearby."

"A friend of yours?"

She nodded. She supposed she could always explain away any questions about the way she treated Lucien by saying they'd had a fight, but she hoped it wouldn't come to that.

The German waved them on. "Enjoy yourselves," he said. Snickering, he headed toward the black car.

"Oh, we will, won't we, Lucien?" she said, kissing the English soldier.

11

"Thirty-two and too old to fight—it's ridiculous!" Guy stopped pacing and leaned against the wall by the window. "Except for these damn headaches, I'm in better shape now than I was ten years ago." He took a drink of the Scotch whisky and rolled it around in his mouth."

"Did you try the navy?" his father asked.

"The navy, the army, the RAF. Didn't bother them a bit I've American citizenship, but as soon as they saw my age, they just laughed." Guy slammed his fist against the sill. A horn squawked, and he glanced out the window. God, London was a noisy place. He pinched the bridge of his nose.

Leaning forward in the wing chair, Richard Chalmers stroked his chin. "Maybe I could help you, son. Let me talk to André Simon. Heard he's here now and involved in some hush-hush operations."

"Fine." Guy resumed pacing. "Anything. I hate sitting on my thumbs while the Jerries squash France and bomb the bloody hell out of England. I even tried to join de Gaulle's Free French, but as soon as they found out I'm American—"

"No good, what?"

Guy shook his head and slumped onto the sofa. Usually he enjoyed visiting London, but it was different this time. He wasn't on holiday; he was exiled. France was his home, had been for years, and God knew when he'd see it again.

"Seen Lydia and Tessie lately?" his father asked suddenly.

"Of course."

"You didn't say anything."

"It wasn't pleasant." Guy gulped down another mouthful of whisky.

His father raised his eyebrows. "Lydia being difficult again? Why don't you just pick up Tessie and bring her over here? I'd like to see that cute granddaughter of mine more often."

"Lydia won't let her out of the house. She's terrified the Germans will bomb London while Tessie is with me." Guy set the empty glass on the end table and reached for his pipe and tobacco.

"That's rot. What if they do? She's just as safe with you, I daresay."

"I know that, you know that, but Lydia has her own way of reasoning. I even tried to persuade her to take Tessie and go to her parents' home in Surrey, but she wouldn't hear of it. She may be scared, but better scared to death than bored to death. Christ!" He rolled his eyes as he lit the pipe. "Frightened as she is, do you know what she complains about the most? The tea ration!"

"What about Charles?"

"He's the reason she won't leave." The muscles in his jaw tightened, and he clamped his teeth onto the pipe. Charles White was a nice enough chap, but, damn, he didn't relish the idea of his becoming Tessie's stepfather. "He works at the Foreign Office, you know, and can't leave London."

"Well, if you'll permit your old father to offer some sensible advice based on practical experience, don't push the girl or you may well end up the way I did. Your mother went back to America to keep you from me." Settling back in the chair, he crossed his legs. "You don't want that."

"Actually, I wouldn't mind if she went to America—at least then I'd know Tessie'd be safe. But it's too late for that now." Guy stood and walked to the window again. The marriage had been a mistake from the beginning—neither he nor Lydia had ever been happy. Tessie's birth had only made things worse: she gave them twice as much to fight about, and the stakes were just that much higher. Even divorce hadn't solved that problem.

Guy exhaled, blowing the bitter smoke at the floor. He'd been in London for two months now, and all he'd accomplished so far was to argue with his ex-wife and get drunk

with Jake. Dad didn't really need him for the London end of
the shipping business—what little there was left of it.

And he was worried about Michou. The news from
France was increasingly more depressing. The Germans occupied Bordeaux and most of France while the Vichy government pretended to occupy what was left. He wondered if
there were German soldiers at Château Bourdet. He hoped
Michou was all right, was playing it smart. She was just too
spunky for her own good.

And here he was sitting on his ass in London, not doing
a bloody damn thing to fight the Nazis.

He faced his father. "I'm going out. See you tomorrow
morning." After he shrugged on his jacket, he emptied his
pipe in the ashtray and stuck it in his pocket.

Richard lifted an eyebrow. "Why don't you and Jacob
have supper at the club with me?"

"Maybe tomorrow." Guy grabbed his hat and jammed it
on his head.

As soon as he reached the street, the air-raid siren began
shrieking. A few people shrugged at him, but no one seemed
particularly worried. Small wonder—"Wailing Willie" wailed
so frequently lately that no one paid much attention to it,
probably because London hadn't suffered much damage. Yet.
Everyone wondered when it would really begin.

Guy strode into the Three Ravens, stopping at the ornately carved bar to order a whisky and water while his eyes
adjusted to the smoky, beer-scented dark. Sipping the drink,
he scanned the booths until a waving hand caught his eye.

Jacob Schweiger sat at a table in the corner. As Guy
approached, he raised his mug. "Cheers," he said. "Here's to
our chaps in the sky."

Guy smiled and sat down. Even though he was German,
Jake's English was flawless. It always had been pretty good,
even when they first met as students in Cambridge. "Any
luck today?" he asked.

Jake shook his head. "I'm too old, I'm German, I'm
Jewish, I'm bald, and I probably have flat feet. What is wrong
with these people? Can't they see Hitler's serious?"

"I guess they don't consider an economist very useful."

"Nor a wine shipper."

"Heard anything from the Red Cross?"

"Nothing." Grimacing, Jake thudded his glass down on the table.

"You will." Guy tried to sound positive, but it was hard. Jake's wife and two children had disappeared one day when he'd been out, and a neighbor had warned him it wasn't safe for Jews to stay in Germany any longer. He'd searched for weeks, finally giving up and escaping to France after he'd almost been captured. He knew they'd been sent to a concentration camp, but he had no idea which one. And the Red Cross wasn't having any better luck.

Jake shut his eyes. "It won't do me much good when I do find out, will it?"

Guy sipped his whisky. He didn't know what to say. Jake was right. More and more horror stories of the Nazis' treatment of the Jews had reached England.

The drone of planes high overhead cut through the din, and Guy glanced at the ceiling as the pub became suddenly quiet. Several distant explosions boomed, followed by the racket of antiaircraft guns.

Then a loud blast shook the room. The lights flickered, and several bottles crashed to the floor as the ack-acks increased their fire.

Guy swiveled in his seat as someone at the bar shouted, "Hooray!" and another deep voice added, "We'll show those buggers!" All at once, everyone started talking and laughing.

Guy turned back to Jake and held up his empty glass. "Another?"

Jake laughed stiffly. "Why not? Doesn't seem to be anything better to do."

As he stood up, Guy nodded. "Pretty damn sad and stupid, isn't it?"

Jake set the heavy book on the nightstand, then slid down under the thin wool blankets. Once again he'd drunk too much with Guy, and Joyce's words made even less sense to him than usual. Perhaps he should just give up. Now was not the right time in his life to take on a project like *Finnegan's Wake*, not when he kept meeting frustration at every turn of the page, at every turn of the corner. Knowing when to quit didn't necessarily make him a loser.

And knowing when to get out didn't necessarily make

him a coward. He snapped off the bedside lamp, and the squalid bedsitting room disappeared into the cold, thick dark. He'd repeated his litany of self-exoneration so often the words no longer meant anything. It didn't matter that there'd been nothing he could do for Hannah and the boys. He'd escaped. He was alive. He was a coward.

He rolled onto his side and curled his legs up to his chest. He could fool himself during the day, but at night the truth was as black as his room. He was never going to see his wife and children again.

His hands in his pockets, Guy stared at the door to Lydia's Mayfair town house. He'd give it one more try. Maybe last night's bombing would help him convince her that London wasn't going to be the safest place for Tessie.

When Lydia opened the door, he raised his eyebrows. He hadn't even expected her to be up, let alone dressed and answering the door. "Where's Mrs. Worth?"

"Oh!" Lydia shook her head so that her smooth dark hair swung about her shoulders. "Oh, she went off to her daughter's. Got all nervous about the bombs. Tried to tell her she'd be just as safe here, but do you think she'd listen?"

Guy resisted the urge to tell her Mrs. Worth had twice her brains. It wouldn't do to begin that way. Once Lydia got her back up, it was impossible to move her. "May I come in? I'd like to see Tessie. She up?"

"Of course. Four-year-olds love the dawn, didn't you know?" She waved him toward the dining room. "She's in there. Help yourself if you're hungry."

"You're not going to join us?" He paused with his hand on the door.

"In a few minutes maybe." She glanced up the stairs and then back at him, patting her hair into place.

"I *would* like to talk to you, Lydia."

She nodded as she started up the stairs. "Fine. A few minutes, then."

He forced his lips into a smile and pushed open the door. Tessie and Nanny sat at the long table.

When she saw him, Tessie jumped down from her seat and ran to him. "Daddy! I'm eating at the big table today! Mommy said I could have breakfast downstairs!"

The tension eased from Guy. He bent down and hugged Tessie, burying his nose in her soft light brown hair. He was glad she still smelled like a baby.

"Will you eat with us, Daddy? Please do!" She tugged his hand and pointed at the sideboard.

"Why not?" He lifted her back into her chair. "Looks as if there's plenty."

"Mommy said we were having company. But she didn't tell me it was you!"

He winked at her. "Guess she wanted to surprise you." He turned to the middle-aged woman sitting across from Tessie. "Isn't that right, Nanny?"

"I imagine so, sir."

Like hell she did. Lydia'd been as surprised to see him as he had her. He dished some eggs and bacon onto his plate and took a piece of toast from the rack. "I hope your mother won't mind if I drink a bit of her tea."

"She has lots! Uncle Charles gave her some!" Tessie bounced up and down in her chair until Nanny frowned at her.

Trying to keep the edge from his voice, Guy said, "That's nice of him." He sat down next to Tessie. "Uncle Charles is a nice man."

"Oh, he is!" Tessie said. "He promised me a pony." She stuck out her lower lip. "But Mommy won't let me go."

"Go where?"

"To Grandmother and Grandpa's."

So even Charles saw the sense in getting Tessie out of the city. Damn Lydia. Damn her selfishness. He wasn't going to put up with it anymore. He rattled the teacup into the saucer. "You'd like to live in the country, then?"

Tessie slid out of her chair. "Uh-huh." She nodded, a serious expression on her face, and then ran to Nanny and whispered something in her ear.

Nanny smiled. "All right, dear."

"I'll be right back," Tessie said, and skipped out of the room.

Chewing on his toast, Guy poked at the clumpy scrambled eggs. Lydia *had* to agree now. Last night's bombing had been the worst so far, and everyone knew Hitler was getting ready for an invasion. He looked up when the door squeaked open.

"Hullo, Guy." Charles stood next to Lydia, looking awkward as hell. He pulled his hand loose from Lydia's and stuck it out. "Glad to see you, old man."

Guy rose as Charles approached. Why had Lydia done this to them? He and Charles and Jake had been inseparable at Cambridge, but now he found it difficult to shake the man's hand. The muscles in his jaw tensed as Charles clasped his hand.

"Perhaps you can help me talk some sense into Lydia." Charles sat down next to Guy while Lydia filled a plate for him. "I've been telling her that if she doesn't send Tessie to Surrey, pretty soon she won't have a choice. If it gets much worse, they're going to send all the children out of London."

Lydia set the plate in front of Charles. "Now, don't you two get started. When we have to, we'll go. Not before." She turned to Nanny. "Would you please check on Tessie?"

After Nanny excused herself, Guy looked at Charles and shook his head. Charles had a lot to learn if he was planning on marrying Lydia. For a minute, he almost pitied him, but the feeling shriveled into a hard little wad in his stomach when he remembered the day he'd discovered their affair. And, fool that he was, he'd thought all of Lydia's visits to England were because she missed her parents. Well, as far as he was concerned, Charles deserved everything he got.

But that didn't matter now—it was Tessie who was important, and they were allies in that regard. Guy leaned back in his chair, balancing his teacup and saucer on his knee.

Lydia flounced into the seat opposite Charles. "I don't want to hear anything more about it." She cocked her head and smiled at Charles.

The muscles in Guy's face tightened again. "For once, Lydia, you have to consider someone else besides yourself." His voice got louder. "Tessie is my—"

The door rattled. "Close your eyes, Daddy," Tessie called.

Swallowing, Guy clamped his mouth shut. He didn't like Tessie to hear them arguing; he'd never forgotten the fights his parents used to have and how unhappy it'd made him.

"Are you ready?"

"All ready."

He heard Tessie scamper across the wood floor. "Boo!" she shouted.

He opened his eyes wide. "Oh, my God, what is it? Where's Tessie?"

Shrieking with laughter, Tessie removed the Mickey Mouse gas mask. "Here I am. Were you really fooled?"

Guy nodded and scooped Tessie into his lap. If Lydia wouldn't listen to reason, he'd just have to fight dirty. "How'd you like to go on a trip with me and your granddad?"

"Really, Daddy? Could we ride ponies?"

"Of course." Guy glanced up.

Lydia's eyes narrowed into black slits. Standing, she said, "We'll discuss this later." She held out her hand to Tessie. "We have to go now."

Charles looked at Guy and shrugged as he stood up. "Sorry, old man," he said.

After they left, Guy fished in his pocket for his pipe. He'd just have to keep trying. But if it didn't work soon, the hell with being civilized. He'd just take Tessie and go. You couldn't call protecting your daughter's life kidnapping.

12

Lucien swirled the cognac in his glass before he answered Kohler. Best to keep the bastard in his place—he was only a sergeant, after all. Still, he was useful and less of a fool than he looked.

"All right. Two hundred francs a week," he said. "But no more." He sniffed the cognac, and the fumes made his eyes water. Pretty rough for a twenty-year-old *grande fine*, he thought. Maybe old Chabot thought his new clientele at Le Chat Noir couldn't tell the difference. Well, he could, and it didn't bother him to remind the son of a bitch. He slammed the glass back on the table and beckoned the waiter.

Kohler shrugged. "No promises. Something interesting might develop. You never know." He winked at Lucien. "One of Stecher's men might want a cut."

Lucien leaned forward. "Do they know about the English soldiers?"

"Not yet," Kohler said. "There's only been one since they got there. But there's bound to be more. And that bald friend of theirs—*der Dummkopf*—he's pretty careless. I heard Valette yelling at him a couple of weeks ago."

Lucien looked up as the waiter approached the table. He pointed to the cognac and spoke quickly so Kohler couldn't follow him. "Tell Chabot he can serve piss to the Germans, but I expect what I pay for. Even if he has to open his private stock. Understand?"

"Yes, Monsieur Desroches," the waiter said. He picked up the glass and returned to the bar.

Lucien turned back to Kohler. "You told me about Tissier last week. Anything new for my two hundred francs?" He pulled a cigar and his ebony holder from his pocket.

Kohler smirked. "You'll like this one," he said. "You didn't go to Valette's birthday dinner, did you?"

"No. I wasn't invited."

"That's what I thought," Kohler said. "Well, according to Stecher's driver, you were there." Looking smug, he clasped his hands behind his head.

"What the hell?" Lucien said. He lit his cigar and took a couple of puffs before continuing. "My father and Berthe were there, but I wasn't. Michou's doing, no doubt."

"That's not what Fischer said." Kohler seemed to be enjoying himself.

"I don't pay you to run a guessing game," Lucien said.

Kohler put his arms back on the table and lowered his voice. "Fischer told me the little blonde was outside necking with her boyfriend that night. And her boyfriend's name was Lucien Desroches."

Lucien snorted. "What did you say to Fischer?"

"Nothing."

"Wise man." And damned greedy, too, Lucien thought. Didn't want to share the loot if he didn't have to. Of course, maybe the others weren't as corrupt as Kohler, and he was protecting himself as much as his money. He'd have to wait and see about Stecher and his men—if they were honest, perhaps he wouldn't have to pay anything for Kohler's information. The fat sergeant probably wouldn't like having his recent activities revealed. He smiled at the thought. "The boyfriend—he was probably an Englishman?"

"*Ja.* I saw them. She took him to the vathouse."

"And I suppose you followed them there?"

"*Jawohl.* I always do."

"Well? What did they do?" Lucien tapped the ashes off his cigar.

"Nothing you'd be interested in." Kohler leered at him, his fat cheeks shaking with suppressed laughter.

"And what's that supposed to mean?" Lucien asked, narrowing his eyes.

Kohler's smile evaporated. "Nothing. She just left him there and went back inside."

"Did you see my sister?"

"*Nein.* I was patrolling the border."

More likely sleeping, Lucien thought. "Well, I talked to her. She's still a little reluctant. She'll come around, though,"

he said. And damn soon if she knew what was good for her.
Stupid cow had no right to be so particular. Especially when
he was doing her a favor. God knows, not many men would
have the hots for her, and Kohler had been after him to
arrange a date since the first time he'd seen her.

Lucien nodded at the waiter as he set a new glass of
cognac in front of him. He swirled the amber liquid again and
sniffed it. "That's better," he said, waving the waiter away.
More like it this time. He raised his glass and toasted Chabot,
who was standing behind the bar watching him.

As he set his glass back down, Lucien caught the eye of a
tall blond Nazi major heading toward his table. Inclining his
head slightly, the Nazi raised one eyebrow and smiled with
closed lips.

When he reached the table, the Nazi bowed to Lucien,
clicking his heels together. "Sergeant Kohler, will you do the
honors?" he asked.

Kohler stood up hurriedly and saluted. "Heil Hitler!
Sir!"

The German returned the salute. "I'd like to meet your
friend," he said.

After he stubbed out his cigar, Lucien rose slowly, keeping his eyes on the Nazi. Not bad—a little stern-looking with
his thin lips and small chin perhaps, but not bad. He knew a
pédé when he saw one, and this one was definitely interested
in him.

He smiled. A major could be much more helpful than a
sergeant—even if he couldn't be conventionally bribed. He
held out his hand and introduced himself before Kohler could
speak.

The Nazi took his hand. "Major Karl Stecher," he said,
bowing again. "May I join you?"

"Of course," Lucien said. He sat back down as Major
Stecher seated himself next to him.

Major Stecher waved Kohler away. "You're dismissed,
Sergeant," he said. Kohler grinned, saluted, and moved off
toward the bar.

"How do you come to know that buffoon?" Major
Stecher asked. He put a cigarette between his lips, pausing as
if he expected Lucien to light it for him.

Lucien quickly pulled his silver lighter out of his pocket.
"I own Château LeClair-Figeac. It's very near where he's

billeted, and the Valettes are old friends of my family," he said, lighting the cigarette.

"Ach so," Major Stecher said. "I remember now. Desroches. I met your father and sister my first night there. But you were not present. Why was that?"

"I had an important meeting that night." At least that part was true, Lucien thought.

"How unfortunate! It was a delightful evening. What could have been more important?" Major Stecher blew out the smoke in a thin stream between his closed lips.

"An emergency session of the local Rassemblement National Populaire. Someone tried to kill Déat."

"Ach! I remember. So you're a member of the Pétainist party. *Sehr gut."* Major Stecher smiled. "Let my buy another drink for a comrade."

Lucien shook his head. "I'd like to buy one for you. I insist." He turned to the hovering waiter. "Two more, please. And be sure it's from the same bottle."

After the waiter set the drinks on the table, Stecher lifted his glass. "To friendship between our countries," he said. *"Santé!"*

Lucien clicked his glass against Stecher's. *"Prost!"* he said.

Michou grabbed an apron from the hook. "Put me to work," she told Berthe. "I'm not much of a cook—Cécile won't let anyone but Maman in the kitchen—but I'd love to help. Just tell me what to do."

Berthe laughed and poured some port into a melon half. "Well, you can peel the potatoes. That doesn't take much skill."

"Perfect," Michou said. "What's the menu?"

"What I could scrape together of Papa's favorites. *Melon au porto, épaule d'agneau à la châtelaine,* and for dessert *pêches Cardinale,"* she said, ticking the items off on her fingers. "Lucien brought us the lamb, Papa traded some wine for the peaches, and the rest came from my garden."

"What a feast!" Michou said. She inhaled the aroma of freshly crushed raspberries and simmering peaches. Berthe had always been a real genius in the kitchen, but Michou hadn't expected this, not when it was getting harder and harder to find decent food. "Thank you for sharing it with me."

"Don't be silly." Berthe ducked her head. "You're my best friend." Suddenly she raised her eyes. "Michou, may I ask you a question?"

"Don't *you* be silly." Michou grinned at her. Even though they'd known each other practically since infancy, Berthe always needed encouragement. She was so timid, so self-effacing—something else to blame on Lucien. "That's what best friends are for."

Berthe tested a large knife against her thumb. "Do you know any Germans?" she asked.

"Of course." Michou said. "Four of them are billeted with us." She flipped a peeled potato into the bowl.

Berthe skillfully trimmed the fat from the lamb shoulder. "I know that," she said. "That's not what I mean. Do you know any of them . . . well, personally?"

"You mean—" Michou stuck out her tongue. "That's disgusting. Why?"

"Because Lucien wants me to—"

"Go out with one? Oh, no, Berthe! You can't be considering it!" Michou stared at her.

"I know. Everyone will say I'm collaborating. I don't want to do it, but—"

"Damn Lucien!" Michou exploded. "He has no right to ask that of you."

"But that's just it—he isn't asking," Berthe said. Still gripping the knife, she rubbed at the tears on her face with the back of her hand. "He told me if I didn't go out with his friend, he'd make sure I never went out with anyone. And you know Lucien, Michou. He'd do it."

"There's a war on, you know. Maybe someone will shoot that brother of yours," Michou said.

Berthe gasped.

Michou clapped her hand over her mouth. "Oh, Berthe, I'm sorry. You know I didn't mean it." Like hell, she thought. But it had been cruel of her to say so. If Berthe loved Lucien a fraction of what she'd loved Alain—

"I know you didn't. It's my fault for—"

"Stop that! I'm tired of you always blaming yourself. Lucien's damn lucky to have a sister like you."

"I am, am I?"

Michou started as Lucien poked his head through the kitchen door. "Yes, you are," she said. "And you know it. I'd certainly never put up with you."

"What are you doing here?" Berthe asked.

Lucien ignored her. "Why not?" he asked Michou. "Just what is it you don't like about me? Why not come right out and tell me?" He lounged against the door frame. "Come on. I'm curious."

Michou threw the last potato into the bowl, and it bounced out onto the floor. She watched it come to a stop next to Lucien's foot. "Because you're *un mac,* that's why. A pimp. Forcing your own sister to go out with a Nazi pig."

Lucien rested his foot on the potato for a moment before stooping to pick it up. He tossed it at Michou. "I'm not *forcing* her." He shrugged. "If she doesn't want to go, *tant pis.* It's her loss. I'm just thinking of her."

Berthe put down the knife and faced Lucien, arms akimbo. "What are you doing here?" she repeated. "You said you had other plans. That's why I invited Michou."

Lucien glanced at her, and she dropped her arms to her sides. "I changed my mind," he said. "Kohler told me the blond fräulein left with my father, and—"

"You know Kohler?" Michou asked, her throat tight. What if Kohler had talked to Lucien about the English soldiers? She turned away and washed off the potato. "How long have you known him?" she said, trying to keep her tone casual.

"Since before he went to Château Bourdet," Lucien said. "We've become good friends."

"Oh," Michou said. For a second she felt as if someone had knocked all the air from her lungs. Then she spun around and faced Lucien. "Is he the one you want Berthe to go out with? You're crazy, Lucien. He's a fat swine."

Lucien smiled crookedly. "Well, Major Stecher certainly wouldn't be interested in her. As I said, I'm just doing her a favor." He paused while he lit a cigar. "By the way, did you hear what they did to that kid who cut the phone wires at La Rochelle?"

Michou shook her head.

Raising his eyebrows, Lucien looked directly into her eyes. "They shot him," he said.

13

❧

Guy paused in front of the tall double doors, waiting for the clank that would signal the shot had been made. "Dad hates to have his concentration broken when he's playing snooker," he explained to Jake. "He claims it puts him off his stroke."

The sound of balls clicking together came faintly through the thick doors. "There," he said. "It's safe now." He opened the doors and motioned for Jake to enter.

He followed Jake into the club's wood-paneled billiards room, the dark wood on the walls made even darker by decades of cigar and pipe smoke. Dad had been coming here when he was in London ever since he could remember—even before his parents' divorce. Guy liked the warm masculinity of Greene's, the aromas of tobacco and old leather and good food; and the billiards room had been a favorite with him since his first visit, on his twenty-first birthday. It had become a birthday tradition—a game of billiards or snooker, then dinner in the club's excellent dining room, followed by cognac in front of the fireplace in the library until late at night.

His father raised his hand in greeting when he saw Guy. "Only a few more strokes, then on to dinner," he said. He took the spider bridge off the rack and placed it on the table. "Extraordinarily difficult shot."

"Good luck, sir," Jake said.

"Thank you." Richard Chalmers slid his cue into the groove on the top of the bridge and lined it up with the cue ball. "Blue to side pocket," he said.

Guy smiled as the ball dropped softly into the pocket. He liked Dad's style—unpretentious, easy, no fancy stuff. Just pot the ball and move on to the next.

"Five points," Chalmers' partner said. "Good shot, Richard."

Guy nodded at the partner. André Simon looked much younger than his sixty-odd years despite his somewhat unruly white hair and deeply lined forehead. He and Richard Chalmers had a lot in common. Both of them loved France, wine, and snooker. Both made their homes in Bordeaux and ran wine-shipping businesses from there until they were driven out by the Germans. Both were British subjects, and both were members of Greene's Club for Gentlemen on St. James' Street.

Several strokes later, the game was finished. Simon clapped Richard on the back. "Excellent game, *cher ami*," he said. "I never mind losing to you." He turned to Guy and shook his hand. "Nice to see you again. I understand it's your birthday."

"Yes, sir," Guy said, and then introduced Jake. "We were at Cambridge together. Then Jake went back to Germany. He has some horrifying stories to tell about his escape."

Simon shook Jake's hand. "I'd be interested in hearing them. Shall we move on to the dining room?"

"Certainly," Richard said. "I'm so pleased you could join us tonight, André. I've told Guy a little about what your son has been doing, and he's extremely anxious to know more."

"I sure am, sir," Guy said. "And I know Jake is, too. We're both bloody tired of being informed we're too old to train." He fell into step beside Simon. "Today I was offered a job as a clerk at an RAF depot. A civilian clerk. That's the closest I've been able to get to the war. And I've at least twice as many reasons to fight as those young kids. You understand, sir, don't you?"

"Rather," Simon said as he sat down at the table reserved for them. "My son André was terribly pleased to have a uniform waiting for him, and he's a bit older than you, I daresay."

Guy waited until his father was seated before he slid into the chair across from Simon. Leaning back, he pretended to study the menu. He was anxious to ask Simon about the clandestine operations Dad had mentioned, but he didn't want to appear rude. Besides, it might be something Simon couldn't talk about in public. It was better to let him take the lead.

"What do you say to the roast beef and Yorkshire pudding?" Richard asked. "It's always been something of a tradition for Guy's birthday, and I have in mind just the bottles to go with it—a nineteen-hundred Latour and an excellent Saint-Émilion, the twenty-nine Clos Fourtet."

"Fine with me, Dad," Guy said. More than fine, actually—since he'd met Michou, he'd become intrigued by Saint-Émilions, wines that shippers from Bordeaux didn't have much association with because they were mostly shipped from Libourne. Dad must have noticed his interest. Guy wondered if he'd guessed at the cause—although he'd told Dad about meeting Michou and taking her to Paris with him, he'd never said anything about how much he'd liked her.

Still, Dad was plenty shrewd enough to figure it out. Guy chuckled to himself. Ordering a Clos Fourtet was just like him—a Château Bourdet would have been too obvious, so he'd suggested a wine from the closest neighbor.

Simon nodded his approval. "The Latour is a superb choice. I drank one last year, and it's holding up marvelously. It's not often that one can drink a wine made from ungrafted vines anymore. And the Clos Fourtet is a lovely, fruity wine."

Although the roast beef was not up to its usual standards, Guy enjoyed the meal more than he'd anticipated. Listening to Dad and André reminisce about some of the extraordinary wines they'd drunk, dinners they'd attended, people they'd met, was interesting enough to keep him entertained even though it didn't take his mind completely off the one thing he really wanted to talk about.

Finally, over the port, Simon turned abruptly to Jake. "And what's your story?" he said without prelude. "Tell me about your escape from Germany."

Keeping his voice low and toneless, Jake recited for Simon the story he'd told Guy. When he finished, he shrugged and looked at Guy. "Did I leave out anything?" he asked.

"Just one question," Simon said. "You're Jewish?"

"Yes," Jake said. He raised his eyebrows. "Did I leave that out?"

"In my business I've learned never to assume anything." Simon paused, stroking his chin. Then he leaned forward. "I think my son might like to talk to both of you. May I have him call you later this week and set up an appointment?"

"Definitely!" Guy nodded vigorously and smiled at Jake.

Suddenly the screech of an air-raid siren boomeranged through the dining room, followed by the clatter of silverware and the scrape of chairs.

Simon picked up the bottle of port and his glass and rose from the table. "To the cellar," he said. "It's not as comfortable as the library, but much preferable to the Green Park tube station."

"Better get some whisky, too," Guy said, sighing as he stood up. "It's going to be another long night."

The sudden silence was like diving into deep water. Perhaps the next bomb would explode right on top of Greene's, sending tons of brick crashing down into the cellar. Jake arched his back and pressed his shoulders against the wall. All around him, older members of the club read or slept restlessly in worn, ratty-looking chairs, but at least they were more comfortable than he was on his hard bench.

He glanced at Guy, sitting on a stool in the corner and staring at the empty bottle of whisky, and guilt prodded at him. It wasn't fair to wish destruction on his friends just because his own life was over. Although he'd been careful to hide it, repeating his story to Simon had only renewed his anguish, not exorcised it. Active involvement in the fight against the Nazis was the only thing that might help.

Jake closed his eyes and stretched, tipping his head back until it rested against the bricks. Simon had offered some hope, but he knew better than to clutch at it. It was better to go on expecting nothing.

"Think they're going to let up?" Guy said.

Jake straightened. Before he could speak, another flurry of ack-ack racket echoed throughout the damp cellar, and several dozing heads jerked upright. "No," he said. He forced his lips into a brief smile as a muffled thud rattled bottles in the shelves lining the room.

Guy shrugged and emptied the last drops of whisky into his glass. He held up his glass. "To tomorrow's headache," he said.

Jake held up his empty snifter. To tomorrow's heartache, he thought, but said nothing.

Guy yawned and pinched the bridge of his nose tightly as he stepped out of the Marble Arch tube station. Last night had been the worst since the blitz started a week ago. The raid had gone on so long, he and Jake had decided to stay all night in the club's cellar. But the new antiaircraft guns had made so much noise it had been impossible to sleep, the loud booms shaking even the cellar and turning his head into a bloody throbbing haggis.

He grimaced and turned the corner onto Park Street. No use blaming the entire headache on the racket—he had to cut down on the whisky. Should give it up, in fact.

And he would—as soon as he got Tessie out of this goddamn city. During the raid last night, he'd made up his mind. He kicked a jagged piece of stone on the sidewalk, raising his head to watch it bounce onto the street.

A makeshift barrier topped by a yellow sign reading DIVERSION blocked the entrance to Brook Street. He sucked in his breath and held it, willing his heart to stop its sudden thudding. In the last week, those barriers and signs had become a familiar sight. Too familiar.

The street must have been bombed.

"God, no!" His breath exploded out of his chest. He climbed over the barrier and started running.

They had to be all right. He was taking Tessie to the country today.

They had to be all right.

All right.

All right.

Dust and smoke clogged his nose as he turned onto Audley. His shoes made hard smacking sounds against the concrete. He stumbled over loose rocks and fell, cutting his palm. He pushed himself up, wiped his hand on his trousers, and forced himself to look.

Lydia's town house was a pile of bricks. The dusty foot of a child poked out of the rubble.

He was sick of waiting. It seemed as if he'd done nothing but wait for the last week—wait for Lydia's parents to return to London so he could make the funeral arrangements, wait for the clods of dirt to fall on Tessie's small coffin, wait for the pain to recede enough so he could cry.

Guy changed his position in the uncomfortable wing chair. Now he was waiting again—this time in the dingy lobby of the Northumberland Hotel—and his inactivity gave him too much opportunity to think about his grief. Why the hell had they made the appointment for three o'clock when they didn't plan to see him until five? Well, if they were testing his patience, he didn't have much left.

He glanced at the open book on his lap: *Stay Me with Flagons* by Maurice Healy, a gift from André Simon after the dinner party last week, sent with a note setting up this meeting. It deserved more attention than it was getting.

Footsteps thudded on the thinly carpeted stairs, and Guy raised his head.

"Mr. Chalmers?" a pale young man asked.

Guy stood up and tucked the book under his arm. "Yes," he said.

"If you'll follow me, please."

He climbed the stairs. Focusing on the orderly's thin back, he willed himself to forget the horrors of the last week. Don't think of Tessie, he told himself. Don't remember how it felt to pick up her little body, wrapped in a coarse green blanket by rescue workers, how her huge brown eyes stared upward, how her arms reached stiffly out before her. My God, she was only four years old.

He clenched his fists. No more. He couldn't afford to choke up now. Not when he needed this chance more than anything.

The orderly stopped in front of Room 211 and knocked on the door before he opened it. "Go on in," he said. "Captain Cranston will be here in a few minutes."

Guy stepped into the small room. Except for two chairs and a makeshift desk, it was empty—no bed, no pictures on the walls, no rug.

"Have a seat," the orderly said. He motioned toward the wood chair in the middle of the room and left.

Guy sat down and rested his chin on his knuckles. Waiting again, damn them. Didn't they know how close to the edge—

He sat up stiffly. No, they didn't. And they weren't going to, either. As he reached down to pick up his book, the door opened and closed softly.

Dropping the book with a clatter, he rose hurriedly. Calm down, he thought. He forced himself to smile when the captain introduced himself.

"Sit down," Captain Cranston said. "From now on we'll speak in French. I'd like to see just how good your command of the language is."

Guy lowered himself slowly into the chair. So that's what it was all about. They were looking for interpreters. He should have known.

For half an hour the captain asked him questions about himself, and Guy answered them uneasily, hoping he wouldn't have to explain about Lydia or Tessie. Gradually, though, Cranston broadened the topics, finally switching to questions about French geography and customs.

Leaning forward, Guy rubbed his chin. Why ask if he knew what it meant to *faire chabrot* if they only wanted a translator? "First, you eat most of your soup as quickly as you can," he explained. "Then you pour a glass of red wine into the bowl, swirl it around, and pick up the bowl and drink it."

Captain Cranston nodded, apparently satisfied. "Your knowledge of French customs is admirable for a foreigner, and your language skills are excellent. One would have no trouble believing you were French."

"You didn't want a translator, then?" Guy asked. He found himself gripping the seat of the chair tightly.

Cranston shook his head. "Is that what you thought?" He smiled briefly. "No, we have something considerably more dangerous in mind: parachuting into France to work against the Germans right in their midst. Are you interested?"

"Christ, am I!" Guy jumped up and walked to the window before he turned back to the captain. "When do I start?"

"I'll set up an interview for you tomorrow with Humphreys. He'll explain about the training. Expect a call this evening," Cranston said, standing up.

Guy stuck out his hand. "Thank you, sir," he said. He picked up his book and turned to go.

"One thing you should know, Chalmers," the captain said.

Guy stopped at the door.

Cranston cleared his throat. "If you get caught, you'll be entirely on your own. And the Gestapo does not take spying lightly."

14

"Do we have any more garlic, Madeleine?" Berthe asked. "I just used the last clove." She slapped the large chunk of beef and smiled. "Can you believe this? I don't know how Lucien does it! Château LeClair-Figeac is going to have the best *soupe des vendages* in Saint-Émilion!"

Madeleine snorted and tossed her another head of garlic. "Too bad he couldn't get a leg of veal as well," she said. "We've been eating pretty well here since he made friends with that major from Château Bourdet."

Berthe continued poking the strong-smelling laurel leaves and garlic cloves into slits in the beef. She knew Lucien had Nazi friends, but she refused to believe what everyone said about him. If he received favors from the Germans, he only did it to help her and Father. Madeleine had always been a complainer, and Michou, well, she had turned against Lucien when Alain died. Even Father had never understood Lucien the way she did. Mother's death had been the hardest on him.

Finally, she was satisfied with the beef. "There," she said, heaving it into the huge pot on the stove. "Now for the vegetables. Are you finished yet?" Lucien had given orders for the grape-pickers' soup to be ready an hour earlier today. He wanted his guest to try it before the harvest workers came in from the vineyards. That was fine with her—Michou was coming for lunch, too, and it gave them extra time to spend together without Lucien. She wished Michou didn't dislike him so much. It hadn't always been that way. Before Daniel and Alain drowned, the two families had spent a lot of time

103

together. After the grief ebbed, though, Michou's bitterness made it difficult for all of them to be together the way they used to. Only her loyalty to Berthe had survived Alain's death.

"*Ouais,* mademoiselle," Madeleine said sarcastically. "Don't forget I've done this a few times before." She dumped a large bowl of turnips, potatoes, onions, and cabbage into the pot.

"I'm sorry," Berthe said. Ducking her head to avoid Madeleine's eyes, she scattered a bunch of grapes and a handful of cloves over the top of the vegetables. "It's just that—" She paused as Lucien strode into the kitchen.

"You finish, Madeleine," he said. "I want to talk to Berthe." He snapped his fingers at her and frowned. "Come on. Can't you hurry it up?"

Hastily, Berthe hung her apron on the peg and followed Lucien through the swinging doors. She'd done everything he'd asked—why was he angry at her now? She wiped her palms on her skirt.

At the bottom of the stairs, Lucien turned and put his hands on his hips. "Have you thought any more about going out with Sergeant Kohler?" he asked.

"N-no," she said, her eyes fixed on her shoes.

"No, you haven't thought about it, or no, you won't?"

"I—I haven't thought about it." She plucked at her skirt. "But I—"

He grabbed her arm. "Well, start thinking. He's here, and he wants to meet you." He squeezed her arm hard before releasing it. "Although why, I can't imagine," he muttered.

"Here? N-now?" she said, raising her eyes.

Lucien's eyes were slits. "Yes," he hissed. "In my room." He pushed her toward the stairs. "Go on up."

"Oh, I—"

"Shut up and go," he shouted. "No more excuses."

Her eyes filling with tears, Berthe trudged up the stairs, grasping the banister tightly. She hated it when Lucien yelled at her. She tried so hard to please him, but he acted as if he were mad at her so much of the time. Even though she loved him, sometimes he scared her.

She stopped outside his room and took her handkerchief out of her pocket. After she wiped her eyes and blew her

nose, she knocked on the door. She did not want to meet this
German, but if it was really that important to Lucien—

"*Kommen sie.*"

When she entered, he stood at the window with his back
to her, hands clasped behind him. She cleared her throat.
"I—"

He swung around and faced her. "You have some hesi-
tancy about seeing a German, *ja?*" he said. "It is very natural. I understand. That is why I asked Lucien to meet you in
private." He offered her his hand. "I am Wolf Kohler."

His fingers made her think of sausages, fat German
sausages. She shook his hand. It was moist and sticky. She
had to stop herself from wiping her palm on her skirt.

She lifted her eyes. Dark blond hair bristled out from
under his cap, and his closely cropped moustache looked
ridiculously small for his large face. Gray-green and
wrinkled, his uniform stretched tightly across his hanging
belly and large thighs. Michou was right—he was a swine.
Why was Lucien making her do this?

"Well, uh, Sergeant Kohler, it's been very nice meeting
you, but—" She backed toward the door.

"I don't think you understand, Fräulein," he said. He
lunged forward, grasping her around the waist and pulling her
toward him. "Your brother promised me—"

Berthe's heartbeat thudded in her ears. She gasped and
clutched at the fingers clawing at her middle. Lucien couldn't
have promised *that* to this pig. He'd just asked her to meet
him, that was all. He'd be mad at Kohler when she told him
he'd touched her. He'd see she was right not to date a German. He had to. *He had to.* Bitter-tasting fear bubbled into
her throat, and she screeched, "Luc—"

Kohler's other hand clamped over her mouth. "*Halte
den mund!*" he wheezed. "Shut up, shut up, you stupid
bitch!" He pulled her away from the door. "Your brother
means for you to be nice to me. Do you understand?"

She widened her eyes and nodded vigorously. As soon as
he released her, she said, "But I can't!" She gulped. "I don't
want to—" She ran for the door.

"*Scheiss!*" The word exploded from Kohler as he
lurched toward her and seized her again. Then he slapped her
hard across her face.

Her ears ringing, Berthe struggled to get away from him. A strange, salty taste filled her mouth. Blood. She swallowed a mouthful and gagged.

Kohler pressed his mouth over hers, and the too-sweet smell of Oriental tobacco and wine made her heave again. Sour bile spewed out of her mouth and ran down his chin.

Spitting, he jerked away. He hit her again, this time with his fist.

Bones crunched in Berthe's face, and her vision fogged. She panted. Kohler's raspy laugh buzzed in her ears as he threw her onto Lucien's bed.

"No!" she screamed, kicking at him.

Pulling down his pants with one hand and holding her against the bed with the other, he grunted. Then he laughed again. His hard fingers poked at her, fumbled with her panties, scratched the soft flesh of her inner thighs.

"No!" Her shriek bounced inside her head. "Don't!"

Suddenly a spurt of pain between her legs pierced the throbbing ache. She cried out again and flailed her legs, but the stabbing deep inside her didn't stop.

It went on and on. She squeezed her eyes shut and stopped fighting.

When Kohler finally stood up, she didn't move. Her breath rattled in her throat. She tried to open her eyes, but one was swollen shut and the other was blurred with tears.

Kohler zipped up his pants. "*Danke,* Fräulein," he said. "You'll like it better next time. Virgins always do."

"She doesn't want to see me?" Michou frowned. "But she invited me for lunch." That wasn't like Berthe at all. Even if she were ill, she wouldn't refuse a visitor. Berthe loved company. Saying no to a friend was almost impossible for her.

Madeleine shrugged. "She got sick. Came on real sudden. Fine as could be until Lucien talked to her. Now she doesn't want to see anybody. Wouldn't even let me into her room."

"I'm going up anyway," Michou said. "Something's wrong."

Madeleine shrugged again and waddled off toward the

kitchen, her fat hips waving from side to side under the black dress. "You do that," she said over her shoulder before she elbowed open the doors. "I got to set up for lunch. Can't be worrying over such nonsense."

The smell of boiling beef, cabbage, and garlic surged into the hallway as Madeleine disappeared into the kitchen. Michou stared at the doors, still swinging back and forth, before she headed up the worn wooden stairs. She clenched her fists. If Lucien had done anything to hurt Berthe—

"Berthe?" she called, knocking on the door. "It's Michou. I'm coming in."

Ignoring the muffled "No!" from the other side of the door, she strode into the small bedroom, the room Berthe had used every summer since her father had bought the château when they were all children. They'd shared a lot in this room: daring plots against their big brothers, secrets about the boys they would most like to kiss, confusion about their changing bodies, plans for the future when they would be too big for anyone to tell them what to do.

Berthe lay on her stomach on the large canopied bed, her face pressed into a pillow. Her plump body shook with sobs.

Michou sat beside her. "What's wrong?" she said, stroking Berthe's soft brown hair. "Did Lucien upset you?"

Berthe's head moved back and forth on the pillow.

"Tell me what's wrong," Michou said. She gave Berthe's shoulders a little shake. "What happened?"

Slowly, Berthe turned her face toward Michou. One eye was swollen shut and purple, a thin trail of dried blood stained her cheek, and her upper lip, red and puffed, almost reached her nose.

"*Mon Dieu!* Who did this to you?" Michou jumped up from the bed. "Did Lucien do this?" she demanded.

"N-no," Berthe said, sobbing.

"Who, then? Tell me right now!" Michou stomped her foot.

"Oh, Michou, y-you can't do anything about it." Berthe pushed her face back into the pillow.

"Tell me, damn it!" She leaned over Berthe. "Look at me. What bastard did this?"

"K-Kohler," Berthe whispered. She rolled onto her side.

"Kohler!" Michou spat the name. "Why would he—" She sat back down on the bed. "Did he try to—"

Berthe pushed herself up on one elbow. She nodded, tears spilling over her cheeks.

"You didn't let him?"

"I—I couldn't help it," Berthe sobbed. She sat up. "He was too strong."

"I would have killed him first!"

"I know. But *I* couldn't. You know that." Berthe buried her face in her hands and cried even harder.

Michou put her arm around Berthe's shoulders. "I'm sorry. I didn't mean it that way," she said. "Where did this happen? Did Lucien finally talk you into going out with him?"

Berthe shook her head. "In Lucien's room. He said Kohler wanted to meet me."

"Damn Lucien! He knew—"

"Oh, no, Michou," Berthe said. "It's not Lucien's fault. Kohler was drunk. He told me Lucien said I should be nice to him. He didn't say anything about—"

"Hah!" Michou said. Why couldn't Berthe see her brother for what he really was? "Does Lucien know what he did to you?"

"Not yet," Berthe said. "He said he had an important guest for lunch today."

The door opened, and Lucien stuck his head in. "Oh, you're here," he said when he saw Michou. He stepped into the room. "How was Kohler?" he asked Berthe.

Without answering, she turned her bruised and swollen face toward him.

"Jesus, Berthe!" His eyes widened and his mouth fell open. "Did that pig Kohler do this to you?" He sounded horrified.

Michou sprang up from the bed and shook her fist in Lucien's face. "Yes, and it's your fault, Lucien Desroches. If you hadn't insisted that she meet him, this wouldn't have—"

"Shut up, Michou," Lucien drawled, grabbing her hand. He curled his upper lip, and his usual mask of indifference crept back over his face. "It was her own damn fault. She probably led him on and then started acting coy."

Michou snatched her hand out of Lucien's grasp. "He raped her!" she shouted. "Don't you even care that a *Boche* beat up your sister and then raped her?"

His voice higher pitched than usual, Lucien laughed as he retreated to the door. "Well," he said, "at least now she won't have to die a virgin." He slammed the door behind him.

Sobbing hysterically, Berthe threw herself down on the bed. "Oh, God, he hates me," she said. "He hates me. I never knew."

Michou patted her back. God would forgive her for lying if it helped Berthe. "No, he doesn't," she said. "It's just hard for him to show sympathy." She knew she didn't sound convincing, but it might work with Berthe. She never could believe the worst of anyone, especially Lucien.

"I want you to come and stay with me until you go back to Libourne," Michou said. "I don't think you should be alone."

Berthe raised her head and turned her swollen face toward Michou. "Thank you," she gasped. "I can't bear to see anyone."

Michou gritted her teeth. Someday, she'd make Lucien pay.

Kohler had to go, Lucien decided as he returned to the dining room. Not just because of what he'd done to Berthe, although that was a part of it. He was just getting out of hand—drinking too much, talking too much, taking too much for granted. There was no telling what he'd do—or say—next. While he didn't really care if the fool got caught and implicated Valette, it wouldn't do for Michou to be arrested, too. You couldn't trust a drunk, and a stupid drunk was even worse.

Kohler leaned back in his chair, puffing on one of Lucien's expensive cigars. "Not bad," he said. He sneered, as if daring Lucien to say anything about either the cigar or Berthe.

"Glad you like it," Lucien said. There was no way he'd give him the satisfaction of mentioning Berthe. "May I get you another glass of wine?" Maybe he could scare the shit out of the bastard if he got him drunk enough.

"*Jawohl.*" Kohler waved his glass in the air.

Lucien filled the glass and set the empty bottle next to the other two on the table. "Another cadaver," he said. "What is it the Americans say—another dead soldier?"

Kohler swigged down the wine. "I haven't heard that one," he said. He belched and hiccuped in rapid succession.

Lucien opened another bottle of wine. Although Kohler certainly looked drunk enough to be impressionable, it was better not to take any chances. "What do you think of Major Stecher so far?" he asked, pouring him another glass.

"Tough man," Kohler said. He nodded as if he considered himself a great judge of character and gulped down more red wine. "Yes, a damn tough man."

"My opinion exactly," Lucien said, resting his elbows on the table. "I've gotten to know him pretty well." He smiled with closed lips and raised his eyebrows. He hoped Kohler wasn't too drunk to understand his implications.

"You have?" Kohler's words were slurred. "He never said anything about seeing you again."

"He's not the kind of man to reveal much," Lucien said. "He sees more than he talks about."

"He does?"

Lucien leaned toward Kohler. "You've been a little careless lately, haven't you?" he said.

Kohler's mouth fell open, and he scooted back in his chair.

Lucien slowly fitted a cigar into his holder. He stared at Kohler as he lit it, inhaled the smoke, and then exhaled out his nose. "Stecher knows," he said. "He's just waiting for a good time to arrest you."

Kohler's breath whistled out between his teeth. Twisting violently toward Lucien, he knocked over his wineglass. "You told him!" he yelled.

"Why would I do that?" Lucien asked quietly, his mouth twitching at the corners.

Kohler jumped up. "Stecher's a fag. If he likes you, he'd tell you everything you want to know. You wouldn't need to pay me."

Lucien pointed at the chair. "Sit down," he said. "And calm down." He paused while Kohler obeyed. "You are right about one thing—Stecher does like me, and he does tell me plenty. For example, he told me about you. I'm doing you a big favor by passing on the information."

Kohler looked as if someone had just punched him in his fat stomach. "What should I do now?" he whined.

"I know what I'd do," Lucien said. "I'd join the next group of Englishmen."

"But that's desertion. They'd shoot me if they caught me."

Lucien nodded. "That's right. And if you stay, they'll shoot you for treason. Which would you prefer?" He thudded down the fourth empty bottle of wine next to the others and smiled. "Another dead soldier."

15

❧

Except for Lucien and the middle-aged barmaid, the small bar at L'Hostellerie was empty. The barmaid glanced at him beneath her lashes and smiled coyly. Stupid bitch, he thought, winking at her. Chantal must have been around thirty or so when he'd slept with her a few times when he was fifteen, and she probably still thought she'd initiated him into *les plaisirs de l'amour*. He'd never bothered to disabuse her. It was more fun to lead her on, let her think maybe, just maybe, she might be so lucky again.

He stared at her as she poured him another Pernod. She'd been pretty good-looking at thirty, but she looked like hell now. He'd just as soon go to bed with fat old Madeleine.

He added water to the *pastis* until it turned a milky yellow and then swirled the glass, blinking as the anise-scented fumes rose to his eyes. If Kohler was going to show up for his regular aperitif, he should be there soon. In half an hour, the bar would be filled with pickers, and he generally preferred to have swilled down two or three before the locals arrived.

Boots clattered on the bare wooden floor, and he twisted around on the stool. Not Kohler, but Karl and his driver. He smiled and stood up. Although Kohler patronized L'Hostellerie frequently, this was the first time he'd seen Karl here. He hoped it meant he was looking for Kohler.

Lucien offered Karl his hand. "Good to see you, Major," he said. "Won't you join me?"

"With pleasure," Karl said. After he sat down, he turned to his driver. "Wait in the car."

"I'd be glad to give you a ride," Lucien said, resuming his seat.

"Wonderful," Karl said. "In that case, you may return to Château Bourdet." He waited until the driver left before he patted Lucien's arm. "It's good to see you again. I thoroughly enjoyed our evening together last week. Perhaps we can repeat it again once the vintage is completed."

"Of course," Lucien said. He nodded in the direction of the barmaid and raised his eyebrow. "You'd like to order something?" he asked Karl.

"Whatever you're having is fine," Karl said. He took the hint and lowered his voice. "I'm looking for Sergeant Kohler. He didn't report for duty this morning, and my aide tells me this place is a favorite of his. Have you seen him?"

"Not today," Lucien said. "And I've been here for a couple of hours. Maybe he went into Libourne." His story must have worked, he thought. He tried to look as blank as he could.

Karl shook his head. "I checked. Stupid drunkard. The transfer I requested for him came through. No good letting a drunk guard a wine château."

"Probably passed out somewhere."

"Perhaps." He paid the barmaid for his drink and took a sip. He made a face. "Ugh. Licorice," he said, pushing the *pastis* away.

"Sorry," Lucien said. He leaned toward Karl. "I know Château Bourdet better than you do. Let me drive you there. We can look around together. You probably didn't check the first-year *chai?*"

"No." Karl stood. "I don't know much about winemaking." He smiled his tight-lipped smile. "I guess it makes about as much sense to send me to oversee wine production in Saint-Émilion as it does to send a lush to guard it."

Lucien finished his drink. "The wine is stored in barrels there. It's not especially good at that point, but all you have to do to get a drink is siphon some off. No one would miss it," he said as he escorted Karl to his car.

Karl snapped his fingers. "I'll bet that's where he is, then."

Smiling, Lucien slid behind the wheel. Kohler wasn't there, but if he was lucky, maybe an Englishman or two might be. "I never bet against a sure thing," he said, starting the car.

Karl didn't seem to be in the mood for chatting during the short drive to Château Bourdet, so Lucien concentrated on his driving. He loved the way the Mercedes took the sharp curves on the windy old road, poorly surfaced as it was. He could break loose all four tires without losing control. He glanced occasionally at Karl to see his reaction, but his face remained impassive, even after a particularly spectacular drift. Maybe he was beginning to suspect the worst about Kohler.

By the time Lucien parked in front of the château, the last few pickers were leaving. Excellent timing, he congratulated himself. The *chai* should be empty while Michou and Alexandre cleaned up before dinner.

He led Karl past the guard and into the *cuvier*. "This is where the grapes are crushed," he said, tapping the *fouloirégrappoir,* a large contraption filled with dull purple-black grapes. "Then the juice goes into this vat to ferment."

Karl wrinkled his nose. "That's what that horrid yeasty odor is, then. Odd—it smells more like bread than like wine. This isn't the stuff Kohler is so fond of, is it? Disgusting."

Lucien laughed. "Not even Kohler could be that desperate." He pointed to the door behind the large cement *cuve*. "There's the first-year *chai,"* he said. "That's probably where we'll find him, snoring away behind a—"

He paused as voices carried in through the open door. Putting his finger over his lips, he motioned for Karl to stand behind the vat.

"Was—" Karl frowned as Lucien knelt beside him.

Two men dressed as pickers walked into the *cuvier*. They looked around nervously, their eyes darting from one object to another.

Finally, one waved toward the doorway opening to the *chai* and whispered something in English. The other nodded vigorously, and they headed into the *chai,* closing the door quietly behind them.

"Englanders!" The words exploded from Karl's mouth. He pulled his gun out of the holster at his side and nudged Lucien. "I will arrest them," he said.

Lucien stepped out from behind the vat. It wouldn't do

him much good if Karl didn't get Valette, too. "They must be waiting for a *passeur*," he said softly. "But how did they know to—"

"*Ach so*," Karl said. He put his gun away. "Let us see if we can catch some bigger fish than two puny Englishmen." He paused, his eyes narrowing. "Perhaps some French fish as well, *ja?*"

Trying to pretend it wasn't yet dawn, Michou stretched again and buried her head in her pillow. She was so exhausted that even getting out of bed seemed like too much work. And with fewer pickers and more grapes than usual, the vintage was likely to last another week.

Stiffly, she pushed herself up. It wouldn't do for Papa to guess how tired she was. She knew he counted on her help more than he liked to admit.

She stared out the window as she put on her work-clothes, a pair of heavy brown trousers and an old wool sweater—the mornings were much cooler now. The vine-yards always looked so peaceful before the pickers arrived. Still, she'd always loved the harvest—the vivid autumn colors, the noise, the sweet smell of the grapes and the ferment-ing must, the hope for the future.

The hope for the future. *Hah!* She rested her forehead against the cold glass. It seemed almost pointless to pretend. Why bother to make wine if the Germans were just going to steal it?

That didn't seem to bother Papa, though. He acted as if this were a normal vintage, pushing himself and everyone else just as hard as if these wines were destined for a con-noisseur's table instead of for swill for the Nazis. There'd even been rumors that the Germans planned to convert much of the wine into industrial alcohol.

A movement in Stecher's car, parked below, caught Michou's attention, and she frowned. Where would he be going at this hour?

Just then, the door at the bottom of the tower clicked shut, and her father stepped into view. As Papa approached the car, Stecher slunk down in his seat as if he didn't want to be seen.

Michou gasped and covered her mouth with her hand.

There were Englishmen in the *chai* waiting for the *passeur,* and Stecher was watching Papa! Kohler hadn't been around for a couple of days—maybe he'd told.

She fumbled around under the chair for her *sabots.* She had to stop Papa before he got to the *chai.* She swallowed hard to hold back her fear.

She finally found the wooden shoes and jammed her feet into them. Then when she reached the steps, she took them off—they'd make too much noise on the bare stone.

She ran down the stairs. At the bottom she opened the door a crack and peeked out. She couldn't see Papa, but Stecher and his men stood at the corner of the *cuvier,* guns in their hands.

She bit her lip. *Merde!* What should she do? If she tried to warn Papa now, they'd know for sure. But she couldn't just stand there and watch.

She put her shoes on and stepped out. Maybe she could distract the Germans, talk to them loudly enough for Papa to hear.

She walked quietly toward the *cuvier,* her ears ringing so loudly that the crunch of the gravel under her heavy shoes sounded far away.

Suddenly one of the Germans shouted, "Halt!" All three of them raised their guns, clasping them with two hands.

Michou stood motionless, but none of them turned around. They hadn't even seen her yet. They were looking at something she couldn't see.

Two figures raced from the *cuvier* into the vineyard.

"Halt!" one of the Germans yelled again.

The men kept running.

A huge roar echoed in Michou's head. One man stumbled and fell. Another roar. The other man leaped into the air before he crashed onto the vines.

Michou's breath exploded between her lips, and her eyes stung. She felt sick to her stomach. She didn't even know them, and it was awful. She wiped the tears from her cheeks. Where was Papa?

The front door slammed and running footsteps thundered behind her and still she couldn't move. A hand grabbed her arm.

"What happened?" Philippe hissed.

She stared at him, her mouth open, but no sound came out.

"What happened?" he repeated, shaking her arm.

"Two men. They shot two men. In the vineyards." Her voice rasped in her throat.

One of the Nazis headed toward the fallen men while the other and Stecher disappeared into the *cuvier*. In a minute Papa walked out.

Stecher followed closely behind him, his gun leveled at Papa's back.

16

❧

Guy shrugged into his tweed jacket and glanced in the mirror. Despite the changes two months of commando training had wrought on his body, the jacket still fit reasonably well. He pulled his arms back. Perhaps a bit tight now through the arms and shoulders—still, not too bad. Marriott had been pleased that the Special Operations executive didn't have to pay for a complete new wordrobe for him. His old things were more authentic than what the SOE's tailor could make—and they were already broken in. Even more important, they were perfectly suitable for the cover he would be assuming once he was in France.

He tapped the gray hat the tailor had bought from a newly arrived refugee onto his head and gazed at his reflection. Perfect. Guy Fournier—a not-too-prosperous wine broker, wearing last year's jacket, worn gray trousers, scuffed black shoes, and a new hat—stared back at him, his thick dark eyebrows pulled together above his brown eyes, a lock of straight gold-brown hair falling onto his forehead. He sighed and smoothed his hair back under the hat. No point in looking seedier than necessary now. He could save that for France.

His father looked up from his newspaper and waved as Guy let himself out. "See you later, Dad," he said. "I'm off to meet Jake at the Gay Nineties."

Richard nodded. "Seems to be your favorite place lately. What is it—a club for spies?" He chuckled.

Guy shook his head, but Dad was closer to the truth than he realized. All the trouble they took at Orchard Court to keep agents apart—even hustling you into the famous black bathroom to avoid a chance meeting in the hallway if the other rooms were occupied—seemed silly when you could walk into the bar on Berkeley Street and spot six or eight at a time. Of course, you had to pretend you didn't know them. "Just a good meeting place," he mumbled.

"Enjoy yourself, then," Richard said. "Come around to the club afterward if you feel like it. Watch me snooker André again."

Guy's lips curved upward in his best imitation of a smile. "Might just do that," he said, forcing himself to sound hearty. Since he'd returned to London a week ago, he'd worked hard to keep his father from guessing just how depressed he really was. He was afraid if Dad realized it, he'd mention it to André and André would mention it to Marriott and they'd pull him from his mission. And he'd be damned if he'd risk that, not now when his reasons for going were even stronger than before. Except for Dad, he had nothing left in England. London for him was just sirens and piles of rubble, reminders of how Tessie had died.

He whistled tunelessly until he caught a cab to Berkeley Street. Well, at least he had Dad. Jake had no one. Word had finally arrived three days ago—his wife and two sons were dead, his father was dead, and his sister and her family had disappeared.

Guy paid the cabbie and shoved his wallet back into his pocket. Jake had made him swear not to tell anyone, not even his father. He was afraid, too, that Marriott might cancel his assignment. The firm didn't like to send in emotionally unstable agents. "I'm fine," he had protested when Guy suggested perhaps it would be safer to wait. "Not a bit unstable. Rock bottom is about as stable as you can get."

The smell of beer and smoke was a relief after the rancid-sweat odor of the taxi. Resting his foot on the brass rail, Guy ordered a whisky and water and glanced at the ornate clock behind the bar. He was early. Good. He'd have time for a couple before Jake arrived.

When his drink was served, he sipped it and grimaced. He'd gotten spoiled on the Highland malts during his training in Scotland, and the bar blend he'd always drunk seemed insipid now. He was still drinking too much, he knew. But after Tessie's death, it didn't really matter anymore; and at Arisaig the instructors had even encouraged the trainees, setting up drinks all around, and then, when everyone was properly smashed, ordering a three-mile run in the dark back to the country house where they were billeted.

Guy gulped down the rest of the whisky and ordered another. Poor Jake. He wasn't much of a drinker and even less of a runner. But he'd made it, flat feet and all, through everything, even the parachute jumping. Not everyone had.

He raised his glass in a silent toast to Tom Liggett, whose parachute had roman-candled during the practice jump at Ringway, where they'd gone after Arisaig. Christ, he hadn't wanted to jump after that, but he'd forced himself. Two of the trainees who'd refused were gone the next day. He hadn't come that far for nothing.

And he'd surprised himself by actually liking it. For a few minutes he hadn't thought about Tessie at all. He hadn't thought about anything except the sensation of extraordinary freedom, a release even greater than drinking himself into a stupor.

Someone jostled his shoulder, and Guy spilled whisky on his jacket. He brushed it off and turned his head slowly. Ian Mapp. He should have guessed. He'd like to punch the son of a bitch in the nose—by the looks of it, it wouldn't be the first time, either.

Mapp nodded and grinned, his thick lips curling up to reveal a missing front tooth. "Sorry, mate," he said. He jerked his head at the bartender.

Guy leaned on his elbow and stared at Mapp. His lean face, small yellow-flecked green eyes, even his bristle of red hair seemed to ooze belligerence. One cheekbone was completely flattened from being broken, and the skin was tinted slightly blue underneath.

After Mapp ordered a Guinness stout, he turned back to Guy. "Where's your friend?" he asked. "The bloody German."

Guy narrowed his eyes. He was sick of Mapp's insinuations. "Just what do you mean by that?" he said, keeping his voice low with an effort.

Mapp snickered and crossed his arms. "Your friend's a German, that's all. Why they let a bloody Jerry in is no business of mine, but—"

"Damn right!" Guy said. "One would assume the Special Operations people know more about the matter than a—"

"Fuck off, mate," Mapp said. He grimaced an approximation of a smile. "Those blokes don't know their ass from a—"

The bartender set a glass in front of him, and Mapp smacked some coins onto the bar. He took a large gulp of stout and swallowed noisily.

Guy clamped his jaw shut and ground his teeth. He'd managed to avoid a fight with Mapp throughout training—no point in starting one now, no matter how satisfying it would be to flatten the other cheekbone. Mapp seemed incapable of comprehending that Jake was Jewish first and German second, that the Nazis had destroyed any love he had for his fatherland when they'd taken away his wife and two small sons.

At least Marriott had been quick to see it, even though the general rule was to recruit only British nationals. And fortunately for Guy, Marriott had been willing to overlook his American citizenship as well.

Guy sighed deeply and took another drink of his whisky. No, he didn't want to ruin things now, risk losing his assignment. In two weeks he'd be in France, and with any kind of luck, he wouldn't see Mapp again. He just hoped they weren't sending him to the Bordeaux area, too. Whoever the firm sent in with him would be compromised from the first—not only was Mapp much larger than the average Frenchman; but his red hair made him stand out, and he had a habit of interjecting English curses into the middle of his French. Guy snickered as he pictured Mapp losing his temper and calling a Nazi a "bloody *con*."

"Something funny, mate?" Mapp said.

"You, mate," Guy said.

Mapp slammed his glass down on the bar, and the dark brown beer spewed into the air and onto his hand. He wiped his hand off on his pants and stood up straight. "Want to explain?" he said.

Guy forced himself to smile pleasantly. "You wouldn't understand," he said.

Mapp's fists shot up in front of his face, and he stepped forward.

Guy felt a hand on his arm and turned, his fists clenched.

Jake stood behind him. "Don't be stupid," he hissed. He nodded toward a table by the door. "Sergeant Barton is watching."

Mapp swiveled his head, and his arms fell loosely to his sides. He turned back to Guy. "Next time, mate," he said.

Guy relaxed his hands and picked up his drink as Jake ordered a pint of bitter. "Nice talking to you, *mate*," he said to Mapp. He followed Jake to a table by the window.

"What the hell was that all about?" Jake asked as he sat down.

Guy slid into the chair opposite him. "I just don't like the bastard," he said. "And I don't trust him. Why they ever recruited him is still a mystery to me."

"He's a radio man and they're scarce," Jake said. "And he speaks French. Besides, I heard he requested the transfer—something about his brother dying in his arms at Dunkirk. I guess he wants revenge." He frowned. "Now, that's something both of us can understand."

Guy shrugged. Leave it to Jake to sympathize with a man who hated him. "Fine. Let him get his revenge. On the Nazis—not you. You're not the enemy."

"I'm German. For a regular-army type like Mapp, that's enough."

"More likely he's brassed off because we were both commissioned captains and he only made it to lieutenant." Guy snorted. "Son of a bitch should be grateful. He'd never have made it that far if he'd stayed put."

Jake looked over his shoulder and then leaned forward. "Forget Mapp," he said, lowering his voice. "I got my orders yesterday. No more waiting."

"Parachute or felucca?" Guy asked.

"Felucca. Somewhere on the Côte d'Azur."

Guy nodded. He didn't want Jake to be any more specific—it was too dangerous. And Jake only knew that he was parachuting into France to organize resistance groups. He'd been careful not to reveal he was jumping into the area between the Dordogne and Garonne rivers.

Jake rubbed the lapel of his jacket. "Did you get your phial yet?"

"Damn stupid, if you ask me," Guy asked. "I threw it

away. Try denying you're an agent if they find that on you."

Jake stroked his chin. "I hadn't thought of that," he said. "Still, there's some comfort in knowing it's there. Just in case." He sat back in his chair and surveyed the room. "Look. Next to Mapp. There's the sergeant from Wanborough."

"The one we cursed after every cross-country run. I'd like to thank him now," Guy said. After the first shock, the physical pain of getting back into shape had been a relief, almost a drug. He knew it had been the same for Jake; he had seen it in his face, the way the deep wrinkles between his eyebrows had gradually smoothed into faint lines and the tight set of his mouth had eased into half smiles. He still wasn't the same Jake he'd known in Cambridge, but Guy doubted he'd ever be.

"I know what you mean. I didn't think I was going to make it. But even that wasn't as bad as Beaulieu," Jake said. "That's why I'm keeping this." He patted his lapel.

Guy took his pipe and a packet of tobacco from his pocket. Jake was right—what they'd learned about Gestapo interrogation techniques during the training at Beaulieu had been pretty sobering. Even Mapp had been impressed with the bathtub torture—half drowning someone, reviving him, then holding him under again.

He scooped the pipe into the packet and tamped it with his forefinger. At least the instructors hadn't gone that far in their efforts to prepare their trainees. He shivered, remembering the night he'd been awakened from an exhausted sleep.

"Chalmers, 'raus!"

Guy had forced his eyes open. It was still dark. Why were they waking him in the middle of the night?

A brilliant light shone suddenly in his face, and he squeezed his eyes shut again.

"'Raus!" Strong hands shook his shoulders.

"What the hell?" he mumbled. His tongue felt huge and furry. Christ, why had he drunk so much? He tried to push the hands away, but they only shook him harder.

Wait a minute. They were speaking German. He opened his eyes slowly and squinted past the light. The silver tips on the collars of the dark uniforms, the twin flashes of light-ning—they were SS. But what were they doing in England?

"Get dressed," the tall, storklike one said in heavily accented English.

All at once Guy's stupor evaporated. So this was what the captain had meant when he'd told them they'd be in training twenty-four hours a day. These weren't really SS officers after all—just a couple of SOE staffers dressed up in the uniform of Hitler's most terrifying corps.

Guy stared at the men with what he hoped was a stu-pefied look. *"Je ne comprends pas,"* he said. At least he wouldn't make the mistake of showing he understood En-glish.

"You understand, all right," the shorter officer said. "Don't play games with us."

Guy sat up and shook his head. *"Je ne parle pas An-glais,"* he said. He bit his lip and shrugged, palms up, a gesture he'd seen many of his father's French employees use when they thought someone in charge was being particularly unreasonable or obtuse.

"Ach so," the stork said. He put his hands on his hips, and his protruding elbows made him look even more like the large, gawky bird. "You want to act stupid, fine with me," he said in French. "Get up and get dressed."

Guy got out of bed and forced himself to dress unhur-riedly. Slowly, slowly, he told himself. It was important to stay calm, his instructors had said, and the best way to do that was to be slow and deliberate and casual. No matter that two SS men waking you in the middle of the night would scare anyone, innocent or guilty.

When Guy finished dressing, the short officer pulled out his gun and waved it toward the door. The gun at his back, Guy had followed the stork down the hall and out to the car. They had taken him to a nearby house and questioned him for four hours.

And that had been plenty unpleasant. He'd managed to perform well enough to satisfy the major in charge, but he had no wish to repeat the experience, especially not with the real thing. Now, Guy lit the pipe and inhaled deeply. "Damn," he sputtered.

"Something wrong?" Jake asked.

"Got Dad's Latakia blend by mistake." Guy waved the heavy burnt-plum-scented smoke from his face and emptied the pipe into the ashtray. "At least I got the right pipe. The one the firm gave me to take with me has a tiny compass in the mouthpiece. Doesn't draw very well."

Jake chuckled. "Better watch out for that. They're pretty thorough, these chaps. Don't they even give you French tobacco before you leave?"

"Yes, unfortunately. Pretty tasteless stuff. But at least it doesn't stink," Guy said.

"It doesn't smell half as bad as the plastic explosive," Jake said. "God, that stuff gave me a headache."

"And you could never trust the detonators to go off on time," Guy said.

"At least they always went off," Jake said. "Sooner or later." He drained the last of his bitter. "Like another? I'm buying."

"Why not?" Guy said. He handed Jake his empty glass. "Have to stay in practice."

Jake carried the glasses back to the bar. The only empty space was next to Mapp, and he hesitated a moment before stepping forward.

"Damn fool," Guy muttered, half rising from his chair. "I should've gone."

Mapp turned to Jake and snarled something Guy couldn't hear above the din. Jake shrugged, paid for the drinks, and picked them up. Both elbows resting on the bar, Mapp glared at Jake as he headed back toward the table.

Keeping his eyes on Mapp, Guy lowered himself slowly back into his seat. Just let the son of a bitch start something. Mapp might outweigh him by forty pounds, but he hadn't been nearly as good at judo.

Mapp pushed himself away from the bar and followed Jake. He stepped up to the table just as Jake sat down. "Just thought you might like to know," he said, staring first at Guy and then at Jake. "Got my orders. Going in soon."

"Oh," Jake said, raising his eyebrows.

"Yeah," Mapp said. He leered. "I'm your bloody wireless operator, mate."

❧

17

"Number six-five-one. *'Raus!'*"

Alexandre shook his head to clear the fog from his eyes and stood. It was going to happen again. Why didn't they just shoot him and get it over with? He didn't know how much more he could stand.

He padded to the cell door and waited while the guard unlocked it. It had been two months since the last questioning, months so dull he'd almost started looking forward to the next session, no matter what it would bring. Maybe if they tried to drown him again, he'd just cooperate this time, swallow water as fast as he could and hope they couldn't revive him. At least he wouldn't have to worry any longer about giving in to their torture.

He followed the guard down the hall. In the seven months that he'd been in the Cherche-Midi prison, he'd gotten used to the procedure. First, they brought you breakfast—a disgusting liquid supposed to be coffee. Then wait, wait for the sound of footsteps and rattle of keys—was it going to be you today, your number barked out in a harsh German accent? Maybe you'd be lucky and sit there until lunch on the hard wooden slats that passed as your bed, breathing in the sour smell of hunger and the stench of the unemptied slop bucket.

He focused on the guard's feet and tried to keep up. *Nom de Dieu,* he was weak, weaker every time he made this walk. Gifts of food were not allowed for prisoners undergoing interrogation. He figured they were trying to starve him into submission. He thought of the lunch that would be waiting for him when he came back this time—if he came back. Whale soup. Phony, tasteless salami. Enough food to keep a man alive, but not enough to ever satisfy the hunger.

He stumbled against the guard. *"Pardon,"* he whispered, then scolded himself for being polite to a Nazi. Talking was too much of an effort to waste on a *Boche*. Better to suffer the inevitable blow in silence.

He stopped and waited. No blow came. Instead, the guard grabbed his arm and shoved him into a room.

"Wait here." The guard left.

He backed up to the wall and leaned against it. What would he concentrate on today? Catherine's face? No, that might make him cry again, and the last time they'd laughed, thinking he was about to break. Maybe he'd remember his favorite food, the rich smell of lamb roasting on a spit, the fat crackling and dripping on the vine cuttings, spurts of garlic-scented smoke—

The door clicked open and he pushed away from the wall, bracing himself for a moment to keep from swaying.

"You may sit, Herr Valette."

The voice seemed to come from far away. Alexandre didn't move.

"Sit down, *bitte*." The soft-spoken officer pointed to a plain wooden chair in front of the window.

Alexandre shuffled to the chair and slumped into it. Was this some kind of trick? He blinked his eyes rapidly to clear the film that always seemed to cover them and stared at the officer. He'd never seen this one before. Tall, gray-haired, blue-eyed—he looked almost kind compared to the others.

That didn't mean anything, Alcxandre reminded himself. They all wanted the same thing—for him to betray the other members of the escape route—Father Francis, Georges, Michou. Michou. No, he couldn't let himself even think their names. He had to think about something else, anything else.

The officer pulled a chair up in front of him and sat down. "I'm Major Gottlob," he said. He offered Alexandre a Dunhill.

Alexandre shook his head. He missed his pipe, and an English cigarette was no substitute. Besides, if they thought this approach was going to work better than the others—

Major Gottlob shrugged, lit his cigarette, and slipped the pack into his pocket. He leaned forward and stared at him. "Are you ready to tell us what we want to know?"

Alexandre kept his mouth firmly closed.

Gottlob gave an exaggerated sigh. "You know that the penalty for your offense is death," he said. "However, I might be able to get it reduced to several years of hard labor if you'd answer my questions. Cooperation is the key." He tilted his head and smiled, tapping his fingernails against his bottom teeth.

"Forget it." Alexandre folded his arms across his chest. "I don't know anything, and if I did, I wouldn't tell you."

Gottlob sat back in his chair and crossed his legs. His eyes narrowed as he blew a stream of smoke upward out of the corner of his mouth. "The game's up, Herr Valette," he said. "We've got the priest. He confessed to everything."

Alexandre clamped his teeth together in an effort to keep his face impassive. Was the major lying? Had they really caught Father Francis? And if they had, and he had talked, whom else had he given up? *Nom de Dieu*, if the priest had even mentioned Michou, he'd kill him himself—

He gripped the edges of the seat with both hands and fixed his eyes on his feet. The tops of his shoes were stained brown with blood from the time they'd ripped out his toenails. The sadistic bastards had made him put his shoes on and walk back to his cell afterward. If they arrested Michou, they'd do the same to her. Maybe worse.

Major Gottlob cleared his throat. "Since the tribunal has already found you guilty and we've reviewed your case, you may as well prepare yourself for your punishment. You have permission to write to your friends and family."

Alexandre relaxed his hands and let them dangle between his legs for a minute before he stood up. So they were through with him now. They must have the priest after all. Please God, he prayed, give Father Francis strength.

He raised his head. He'd write to Henri as well, ask him to watch over his family, to take care of Catherine. Catherine. Leaving her was almost the hardest part.

Gottlob rose, strode to the door, and flung it open. "Guard," he shouted. He stubbed out his cigarette and turned back to Alexandre. "You will have to write fast, though."

Alexandre pulled his shoulders back. God would give him the strength he needed, too.

Gottlob smiled. "You will be executed this afternoon at four."

As the last note of Debussy's "Rêverie" faded, Michou opened her eyes and raised her head. "Play another, Maman," she said, blinking back the tears. "But play something more rousing this time." She'd always loved listening to her mother play the piano, but the slow, sad "Rêverie" made the waiting even harder, especially since Maman had played it over and over since Papa had been arrested.

Maman turned away from the piano and stared at her, a faraway expression on her face, as if she hadn't quite understood.

"How about Chopin's *Revolutionary* Étude?" Mémé Laure asked, looking up from her crocheting. "Isn't that the one he wrote when he heard that Warsaw had fallen?"

Maman nodded as she thumbed through her music books.

"Of course, that might be a little risky," Mémé Laure said. "Major Stecher could walk in any time, and he is quite an educated man, you know." She looked over the top of her glasses, first at Maman and then at Michou. Her lips twisted in a wry smile, the one she always wore when she was about to expose a lie or deflate an ego.

"Yes, quite educated," Maman echoed.

"And *so* attractive," Philippe said, pitching his voice an octave higher than usual. "All the boys just *love* him." He patted his hair and inspected his fingernails in a perfect caricature of Stecher. "And he loves all of them."

"Especially Lucien," Michou said.

Philippe snickered. "Wondered if you'd noticed. You aren't too jealous, are you, *schatzie?*"

"Don't be an ass," Michou said.

"Enough, children, please," Maman said. She spread her fingers over the keys. "We really shouldn't be talking like this."

Philippe stood up and, cracking his knuckles, walked to the window. "Is it all right if I go see Édouard, Maman? Waiting for Henri is making me nervous. The letter will still be here when I get back, won't it?"

Michou narrowed her eyes and glared at Philippe. "You're a fool," she said. "Sit down and shut up. Can't you see we're all nervous?"

"Don't be so hard on him, Michou," Maman said, her hands dropping back into her lap.

"He's just a boy," Michou mimicked bitterly. "Well, it's about time he grew up, took some responsibility around here. I'm sick of doing everything by myself while he plays soldier with Édouard."

Philippe wheeled around and put his hands on his hips. "We're not *playing* anything. All you think about is the damn wine. Why bother? The *Boches* are going to take it all anyway."

"I'm only trying to keep things going until Papa returns. I want everything to be perfect when he comes back."

"*You* grow up. Papa isn't coming back!" Philippe shouted. He ran out of the salon, and a few seconds later the front door slammed.

"Don't do this now," Maman said. "Not now. I can't stand it." Her eyes filled with tears.

Michou bit her lip. She hated it when Maman got upset, and this time it was because of her. Lately, it always seemed to be her fault. She got up and patted her mother on the shoulder. "I'm sorry, Maman," she said.

Maman wiped the tears off her cheeks. "It's all right, *chérie*. I know how hard you've been working. I wish you wouldn't. Your papa wouldn't like it. I—" She broke off and stared into space. Her hands moved automatically to the keys, and she began to play "Rêverie" again.

Mémé Laure shook her head and beckoned Michou. "Sit down, child," she whispered, putting her crocheting into the basket at her feet. "It's her way. You have the vineyards; Philippe dreams of being a soldier. You must be more patient with your family. We are all you have."

Michou leaned her head against Mémé Laure's shoulder. She was right. And Philippe was right, too. Papa would never come back. They all knew it.

The front door opened, and Michou lifted her head as footsteps clattered in the entry. The tall double doors flew open, and Philippe rushed in, followed by Henri Desroches. Maman's hands crashed down on the keys.

"I met him on the road," Philippe gasped. "I ran all the way back. He's got the letter!"

Henri looked down at his feet and slowly pulled an envelope from his pocket. He held it out, and Philippe grabbed it and ripped it open.

Michou jumped up. "Philippe!" she yelled. "What are you doing? Give it to Maman!" She rushed at him and grasped at the letter.

Philippe held the letter above her outstretched arms and looked first at Maman and then at Mémé Laure.

Mémé Laure glanced at Maman. She held out her hand. "Give it to me, Philippe," she said. "I'll read it aloud."

Philippe shoved Michou aside and handed Mémé Laure the letter.

"Everyone sit down," Mémé Laure said. She peered over her glasses at Michou and Philippe and then turned her gaze to Henri. "You, too, Henri," she said.

Michou sat down on the piano bench next to Maman and slipped her arm around Maman's waist. Her stomach contracted into a tight knot.

Mémé Laure cleared her throat and waited while Philippe and Henri settled themselves. She pushed her glasses back up on her nose and read:

"'I send this letter by my dear friend Henri because he has promised me to take care of you when I am gone. I will say the hardest thing first.'"

Mémé Laure gasped, and when she continued reading, her voice was hoarse.

"'I will be dead by the time you read this.'"

"No!" Maman cried out, and gripped Michou's hand tightly. "No!"

Michou clenched her teeth to keep from shrieking, and squeezed her eyes shut. Her throat closed around the screams bursting in her chest, and she choked them back. Papa dead? No—no—no! It wasn't true! It was a trick!

Her voice barely a whisper, Mémé Laure kept reading.

"'I no longer feel any anger about this. I have been waiting for it for a long time. I only feel much sadness that I cannot see the ones I love so much once again before I die.

"'I am not sorry for what I have done. I love France, and for her I give my life.'"

Mémé Laure drew a deep breath, and Michou gripped the piano bench with both hands, ignoring the hot flow of tears washing her cheeks. First Marc, and now Papa. Both dead, both giving their lives for France. She gulped, and searing hatred filled her.

Mémé Laure looked at Maman before she continued. "'My beloved Catherine, be courageous. You were always my strength. Be strong for yourself and our children now. I love you.'"

Michou's body shook. She leaned forward and wrapped her arms across her chest, rocking back and forth. Howls of anguish bounced inside her head, and she clenched her jaw to keep them inside. If one sound escaped her lips, she knew she wouldn't be able to stop the screams.

Maman sobbed even harder, and Mémé Laure waited. "Shall I finish it?" she asked.

Maman nodded, her face white.

"'Michou, my little one, try not to grieve too hard. You will be angry. Do not let this bitterness control your life. I love you.'"

Waves of pain battered Michou's chest. Papa was right. She felt poisoned with anger, with hatred. She moved her crossed arms down to her belly and clutched herself more tightly, bending forward until her forehead touched her knees.

Mémé Laure cleared her throat noisily. "'My hotheaded Philippe. You are still so young. Give yourself time to grow up. Walk slowly. Take the time to think. I love you.'"

Philippe choked and sobbed, and Michou slowly raised her head and glared at him. She hated him, even though she knew it was irrational. Why hadn't he done something to save Papa? Why hadn't she? She hated herself, too.

Tears streaming down her face and her lips moving slightly, Mémé Laure read the rest of the letter to herself. Finally, she cleared her throat again. "'My dears, I take with me the happiest moments in my life, the memories of my family. I bless this life, which has given me such great gifts. I love you all. Pray for me.'"

Mémé Laure slowly lowered the letter to her lap and bowed her head. Maman clutched Michou's hand.

Michou pulled her hand from Maman's grasp and

jumped up. Her cheeks were wet with tears. "I can't!" she cried, and ran out of the room.

Catherine put the silver-framed photograph of Alexandre back down on the dressing table and picked up her brush. She stared at the picture as she slowly ran the brush through her hair. It had been taken on their wedding day, twenty-seven years ago tomorrow.

She leaned forward and inspected her face in the mirror. It was difficult to believe that she was actually forty-five years old. Before Alexandre's arrest she'd never really thought much about growing older; she still loved him in the same headstrong way she had as a girl. Three children hadn't changed that.

It had been at a garden party in honor of Julien's graduation, on a warm June day in 1911. She had been fifteen, and her white party dress had swirled around her ankles. She wanted to wear rose, she remembered, but Mère insisted on the white.

She stood at the refreshment table, not quite sure of what to do. The guests moved in colorful waves through the garden, gathering in scattered bunches, then quickly flowing into new configurations. She wanted to join them but didn't know how. Would they laugh at Julien's little sister, trying so hard to be grown up? She'd heard Mère complaining that his friends were fast, that the girls smoked and the boys drank.

She sat down and rested her cheek on the palm of her hand. The girls all looked so sophisticated, while her dress made her look like a baby. Damn Mère!

She gasped and clapped her hand over her mouth. She shouldn't even think such a thing. What would Mère say? She giggled. Mère would never know if she didn't tell her.

"They do look pretty funny, all right."

She jumped, knocking her glass of punch off the table and onto a pair of gray trousers. "Oh, I'm so sorry!" she said. She stood up and looked directly into the softest brown eyes she'd ever seen.

He wiped off his pants. "Don't worry," he said. "I'm sure no one saw." He held out his hand. "I'm Alexandre Valette."

She had put her hand in his. It had been sticky from the punch, and she had laughed.

Catherine's smile faded now, and she set the brush back down next to the photograph. The laughter was what she missed the most. Only Alexandre knew how to make her laugh. That was why she'd fallen in love with him. Not because he was handsome or rich. He wasn't either, and that was why Mère had never liked him. He was honest, though, and funny and brave, and she missed him so much.

She put her head on her arms and cried. How could she be strong now that he was gone?

A soft tap sounded at the door. She hastily dabbed at her eyes with a rose-scented handkerchief and sat up stiffly. "Yes?" she called.

Michou opened the door. "May I come in?" she asked. She ducked her head, and her tangled platinum curls fell around her face.

"Of course," Catherine said.

Michou ran to her. She dropped to her knees, flung her arms around Catherine's waist, and buried her face in her lap. "Oh, Maman, I'm so sorry," she said.

Stroking Michou's soft curls, Catherine raised her chin. Alexandre was right. She had to be strong for their children. No more daydreaming, no more denials, no more endless hours at the piano or in her studio or in the rose garden. Michou and Philippe needed her, now more than ever.

Michou's tiny shoulders shook with sobs. She raised her face. "Will the world ever be right again?" she asked.

18

The wind tore at Guy's legs as he dangled them through the hole in the floor of the lumbering Whitley bomber. In another minute or two he would be floating free, and a few seconds after that, he'd be back on French soil for the first time in a year.

"Lights ahead!" the dispatcher shouted. "Signal correct." He paused. "Go!"

Guy clamped his feet firmly together and pushed forward. He held his breath until the static line jerked his parachute open. When you were dropped from only six hundred feet, any delay could mean death.

He blinked rapidly to clear the watery film from his eyes. Except for the flickering signal lamps, the moonlit countryside below looked peaceful and deserted. The road glowed shiny and white and close.

Too close. His chute had barely opened. Guy grunted as he landed with a thud and rolled. Chalky dust filled his nostrils, and he gasped. Something had gone wrong. The bloody RAF must have dropped him too low. He'd never felt this kind of pain during his practice jumps.

He tried to stand, and the pain quickly localized. Christ, he must have broken his ankle. Collapsing back on the road, he clenched his teeth to keep from cursing. What goddamn luck. Ankle injuries were the commonest sort for parachutists. The Germans knew that. Now he'd have to stay hidden until he could walk.

Hoarse whispers and the sound of running feet broke through the buzzing in his ears. Hands pulled at his harness and chute, and he flailed his arms. Someone hauled him to his feet.

"*Merde!*" he sputtered. "My ankle! Watch out!"

The man removed his black beret and ran his hand over his bald head. He patted the beret back on and worked his glowing cigarette to the other side of his mouth. "Lean on me," he said. "The car's just over there. My men will round up your partner and bury your gear."

Guy rested his arm on the shorter man's shoulder and hobbled beside him. "A car?" he asked. "Isn't that a bit dangerous?"

The man chuckled, his plump cheeks almost touching his eyes. "Got an after-hours *Ausweis,*" he said. He winked. "You know how the *Boches* are—a permit can make anything correct."

"You have a place I can stay until this damn ankle heals?" Guy asked. "Somewhere quiet, safe, out of the way?"

"Thinking on it," the man said. He brushed aside some branches. "Here's the car. Get in while I finish clearing it off. Pierre and Jean should be through in a minute." He opened the door.

Guy heaved himself into the back seat. His ankle throbbed, sending bolts of fire up his leg. Stupid son of a bitch, he cursed himself silently. He hoped René had had better luck. Couldn't afford to have anything happen to his wireless operator. Or the wireless. Closing his eyes, he rested his head against the back of the seat.

The car door slammed, and Guy's eyes jerked open. The plump man's face, lit by the full moon and the cigarette still dangling from his lips, peered at him over the front seat. "You going to make it?" he asked. He opened the glove compartment, took out a flask, and handed it to Guy. "Have some of this."

Guy unscrewed the top and gulped down a mouthful. The strong marc burned its way down his throat and warmed his stomach. He coughed and drank again before handing the flask back. "Thanks," he said.

The man threw his cigarette out the window and took a drink. "Not quite sure what to do with you now. First thing, you need a doctor. That's no problem. Young Bertrand will be glad to help. Won't ask any questions. Hates the Germans."

"Forget the doctor," Guy said. "I can splint and wrap it if it needs it. No point in involving anyone unnecessarily."

The man shrugged. "If you say so," he said. He rubbed his chin. "Think I know the ideal place. Get you across the line at a moment's notice if necessary. Too bad—"

"Any children there?" Guy asked.

The man shook his head. "No. A few Germans billeted there, but no children. Germans aren't the problem, though. Young lady in charge refuses to cooperate with us since the Nazis executed her father. Blames us as much as she blames the *Boches*."

"Could I hide there without her knowing?"

The man snapped his fingers. "That's it! I've heard young Philippe has been itching to help out. Should have thought of him before. We can hide you in the *chai* tonight, tell him in the morning." He swiveled his head around and cocked it to one side. *"Bien.* Here they come."

Two swarthy young men escorted René toward the car. After he put a small suitcase in the trunk, he got into the front seat while the other two slid into the back beside Guy.

"You land all right?" Guy asked, leaning forward.

René nodded. "No problem. They said you're hurt."

"I'll be okay," Guy said. "What about the wireless?"

"Seems to be fine," René said.

"Good." Guy settled back and glanced at the man on his right. Even in the semidarkness he looked curiously misshapen, as if he were wearing a lifesaver around his waist. Guy frowned. "What do you have there?" he asked.

The young man grinned and opened his shirt. Swaths of soft white material were wrapped around his waist. "Make a nice silk blouse for my girlfriend," he said.

"You damn fool!" Guy shouted. "You want to get us all killed? The Germans aren't stupid. Get out and bury that. Now!" He sank back against the seat as the youth sulkily obeyed. Christ, what a nightmare this was turning out to be. He just hoped it wasn't an omen—if it was, his mission was doomed from the start.

* * *

Michou wiped the sweat from her forehead with the back of her hand. Midnight, and it was still hot, and the grapy fumes of the young wine filled the air. Two more barrels to rack tonight and she'd go to bed. Tomorrow she still had to thin and tie the young shoots in the lower vineyards. Without any help, it was going slowly. Too slowly.

She moved the hose to the next barrel. Well, she'd just do it all herself if she had to. This was Papa's last wine, and she wanted it to be perfect. And the young grapes in the vineyards would make her first wine. She wanted that to be perfect, too.

She sighed and leaned against the barrel just emptied. It all depended on the weather, on chance. With no sulfur to spray this year, mold was going to be a problem when the nights turned cool. If the summer stayed hot and the grapes matured early, everything might be all right. If not—

No point in thinking about it, she told herself. She slipped the hooks into the bands at both ends of the barrel and pulled on the line attached to the pulley overhead. The barrel tilted sideways, and she scraped the lees out into a bucket.

She yawned as she scrubbed the inside of the barrel. If Maman knew what she was doing, she'd be angry at her. Too bad she didn't get mad at Philippe instead. Even though he had helped expand the block-and-tackle system for moving the barrels, he'd only done it so she could handle the heavy work by herself. Ever since Papa's arrest, it had been hard to get him to help her; and after the execution, he'd refused to do anything. He and Édouard were always off whispering in some corner. God knew what they were planning.

The sound of footsteps interrupted her thoughts. The *cuvier* door scraped open. Perhaps Philippe was coming to see if he could help after all. Hah! Her lips turned down at the corners. That was unlikely. Maybe it was Maman checking on her.

Clutching the long-handled brush, she tiptoed to the door and opened it a crack. Several shadowy figures stood next to the vat. The one in front whispered to the others, and they followed him toward the *chai* entrance.

Michou dropped the brush, and it clattered on the stone floor.

"Who's there?" one of the shadows whispered.

Whoever it was, he was French, Michou decided. She stepped forward and put her hands on her hips. "I belong here," she said. "Who are you?"

"Merde!" one of them said under his breath. "Is that you?" He walked quickly toward her.

"Georges?" she asked as she recognized the short, plump man. "What the hell are you doing here?"

"We need help," he said, holding out his hands, palms up.

"Goddamn you!" she hissed. "What are you trying to do—get the rest of us killed, too? You're not satisfied that Papa's dead?" She doubled her fists and pummeled his soft chest. "Get out of here!"

Georges grabbed her by the wrists. "I'm sorry, Michou," he said. "Alexandre knew the risks. He thought it was worth it."

"Well, I don't anymore," she said. She jerked her hands away and rubbed her wrist.

"Michou? Michou Valette?" whispered one of the figures behind Georges. He hopped forward on one foot.

The husky voice sounded familiar. She squinted into the darkness. "Do I know you?" she asked, backing into the *chai*.

Georges stepped aside as the tall man brushed by him. "He needs help," he said. "He broke his ankle."

The man hobbled over the threshold and into the light. "It *is* you," he said. He tried to smile, but his thick eyebrows pulled together in a grimace of pain. He braced himself against the vat.

"Guy!" she said. Her cheeks burning, she stooped quickly and picked up the cleaning brush. "But I thought you were going to Eng—"

He shook his head and glanced over his shoulder. "I'm sorry about your father," he said. "But I'm glad you're okay." He reached out and stroked her cheek.

Michou ducked her head. Twisting the brush in her hands, she said, "You must think I'm terrible."

"No," he said. "I think you've been hurt. I'll have them find another place for me. I don't want to put your family in any more danger." He pushed himself away from the vat and turned to go.

She grabbed his arm. "Please don't go," she said. She pushed by him and faced Georges. "I'll hide him. But not for you. Now, take your friends and get out. And don't ask anything more of me."

Georges grinned and winked at Guy. "Watch out for that one," he said, jerking his head at Michou. "Regular little spitfire, she is." He shook Guy's hand. "Good luck."

Michou waited until Georges and his men were gone before she turned back to Guy. His face was pale and beads of sweat stood out on his forehead. "Let me see your ankle," she said, bending down.

She pushed up his trouser leg and pulled down the sock. His ankle was swollen and already turning black and blue. "I can't tell if it's broken or sprained," she said. "At least it's not crooked."

"Doesn't matter," Guy gasped. "I just need a place to lie down. The foot has to be elevated." He shivered. "And I need a blanket."

She stood up and put her arm around his waist. "I'm going to take you to my room. You'll have to climb some stairs, but you should be safer there than here. This is where Papa used to hide the soldiers." She turned out the lights.

He laid his arm on her shoulders. "I'll be out of here as soon as I can walk," he said, limping beside her.

She paused by the door and put her finger to her lips. "No talking until we get to my room," she said. "Stecher still orders patrols sometimes."

Sticking to the shadows, she walked slowly toward the tower. When she reached it, she carefully opened the door so it wouldn't squeak and helped Guy inside. One step at a time, she supported him until they reached her room.

He collapsed on her bed, and his breath exploded out of him. "Christ!" he groaned. His teeth chattered uncontrollably.

Michou stripped off his shoes and socks and propped his swollen ankle with a pillow. She threw a quilt over him and then poured some water into a basin and soaked a small towel. "This should help the swelling," she said as she wrapped the towel around his ankle.

Guy's lips turned up slightly. "Thanks," he said. "I'm glad it's you." His eyes closed.

She curled up in the chair beside the bed. For some reason she didn't understand, she felt almost happy. Resting her chin on her knees, she watched him for a few minutes before she switched off the lamp on the nightstand. "And I'm glad it's you," she whispered.

Something was poking her in the neck. She tried to push it away, but it wouldn't go. She lifted her head from the back of the chair and rubbed her neck. No, it was just stiff from sleeping sitting up. But why wasn't she in her bed?

Her eyes popped open. Of course. Guy was sleeping in her bed. Massaging her neck, she carefully turned her head.

He lay sprawled on top of the coverlet, his foot sticking up under the faded blue quilt she'd thrown over him last night. His gold-streaked brown hair was tousled, and his large brown eyes stared back at her. He smiled and raised an eyebrow. "Sleep well?" he asked, laughing. "Sorry I did you out of your bed."

Michou tried to smooth her unruly hair into place with her fingers. She stretched and stood up. "Actually, I did sleep well," she said. "Better than in a long time. In fact, I'm afraid I may have overslept." She pulled aside the heavy curtains and peeked out. "Looks as if the sun's been up for hours."

She turned back to Guy. "Are you feeling better?" she asked.

He propped himself up on his elbows. "Some," he said. "But my ankle still throbs. I'm afraid it'll be a few days before I can put any weight on it."

Michou felt her cheeks get hot, and she twisted her ring around her finger. "That's not what I meant," she said. "Don't even think about leaving until you're perfectly well."

"Of course not," he said. "We're all doing what we can."

She stared at her bare feet. He'd heard her outburst last night, but he was pretending she was risking her life as willingly as he was. If it had been anyone else, she'd have left him to the Germans. Or would she? Maybe he was right after all. She just didn't know anymore.

"Are you hungry?" she asked.

"Ravenous."

"I'll go steal something from the kitchen," she said. "We don't have anything fancy, though." She headed toward the door.

"I'm not used to fancy," he said. "England is at war, too."

"Too," she echoed. She turned back to him and smiled. "I like that. Vichy wouldn't agree, of course. But I like that."

19

❧

Guy groaned as a sudden jolt awakened him. He wasn't used to sharing his bed with anyone, and neither, it appeared, was Michou. She sprawled on her stomach across most of the bed, her face turned toward him and her leg flung over his thigh. That must have been what woke him up.

He lay still and listened to the sound of her breathing. He'd felt so guilty seeing her curled up in the chair every morning for the last week that he'd insisted she sleep in her bed. She'd put up quite a fuss about it but had finally given in when he'd sworn that if she didn't, he'd sleep in the chair. He smiled. Since he'd been sitting in the chair at the time, she didn't have much choice—it was either the bed or the floor.

She was sensible. He liked that. As soon as she saw he wasn't going to back down, she'd agreed—but only if he'd sleep in the bed, too. It was big enough for both of them, and besides, she knew he was a gentleman.

He stifled a chuckle. He didn't feel like much of a gentleman. Good thing she was asleep. He'd awakened with the beginnings of an erection, and now his penis was straining against the too-small pajamas Michou had found for him.

He clasped his hands together behind his neck. Christ, he wanted to touch her. He breathed deeply. The lavender scent of the sheets mingled with the sweet vanilla smell of her skin. He imagined stroking her soft breasts, thighs, belly.

She stirred and moaned, and his body stiffened. Don't move, he prayed silently. Not yet. He wasn't ready to let go of the fantasy.

He sighed. And fantasy it should stay. It wasn't safe for either of them; it wasn't practical; it would be downright stupid for him to fall in love with her now. And he was so close, had been ever since he'd turned the car around that day in Poitiers. Images of Michou—huddled on the hospital steps, lying asleep in bed after her miscarriage looking so pale and fragile, rising from the ditch after the strafing, anger blazing in her eyes and her face streaked with tears and dirt, waving as he drove away from the château—cut through the blur of desire.

Holding his breath, he turned his head slowly toward hers. In the dim early-morning light, he could just make out her features. Her long lashes, unusually dark for so fair a blonde, seemed to float above her rounded cheeks, and her soft full lips parted and curved upward in a half smile.

Slowly, he pushed himself up on one elbow. If only he could kiss her without waking her. The ache in his groin was almost as bad as the throbbing of his ankle, and it wasn't just because it had been a couple of weeks since he'd slept with a woman. Since his divorce from Lydia—and maybe even before—he'd only satisfied his physical needs. Making love with Michou would be more than that; it would be—well, making love.

He ran his hand across the curls that spilled over her pillow, stopping before he touched her cheek. What would she think? It was hard for him to tell—she was polite but withdrawn. Perhaps it was just her sense of obligation that compelled her to help him at the risk of her own life. Still, there had been a few times when—

Stop, he told himself. He lowered his head back to the pillow. Don't even think about it. Think about something else. Think about garbage. Think about jumping out of another airplane. Think about war.

War. Bombed cities. Dead children. Tessie.

His desire slipped away.

Gently, he pushed Michou's leg off his. She moaned again and rolled over, and he scooted closer to the edge of the bed, gingerly moving his ankle.

He squeezed his eyes shut. He couldn't afford to think of Michou except in terms of how she could help him with his assignment; otherwise, he might get foolish and soft. His instructors had stressed it over and over during training— agents who fell in love ended up in jail—or dead. Neither would do much to help win the war.

And that was what was important right now. If he lived and England survived, there'd be time enough for love.

Lucien slammed on the brakes in front of the steps, and a cloud of dust swirled around his car. Curling her upper lip, Michou stood and brushed off the back of her pink-and-white-striped dress. If she had time, she would have much preferred to bicycle to Libourne to see Berthe.

But time was something she didn't have, not even at the end of June, when the bulk of the work was usually finished until preparations started for the harvest. Papa had always been so happy at this time of year. "Just watching the grapes grow," he'd always said.

She put her hands on her hips and waited for the dust to settle. This year nobody would be watching the grapes grow. Philippe didn't care, and she was just too busy. When she wasn't working in the vineyards or *chai,* she was visiting Berthe or taking care of Guy.

She frowned. This was the first time she'd left Château Bourdet since he'd arrived. He'd assured her he'd be all right for the afternoon. She hoped he was right—and not just for her sake. She cared for him more than she wanted to. What he was doing was dangerous, she knew, and she didn't ever want to have to grieve again.

Lucien waved. "Get in," he shouted.

She ran down the steps and climbed into the car. Leave it to Lucien to always have plenty of gas when no one else had any. Another sign of Stecher's favors, undoubtedly.

"How's Berthe?" she asked.

"The same," he said. "Fat, ugly, pregnant."

"And you're the same, too," she said. "Mean, cruel, and disgusting."

He popped the clutch, and the car spun out. "You haven't changed either," he shouted above the roar of the engine and crunch of gravel. "Snotty, belligerent—" He turned his head and leered at her. "And beautiful. Come to dinner with me after you console Berthe."

"No." She clamped her mouth shut. It was the same routine every time. Why didn't he just give up? She didn't care how handsome he was or what a nice car he had or how much money he made. She was tired of fending off his advances, turning down his offers. If it weren't for Berthe, she'd forbid him to come near her.

He narrowed his eyes and stared at her for a second. Then he shrugged and looked back at the road. *"Tant pis,"* he said.

She gazed out the window as the spiraling rows of vines clicked by. Poor Berthe. It was only for her sake she put up with Lucien at all. And with the baby due any day, Berthe needed all the support Michou could give her. Half an hour a week driving to Libourne and back with Lucien wasn't much to endure for a friend.

She hung on to the seat as the car careered around a sharp curve. Dust clogged her nostrils, and she coughed. "Slow down!" she shouted.

He smiled. "Am I scaring you?" he asked, stomping on the brakes.

Her body jerked forward. "Goddamn you, Lucien," she said. "Just let me out. I'd rather walk."

He shook his head and speeded up again. "You'll have to jump," he said, grinning even wider.

Gritting her teeth, she sank back in the seat. "What makes you so nasty?"

"My father has always hated me," he said. He laughed abruptly. "You know that. I'm just trying to get even with him."

Michou opened her eyes wide and raised her eyebrows. He sounded almost sincere. It was true that Henri Desroches had never treated Lucien with the same warmth he had lavished on his younger son, Daniel, and after Daniel's death, he had seemed even colder toward Lucien. Of course, he never really neglected him—whenever Lucien got in trouble, Henri just sighed, rolled his eyes, and paid whatever was required, complaining to his friends, even in Lucien's presence, that his son was *"un débauché."* She'd heard him more than once describe Lucien's latest indiscretion to Papa, not the least trace of paternal amusement in his voice.

Still, even if there was some truth in Lucien's claim, it didn't give him the right to act the way he did. She snorted and tossed her head. Nothing could excuse the way he treated Berthe.

"You arranged for Berthe to get raped to get even with your father?" she said sarcastically.

He pulled up in front of the Desroches's gray stone house. Smiling crookedly, he pulled out a cigar and lit it. "No," he said. He blew the smoke downward out of the corner of his mouth. "That was to get even with my mother."

Berthe pulled aside the lace curtains and peeked out the window. Thank goodness Michou was finally here. It seemed like hours since Lucien had left and much longer than a week since their last visit. If she didn't have Michou, she didn't know what she'd do.

As Michou came up the walk, Berthe let the curtains fall back and lumbered to the door. She was so big now that walking even a short distance was hard. Her hips hurt; her back ached; the baby felt as if its head was butting her in the ribs.

She opened the door before Michou could knock. "I'm so glad to see you," she said, kissing her on both cheeks to hide the tears filling her eyes. She brushed at her eyes with her hand and stepped back. "You look so pretty in that dress," she said. She tried to smile and burst into sobs instead.

Michou put her arm around her shoulders and guided her to the sofa. "It'll be all right," she said, stroking Berthe's hair. "People have babies all the time."

Berthe slowly lowered herself to the sofa, bracing herself with one hand. "I'm so mixed up. I hate this baby and I love it. Sometimes I wish it would die, and then I feel awful."

She paused. "I went to the doctor this morning. He said the baby's turned upside down. And if it stays that way, it might—" She buried her face in her hands.

"Can't he turn it around?"

Sobbing, Berthe looked up. "He tried. It wouldn't turn. And I feel as if it's my fault, as if the baby somehow knows and doesn't want to come out."

"Don't be silly. Forget Kohler. This is your baby," Michou said quietly.

Berthe's chest tightened and her voice soared. "Could you? Could you forget how the baby got there? Who its father is?" She clasped Michou's hand and kissed it. "I'm sorry," she said, lowering her voice. "I just don't want this baby to ever find out—"

"And you're afraid of what Lucien might say," Michou said.

Berthe nodded. "He's been so nice to me since this happened. I'm sure he had no idea what Kohler was going to do. But—" She dropped Michou's hand and hunched forward.

"But if he gets mad, he might tell."

"And I always seem to make him mad," Berthe whispered. "He's going to say something. I know he is. Sooner or later."

"Then you'll just have to tell the child yourself when it's old enough to understand. But that's a long time away. Don't worry about that now."

Berthe took a deep breath. "I know you're right. I'm so glad I have you." She tried to control her tears. Michou looked so exhausted she hated to ask for anything; but except for Gabrielle, Michou was her only real friend. And Gabrielle was just too flighty to handle anything serious.

Berthe blew her nose on the jasmine-scented handkerchief Michou offered. She couldn't even count on her own father anymore. After she refused to tell him who had gotten her pregnant, he'd barely spoken to her. She hated to think what he'd do if he ever found out his grandchild's father was a Nazi deserter.

She hiccupped. "W-will you be with me when the baby comes?" she asked.

"Of course," Michou said. "Even if I have to break curfew to get here."

Berthe gasped. "Don't do that," she said. "Lucien told me about the people they shot in Bordeaux. Some of them had been picked up for being out after curfew."

"I didn't really mean it." Michou patted her hand. "You're always so serious, Berthe. Don't worry. If it's necessary, Lucien can ask his friend Stecher to get me an *Ausweis*, can't he?"

Berthe grunted as the baby kicked. She spread her hands over her huge belly. It felt solid and hard.

"Look!" Michou exclaimed. "He's trying to do a somersault. He doesn't want to be born upside down."

Berthe forced herself to smile. Michou tried so hard to

make her feel better. "You're such a good friend," she said. "I don't know how to thank you."

Lucien stretched and sprawled across the bed. Thank God Karl had finally gone. Every night he stayed longer, and tonight he'd even fallen asleep afterward. Lucien hoped he didn't make a habit of it. He didn't like sharing his bed with anyone.

He groped on top of the nightstand until his fingers found the pack of Dunhills Karl had left behind. Maybe he should amend that generalization slightly. He wouldn't mind sharing his bed with Michou. He couldn't imagine her snoring like Gabrielle, or flailing about like Karl. Michou would sleep delicately, a half smile curving her lips, pale hair tousled about her face, one small hand tucked under her cheek. He fumbled a cigarette from the pack and put it in his mouth, then patted the nightstand in search of his lighter.

He found it and lit the cigarette, staring at the spurt of flame glowing in the dark room for a moment before he clicked it off. He still remembered with total clarity the moment he'd realized how much he wanted her. She'd been staying with Berthe, and the two of them had just returned from the cinema, where they'd seen *La Belle Équipe*. He'd been sitting in the salon, smoking in the dark, just like tonight, and they hadn't seen him as they stood laughing and arguing at the base of the stairs.

"Isn't Gabin wonderful?" Berthe said. "So handsome."

Michou shrugged. "I guess so. If you like that type."

Berthe giggled and elbowed her as they started up the stairs. "I know what your type is. I saw the way you looked at Marc. And I think he noticed, too. He seemed pretty interested."

He hadn't heard Michou's reply, but for a second she'd turned her head back toward the salon. She hadn't seen him, and the look of yearning on her face had pierced his soul. Nasty little Michou had grown up while she'd been away in Paris, and suddenly he'd wanted her to look like that for him.

That had been five years ago, and his desire for her had only grown stronger. He exhaled the bitter smoke and stubbed out the cigarette. There had to be some way he could make her want him as much as he wanted her.

20

Christ! Guy winced as he stepped down on a large stone. Although he could walk without much of a limp, his ankle was still tender. If he wasn't careful, he'd end up back in bed and he couldn't afford to waste any more time laid up. He was already so late in making his contact in Libourne that his wireless operator must surely think he'd been caught.

He reached the *cuvier* and groped for the door. He'd thought about leaving without saying good-bye to Michou but just couldn't bring himself to do it. For two weeks she'd nursed him, stolen food from the kitchen for him, emptied his chamber pot, shared her bed with him. He owed her a farewell.

Cautiously, he edged his way through the dark *cuvier* toward the *chai*. Admit it, he told himself. He hadn't been one damn bit successful in curbing his feelings for her—in fact, they'd grown stronger than ever. He *had* to see her before he left.

A crash and a murmured curse made him hurry to the door. "Are you all right?" he asked.

"What are you doing here?" Michou frowned at him. "Are you crazy? You don't have a pass; you probably don't even have any identity papers."

Even though she'd changed a lot in the last year, she hadn't lost any of her feistiness. She may have thought she'd given up, but she really hadn't. She'd just been catching her second wind, regrouping for the battle.

He patted his jacket pocket. "As a matter of fact, I do. Don't worry about me. What happened?"

She pointed to her foot. "I let go of the rope and the barrel dropped on it. At least it was empty."

He laughed. "Now we have something in common."

She grinned at that. Then her smile faded. "You didn't answer my question. It isn't safe for you here. Go back to my room." She jabbed the brush into the barrel and scrubbed it vigorously.

"I've just come to say good-bye."

"Wh-what?" Her head snapped up. "But—but you're still limping. You said it was important you didn't limp."

"I can manage fine. And the war keeps going. Now the Germans are in Russia. Things are happening too fast for me to stay here any longer."

She straightened and put her hands on her hips. "Just what is it you're doing here, anyway? I think I deserve to know."

"You're probably right," Guy said. "But I think you're safer if you don't know. You said you didn't want any more involvement in the Resistance." Raising an eyebrow, he leaned against a barrel. "Do you still mean that?"

She gnawed at her lower lip and stared at him, her violet eyes opened wide. Finally, she shook her head. "I don't know," she said. "I'm just not sure."

"Then I can't tell you."

"Are you working with Georges?" she asked, turning to the next barrel.

"No," he said. "He was part of the local reception committee. His work is quite separate from mine. My work involves a lot of traveling between here and Bordeaux."

"If I could help just you, I would," she said. "But I don't want anything to do with Georges. As far as I'm concerned, it's his fault Papa was caught. He acts as if the whole business is a game. And he does stupid things."

"That's good to know." He took the brush from her and set it down. As much as he'd like to protect her, she *would* be useful. She could help him establish his cover as a wine broker, and her outspoken reluctance to help the Resistance since her father's death would set her up perfectly to run a safe house.

Stroking his chin, he stared at her. No matter how much she could do, he still hated the idea of her risking her life any further. He shook his head. "No," he said. "You can't do it just for me."

Michou blushed and lowered her head. "That's not what I meant," she said. "Not just *for* you. *With* you. I don't want the others to know."

He nodded slowly. "I think I understand now," he said. He raised his eyebrows again and squinted. "You know, I really think it might work better that way. And your help would be even more valuable if your friends believed you were collaborating."

"Collaborating!" She spat out the word. "I won't do that!"

"Now *you* don't understand." He grinned at her vehemence, remembering her reaction a year ago when he'd suggested she might be safer smiling at Germans than snarling at them. "Of course, you wouldn't *really* be collaborating, but just continuing not to cooperate with Georges and his friends."

She sat down on a barrel and pushed her hair back off of her face. "That's easy," she said. "But why?"

"I need two things from you," he said. "Introductions to your neighbors as Guy Fournier, a wine broker from Bordeaux, a friend of your father's. And a safe house, a place to hide if I need it. Or if someone I know needs it."

Her shoulders hunched forward, she twisted her ring around her finger. "All right," she said. She lifted her head and looked at him. "You're really leaving tonight?"

"Have to," he said. "But I'll be back. Often. You can count on that."

She stood and offered him her hand. "Won't it be dangerous to come here openly? Don't forget Stecher and his men."

He grinned at her. "Safest place for a thief to hide is in a police station. Who'd ever think of looking for him there?" He shook her hand and turned to go.

When he reached the door, he looked back over his shoulder. *"Au revoir,"* he said.

Her smile wavered. "I hope so," she said.

Michou rested her head against the back of the leather car seat and yawned, covering her mouth with her hand. It had been a long night, and she was glad it was over. She smiled. But not as glad as Berthe, she bet. The doctor said she'd been lucky to have such an easy time with a breech baby.

She shook her head. It hadn't seemed easy to her, but at least both Berthe and the baby were all right. And the terrible conflict was over for Berthe—it had been obvious from the moment she saw the red and squalling little Daniel that she loved him. Michou had never seen her look happier.

She glanced sideways at Lucien. The wind swept his black hair back from his too-handsome face, and a slight smile hovered at the corner of his mouth. Could it be that he was actually going to enjoy being an uncle?

Hah! She snorted. More likely he was going to enjoy having a secret to torment Berthe with. Berthe's love for her baby was going to make her more vulnerable than ever. That realization wasn't something Lucien was likely to miss.

Lucien looked away from the road. "Something funny?" he asked.

"No," she said. "Something sad."

"Oh?" he said. "What?"

"You."

He shook his head as he turned the car into the drive. "Come on," he said. "Can't we even have a truce on my nephew's birthday?"

She snorted again. "I just can't picture you as a doting uncle. You're planning on drowning this Daniel, too, perhaps?"

His eyes narrowed and he stomped on the brakes. "You've always thought that, haven't you?" he said. "That it was my fault Daniel and your precious brother drowned?"

"Wasn't it?" She opened the car door. "You hated both of them, didn't you?"

Ignoring her question, he stared past her. "Who's that?" he asked, nodding toward the entrance gates.

She looked over her shoulder. An ancient Renault *gazogène* sputtered into the drive. As it emerged from the shadows of the plane trees, she recognized Guy behind the wheel.

She stifled a gasp. What a terrible time for him to pick for his first visit! Her heart thudded in her ears. Calm down, she told herself. Lucien wasn't dumb. If she didn't act perfectly normal, he'd notice right away.

Guy waved and pulled his car up behind Lucien's red

Mercedes. It shuddered and died, and a cloud of wood smoke puffed out of the furnace in the rear. "Good morning," he called, poking his head out the open window. "Are you coming or going?"

She stepped out of the car and slammed the door. "Just got back," she said. "Berthe finally had her baby." She smiled broadly, as if he would be expecting exactly this information.

Guy didn't miss a beat. "Wonderful!" he said as he got out of the car. "Boy or girl?"

"A boy," she said. "Daniel." She kissed him on both cheeks before turning back to Lucien. "And this is his uncle, Lucien Desroches. Guy Fournier, a friend of Papa's from Bordeaux. He's a wine broker."

Guy walked over to the car and shook hands with Lucien. "Nice to meet you. You're Henri Desroches's son, then?"

Lucien nodded. "You know my father?"

"Not yet," Guy said. "But I hope to. Expanding my territory a bit." He turned to Michou. "You have some samples for me to taste today?"

"Of course," she said. "I think you're going to like Papa's last wine. It's coming along quite nicely—what there is left of it after the *Boches* took their share."

She put her arm through Guy's. "Come along," she said. "Lucien has to get back to his sister and new nephew, don't you, Lucien?"

"I'm in no hurry," Lucien said. "Besides, I'd like to tell Major Stecher the good news." He looked over her shoulder, smiled, and waved. "Hello, Karl," he said as he got out of the car.

Michou tightened her grip on Guy's arm, and her throat constricted. God help them now. Ever since Stecher had caught Papa with the English fliers, it seemed to her he'd watched her suspiciously.

Guy patted her hand and smiled at her. "Relax," he whispered as Lucien shook Stecher's hand and told him about the baby. Guy smiled pleasantly at Stecher and nodded at his driver standing behind him.

Inclining his head, Stecher clicked his heels together. He looked at Michou, his eyebrows raised.

He expected her to introduce Guy, she realized. She

swallowed hard, willing her voice to sound natural; but before she could speak, Guy stepped forward, offered his hand, and introduced himself as casually as if he were another German officer.

"You're in charge of local wine requisitions?" Guy asked Stecher.

"Yes," Stecher said. "An assignment I've learned to enjoy." He inspected his fingernails and then smiled at Lucien. "Are you returning to Libourne right away?" he asked.

The flutter in Michou's stomach faded. Stecher didn't seem particularly interested in Guy. Thank God for his obvious infatuation with Lucien. She glanced at Guy out of the corner of her eye, and he gave her a little half smile.

Lucien bowed. "At your service." He flung open the passenger door.

Stecher turned to his driver. "You needn't take me after all." After he slid into the seat, he touched his cap and nodded at Guy. "I'll be seeing more of you, undoubtedly," he said. "I compliment you on your excellent taste." He smirked at Michou.

Lucien glared at Guy for a second before getting into his car. He started the engine with a roar.

"Thank you, sir," Guy said. "The shippers who buy from me count on it."

Michou's mouth fell open, and she stared at the red car as Lucien sped down the drive. When it pulled onto the road, she turned to Guy. "He thinks—"

Guy jerked his head toward the German driver still standing on the steps. "I'd like to try some of the thirty-nines as well," he said, grinning and offering his arm. "Show me to your *chai*, mademoiselle."

It had been a long time since she'd enjoyed a day so much, Michou thought, draping her clothes over the armchair next to her bed. Maman and Mémé Laure had both seemed to like Guy, and by the end of the evening, Philippe practically panted with adoration.

She laughed aloud at the comparison. Philippe *was* like a puppy, irrepressible, happy, always making messes for other people to clean up. And he missed Papa just as much as she did. Mémé Laure was right—she was going to have to be more understanding.

After she splashed water on her face and wiped it dry, she rummaged through a drawer in the old armoire for her nightgown. Someday when she had time she'd fold everything, she promised herself. If Maman opened it, she'd shake her head sadly and make a comparison between an untidy drawer and a confused mind. Well, Maman was probably right. But at least now the confusion was tinged with a bit of happiness.

Her fingers touched something slick, and she pulled it out and turned it over. Marc, smiling in his uniform, stared up at her. It was the only picture of him she'd left in the drawer. She'd returned the others to the top of her bureau months ago, but the uniform had been too much then. She smiled back at him, her lips trembling slightly. He wouldn't want her to spend the rest of her life mourning him—he'd always been practical. She ran her fingers across the photograph and slid it back into the drawer, then pulled out the nightgown.

She paused for a moment, enjoying the faint scent of jasmine. It still seemed odd coming back to her room and finding it empty. As nervous as she'd been at first, after a couple of nights she'd found herself looking forward to slipping into bed alongside Guy. Watching him sleep, sometimes she pretended they were married.

She sighed, thrust her arms into the sleeves, and pulled the nightgown over her head. *Mon Dieu,* she'd wanted him to wake up and kiss her. But he'd been polite and distant, scooting carefully to the edge of the bed when she got in, treating her more like a little sister than a—

Lover.

Sliding between the cool sheets, she whispered the word aloud.

"Lover."

She rolled onto her stomach and buried her face in the soft pillow. It wasn't going to happen. He treated her exactly the same as he did the rest of her family. The pleasant tension of her happiness fizzled away, like the bubbles in an untouched glass of champagne.

21

❦

Standing in the doorway and squinting into the morning sun, Lucien stared at Guy's back as he walked away from the table. He waited until Guy turned the corner before he stepped out onto the *terrasse* and approached Michou.

"What did he want?" he demanded. He'd seen too much of that one lately. He sure as hell would hate to have her fall for anyone else again now that Marc was out of the way. It wouldn't help, either, if Karl suspected the same thing he did about the two of them—although *that* wasn't likely to happen, the way Karl had been acting lately. Lucien smirked. The mighty Major Stecher had turned into a lovesick idiot.

Michou twisted her cup around in her hand before she looked up. "What do *you* want?" she said, narrowing her eyes.

Lucien settled himself into the chair opposite her, tilting it back and stretching out his legs in the narrow space between the tables. He clasped his hands behind his neck, surveying the other patrons of the sidewalk café. "Who is he, really?" he said, keeping his voice low. No point in letting anyone else in on his suspicions.

"A *courtier*. You know that." She banged the cup back down in the saucer and started to get up.

"Sit down," Lucien said. He grabbed her wrist and pulled her back into her chair. He had no intention of letting her leave until he'd found out more about this Guy Fournier. Wine broker, like hell. If Fournier had been so chummy with old Valette, why hadn't he ever met Father, too? Perhaps Valette's common interest with Fournier hadn't been wine.

"You know as well as I do he's involved in the Resistance. Sure you're not helping him out the same way you helped your father?" he said.

Michou jerked her arm out of his grasp and looked down, rubbing her wrist until it was even redder. She didn't speak for a minute and then she said slowly, "You're an ass, Lucien. What makes you think I helped Papa? Did one of your *friends* tell you? Why haven't I been arrested, then? Not because I'm a woman, surely? We both know that makes no difference."

Merde! Why had he said that? He didn't want her to start thinking about Kohler's disappearance, to realize it coincided with her father's arrest. If she guessed Kohler had kept him informed of her actions—

He waved his hand and rocked the chair back onto four legs. "Forget it." He pushed away from the table and stood up. "Just don't see too much of him. I've heard talk. A friendly warning."

Michou stared up at him and opened her mouth as if intending to speak, but she didn't utter a word. She clamped her lips shut and stood up. Spinning on her heel, she walked away quickly, her wood-soled shoes clomping loudly on the sidewalk.

Lucien sat back down. Had she guessed? He shrugged. It was too late to worry about that now. Even if she had, what could she do about it? Turn herself in to get even with him?

He stuck his hand into his trouser pocket and fingered the lace-edged handkerchief he always kept there. Michou's handkerchief. She'd left it at Château LeClair-Figeac once after a visit with Berthe, and he'd picked it up, saying he would return it to her. He never had. It had joined other things of hers he kept—the corkscrew, a pair of panties, letters she'd written to Berthe. Sometimes he gathered them all about him, imagining they belonged to him because she did.

He let go of the handkerchief, pulled his hand from his pocket, and glanced at his watch. Karl should be joining him any minute. At least everything was going smoothly with him. Perhaps a bit too smoothly—the last few times they'd met at L'Hostellerie there'd been a sudden brief quiet when Karl entered, followed by a quick resumption of conversation pitched higher than before and undercut by more than a few snickers after he seated himself at Lucien's table. Even Karl had noticed it—that was why they were meeting in Libourne instead.

Karl rounded the corner from the same direction Michou had stomped off, and Lucien waved. He stood up as Karl walked toward him and offered his hand when he reached the table.

"It is extremely pleasant to see you again," Karl said, shaking his hand. Keeping his eyes fixed on Lucien's, he smiled as he slid into the chair just vacated by Michou.

"Yes, very." Lucien forced himself to sound pleased. As useful as Karl was, he was getting tired of him. He had as many moods as a woman and was even more possessive. "Let me order us some coffee."

"Or at least a close facsimile," Karl said. "Won't it be lovely when the war is won and we can drink real coffee again?"

"Lovely." Lucien signaled the waiter and ordered.

"And how is your little nephew?" Karl asked after the waiter disappeared through the swinging door.

"Fine," Lucien said. No point in letting Karl know his nephew was the son of a German traitor and deserter. He'd save that little piece of information until he needed it.

Karl patted his hair and leaned forward. "I'd like to see you again," he said. "Someplace private. Perhaps dinner at your home? Tonight?" He paused as the waiter set down the cups.

Lucien dropped three sugar cubes into his coffee and stirred it. He supposed he could cancel his date with Gabrielle. It didn't really make that much difference. Stupid cow. He was even more bored with her than he was with Karl.

"Of course," Lucien said. "I'll tell Madeleine to fix something special." He took a sip of the hot, bitter coffee and added another sugar cube.

"I've got just the thing," Karl said. "*Foie gras* and Sauternes to start, baby partridges, a filet of beef. I'll have my aide deliver them this afternoon." He lit a cigarette and leaned back, blowing the smoke out in a stream between his thin lips.

"Very nice." Lucien pulled his silver cigar case out of his pocket and opened it. Only one cigar remained. Leaving the case open on the table, he removed the cigar and fitted it into the holder. Maybe Karl would replenish his dwindling supply of Davidoff Havanas as well.

He smiled as Karl hurriedly flicked on his lighter. No, he wasn't ready to give up Karl yet. It was just too damn lucrative.

Crossing his legs, Lucien inhaled the rich smoke and gazed into Karl's blue eyes. As long as the smitten fool supplied him with enough luxuries for himself and his black-market trade, he'd put up with him.

As the last of the grape pickers straggled through the gate, Michou frowned at the cloudy sky. They were never going to beat the threatening rain with so few workers. Worse than last year, even. Damn the Nazis to hell. They took all the best wine, they refused her the chemicals she needed all summer, and now they made it almost impossible to find help.

She followed the pickers toward the vineyard. The two men hoisted the large conical containers to their backs and adjusted the straps while the woman grabbed a basket from the pile. They joined the others already at work.

The chug of a *gazogène* reached her ears, and she spun back again toward the road, holding her breath to ease the sudden pounding in her chest. An old gray Renault pulled into the drive, and she let her breath out with a slow hiss. It was Guy, and he wasn't alone. He'd kept his promise.

She walked slowly to the car as Guy and three other men climbed out. "You came," she said. "Look at the sky. It even smells like rain."

Guy laughed and kissed her cheeks. "If it rains, we'll just carry umbrellas." He introduced her to his friends.

Michou shook hands with each. "Thank you for helping," she said. "I can't pay you much, but you'll have all the soup and bread you can eat and all the wine you can drink."

The stocky one, whom Guy had introduced as René, cleared his throat and spat. "We just came for the food and drink. Pay him whatever you can afford." He jerked his head at Guy and then walked off toward the vineyard, the other two following him.

Michou glanced up at Guy. "I didn't think you were going to make it." She ducked her head, stirring the dusty gravel with her shoe. She hated the way he always looked at her, as if he found her as amusing as a kitten. He was just like everyone—he didn't take her seriously because she was small.

Michou kicked at the rocks. She'd show him. Even kittens had sharp claws, and only a fool would think an adder harmless because it was tiny.

"Something wrong? I thought you'd be pleased," Guy said. He put his hand under her chin and lifted her face toward his.

She narrowed her eyes and jerked away from him. "Stop treating me like a child. I'm not your daughter. My father is dead." She whirled around and started after the men.

"So is my daughter."

She stopped abruptly. "Oh, no," she gasped. He'd told her about his wife, that they were divorced and that she'd been killed during a bombing raid, but he'd never mentioned anything about his little girl and she hadn't thought to ask him. *Mon Dieu*, how selfish she'd become.

She turned slowly. "I'm so sorry. You didn't tell me."

He shrugged, the smile gone from his eyes. "A year ago," he said. "The same bomb that killed her mother."

"You didn't tell me," she repeated. She didn't know what else to say. She'd hurt so badly over her miscarriage, and she hadn't even known her baby. To lose a child, one you'd held and fed and loved—she didn't even want to imagine how it would feel. Sudden tears blurred her eyes.

He dug his hands into his pockets and looked down at his feet. "I shouldn't have told you now, either. We have work to do." Walking quickly, he passed her and headed after his men.

Michou brushed the tears from her eyes with her sleeve. "Wait!" she yelled. She sprinted after him until she caught up and then tugged at his arm. "Please stop. Don't be angry with me."

He faced her. "I'm not. It's just that I try not to think about it. Makes me want to strangle every Nazi I see."

Glancing toward the soldier leaning against Stecher's car, she curled her lip. "I'd rather shoot them all," she said. "And the collabos, too. Lucien first."

Guy lifted an eyebrow. "He *is* rather repulsive, the way he makes up to that Stecher. But he hardly deserves death for that. Why do you hate him so much?"

"Because he killed my father."

Guy frowned. "I thought your father was executed," he said. He took her hand and pulled her around the corner of the *cuvier*.

"He was. But Lucien turned him in."

Guy propelled her through the door. "How do you know that?" he asked when they were out of sight of Stecher's aide.

"He told me he knew I'd been helping Papa hide the Englishmen."

"If the Germans had known that, they'd have arrested you, too," he said.

She nodded. "Before Stecher got here, Lucien was a great pal of a sergeant named Kohler, a fat, disgusting drunk. He disappeared right before Papa was arrested." She clenched her fists so hard her nails cut into her palms. "Kohler must have told Lucien about what we were doing. Then Lucien somehow got rid of him and turned Papa in."

"Leaving out your involvement?" Guy frowned. "But why?"

"He wants me," she said. "He always has. But I've always hated him. And now I'm going to kill him."

Guy shook his head as two men dragging a small cart filled with grapes made their way toward the *cuvier*. He helped them hook the cart to the pulley, hoist it overhead, and dump the grapes into the crusher.

Michou didn't speak until the men and the cart were headed back toward the vineyard. "I mean it," she whispered. "Papa kept a gun hidden in—"

"You little fool!" He shook her by the shoulders. "Even I don't carry a gun. It's too dangerous. Get rid of it!"

She wrestled away from him and backed up, crossing her arms tightly against her chest. "No," she said. She shook her head.

He leaned against the crusher and pinched the bridge of

his nose. "Georges was right," he muttered. He raised his head. "Fine. They could arrest your whole family."

Michou put her hands on her hips. "They can arrest my whole family anytime they want, gun or no gun. You know that."

He sighed and held out his hands. "Keep the damn gun, then. Just promise me you won't kill Lucien."

"No."

"Look," he said, "I know how you feel. But think about it. What good would it do? It wouldn't get rid of the Nazis any sooner. They might even decide to shoot some hostages in reprisal. Would you want to be responsible for that?"

"I don't care."

"Yes, you do." He rested his hands on her shoulders. "And I care about you. Don't do it."

Michou stared into his eyes for a few seconds before she turned away. "If you knew who had done it, you'd kill whoever killed—"

"I'd want to," he said, his voice clipped. "But I wouldn't. Winning the war is more important than personal revenge." He stalked out the door.

Michou stuck her tongue out at his back. He was too old to understand. He sounded just like Papa.

Her eyes filled again with tears. Guy *was* right, she knew. But she was going to kill Lucien anyway. Maybe not right away. She could wait. She only hoped someone else didn't kill him first.

22

Catherine propped the unfinished watercolor against the wall and stepped back. Not too bad, she decided. All she had left to paint were the leaves on the vines and the two figures in front of the *cuvier*—Alexandre, standing as he always had, one hand shading his eyes as he gazed across the vineyards, and Michou, clinging to his other hand.

She set the heavily textured paper back down on her drawing board and selected a thin sable brush for the leaves. This painting had been Mémé Laure's idea. She'd suggested it as a good Christmas present for Michou because she'd always loved the harvest watercolor in the entry. "Paint it again," Mémé Laure had said. "But put Alexandre and Michou in it this time."

A slight smile twitched at the corners of Catherine's lips as she squeezed a dab of ocher on the white porcelain plate she used for mixing colors. It hadn't taken her long to figure out the real reason for Mémé Laure's proposal: painting helped her forget the pain and remember the happiness.

After she dipped the brush into the water cup, she smeared it into the paint and spattered on the leaves with short, quick strokes. It felt good to be painting again after so many months. There was reassurance in the smell of the paints, the pressure of the brush in her hands, the rough texture of the rag paper. Her life would never be the same without Alexandre, but at least she could make it appear normal. She still had her children, her roses, her piano, her painting. She still had the home Alexandre had loved so much.

The brush in the air, she paused and sighed. It was too bad Michou couldn't find the same kind of release. Ever since Alexandre's death, she had worked in the vineyards and the *chai* with such frenzy that it hurt to watch her. The dark shadows under her eyes never faded, not even after Guy's sudden appearance.

The smile pulled at her mouth again as she added a few more leaves. Those two—pretending to each other, to everyone else, probably even to themselves, that there was nothing between them. Even Philippe had noticed, and for him to slow down long enough to see anything was unusual.

"There," she said. She put the brush down, picked up a thicker one, and swirled it into the umber. She hadn't said anything when Michou had introduced Guy as a friend of Alexandre's, but she was sure he couldn't have been. Alexandre had always told her everything. Guy couldn't have had a friend she'd never even heard of. If they were involved in something dangerous—

She took a deep breath. All she could do was go along with Michou. She'd welcomed Guy as a longtime friend of the family, inviting him to dinner whenever he showed up. He'd been around so much lately it was even beginning to seem natural. But what were they up to?

She shook her head. Whatever it was, at least it wasn't as awful as what Sylvie was doing. There wasn't much danger of that with Michou, though, not the way she hated the Germans. Mère had sounded so disappointed with Sylvie in her last letter, so angry, so old. "She's taken up with a German officer," she'd written. "We no longer allow her in the house."

Squinting, Catherine applied the paint carefully. She didn't even want to think about that now. This was the most important part of the painting. One slip and the whole picture was ruined—one couldn't paint over a mistake as easily with watercolors as one could with oils. The two small figures silhouetted against the vineyards had to be perfect.

A knock at the door interrupted her concentration. She sighed again and put down the brush. "Come in," she said.

Mémé Laure stepped into the studio, her chest heaving and her breath rattling in her throat. "Just wanted to see the picture," she gasped.

Catherine put her arm around Mémé Laure's soft waist and helped her into the chair next to her drawing table. "You're going to wear yourself out climbing all those steps to the top of the tower," she scolded, shaking her finger. "I'd have brought it to you when I finished. You know that."

"Nonsense," Mémé Laure said. "Need to walk a little. Get tired of that silly room after a while." She coughed and cleared her throat. "Well, let me see it."

Catherine held the painting up against her chest. "Is it all right?" she asked.

The only sound for a few seconds was Mémé Laure's raspy breathing. Finally, she said, "Oh, Catherine. Call it *Winemakers After the Harvest*. Michou will love it."

"I hope so." Catherine laid the painting down. "I've been so worried about her."

"She'll be fine," Mémé Laure said. "She's angry and that's natural, *n'est-ce pas?*"

"I know. I felt the same. Can you believe I spent hours thinking about how to poison Stecher? And that was during my more lucid moments." Catherine shook her head. "As if that would help Alexandre or stop the hurting. But the anger faded months ago for me. Why is she still so bitter?"

Mémé Laure looked over the top of her glasses. "She's got a lot of her grandfather in her—and Patrick never forgave an insult. I loved him, but he could be a hard man, an unforgiving enemy. Thank God Alexandre wasn't the same." She coughed. "And the hatred is kept alive for her. Every day she has to see the man who arrested her father, watch him enjoying the life her father built."

Catherine rested her elbows on the windowsill and gazed out. "I don't think too much about Stecher any longer, but sometimes I still get mad at Alexandre. Why did he do it? Then I feel guilty. We both know he *had* to help those poor men."

"When the Germans came, I knew Alexandre wouldn't live quietly to save himself. Principles were always too important to him." Mémé Laure chuckled. "He and his father used to argue for weeks about some silly idea. Neither would ever give in. It would have been impossible for Alexandre to do nothing, *n'est-ce pas?*"

"Michou is like *both* of them," Catherine said, turning

away from the window. "After all these years, she's never forgiven Lucien for not making an attempt to save Alain and Daniel."

Mémé Laure nodded. "Another problem—that Lucien. If only he weren't here so often with that German friend of his. Every time Michou sees them together, she gets angrier."

"Poor Henri," Catherine said. "He's so disappointed in that boy."

"Wouldn't you be?"

"It's hard to imagine Alain ever turning out like that. He always cared more about other people than he did about himself." Catherine shrugged and sat down opposite Mémé Laure.

"Unlike Lucien, who's always cared more about himself than anyone else in the world." Mémé Laure's lips twisted into a wry smile. "He, obviously, does not take after *his* father. Nice man, Henri Desroches."

Catherine looked up quickly. Mémé Laure might spend a lot of time in her room, but she never missed a thing. Henri *had* been stopping by a lot more frequently than usual.

Mémé Laure's sparkling brown eyes smiled at her over the top of her glasses. "You can't fool me, Catherine de Bacqueville Valette. You think he's a nice man, too."

"Of course," Catherine said. "He's always been a good friend of ours."

"And now he wants to be a good friend of *yours*." Deep wrinkles creased Mémé Laure's cheeks as she grinned. "Just like Patrick after Robert died." Laying her head against the back of the chair, she closed her eyes for a minute. "So many years ago."

Catherine raised her eyebrows. Mémé Laure seldom spoke of Robert, her first husband, or of Patrick's courtship. "I'm not ready yet for anything like that," she said. "But I do enjoy his company. And he needs my friendship, too. Especially now."

Mémé Laure lifted her head. "Has he forgiven that daughter of his yet? He'll never be happy until he does."

"She still won't tell him who little Daniel's father is." Catherine lowered her voice to almost a whisper. "I think he suspects Lucien. It's been eating at him."

Mémé Laure snorted and waved her hand in the air. "That's ridiculous! Sister or not, Berthe's not nearly pretty enough for Lucien. She probably had an affair with some German who got transferred away, and she's just too ashamed to admit it."

"That's what I think, too," Catherine said, tapping her fingernails on the arm of the chair. "And I've told him so. He always seems to agree, and then the next time I see him, he has another story about something or other the baby has done that was just like Lucien as an infant."

"For God's sake!" Mémé Laure coughed until she gasped for breath. "Lucien *is* the baby's uncle," she said when she could speak again. "Of course the child is going to resemble him in some ways."

Footsteps echoed on the tower stairs. Catherine laid her fingers over her lips, stood up, and walked to the door. "Only Philippe runs up the stairs that way," she said as she opened the door.

Philippe flung himself into the room. "I just heard the news," he gasped. "The Japanese attacked Pearl Harbor. The Americans are in the war!"

Michou stuck the pruning knife in her belt and peeled the glove off her right hand. Rows and rows of vines to go, and her hand was already a mass of blisters. No more today. Tomorrow she'd have to use her left hand unless she could get Philippe to help.

Someone whistled, and she snapped her head up. Maybe Guy had come early. He'd be glad to help her—the way he had with the harvest, the racking of Papa's last wine, the fining and bottling of the wine from the second-year *chai*. Even if he came only to make sure she didn't get carried away with her hatred for Lucien, his help was welcome. There just wasn't enough time to do everything herself, and she couldn't afford to hire workers.

The cold wind whipped tears into her eyes, and she blinked and squinted. A red car was parked in the drive. Damn! It wasn't Guy after all.

Lucien waved as he approached her. "You must be freezing," he said. He put his arms around her and kissed her cheeks. "Why don't you let me warm you?"

He smelled like his fancy cigars and cognac. She pushed him away. "You've got the wrong person," she said. "Go warm up Stecher. He likes you. I don't." She turned and stomped to the end of the row.

Lucien's footsteps crunched behind her, and she increased her speed as she crossed the graveled drive to Papa's office. Perhaps if she ignored him, he'd give up and go find someone else to bother. She snorted. Of course, Stecher wouldn't consider Lucien's presence a bother.

She opened the door with her left hand and stepped into the little room lined with large-scale plans of the entire vineyard. She flung the door shut, but it didn't clatter.

"I want to talk to you." Lucien shut the door quietly and lounged against it.

She threw her gloves down on Papa's desk. "Go away," she said without turning around. "I *don't* want to talk to you."

"Look at me!" Lucien grabbed her arm and spun her around. "Stay away from that Fournier. He's only going to cause trouble for you. You'll see. I'm doing you a favor."

"The only favor you could do me is to die," she said. She tried to shake his hand loose, but he tightened his grip.

"You don't mean that," Lucien said. "I know you don't mean that. You've always pretended to hate me, but you don't really. You're just scared of your feelings." He grasped her other arm and pulled her closer.

Michou stared up at him. His icy blue eyes were half closed, and he ran his tongue along his full lower lip. She took a deep breath and jerked both arms away, backing up to Papa's desk.

"I may be scared of my feelings," she said. "Hatred *is* pretty scary. But I'm not scared of you." She moved her hand slowly to the pruning knife in her belt.

He stroked her hair. "You don't have any reason to be," he said. He bent his head toward her.

She leaned away from him, and the edge of the desk sliced into the back of her legs. "Get away from me," she hissed, working the knife loose.

He pressed his thighs against her. "You know you want me to do this," he said. He gripped her arms tightly and kissed her.

She bit his lip, but he didn't stop. Her mouth filled with the salty taste of blood, and she spat at him.

He pulled his head away, blood and saliva running down his chin and his eyes open wide. *"Sale pute!"* He released one of her arms and wiped his face.

Behind her back she switched the pruning knife to her free hand. If he didn't let go of her, she'd—

He looked over her shoulder. "What have you got there?" he asked.

She flailed the hooked knife at his face. He jerked away quickly. A thin red scratch appeared on his cheek, and his eyes opened wider still.

He clasped her wrist. "No!" he yelled. "Drop it!" He banged her hand against the desk.

The knife clattered to the floor, and he kicked it away. "That was stupid," he said, lowering his voice. "I want you and I'm going to have you." He pulled her tightly against him.

"Really?" she said. "You had me fooled. All this time I thought Stecher was the one you wanted." She curled her lip. If he tried again, there was still Papa's gun. She groped toward the drawer where it was kept.

"I'll show you I'm no *pédé,*" he said, slapping her across the face.

The blood in her mouth this time was her own. She swallowed hard and pressed her lips together. Perhaps if she stopped struggling, she could get to the gun. She made herself go limp in his arms.

He loosened his hold and looked at her, his lips curving into a half sneer, half smile.

"I believe you," she gasped, fumbling at the latch on the drawer. Damn her shaking fingers! He'd realize what she was doing if she didn't hurry.

"Good." Wrapping one arm around her, he rubbed his pelvis against her. Then, suddenly, he forced his hand under the waistband of her trousers. He entwined his fingers in her pubic hair and tugged sharply.

"Don't!" She dropped the latch, and it clanked against the drawer. Her eyes blurred with tears of pain, and she struggled to escape his groping fingers. His hoarse grunts rattled in her ears as she pummeled his kidneys with her fists.

He laughed and pushed his fingers deep inside her.

"No!" she screamed. She clutched at his wrist and tried to wrench his hand out of her, away from her.

Clamping his free hand over her mouth, he bent her backward over the desk until her head bumped the wall. His long fingernails scraped her as he slowly withdrew his hand.

The front door of the château slammed, and someone spoke loudly in German.

"Karl," Lucien whispered. Keeping his hand over Michou's mouth, he straightened and pulled her back up.

She jerked his hand away and narrowed her eyes. "He's looking for his lover," she hissed. "You'd better go before he finds out you've been unfaithful to him."

Lucien slapped her again, and she fell against the desk. "You say anything, and I tell him my suspicions about Fournier," he said, spinning on his heel and heading for the door. He pulled a handkerchief out of his pocket and rubbed at the scratch on his cheek.

"Just like you—"

The door banged shut behind him.

"—told about Papa."

Sobbing, she jerked open the drawer and snatched up the gun. She ran to the window and wiped it clear of condensation.

Lucien and Stecher stood next to the red car, smiling and nodding.

She raised the gun and aimed it at Lucien's head. "Bang," she whispered. "You're dead."

❧

23

Mémé Laure coughed. "Pour me another glass of water, child," she said. "Then tell me what's happening out there."

Michou dropped the curtain and turned back to Mémé Laure. After she filled the glass and handed it to her, she sat in the chair by the bed. The pungent fumes of Mémé Laure's chest ointment made her eyes sting, and she blinked. "Stecher's leaving. It looks as if Lucien is taking him. They're loading bags into his car," she said. "Thank God I'll never have to look at Stecher again." She never saw him without remembering the day he had arrested Papa, without experiencing the same shocks of terror, helplessness, hatred.

Mémé Laure gulped the water and coughed again. She handed the glass to Michou. "Thank you, child," she said, lying back on the pillow. "It's hard getting old. I hate being—"

"Stop," Michou said. "I don't want to hear it. Summer will be here soon, and you'll be just fine." She squeezed Mémé Laure's hand. "I know you will."

"Of course." Mémé Laure wheezed. "Now tell me the news. I may be dying, but I'm still curious as hell."

Michou tried to smile. "You're not dying yet. I know you. You couldn't—not without knowing France is free again." She hated it when Mémé Laure talked like that, but she understood why she did. Every winter her bronchitis got worse, and every spring it took her longer to recover. She'd never survive another bout of pneumonia like the one she'd had two years ago. And with heating fuel so scarce since the occupation, she was even more likely to come down with it.

"You're probably right." Mémé Laure's chuckle led to

another coughing spell. When she finished, she said, "Are all our guests leaving with Stecher?"

Michou shook her head. "No. Lucien told Berthe another one is coming to replace him. Probably just as awful. But at least I won't have a *special* reason to hate this one. I can detest him simply because he's a *Boche*."

A car rumbled up the drive, and Michou stood and walked back to the window. "Maybe that's the new one." She pulled aside the musty-smelling rose damask drape. "Must be. He's getting out of the car. Saluting Stecher. Shaking hands with Lucien. He's taller than either of them, but I can't see his face." She snorted. "You should see Lucien. He looks like a fish gasping for air. Wish I could see why."

Stecher's replacement turned toward the window. "*Mon Dieu,*" Michou said. "He looks like a god, like one of those beautiful young Nazis in the posters they plastered everywhere at the beginning. Square jaw, strong chin, straight nose. I can't see what color his eyes are, but I'll bet they're blue. The perfect Aryan."

"Just like you, child."

Michou spun around and put her hands on her hips. "I'm not—"

"Now, don't get excited. I just meant that it's hard to tell much about people from the way they look. Most of us don't have much choice."

"He has a choice in how he dresses. And he's wearing a Nazi uniform."

Mémé Laure shrugged. "You have reason to hate Stecher. We all do. But you have no reason to hate his replacement. Ignore him. He doesn't exist. Hatred takes so much effort." She patted the bed. "Come back here, child. I don't care what they're doing out there anymore."

Michou sat on the edge of the huge four-poster. Mémé Laure was usually right, but not this time. Hating the Germans took no effort at all. It was as natural as the fermentation that turned grape juice into wine.

"Your mother has been worried about you. What have you been doing?" Mémé Laure asked.

Michou twisted her hair around her finger. Not this again, she thought. She didn't want to upset anyone, especially Maman, but why couldn't they just leave her alone?

It was much safer for no one to know about the four English airmen she'd hidden for Guy during the last few months.

"Nothing," she said, rolling her eyes. "I'm fine. Just tired. Philippe's not much help, and it's hard keeping everything going. You know that." Mémé Laure had run Château Bourdet during the first Great War.

Mémé Laure smoothed the coverlet. "That's not what I meant. But perhaps it's best not to talk about it after all, *n'est-ce pas?* Tell me the news Philippe learns from his secret radio instead."

"How do you know about that?" Michou sputtered.

"I know a lot more than I tell about." Mémé Laure winked. "I may be old, but I'm not stupid and I'm not blind. Do you remember when you and Alain were children playing together how I used to call from another room for you to stop your mischief?"

Michou smiled. Alain had always been the general and she his willing and obedient soldier. "We always wondered how you knew what we were doing. For a long time we suspected you could see through walls."

"I know you did, and I let you believe it. Actually, though, I'd just listen for quiet. When you two were noisy, I didn't have to worry. But a sudden silence meant you were up to something." Mémé Laure raised her eyebrows and looked over the top of her glasses. "You just got bigger. Nothing else has changed." She paused to catch her breath. "But enough of that. What's this I hear about a new cabinet?"

"Laval's made himself chief of government. And Darlan is now the supreme commander of the armed forces. But that's in all the papers. Did you know someone tried to kill Doriot a couple of days ago?"

"That awful fascist leader?"

"Lucien's hero." Michou snorted. "Too bad it wasn't successful."

"What about General Giraud? Philippe told me he escaped from Germany. Did you know he did the same thing in the last war? Made it all the way to England disguised as a tram conductor." Mémé Laure's face creased as she smiled. "Quite a man."

"It was on the BBC broadcast last night," Michou said.

"He's in Switzerland. Hitler gets to keep his reward money after all." She sighed. "More hostages were shot yesterday—twenty of them at Saint Nazaire."

Mémé Laure rested her head on her pillow and closed her eyes for a minute. When she spoke, her voice sounded flat and far away. "So much sadness. And so much bravery."

Michou stood. "I've tired you." She kissed Mémé Laure's forehead. "Rest. I'll come see you after I get back from Libourne."

Mémé Laure raised her head and opened her eyes. "Give Berthe my regards." Her hand fluttered weakly on the coverlet, and she dropped her head back on the pillow. "So much sadness," she murmured.

Michou let herself out and closed the door softly behind her. It was still hard to see Mémé Laure like this even though she'd spent most of the winter in bed. For a few minutes of each visit, she was her old self, but every day she tired more quickly and grew sad more easily.

Well, Mémé Laure certainly had the right to be sad, Michou thought as she ran down the stairs. She'd outlived two husbands, her only son, and a grandson. No matter how hard she tried to hide it, Papa's death had taken the fight out of her.

Michou clenched her fists. But she'd never let that happen to her, not even if she lived to be ninety and had no one else in the world left to love. As long as she had Château Bourdet, she had something to fight for.

The front door opened, and she stopped at the bottom of the stairs. The new German officer and the two aides strode into the entry. Damn! She should have gone out the other way. She lifted her chin and stared straight ahead.

"Mademoiselle Valette, I believe?" The new officer tucked his cap under his arm and clicked his heels softly. "I'm Lieutenant Erich Mueller. I shall be taking the place of Major Stecher," he said, his French perfectly accented. He offered his hand.

Ignoring his outstretched hand, Michou stared at his chest. She nodded curtly and stepped to the side.

"Good day, then, mademoiselle," he said, letting his hand drop back to his side.

Michou glanced up at him. Cornflower-blue eyes sparkled back at her. She'd been right.

He pushed back his thick blond hair and settled his cap
on his head. He nodded at her before he turned to his men.
"Let's go," he said.

She watched him walk up the stairs, the aides following
with his luggage. This one was different from Stecher, she
thought. Some men looked right in a uniform, as if they were
born to wear one. This lieutenant didn't. His walk was easy,
natural—not precise and stiff.

Still, he was a Nazi. And the Nazis had killed her lover,
her baby, her papa, had conquered her country, invaded her
home. She didn't even have to think about it anymore. She
hated them all.

She slammed the door behind her and ran to the red
bicycle Papa had bought for her after her return from Paris.
Since Lucien's attack on her four months ago, she'd refused
to let him drive her to Libourne to visit Berthe and Daniel.
She didn't see them as often now as she'd like to, but the
bicycle ride was relaxing and pleasant when she had the time.
And anything was better than sitting next to Lucien, alone.

She threw her leg over the bicycle and pushed off, the
tires crunching and bouncing over the gravel drive. Lucien
had always been wild, but his wildness was different now.
Except for the time when they were children that he'd pushed
her down and she'd cut her eyebrow, he hadn't touched her
until he almost raped her at Christmas. It was as if he'd
always been scared of Papa, and now that he was dead, there
was nothing to stop him.

She frowned at the rows and rows of gnarled brown
vines lining the road. Tiny bits of green were just beginning to
emerge, encouraged by the unusually warm spring. A late
frost could shrivel and blacken the baby leaves overnight,
turning them into twisted caricatures.

She shook her head. What kind of frost had shriveled
and blackened Lucien? He'd always been mean to her and
Berthe, refusing to let them play with him when they were
children and plaguing them when they were teenagers. Had
he just been born a bastard?

The bicycle jolted over a large rock, and she tightened

her grip on the handlebars. Alain had told her once that
Lucien hadn't been so nasty when his mother was alive.
Michou had only been five when Lucien's mother died giving
birth to Daniel, so she didn't remember, but it was hard to
believe he'd ever been nice. And the war had only accentu-
ated his rottenness.

Michou stood and pedaled rapidly over the small rise at
the edge of Libourne, gulping in the fresh spring air. With any
luck, Lucien would still be delivering Stecher to his new
residence in Bordeaux while she visited with Berthe and
played with the baby. It was almost impossible for her to
control her disgust when she saw him, and she'd never told
Berthe—or anyone else—about the attack.

And she didn't plan to, at least not right away. Everyone
had too many other worries.

After rounding the corner to the Desroches's house,
Michou pushed on the brakes, swung off the bicycle, and
leaned it against the fence. The lace curtains at the largest
window swayed, and she waved. As usual, Berthe was waiting
for her.

Berthe threw open the door and stood on the porch, the
baby riding at her hip. "It's been too long," she said. She
kissed Michou's cheeks and handed her the baby. "See how
much he's changed!"

Michou cradled Daniel to her chest. "He's so beautiful,"
she said.

"I know." Berthe nodded. "He looks just like Lucien
did as a baby. Father says so all the time." She held out her
arms. "Here. Let me take him. He's getting so heavy, and he
won't hold still."

Michou squeezed Daniel and returned him to Berthe.
"He's going to be walking soon." Just like David, she
thought. She remembered David's first steps on the day she'd
lost her baby, the day before the German army had entered
Paris. He was almost three now, and in her last letter, Rachel
had said he was a handful.

Michou followed Berthe into the salon. She was so worried about Rachel. In her letters she always made fun of
everything, even the yellow star the Nazis had ordered all
Jews to wear. After Guy told her about his friend Jacob and

the terrible things that had happened to his family, she'd written to Rachel, begging her to leave Paris. But Rachel always refused—she had to stay with Joseph.

She rolled her eyes. She couldn't think about that now, not when Berthe needed her to be cheerful.

Henri Desroches rose from the chair by the fireplace. He straightened his tie and smoothed his gray-streaked black hair. "Hello, Michou," he said, offering his hand. "It's always nice to see you."

Smiling, she shook his hand. "Maman sends her regards, too," she said.

"You don't say!" The sad look left his light blue eyes, and he sounded pleased. "How is she?"

"Fine," Michou said. "And busy. Mémé Laure's still not well."

"I'm sorry to hear that. I must get out to see her soon," he said. He picked up his newspaper and tucked it under his arm. "I'll leave you two to chat." He patted Daniel on the head and left.

"I think he's fallen in love with your mother," Berthe said after the door shut.

Michou's mouth dropped open. So that's what was going on. She'd noticed an awkwardness between the two of them since Christmas, but she'd been so involved with her own frustration over Guy and anger at Lucien that she hadn't given it much thought. And now she didn't know *what* to think about it. As much as she cared for Berthe and Henri, the idea of Maman loving someone besides Papa was painful.

"Oh," she said. She sat down on the sofa. "I'm afraid you're probably right."

Berthe put Daniel on the rug and sat beside her. "Afraid?" she asked.

Michou twisted her ring around her finger. "I don't know," she said. "It just seems so odd. I mean, they've been friends for years and years. And Papa *was* your father's closest friend."

"Sometimes I think my father has been in love with your mother for a long time," Berthe said. "Ever since he got over my mother's death."

"Do you think Maman knew?"

Berthe shook her head. "I don't think even Father knew.

He loved Alexandre, too." She reached out and pulled Daniel from under the table where he'd wedged himself. "And he never really stopped missing my mother."

"Do you remember much about her?" Michou asked.

"A little," Berthe said. "She was soft, and she always smelled good, like flowers. Lucien remembers more, but he was ten when she died. I was only five." She sighed and gazed at Daniel. "I love him so much. It's sad to think he wouldn't remember me if I died. But maybe it would be best that way. Maman's death hurt Lucien much more than it did me, and Daniel, of course, never knew her at all."

Michou raised her eyebrows. It was hard to imagine Lucien loving anyone or being hurt by anything. "Lucien was close to your mother?"

"Very." Berthe nodded emphatically. "I think he always blamed Daniel for her death. Lucien wouldn't even look at him when he was a baby." She frowned. "Funny. Daniel always adored him, followed him everywhere as soon as he could walk. Just like this Daniel." She scooped the baby up and hugged him against her large breasts. "He loves his uncle."

Michou stood up and walked to the fireplace. She would never understand Berthe's feelings for Lucien, her inability to see him as he really was even though he treated her with total disregard. Berthe had no capacity for hatred, no taste for revenge. She never had, and she probably never would.

Michou crossed her arms tightly against her abdomen. Well, *she* had a capacity for hatred as well as a strong taste for revenge. Even talking about Lucien made her feel as angry as she had on the day she discovered his betrayal of Papa, as outraged as she had on the day he'd violated her.

But she couldn't let Berthe know. She forced her arms to her side and turned around. "Let's take Daniel for a walk," she said. That way she could just jump on her bicycle and leave if Lucien's car was there when they got back.

"What a good idea!" Berthe said, standing up. "We can go see Gabrielle and cheer her up a bit. She hasn't been herself late—"

"No, damn it!" Michou clenched her jaw. How could Berthe be so naïve? As if Lucien's sister and her baby could make Gabrielle feel better after what she'd been through. It was just too much. "You don't know why?" she asked, her throat tight.

Berthe tilted her head. "No," she said. She wrinkled her nose. "Has she had another fight with Lucien?"

"You might say that," Michou said sarcastically. "He got her pregnant." She bit her lip. It wasn't fair to be mean to Berthe because of Lucien. "She didn't tell you?" she asked more gently.

"No," Berthe whispered, shaking her head. "When are they getting married?"

"Never," Michou said. "He told her the baby probably wasn't his."

24

Erich stood at the window a moment longer, staring at the tiny figure in the vineyard below. "'Even when she walks, she seems to dance,'" he murmured. Did she ever rest? Every morning when he got up, there she was, dressed in old brown trousers rolled to her knees and a thick blue sweater. The vineyards seemed to be her whole life. *Mein Gott,* he admired her strength, her obvious love for what she was doing. It had been a long time since he'd cared that much for anything.

Or anyone. He ran his fingers through his hair. But that was beginning to change. During the week he'd been billeted at Château Bourdet, he'd tried to speak to her on several occasions, but each time she'd just looked right through him. A nod was the most acknowledgment he'd received, and even that had been accompanied by a blank stare.

He sighed and let the curtain drop. "'Sudden as a knife you thrust into my sorry heart,'" he recited aloud. He hadn't felt so enamored since he was a teenager in love with his cousin Gisele. That, of course, had been ill-fated from the beginning; both sets of parents had been quick to react, forbidding them to see each other until they had outgrown their foolishness.

He combed his hair and put on his cap. At the time he'd been sure he'd never get over the love he felt for Gisele; he'd moped in his room for weeks, devouring the Symbolist poets and thinking about suicide.

"Stupid young idiot," he said to himself in the mirror. "Always so full of grand sentiment. Always so incapable of actually doing anything grand."

He squared his shoulders and walked stiffly to the door. Gisele had fallen in love with someone else, and he hadn't killed himself over her. In fact, he hadn't thought of her in years. Now he felt the pain all over again, as if it were only yesterday that he'd watched her being escorted down the front steps by her parents.

He let himself out and closed the door softly behind him. Odd how a new feeling could call back an old one, entwining with the other until it became impossible to separate them, each seeming larger because of the other. It wasn't that Michou Valette reminded him of Gisele. No, they didn't resemble each other at all, tiny Michou with her halo of silver-blond hair and Gisele a fiery-haired Valkyrie. That wasn't it at all.

He closed his eyes and leaned against the door. He'd been numb for so long that it hurt coming back to life again, just like the prickling of a limb long asleep. This time, though, he wasn't going to give up. She couldn't ignore him forever.

She could just strangle both of them, Michou decided as she dragged another scratchy armful of vine prunings to the edge of the vineyard. She had enough to deal with already without Philippe's damn high spirits and Guy's infernal stupidity.

She threw the prunings on the pile and stomped back for more. What was Guy thinking of, bringing her another flier to hide when there was a new German officer snooping all over the place? Wherever she went, there he was, watching. He stared at her all the time. When she told Guy, he'd just laughed. "Probably thinks you're the most beautiful girl he's ever seen," he'd said. Then he'd been serious: "If I had anywhere else to hide him, I would." She couldn't refuse.

Philippe was a different matter, though. She scooped together another armful and returned to the pile. Not even Maman's pleas had worked. He'd helped with the pruning for a few days and then just didn't show up anymore. The vines had been sprouting before she finished, and instead of removing the suckers, she was still cleaning up the vineyards. There'd been no time at all to plant the new cuttings.

After she dropped the awkward load, Michou took off her cap and wiped the sweat from her face. Looking out over the vineyards, she sighed. Almost done. Papa would be proud of her, appreciate what she'd done even if no one else seemed to.

But she wasn't being fair. She put her cap back on and hitched up her trousers. Even if they couldn't do anything in the vineyards, Maman and Mémé Laure had helped with the bottling and labeling until Mémé Laure had gotten sick. Not that there'd been much left to bottle, though, after the Nazis got through with their requisitions.

Shading her eyes with her hand, she squinted into the bright spring sunlight. Someone was coming through the vineyard. She hoped it was Guy with arrangements for the *passeur*. The sooner she got rid of the airman hiding in the tower room below hers, the more relaxed she'd feel.

The tall figure waved. "Good day, mademoiselle," he called.

Damn! It was the new officer, Lieutenant Mueller. She hastily bent over and gathered together another load of twigs so she wouldn't have to acknowledge him.

"Let me help," he said, taking the prunings out of her arms. He strode to the heap of debris at the edge of the vineyard.

Michou was silent as she watched him toss the load onto the pile. If he thought she was going to thank him, he was certainly wrong. She hadn't spoken a word to him in the two weeks he'd been billeted at Château Bourdet, and she had no intention of breaking her habit.

As he started back toward her, she moved to the next row. Even if he was a *Boche,* at least he was an improvement over Stecher. Of course, that wasn't saying much for him. *Anything* would be an improvement over Stecher. She glanced at him as he started cleaning up the row beside her.

He smiled, his cornflower-blue eyes gleaming. "Beautiful d-day, isn't it, mademoiselle?" he said. Without pausing for an answer, he added, "When I was a child, spring was my favorite season. I liked it even better than summer. Spring was the promise; summer, the fulfillment; and promises are always so much more lovely than any reality, d-don't you think?" His laugh was soft and shaded with irony. "Somehow the summers were never quite as wonderful as the springs promised."

Straightening, Michou stared at him. He certainly didn't sound like a soldier. Except for a tiny hesitation, his French was rapid and flowing, with only the slightest accent. There was no trace of the authoritarian superiority of Stecher and the others.

"Perhaps this spring will be different," he said, staring back at her. "Perhaps it will keep its promise."

She ducked her head and fumbled with the rotten stake at the end of the row. Maybe Guy had been right about him, after all. Something in his eyes when he looked at her made her think of Marc, of the softness in his face after they'd made love the first time. It just wasn't the look of a suspicious conqueror searching for evidence of wrongdoing.

Merde! She jerked out the stake, and a splinter poked through her glove and into her palm. Lucien had been obsessed with having her since she was sixteen, and now this idiot seemed to be infatuated as well. She detested both of them. She tossed the stake onto the cleanup heap.

Stripping off the glove, she gritted her teeth. If only Guy would look at her like that. But he treated her as if she were one of his comrades, not a desirable woman. She pulled out the splinter and sucked the blood from her hand.

"You hurt yourself." Lieutenant Mueller hurdled the vine support. "Let me see." He grabbed her hand.

"Don't touch me!" She yanked her hand away.

"So you *can* talk," he said, and smiled. "Corporal Fischer swore he'd heard you speak, but I was beginning to wonder."

She turned away, slipped the glove back on, and stalked to the other end of the row. Those were the last words he'd hear from her.

"I'm from Johannisburg, you know. We make wine there, too. Not red wine, of course, but excellent wine nevertheless. My father was a winemaker for the Metternich family at Schloss Johannisburg. He was quite disappointed when I showed no inclination for the profession. I did learn a lot from him, though. Th-that's why I'm here."

Keeping her back to him, she continued working. She didn't care what his father had been. Winemaker or butcher, it made no difference to her. His son was a German soldier— that was the only thing that mattered now.

His voice followed her. "I chose to become a teacher

instead. French literature. I got my diploma, but I never had a chance to teach. I was called up. And that's also why I'm here."

What was he trying to do—excuse himself for being a Nazi swine? Or show that he was different from the rest? She scraped at a weed with her heel. As long as he was in Hitler's army, he was one of them. He was just the same as Stecher and the rest—murdering bastards, all of them.

"My father was killed last month in a bombing raid on the Rhine. It's still hard for me to believe he's dead. It doesn't make sense. Why would anyone want to bomb vineyards? Why would anyone want to kill an old man?" He paused. "Wh-why would anyone want to kill my father?"

Michou glanced back at him. Even though his words were softly spoken, there was authentic grief in his tone. It seemed peculiar to think of a Nazi as having feelings.

She clasped the armful of vines tightly against her chest. Well, her father was dead, too. The Nazis had killed him. And this soldier following her about the vineyard was a Nazi. Nothing could change that.

"Corporal Fischer told me about your father," he said. "I'm sorry."

Michou shrugged. Apologies meant nothing.

He returned to the row he'd been working on. "I've been watching you," he said after he finished clearing it. "You work too hard."

She ignored him. Another figure approached the vineyard, and she caught her lip between her teeth. Leave it to Guy to pick the worst possible time. It seemed to be a habit with him.

Guy waved at her. "Hello," he shouted. "I've been tasting some wines at your neighbor's and thought I'd just come by and see how things are going. You look busy, as usual." When he reached her, he kissed her cheek. He nodded at the lieutenant.

Lieutenant Mueller introduced himself. "I've just been telling her she works too hard," he said, offering his hand.

Guy shook his hand and smiled. "She won't listen. I've given up."

"You've known each other for a long time, then?" Lieutenant Mueller asked.

"Years," Guy said.

Michou glared at him. How could he just stand there and chat pleasantly with an enemy soldier when he knew how she felt? She spun around and headed for the refuse pile. They could smile and talk until they ran out of breath. She wasn't going to stay around to watch.

She dropped the prunings and strode toward the *chai*. When Guy finished, he could find her there.

"Michou! Wait!" Guy called. "Nice to meet you, Lieutenant. I'm sure I'll see you again."

His steps pounded behind her, and she increased her pace. He grabbed her arm. "You're a little fool," he hissed in her ear.

She shook her arm loose and brushed the dirt from the front of her blouse. "You're the fool," she said. "Why didn't you wait until he'd gone?"

"I've been watching you two from your grandmother's window," he said. "I doubt he would have left. Besides, I wanted to meet him."

"But I didn't hear your car." The strong smell of wine and wood greeted her as she stepped into the *chai*.

"It blew up. I bicycled."

She whirled around and he bumped into her. "You weren't hurt, were you? I told you *gazogènes* were dangerous." Her whole body suddenly felt cold.

He held out his arms. "See—not a scratch. Fortunately, I wasn't in it at the time. I started it up and then went back to my room for this." He pulled a small silver funnel from his pocket and handed it to her. "An old decanting funnel. It's for you. For your collection."

Squinting, she turned the funnel around in her hand. The bowl was cool and smooth, and she pressed it against her cheek. "Thank you," she said, inspecting the unusual border. Tiny cats chased each other's tails all around the rim. Guy would never know how much this meant to her. It had saved his life.

"I found it in a little shop in Libourne," he said. "Something about it made me think of you, and I bought it."

She breathed deeply, pushing the image of the exploding car from her mind, and put the funnel in her trouser pocket. "And I'll think of you every time I look at it," she said, trying to sound flippant so he wouldn't guess how hard her heart was pounding in her ears.

Guy poked his head out the door. "He's gone," he said. "But he finished clearing the vineyard. Good worker. You should hire him." He drew his head back in and closed the door.

She folded her arms across her chest. "Well?" she said. "When do I get rid of the parcel?"

"Tonight. Your mother invited me to stay for dinner. I'll take him afterward." He leaned against the door.

"You?"

"Me." Raising his eyebrows, he stared past her. His voice was calm and distant, as if he were explaining something to a small child. "You see, I didn't start out alone. The guide was in the car."

Erich waited on the steps until Michou and the wine broker disappeared into her office at the side of the château. That was the third time this week Fournier had come to see her. His dedication to his job was certainly commendable.

Frowning, he rubbed the back of his neck. More likely, it was dedication to Michou. But at least Fournier had a job it was possible to like—and even more important, a job that didn't make her hate him.

He nodded at Corporal Kaufmann and trotted down the stairs to the noisily idling black Mercedes. Not that he blamed Michou for hating him. He didn't like himself much, either. Officer in charge of wine requisitions, hah! It was simply a euphemism for stealing; and no one was fooled, most certainty not the *vignerons*, even though the German army paid for what it took. After all, it was the German army—and Vichy—that determined the prices.

Corporal Kaufmann held the door open, and Erich climbed into the back seat. The *Weinführer* in Bordeaux had asked him to check Major Stecher's ledgers on Château LeClair-Figeac. Apparently there was some suspicion that he had falsified the records, paying for more wine than was actually delivered.

Erich leaned his head against the back of the seat while Corporal Kaufmann slid behind the wheel. He'd heard Kaufmann and Fischer cackling about Stecher, but he hadn't encouraged them to include him in their gossip. In fact, one raised eyebrow had discouraged them from continuing in his presence. Even so, he'd heard enough to guess why Major

Stecher had made "special allowances" for LeClair-Figeac, if he had indeed done so.

It was certainly foolish of Stecher, but his reasons were perfectly understandable. Erich sighed as Corporal Kaufmann steered the car through the gates. He hoped his guess about Michou and Fournier was wrong. As strongly as he felt for her, he almost preferred to think the two of them had been going for a lovers' stroll the night last week he'd seen them together. If that was the case, though, why was there someone else with them?

He shook his head. Perhaps it had been her brother. Perhaps not. After all, her father had been shot for aiding Englishmen. He'd just have to watch her more carefully. It was his duty.

25

Erich set down the crystal snifter and held his hands up to the fire. *Mein Gott*, it was cold tonight, and even though Lucien's drawing room was pleasantly furnished, it was certainly drafty—worse even than the dining room, which at least benefited from the warmth of the kitchen. He could understand why Lucien spent so much time in Libourne and Bordeaux.

Lucien immediately stood and threw another log into the fireplace. "I'm terribly sorry," he said. "Even Karl can't do much to help me keep this place warm."

Major Stecher lifted his head from the back of the wing chair. "Not *this* room, anyway." He giggled and hiccupped. "Excuse me," he said, forcing his eyes open wide. "Excellent cognac, Lucien."

"Actually, it's not," Lucien said. "It's some of my father's favorite Armagnac. I find it much richer than cognac. Would you like some more?" Raising his eyebrows, he held up the bottle. "Erich?"

"It was quite delicious," Erich said. "Everything has been, in fact. But I'm afraid I've already drunk too much. I really should be getting home." He stood.

"Nonsense," Lucien said. He pushed Erich gently back into the leather chair. "Just one more. I insist." Without waiting for an answer, he splashed the liquor into the snifter.

Major Stecher waved his glass in front of him. "I'll take some more as well," he said.

"Of course." Lucien smiled at Erich while he filled the glass. He set the bottle down and picked up a small box. "Would you care for another cigar?"

"No thank you," Erich said. He'd only smoked the first to be polite, and now his throat felt raw.

Lucien shrugged and offered the box to Major Stecher. "Karl?"

"*Bitte.*" Major Stecher fumbled in the box, drew out a cigar, and dropped it on the floor.

Lucien rolled his eyes at Erich and retrieved the cigar. "Let me light it for you, Karl," he said.

Major Stecher slumped back in the chair. "*Bitte,*" he mumbled again.

After he prepared the cigar, Lucien lit it and handed it to Major Stecher. He poured himself another glass of Armagnac and sat back down next to Erich. "Life is pleasant for you at Château Bourdet?" he asked.

"More or less," Erich said. "It is a lovely place, anyway." He sipped the fiery Armagnac and tried not to look at Major Stecher. Excess always embarrassed him, and this evening had certainly been full of it, especially on the major's part. His devotion to Lucien made him look foolish.

Cupping the smooth bowl of the glass in his hand, Erich swirled the amber liquor and sniffed the oaky fumes. Although he didn't share Stecher's sexual preferences, Erich could see why he was so infatuated with Lucien. He was handsome, intelligent, charming.

Still, something wasn't quite right about him. Erich took another drink. At times Lucien seemed to be mocking his lover with his assiduous attentiveness, almost like Mephistopheles serving Faust, leading him deeper into damnation with every wish granted.

Erich stared into the fire. At least he hadn't found anything out of the ordinary in Major Stecher's ledgers. If he'd made special provisions for Château LeClair-Figeac, he had hidden them well. It was unfortunate he couldn't do the same with his too-obvious passion for Lucien.

"I imagine Michou is somewhat friendlier to you than she was to Karl," Lucien said.

Erich started. "Pardon?" he said.

"You're enjoying the company of the beautiful Mademoiselle Valette, I imagine?"

Erich shook his head. "She barely acknowledges my presence, and then only when necessary. She ignores me so convincingly that sometimes I even wonder for a moment if I'm really there, if I actually exist."

Lucien glanced at Major Stecher, whose head rested against the chair back, his mouth slack and his cigar hanging loosely between his fingers. "Let me assure you that you do," he said, reaching over and removing the cigar from the major's hand. He stubbed it out and turned back to Erich. "Most definitely."

Crossing his legs, Erich looked away. So that was Lucien's game. *Mein Gott,* he didn't want to play it. He uncrossed his legs and stood. "Thank you for your hospitality," he said. "This time I really must go."

Lucien rose also. "I'll drive you, then," he said. "Karl won't miss us." He snickered.

"I don't mind walking." Erich set his glass on the mantel and picked up his cap.

"And I don't mind driving. In fact, you'd be doing me a favor—I enjoy the opportunity to violate curfew safely." Smiling, Lucien held open the drawing-room door.

There was no graceful way out of it. "In that case, I won't deprive you of your pleasure," Erich said. He put on the cap.

Lucien held out Erich's field-gray greatcoat. "You have my deepest appreciation," he said, tilting his head and raising his eyebrows.

Erich pushed his arms into the sleeves and shrugged on the coat. Lucien's charm was rapidly turning to unctuousness. Damn Stecher for falling asleep!

Lucien rested his hand on Erich's shoulder for a minute before he slipped into his own coat. "This way," he said, escorting him to the door.

Erich pressed his arms close to his sides as the cold air hit his face. Since he'd been in the army, he'd been propositioned by men several times, but it still made him uncomfortable. He always wanted to explain that his rejection wasn't personal, but even that seemed like an insult. So instead he usually just smiled politely and offered some sort of excuse, hoping its lameness would indicate his lack of interest. It had worked so far.

He slid into the car. But he wasn't so sure it would work with Lucien, and even the thought of having to make a direct refusal made him uneasy.

"Cold night," Lucien said as he started the car. "Not good for the vines." After he shifted into gear, he laid his hand on Erich's leg.

The car bounced over a rut, and Erich jostled his leg away from Lucien's touch. Sensing his gaze, Erich turned his head and stared out the window.

"Beautiful sky," Lucien said. "Clear. Stars and moon. That's why it's so cold."

"You don't plan to use stoves tonight?"

Lucien shrugged. "Too much bother. Besides, there isn't any coal. If the vines freeze, they freeze." He jerked hard on the wheel, and the car lurched through Château Bourdet's gates.

"You couldn't burn something else?"

"Could," Lucien said. "But don't want to. I've got other things to do tonight."

As the car sped down the drive, Erich stiffened and held his breath. Several shadowy figures lit by the moonlight spilling over the vineyard hurled themselves to the ground. Was it Michou firing up the stoves to keep the vines from freezing? But there had been at least three shapes. And why would they try to hide?

Mein Gott, he had to do something to distract Lucien. Currying favor seemed far more important to him than loyalty to his countrymen. From what he'd seen tonight, Lucien would undoubtedly go straight to Major Stecher if he saw anything suspicious going on at Château Bourdet.

Lucien slammed on the brakes in front of the steps. "Let me see you to the door," he said.

Erich jumped out before Lucien could open the door for him and staggered against the car. Bending over, he stuck his finger down his throat and gagged.

It didn't take much. Rich food, liquor, and cigar smoke combined with a jolt of fear, and he spewed vomit all over the ground.

Within a second Lucien was standing over him, patting his back. When Erich stopped retching, Lucien put his arm around his waist. "I'll help you to your room," he said.

Erich squeezed his eyes shut and nodded. He forced his body to go limp and let Lucien half drag him up the steps.

At the top of the stairs he opened his eyes and looked

over Lucien's shoulder toward the vineyards. The shadows were gone. In their place, a small figure leaned over a smoking pile of twigs.

Had he been seeing things? Erich straightened. He certainly hoped so. "I can manage now," he said. "I'm feeling much better."

"You're sure?" Lucien said. "I don't mind helping you to your room." He tightened his grip around Erich's waist. "Don't want you to fall down the stairs and wake everyone."

Erich pushed him away. "I'm fine," he said. The proper German soldier returned. "Thank you again for a most pleasant evening." He marched stiffly up the stairs.

Lucien frowned. "Good evening then, Lieutenant Mueller," he said to the retreating uniform, a touch of sarcasm in his voice. "So kind of you to come."

Lucien wheeled around and ran down the steps to his car. *Merde!* He'd been wrong about Mueller—the man was a prig. He was never going to be able to manipulate him the way he could Karl.

Lucien climbed into his car and slammed the door. He hadn't done anything wrong, he decided. He'd been on his best behavior the entire evening, playing the charming host to perfection. The roast duckling had been exquisite, the skin thin and crackling and the *sauce à l'orange* limpid and tangy; the mint-scented peas couldn't have been fresher; no one made better *pommes duchesse* or *profiteroles au chocolat* than Madeleine. He'd broken his balls to provide the best food, wine, cigars, Armagnac.

It hadn't worked. Mueller ate his food, drank his wine, smoked his cigars, said thank you and good evening, and that was it.

Lucien cranked the starter and snickered. Actually, Mueller had eaten Karl's food, drunk Karl's 1920 Château Lafite, smoked Karl's Davidoff Havanas. He shoved the stick into first and let out the clutch. The wheels spun out in the gravel, and the car lurched forward.

As he rounded the drive, the headlights swung briefly across the vineyard. Several small fires smoldered between the rows. So that's what she was doing. But he could swear there'd been more than one person out there when he'd driven up.

He turned onto the road. Well, Mueller hadn't seen anything. Or had he? he'd seemed awfully interested in Michou, pressing for details about her, sounding genuinely sad because she ignored him.

Lucien frowned. Could that be why Erich hadn't responded to him? If he was in love with Michou, might he have pretended not to see anything in order to protect her?

Lucien tapped his fingers on the wheel. No, he couldn't have. Mueller just didn't seem the sort to let his emotions interfere with his duty. He seemed obsessed with propriety.

Jesus, what a bore! Lucien sneered. All that talk about literature and theater and music, as if they were the only important things in life. And Karl had loved it. Except when Lucien was lighting his cigars or pouring his drinks, Karl's eyes had been riveted on the handsome bastard all evening. Damn good thing Karl had passed out when he did.

Lucien pulled up in front of his house and turned off the motor. Karl would probably still be snoring away in the chair in front of the fireplace. Maybe he should just leave him there.

No, that wouldn't be wise. Karl had seemed much too interested in Mueller. Best to treat him with care. Lucien let himself in, pausing for a moment in the entry.

He raised his eyebrows. Maybe that was why Mueller hadn't been interested in him—a Nazi major could do a lot more for him than any Frenchman. Maybe it wasn't Michou he wanted at all.

In that case, Mueller must not have seen the odd goings-on at Château Bourdet. What better way to win favor for himself than by rounding up some Resistance workers?

Lucien took off his coat and tossed it on the chair by the front door. Either way, he'd be smart to keep an eye on the pretty son of a bitch.

He smiled, his lips pressed tightly together. And if it turned out it was Michou the lieutenant wanted rather than Karl, so much the better. Perhaps he could arrange the same sort of party for Mueller that he had for old man Valette.

26

Guy wiped his damp, sticky forehead with the back of his hand and sniffed. The apartment reeked of stale tobacco, unwashed dishes, and soured sweat. He'd finally completed another transmission, this time without any of the power interruptions the Germans used to locate illegal wireless operations.

He pinched the bridge of his nose and winced. Every time he used the wireless, he increased his chance of being caught. It was a good thing he was going to Bordeaux for a couple of months. Still, when he came back, he would have to find another place for it right away.

He returned the wireless to its small suitcase, carefully wrapped his crystals and placed them on top of the set, and shut the lid. After his last transmission, a wireless detection van, a circular listening device attached to its roof, had cruised slowly down the street. Fortunately, he'd already received the coded acknowledgment signifying that his message had been understood and had stopped transmitting. Bloody luck, that was all. If today's message hadn't been so important, he wouldn't have chanced it again.

A light tap sounded at the door, and he froze. He wasn't expecting anyone. He slid the suitcase under the bed.

He took a deep breath. "Who is it?"

"Michou."

Damn! His breath exploded in a hiss. He flung open the door. "What the hell are you doing here?" He grabbed her arm and pulled her into the room.

She tossed her head and narrowed her eyes. "Nothing. I'm sorry I came." She jerked her arm out of his grasp. "I'll leave."

"Nonsense." He reached behind her and shut the door. "If you're here, you must have a reason. Tell me."

She shrugged. "Nothing important. I was just visiting Berthe and decided to come and see you. That's all. I made a mistake. I'll go now." She pivoted on her heel and reached for the doorknob.

Guy's hand covered hers before she could turn the knob. He pulled her close to him for a second. Christ, he wanted to kiss her sulky mouth, feel her thighs pressed against his.

Instead, he gave her a little shake, and the blue kerchief covering her platinum hair slipped off. "Stop acting like a child," he said, picking it up and handing it to her. "I know something's up. What is it?" He steered her to a rickety chair. "Sit down and tell me."

Michou flopped onto the chair. "I don't want you to come to Château Bourdet so often," she said. "I think it's too dangerous." She twisted the kerchief in her hands.

"That's all?" He laughed. "Haven't I told you that the more familiar a sight I am, the less I'll stand out? It's harder to be suspicious of someone you see all the time."

"That's what you say. But I don't believe it." She crossed her arms. "And it's different now anyway."

He raised his eyebrows. "Why?"

"Didn't I tell *you* that the new lieutenant follows me everywhere?"

He nodded. "So? Did something go wrong last night?"

"No." She lifted her head and glared at him. "But it could have. I went out at midnight with the new *passeur* and the parcel to show them the best place to cross. We were in the middle of the vineyard when Lucien drove up. You know who was with him?"

"Not Lieutenant Mueller?" He grimaced.

"Lieutenant Mueller. I don't know if he or Lucien saw the other two, but I know they saw me. It was cold, so I stayed and lit some frost fires between the rows while Paul and the Englishman ran across the line and hid in the ditch. I figured if they had seen something, it was better that it be something plausible."

"Good," Guy said. "Damn quick thinking. Everything turned out fine, then. So what's the problem?" He straddled the chair and rested his arms on the back.

"Lucien helped him up the stairs as if he couldn't walk. I figured he was drunk or something. Then Lucien drove away." She paused, wrapping the kerchief around her hand. "As soon as I couldn't hear his car anymore, the front door slammed again. It was Mueller. He insisted on helping me with the fires for the rest of the night. He wasn't a bit drunk and he could walk perfectly."

"Hmmm." Guy stood and put his hands on his hips. "You think he suspects?"

"I don't know," she said. "But he's always there."

Guy stroked his chin. Maybe she *was* right. Even if Mueller followed her just because he was infatuated with her, it was getting too damn risky. "All right," he said finally. "I'm going to have to find another safe house for the time being. No more parcels. But—"

He frowned and walked to the dirt-streaked window. If he didn't have to worry about compromising Château Bourdet as a safe house, it might provide the answer to his latest dilemma. It would be ideal: out in the countryside detection vans were less common and easier to spot, and hiding the long aerial—a dead giveaway in the city—wouldn't be difficult at all.

He ran his finger along the dirty sill. He hated exposing Michou to any further danger, but it was the perfect solution. He couldn't risk the alternative: if he got caught, there was no one else to organize the new *réseau* after he finished the sabotage mission in Bordeaux, not now, after the Germans had crashed the Autogiro circuit and arrested his contact in Paris.

Still, he hesitated. If he didn't propose it to her, what he'd been battling with himself about all these months would win out. The fight against the Nazis had to come before his love for her, before his desire for her safety. He had to ask.

"Well?" she said.

He turned around and crossed back to the bed. Bending over, he pulled the suitcase out and laid it on the bed.

"What's that?" she asked, getting up and standing behind him.

"A wireless." He opened the case.

Michou furrowed her brow. "Why do you have it?" she said. "I thought René was your radio operator."

"They arrested him right after the harvest," Guy said. "I didn't tell you. I was without a radio until last month, when the RAF dropped this one in. Only one thing—they didn't send an operator. Guess they're short of them back in London—too many getting caught."

"You know how to use one, then?"

He nodded. "It wasn't my specialty, but it was part of my training."

"So now it's all up to you?"

"Yes," he said. "But I thought—"

"You want me to help."

"If you're willing. It would be far less dangerous than keeping a safe house, especially with your German shadow constantly hanging about." He hoped it was the truth. He closed the case and sat on the bed next to it.

She closed her eyes and sighed. "All right," she said at last. "I'm willing."

"You know what the penalty is if you're caught with it?"

"Death," she said.

"Exactly," Guy said. He patted the bed. "Sit down. Are you sure you can handle this?"

Michou sat next to him. No! she wanted to shout at him. She wasn't sure. But she owed it to Papa and Marc to keep fighting. Guy had made her see that. He'd risked his life to come back to France. She owed it to him, too.

He put his finger under her chin and turned her face toward his. "Are you sure? I don't want you to do it unless you are." His voice was low, husky.

She stared at him. His expression showed deep concern—concern, but not love. She was still only a fellow resister to him, not a woman he desired.

Michou pulled away and thrust her chin out. "Of course. I doubt it's any more dangerous than hiding English fliers. There's the death penalty for that, too. Or had you forgotten?"

Guy's hand fell to his side. "No," he said softly. "That's not something I'd be likely to forget."

"I'm sorry," she said. "I didn't mean to be so sarcastic.

Maman says I sound terrible when I talk like that. Sometimes I can't help it, though. I still feel so angry. It's not your fault."

Guy squeezed her arm and then stood up. "I know," he said. "I won't need to bring it out for a while, but we still should decide how to get the damn thing up to your room. I think that's the best place for it. I can lay out the aerial on the roof of the main part of the château."

She bit her lip. If he kept the radio in her room, he'd have to come there to operate it. As much as she wanted to see him, it just wasn't safe. "Teach me to use it," she said. "You're already doing so much."

He raised his eyebrows. "You mean that?" he asked. It would be perfect—she could learn code while he was in Bordeaux, and be ready to operate the thing as soon as he brought it out.

She nodded, keeping her eyes on his.

He blew his breath out between his teeth and looked sideways. "It would sure help," he said finally. "That way we could meet here or in Saint-Émilion and I could pass you the messages."

He looked out the window. "Another thing," he said without turning around. "I know you're not going to like this. But I think you should be friendlier to Mueller. Lead him on a little, make him think you're interested in—"

"What?" Her mouth dropped open. He had to be crazy if he thought she'd encourage a German.

"No, I mean it. Listen," he said, coming back toward her. "Two good reasons. First, maybe you'll find out something useful if he talks to you. Second, if he thinks you care for him, he's far less likely to do anything about his suspicions."

She clamped her mouth shut. "Fine," she said. She'd do what he wanted, all right. "You want me to sleep with the swine, too?"

Guy's eyebrows pulled together. "That's not what I meant. You know that."

She stood and fumbled the kerchief back over her hair. She wasn't so sure she did know what he really wanted, and if she stayed any longer, she was going to lose her temper. "I have to go," she said, clipping her words short. "Meet me in Saint-Émilion tomorrow and we'll discuss my lessons for the wireless." She stalked to the door. "Perhaps you'd also like to include some pointers on how to be *friendly* to Germans."

She slammed the door and ran down the stairs. Damn him! Didn't he care about her at all? She jumped on her bicycle and pedaled as hard as she could down the street. Maybe he *was* right, but he could at least sound more reluctant about it. Everything was so matter-of-fact with him, the coldhearted bastard.

Panting, she rounded the corner in front of the church and pressed back on the brakes. She braced both feet on the ground and studied the old stone building for a minute. She hadn't been inside since Marc's death. But something about the church drew her today. It would be a good place to think, to cool off. She leaned her bicycle against the wall and went in.

The church smelled faintly acrid from the hundreds of votive candles burned there, and it was dark inside. It took her eyes a moment to adjust. She was alone.

She dabbed her fingers into the urn of holy water and crossed herself. "Father, Son, Holy Ghost," she murmured, kneeling briefly before walking down the aisle. About half-way to the altar, she turned into a row and sat down on the wooden pew. She still wasn't ready to offer a prayer—all she needed to do was sort her feelings out.

She closed her eyes and leaned back. Marc had been dead for two years, Papa for a year and a half. It seemed like a different lifetime now when she thought about them. Everything had been so easy when they were alive. She would have married Marc in this church, christened and baptized her children here. Now it only reminded her of the death of the three men she'd loved the most: Alain, then Marc, and finally Papa.

She ran her fingertips along the smooth, cool wood. Loving Guy had helped her forget some of the pain of losing them, but now her feeling for him was bringing her a new kind of grief. When she wanted him to hold her, all he did was smile and joke until she felt like shouting, "I'm not your little sister. Look at me. I'm a woman, and I love you."

She sighed. She'd never be able to say it, not while he wore that half-mocking expression he saved just for her. Sometimes when he thought she wasn't watching, the look on his face was different, sad and serious, almost as if he'd been acting in a play before and thought the curtain had fallen. It was those times that had given her hope.

Until today. She bit her lip. The same refrain kept coming back to her, repeating over and over in her head:

Be friendlier to Mueller.
Be friendlier to Mueller.
Be friendlier to Mueller.

Michou jumped up and ran out of the church. She'd show him. She'd be friendly, all right, so friendly no one would have any doubts, least of all Guy.

She was going to make Lieutenant Erich Mueller a very happy man. If it made Guy unhappy, so much the better. She was only doing what he'd asked.

27

Michou wiped the rain from her face and frowned. Her wet wool sweater stank like an old sheep. She stripped it off before she stepped into L'Hostellerie. Although it suited her mood perfectly, the sudden storm during the bicycle ride to Saint-Émilion had been a surprise. The sky had been clear and blue when she'd awakened; and even though the clouds had moved in while she was working in the vines, she'd only grabbed the sweater as an afterthought before she climbed on her bicycle and pedaled off. Good thing she had—otherwise she'd be soaked to the skin.

The sweater draped over her arm, Michou peered into the small room where Guy had arranged to meet her. He wasn't there yet. Good. At least she had time to comb her hair.

She waved to the barmaid and stepped into the rest room. Grimacing at her reflection in the mirror, she finger-combed her curls and dabbed on lipstick. She looked alive and healthy, anyway—the exercise and wind had brought some color into her cheeks, and her eyes gleamed.

Then she stuck her tongue out at the mirror. "Not going to make much difference anyway," she said aloud. A man who suggested she seduce another obviously wasn't interested in her, no matter how smooth her hair or how red her lips. She doubted he even knew what color her eyes were.

She shrugged. Fine. She'd made up her mind to play her part and play it she would. If Guy didn't like the way she went about it, so much the better.

When she returned to the bar, Guy was waiting at a

table. He nodded at her and stood up as she approached. "Michou!" he said, kissing both her cheeks. "How nice to see you again. It's been too long. Are you meeting someone?"

She stared at him. More games. Well, he must have a reason. She shook her head.

"Then please join me." He pulled out a chair and signaled the waitress.

Michou slid into the seat. "Are they serving wine today?" she asked. "I don't keep up with it."

"No." He smiled. "You don't have any reason to." He ordered two *citronnades* from the waitress and turned back to Michou. "Horrible way to ration wine, don't you think?"

She shrugged. "Doesn't hurt anyone to be sober for a day." She paused as the waitress set the glasses on the table. "Well?" she said, raising her eyebrows. "Did you bring it?"

"Not yet," he said. "I'm going to Bordeaux for a couple of months, and I'll need it while—"

"Bordeaux?" Her voice soared.

He frowned and shook his head.

She swallowed. "But why?" she asked.

"I have business there," he said.

"And you can't tell me what it is. I know. Sorry I asked." She drained the glass of sour *citronnade*. "Do you think it's still raining? I should be getting back."

"Sit still," he said. "You just got here. Besides, I have some things to give you."

"But I thought—"

He pushed a book across the table. "Inside, there's a piece of paper with the alphabet in Morse code. Can you learn it by the time I return?"

She picked up the book and thumbed through it. It smelled musty and old. *"Les Fleurs du Mal,"* she said. "How appropriate."

"It was René's. I've never cared much for Baudelaire. Too depressed—and depressing. Anyway, you could always practice putting the poems into code. He told me that was what he used to do."

She opened the book in the middle. "This ought to be amusing," she said. "'The Soul of the Wine' in dots and dashes."

Laughing, he glanced over her head toward the door. Then his smile froze on his face, and he reached over and closed the book.

"G-good day."

She twisted her head and looked up. Lieutenant Mueller stood in back of her, his cap tucked under his arm. She took a deep breath and forced a smile onto her lips. "Hello, Lieutenant," she said. Oh, God, she wasn't ready, but she'd flirt with him in front of Guy even if it choked her.

Guy rose and offered his hand. "Glad to see you again," he said.

"You, also," Lieutenant Mueller said, looking past him at Michou. "May I j-join you for a few moments?"

"Of course." Guy pulled out a chair for him, and they both sat down.

Lieutenant Mueller laid his cap down on the table and picked up the book. "Baudelaire," he said. He sounded surprised. "I wrote my dissertation on his poetry. May I ask which of you is reading it?"

Michou sighed and glanced at Guy. What if the lieutenant opened the book? How could she explain the paper full of the all-too-obvious markings? Even an idiot would be able to figure out what they were, and Lieutenant Mueller wasn't stupid. Guy shook his head slightly as the lieutenant turned to the table of contents.

Michou cleared her throat. "I am," she said.

Lieutenant Mueller glanced up, a pleased smile on his face. "You are?" he said. He ran his finger down the list of poems. "Here it is—'Hymn to Beauty.'" As he held the book up and turned to the place, a small sheet of paper slipped out from between the pages.

Michou held her breath, every muscle in her body rigid. Don't, *don't*, she prayed silently.

Lieutenant Mueller shoved the paper back into the book without looking at it. He glanced sideways at Michou and then read:

> Do you descend from heaven or rise from hell,
> O Beauty? Your gaze, infernal and divine,
> Showers indifferently both favor and crime,
> And one can for that compare you to wine.

He paused, staring at her, before he continued:

Your eyes hold the twilight and the dawn;
You scatter perfumes like a stormy night;
Your kisses are a drug and your mouth the urn
From which boys drink courage and heroes, fright.

Mueller closed the book and returned it to the table. "There are s-several more stanzas, but I won't bore you with them. I realize not everyone shares my enthusiasm for Baudelaire, but I am so happy you do."

Guy raised his eyebrow. "The poor man sounds awfully confused to me," he said.

Lieutenant Mueller sighed.

Her cheeks burning, Michou fixed her eyes on the book, resisting the impulse to snatch it up. She wasn't quite sure what the poem meant, but the anguish in Lieutenant Mueller's voice had been impossible to misinterpret. She raised her head and found herself looking directly into his intense blue eyes. She hurriedly shifted her gaze toward Guy.

A half smile curving the corners of his lips, Guy raised his eyebrows, and his face took on the mocking expression she hated so much. "What do you think, Michou?" he asked, his voice serious. "Did you enjoy the poem?"

She narrowed her eyes at him. "Yes," she said. She turned to Lieutenant Mueller and smiled. "Thank you. You read our language beautifully."

"Thank *you*," he said. "The ultimate compliment." He stood up, his cap in his hand. "I will not intrude on you any longer. *Au revoir*." He shook Guy's hand and nodded at Michou before he strode to the bar.

Michou rested her cheek on her hand and watched until he sat down. She turned back to Guy. "Well," she said, "was I *friendly* enough for you?"

Erich finished tying the new vine shoot to the wire and straightened. Sweat prickled his back, and he pushed his hair off his damp forehead. It was a good thing he'd dressed in mufti today. His uniform would have been unbearable in the hot spring sun. Besides, as pleasant as Michou had been lately, she seemed even warmer when he was out of uniform.

He supposed it was only natural; she loved France as much as he loved Germany. He certainly wouldn't like French soldiers living in his home.

He pulled the clippers from his pocket and moved to the next plant. It felt good to be working in a vineyard again after so many years spent in dusty libraries and cold lecture halls. Vater had been right—he should have come home during the summers. But somehow he couldn't. He sighed. Maybe he'd been afraid he'd never return to the university.

After he finished cutting away the weakest shoots, he glanced over his shoulder. Hands on her hips, Michou was watching him from the next row. When she saw him looking at her, she smiled.

"Hungry?" she asked. "I brought a little picnic." She nodded toward a basket at the end of the row.

"What an excellent idea," he said. He put the clippers back in his pocket and walked toward her. "Why don't we eat right here, in the middle of the vines?"

Michou laughed. "All right," she said as she retrieved the basket. "But I didn't bring anything to sit on."

"The soil that grows such wonderful grapes is good enough for me." Erich lowered himself to the ground and dug his fingers into the sandy dirt. "Amazing, isn't it, how the vines flourish where nothing else will."

She sat down across from him and removed an unlabeled bottle of red wine, two stubby glasses, and a round loaf of dark bread from the basket. "Papa always said the harder the vine had to work, the more flavor each grape would have." Bending her head, her thick curls obscuring her face, she inserted the corkscrew and tugged.

Erich stiffened, sitting motionless as she extracted the cork. Did she still think him personally responsible for her father's death because he was German? This was the first time she'd ever mentioned him. *Mein Gott,* he hoped it wouldn't destroy the pleasant mood.

She poured a glass of wine and handed it to him. Her smile was gone, but there were no traces of bitterness in her expression. "He also said that the best people were like the vines, sending down deep roots, growing even stronger when they had to struggle." She paused, looking toward the château. "Like Mémé Laure."

"Like you," Erich said. "Your father was a wise man."
He held out his glass. "To your papa."

She clicked her glass against his and looked directly at
him with her incredible violet eyes. "And to yours," she said.

Narrowing her eyes at Philippe, Michou jumped up from
the sofa. She'd be damned if she sat and listened to his
lecture any longer. Why did he always think he knew everything? "Mind your own business," she shouted at him.
"Why shouldn't I let him help me? I don't get any from you."

Philippe glared back at her. "That's not what I was
talking about," he said. "Let him help you all he wants. Fine.
But you don't have to sit around drinking wine with him—not
where everyone can see. I don't want my friends telling me
my sister's making up to a Nazi."

Michou crossed her arms tightly against her chest and
turned toward the fireplace. "So that's all you're worried
about—what your friends will think." She spun to face him,
her hands on her hips. "Well, I don't give a damn what you *or*
your friends think about me. I have my reasons. And I don't
want to talk about them."

She strode to the narrow window at the end of the salon
and rested her forehead against the cool glass. What was
wrong with her? It was only natural for Philippe to be upset
with her for picnicking in the middle of the vineyard with
Erich. A month ago she'd have said the same things he had.

She closed her eyes. She knew why she was being so
defensive, but she hated to acknowledge it, even to herself.
She had actually enjoyed herself today. Erich hadn't been
wearing his uniform, and when he was in civilian clothes, she
sometimes found herself forgetting he was a Nazi. Then she'd
remember with a jolt and feel guilty.

She sighed and turned back to Philippe. Even though
she couldn't tell him what was going on, she could at least
understand his concern. After all, he'd just turned eighteen.
She'd been even worse at that age, always so sure she knew
exactly what was right. And wrong. Now, the difference
sometimes seemed fuzzier. Things weren't always like wines,
either red or white.

Michou wrinkled her nose and almost smiled, imagining
a world where all moral issues became like *vin rosé*. "Sorry I

yelled at you," she said. "I do like Erich. He's different from the others." That at least was true, thank God. She'd always been a poor liar and a bad actress.

"I imagine that's the same thing Sylvie says about her German lover," Philippe said.

Michou clamped her jaw. "Don't push me," she hissed. "There are some things you just don't understand."

"I can understand what you're doing with that—"

The door clicked softly, and Maman stuck her head into the room. "Did I interrupt something?" she asked.

Michou shook her head and sat back down on the sofa, resting her chin on her hand.

"You two have been fighting again." Maman came into the salon and let the door close behind her. "I wish you wouldn't."

"I'm sorry, Maman," Michou said. She held out her hands. There was no point in explaining.

"Well, I'm not!" Philippe glowered at Michou before he ran from the room, slamming the door after him.

"Oh, dear." Maman sighed. "This isn't starting out well at all. I'd hoped—" She paused. "I mean—I wanted to explain—"

Michou frowned. "Explain what?"

Maman took a deep breath. "I think I'm falling in love with Henri," she said.

28

Guy held his breath. Except for the scratch of the crickets and the guard's low whistle, the night was quiet, so quiet that even his own heartbeat seemed noisy by contrast. It didn't matter that he had been watching the factory exactly the same way every night for the last week. Tonight he was going to do more than watch.

The whistle faded as the guard rounded the corner. Guy exhaled slowly. He glanced at his watch. The radium dial glowed in the dark: 2:17. Good. If the guard followed his regular pattern, that gave Guy at least half an hour to set the charges and get the hell out.

He climbed up the gate, the hard wire cutting into his palms. As he swung over the top, the buzz inside his head increased until the only sound that pierced it was the rasp of the guard's off-key rendition of "Lili Marlene."

Suddenly the whistling stopped. Quick footsteps crackled toward him. Guy flattened himself on the ground in front of the gate and shoved his face into the oily dirt. His stomach clenched into a fist. Bloody hell. He must have made too much noise.

A door slammed, and he raised his head slowly. A thin blade of light sliced across the gravel. Two men stepped into it, briefly illuminated before the door behind them closed. Guy frowned. This wasn't right. There wasn't supposed to be a change until six o'clock, right before the workers arrived. Slowly, silently, he drew his knife from his pocket.

The taller shadow laughed and rested his arm on the other's shoulder. "So what is it this time, Dieter?" he asked. "Are you sneaking in or is she sneaking out?"

Dieter chuckled. "She's leaving the door unlocked." He held out his hand. "Thanks again."

The tall soldier shook his hand. "Just hope her bed doesn't creak too much," he said.

Dieter stepped back and saluted. The other guard turned on his heel and walked briskly around the corner of the factory.

Whistling loudly and enthusiastically, Dieter headed toward the gate.

Guy gritted his teeth and waited, his mouth dry, every muscle tense, blood roaring in his ears. At the same moment the German spotted him, Guy flung himself up. He threw one arm around the guard's face, snapped his head back, and pushed the knife blade against his throat. An electric shock jolted Guy's elbow. Dieter's body jerked, and he gurgled.

Warm blood spilled over Guy's hand. He tossed the knife into his pack and wiped his hand in the damp grass before he dragged the limp body to the fence and dropped it. Crouching beside the dead German, he tried to listen for the new guard, but thunder cracked inside his skull.

He shook his head. Be still, still. He had to go now, before the new sentry finished his round. He put on the dead German's cap and walked to the door. If he was unlucky enough to attract the guard's attention, perhaps he'd be mistaken for his friend.

Guy reached the door and paused. Nothing. Carefully, he opened it and eased inside. It was dark and empty. His guess had been right. Apparently the Germans didn't expect any real problems at the propeller factory. Only one guard patrolled the perimeter, and his replacement wasn't due for hours.

Guy shrugged his pack off his shoulder and opened it. The strong almond fumes of the plastic explosive burned his eyes as he pulled out the charges he'd prepared that morning. Working quickly despite the dark and his shaking hands, he inserted the time pencils. From the moment he squeezed their tops and released the acid that set off the charge, he would have fifteen minutes to get away from the area.

He unclipped his flashlight from his belt and swiveled the beam around the cavernlike interior. He didn't know much about making propellers, but it seemed smartest to blow up the most intricate-looking pieces of machinery.

After he attached the first lump of PE to a large machine, he checked his watch again: 2:31. He pinched the tube and placed the other four charges. If they all went off, this place wouldn't be turning out propellers for German airplanes for a long time. Fewer airplanes, fewer bombs dropped, fewer dead children.

He cracked open the door and peered out. The courtyard was clear. He stepped out and, crouching low, ran to the gate. When he reached the dead Nazi, he tossed the cap down beside him.

Guy hoisted the pack onto his shoulders and scaled the gate. He landed with a soft thud on the other side, wincing as pain streaked up his still-weak ankle. Hobbling to the bicycle he'd left leaning against a tree, he cursed silently.

After he'd ridden a couple of blocks, Guy stopped and dragged the bicycle behind a large hedge. He knew it was foolish, but he had to be sure the charges went off. He hunched down beside the bicycle and waited. Gradually, his breathing slowed.

He closed his eyes and leaned his head against the fender. His head pounded, his ankle throbbed, and his stomach rolled. He ground his teeth to keep them from chattering.

He opened his eyes and looked at his watch: 2:45. Everything was quiet. Even the crickets had stopped chirping. It was as if the whole city were listening, waiting—

A loud blast interrupted the silence, followed quickly by another, then another. Five altogether. Good—they'd all gone off. The place would be a shambles.

He peered around the hedge. The street was still empty. The room he'd rented was only a few blocks away. Now all he had to do was get there before German patrols came to investigate.

He jumped on the bicycle and pedaled rapidly down the deserted street, keeping close to the hedges. If he got stopped now, it would all be over. Not only was he breaking the eleven o'clock curfew, but one sniff inside his knapsack and—

He ripped the pack off his shoulder with one hand and

flung it into a bush. The bloody knife was still inside, too. If he'd been using his head, he'd have left it back at the factory. Goddamn, he was dumb. What had he been thinking of?

The bicycle wobbled, and Guy gripped the handlebars tightly with both hands. Only one more block to go. The cold wind whipped against his face as he stood and pumped the pedals. He was going to make it. For the first time since he'd received his orders, he allowed himself to think that the mission was going to be completely successful. No more nightmares about the charges exploding in his hands or not exploding at all or ten Jerries arresting him for curfew violation before he even got to the factory.

Suddenly the street vibrated with the low whirr of a speeding car. Headlights swung toward him as he turned into the alley leading to the back entrance of the rooming house. He pulled behind a large shrub and flung himself off the bicycle. Had they seen him? He tried to swallow but couldn't, and his mouth puckered with the coppery taste of fear.

The car raced down the street, and Guy eased up slowly. He stared at the vanishing taillights for a minute before he pushed his bicycle up to the back steps. He forced himself to take slow, deep breaths as he locked the bicycle and climbed the stairs to the back door.

His fingers stiff, he fumbled in his pocket for the key. Quietly, he inserted it and opened the door, peering into the dingy, urine-stinking hallway before stepping in and pulling the door shut with a soft click.

A loud snore erupted from the room next to his. Guy started and pressed himself against the wall. The snore subsided, and Guy let his breath out in a rush. Jesus, he was jumpy.

He edged down the hall and into his room. He'd really done it. He'd blown up the factory, and he was still alive. He closed his eyes and leaned against the door for a few minutes, just listening to the sound of his own breathing.

He pushed himself away from the door and eased the light switch on, twitching at the loud click. Wincing at every creak of the wooden floor, he crept to the bureau and poured water from the pitcher into the dirty glass. He gulped a mouthful, swirled it around, and spat it back into the glass. He still couldn't swallow.

He set the glass down and peered into the dusty mirror propped against the wall. Jesus Christ! His forehead was streaked with blood, the German's blood. He jerked his hand up. Dried blood and pieces of grass clung to it. If he'd been stopped—

He splashed water into the basin, leaned over it, and rinsed his face. Then he scrubbed his hands and wiped them against his shirt as he inspected his face again in the mirror. The blood was gone, but under the tan his skin was almost blue and his lips were pale and chapped. He looked as if he'd been on a three-day drunk.

Shuddering, he dumped the filthy water from the basin back into the pitcher. First thing in the morning, he'd have to throw it out. He just wasn't up to it now. All he wanted to do was lie down, try to sleep, if his body would let him.

He stripped his clothes off and threw them in a heap on the room's only chair. Good God, what if they had blood on them, too? He grabbed them up and stuffed them under the mattress before he turned off the light and slid into bed.

He pulled the thin covers up to his chin. "Stupid son of a bitch," he murmured. He'd always prided himself on his sangfroid, his levelheadedness, his absolute control under pressure. What had happened to him tonight? He may have blown up the machines, but he'd made too many mistakes.

He rolled onto his side, and the springs squeaked. The Germans had joked about a creaky bed, then two minutes later one of them was dead. Guy had never killed a man before. It had shaken him at the time, but in a way, it was worse now that it was over. Where was the satisfaction he'd imagined he'd feel afterward? All he felt now was horror. Disgust. Sadness.

He squeezed his eyes shut. If he hadn't killed the German, the German would have killed him. Or arrested him, taken him to the Gestapo and their tortures. He might have talked, given up people he cared about, maybe even someone he loved.

He shook his head. Christ, he was getting soft. He hadn't started this bloody war. His four-year-old daughter lay buried in a tiny coffin because of a German bomb, her body as lifeless as the rag doll she'd been clutching when he'd clawed her out from under the bricks and rubble. He'd kept the doll, but he didn't need it to remind him of what he'd lost. All he had to do was think of her lively face, her joyous laugh, the way she entwined her arms around his neck, her fresh baby smell when she hugged him.

And Michou, her father executed by a Nazi firing squad. No, he just couldn't justify his reaction to killing a German. The man had been a soldier, and now he was dead. If Dieter had killed him tonight, Michou would never have known he loved her.

He rolled over onto his stomach and buried his face in the pillow. He'd made himself a promise if he survived tonight, and by God, he was going to keep it. No more pretending—not to himself, not to Michou. He loved her, he wanted her, and he hoped she wanted him. He'd do what the firm ordered, live in filthy, smelly places, risk his life to send wireless messages or blow up factories. But he couldn't go on denying what he felt for Michou.

Guy flopped over onto his back again. Why had he gone on this long? Forcing himself not to think about her took more energy than allowing himself to love her. The next time he saw her, he'd tell her.

He snorted. The next time. How confident he was now that the mission was over and he was lying in his bed, safe and alone. Alone.

"Alone." He whispered the word.

He was tired of being alone. Maybe he just didn't have the strength to do it all by himself after all. It had never been easy for him to admit he needed anything. But he was admitting it now. He needed Michou.

29

Lucien smiled as he helped Jacques unload the bags of powdered sulfur from the trunk of the black Mercedes. Karl had come through again for him, after all. Perhaps he was feeling guilty—ever since that disastrous dinner party in April, Karl had been a bit distant, and it had been over a month since they'd seen each other.

Lucien tossed another foul-smelling bag onto the pile. Whatever the reason, he didn't care. He'd be the only one in Saint-Émilion who didn't have to worry about mold on the vines this year.

After Jacques removed the last bag, Lucien slammed the trunk lid shut. "Please tell Major Stecher how much I appreciate this," he said to the young soldier behind the wheel. "But wait. Let me write a note." He fumbled through his pockets and found an old wine label. "Do you have a pen?"

"Ja." The driver nodded, unbuttoned the flap on his breast pocket, and pulled out a pen. He smiled as he handed it to Lucien.

Lucien quickly scrawled his thanks and an invitation for dinner on the back of the label. He was down to his last tank of gas, almost out of cigars, and in another month or so he'd need more chemicals for the vineyards. It wouldn't do to let Karl's infatuation fade too much, no matter what a relief it had been not having to put up with him during the last month.

He folded the note and gave it and the pen to the soldier. *"Danke,"* he said.

"Bitte." The soldier started the car and headed down the drive. He pulled to the side of the narrow lane to allow

another staff car to squeeze past, waved, then turned onto the main road.

When he recognized the car, Lucien frowned. What did Mueller want now? Ever since Lucien had made that pass at him, the bastard's visits only meant trouble. Mueller seemed to have it in for him.

Approaching the car, Lucien forced what he hoped was a pleasant expression onto his face. "Good day," he said, and opened the door for Mueller. "It's so nice to see you again."

Mueller nodded and stepped out of the car. "Hello." He glanced at the pile of bags and raised his eyebrows. "Sulfur?" he asked, wrinkling his nose. "Quite difficult to procure, isn't it?"

Not if you know the right people, Lucien thought. He shrugged. "Oh?" he said. "I had no idea." He jerked his head at Jacques. "Put it in the barn."

Jacques shrugged, hefted a bag to his shoulders, and shuffled off.

Mueller stared at Lucien for a moment. Finally, he reached back into the car and scooped some papers off the seat. "Bad news, I'm afraid. We're going to need forty barrels of wine. The truck will be here later this afternoon to pick it up." He shuffled through the papers and extracted one. "You need to sign this," handing the requisition and a pen to Lucien.

Forty barrels! *Merde*. Lucien clamped his mouth shut and took the paper from Mueller. He'd bet anything Château Bourdet didn't have to give up forty barrels. He was probably contributing Michou's share as well as his own. He'd heard the local gossip about the two of them.

Lucien put the requisition on the hood of the car and scribbled his signature. "Here you go," he said, returning the paper and pen. "Glad to help." He smiled.

Mueller nodded and got back into the car.

Lucien closed the door and leaned in the open window. He didn't want Mueller to think he was annoyed. As long as the son of a bitch was in charge, it was best to stay friendly. "I'm having several friends to dinner Saturday night," he said. "May I count on you as well?"

Mueller's face remained impassive. "I'm sorry," he said. "I've already got plans for that evening."

"Perhaps some other time, then," Lucien said, straightening.

"Most certainly," Mueller said. He leaned forward. "All right," he said to the driver.

Lucien let his smile fade and narrowed his eyes as the car drove away. He'd managed to scare Fournier off easily enough—a little tampering with that old *gazogène,* and boom. Too bad Fournier hadn't been in the car at the time. At least, though, he hadn't been around in a while.

Pulling the silver corkscrew from his pocket, Lucien snarled. Now he had another one to worry about. He flipped the blade open and scraped under his fingernails. If what he'd been hearing was true, he'd bet Mueller's plans for Saturday night included Michou. He hoped she wasn't falling for the German bastard. That wouldn't do.

He gritted his teeth and thumbed the blade shut. That wouldn't do at all.

The car turned into the drive leading to Château Bourdet, and Erich sighed. The setting sun warmed the white stones of the château into a lovely pink, and the towers at either end stood like friendly giants guarding the princess's castle. He leaned his head against the back of the seat. *Mein Gott,* what a day it had been. It felt good to be back home.

Home. He snorted. He was an enemy soldier billeted on an unwilling French family. Nothing was going to change that, not even Michou's recent friendliness. Only a fool would expect anything different.

Still, it was a relief to be here after the day's unpleasant business. He stretched and got out of the car. "You go ahead," he told Corporal Kaufmann. "I'm going for a stroll first."

"Yes, sir," Kaufmann said. He saluted and trotted up the stairs.

Erich waited until the large doors slammed shut and then ambled toward the lower vineyards. For the first time that day, he could think about Michou without interruption, without reminders of all the reasons she had to hate him. When he helped her in the vineyards, he was simply Erich and she was the woman with whom he was in love.

Frowning, he passed his hand over the new leaves. That

was the problem. He was in love with her, but she still gave no sign of any feeling deeper than friendship. He'd been pleased enough with that at the beginning, but now he wanted more.

A soft thud came from the vat room, and he paused at the end of the row. Was she at work so late? He smiled as he walked toward the squat building. Then he stopped short. What if she wasn't alone, if she was doing something he shouldn't know about—

His smile faded, and he turned away. It was a chance he didn't want to risk, a choice he wasn't ready to make.

A scream echoed from the *cuvier*.

Erich spun around.

Another scream, this one cut off in the middle.

He sprinted toward the vat room, his heart racing, and threw open the door.

"Let go of me!" The low, angry voice hissed from the back of the room.

Erich stalked past the fermenting vats. "Michou?" he called. "Is that you?"

"Erich! Oh, thank God." Michou burst out of the *chai*. Her hair sprang out wildly from beneath her scarf, and her blouse was unbuttoned. Tears streaked down her dusty cheeks. She ran to him and threw her arms around him.

Lucien strolled behind her, his lips twisted into a smug smile. "Lieutenant Mueller," he said, enunciating carefully in the manner of a drunk who wants to sound sober. "We meet again. Perhaps you've some of those requisition papers for Michou to sign as well? I was just telling her about them." Crossing his arms, he lounged against the doorway.

Erich tightened his jaw and his grip on Michou. "I'm sure she informed you, then, that she has already done so." He raised his eyebrows and looked down at her.

Michou pulled away and glared at Lucien. "Get out," she said. "I want you to leave. Now."

Lucien shrugged. "Fine," he said, uncrossing his arms and straightening. "I'm going." He edged past, pausing in front of Michou. He took her chin in his hand. "Sorry if I upset you."

She jerked away and stepped closer to Erich.

Lucien turned to Erich and offered his hand. "Hope to see you again soon," he said.

Erich stared at his hand for a second before he shook it briefly. "Good-bye," he said. He turned back to Michou after Lucien had disappeared behind the large vats.

"Are you all right?" he asked.

She nodded, buttoning her blouse with shaky fingers.

"Did he attack you?"

She swallowed and nodded again.

"Bastard! I'd like to—"

Michou grabbed his arm. "Don't," she said. "He didn't hurt me this time."

"You mean he's done this before?"

"Yes."

"He'll never do it again. I promise you." Erich stared into her eyes before he pulled her close. "I promise you," he whispered, his lips brushing her soft, jasmine-scented hair.

Michou relaxed against Erich's chest. If he hadn't come looking for her, Lucien would have forced a lot more on her than one disgusting, slobbery kiss. She shuddered, remembering the glassy, insane stare of his pale blue eyes when he'd found her working alone in the *chai*, his drunken, incoherent mutterings about barrels of wine and requisitions while he pawed her, the sour, vile smell of his breath as he bit at her lips.

Erich hugged her closer. "It's all right," he murmured.

"Thank you," she said, looking up at him.

His eyes widened and darkened, and he bent his head toward her.

She ducked her head and pulled away. As much as she liked him, she just wasn't ready. Not yet. "I have to go," she said.

His eyebrows drew together, and his face stiffened. He stepped back and nodded. "Of course," he said. "But let me go out first. I want to make certain he's gone."

"If you want," she said. "But I'm sure there's nothing to worry about now."

"Nevertheless—" Erich shrugged and headed for the door.

Michou followed him outside. "See," she said, pointing

to a figure disappearing around the château. "I've known Lucien since we were children. He's a bully and a coward."

She turned to him and rested her hand on his arm. "But be careful," she said. "He always gets even."

Erich emitted a short, humorless chuckle. "I'm not worried. He's quite aware that the German army does not appreciate acts of revenge on its soldiers."

She jerked her hand away as if he had suddenly turned into a spider and walked quickly toward the tower. More and more often she found herself forgetting what Erich was. A German soldier, an enemy. And what she was. A Frenchwoman, leading him on, using him.

Using him. She couldn't let him think she was angry with him. When she reached the tower, she turned and waved.

He stood silhouetted against the *chai,* his shoulders slumped. He lifted his hand.

"Good night," she called. "And thanks again."

His hand dropped. *"De rien,* mademoiselle," he said. He pivoted and headed toward the vineyard.

Shaking her head, Michou plodded up the stairs to her bedroom. She still hated the whole business, but for different reasons than she had at the beginning. She'd been clear then about what she was doing. Now her own attraction to Erich was getting in the way. If Guy didn't come back soon, she might even—

To push the thought out of her mind, she raced up the last steps, threw open her door, and flopped onto her bed. She didn't want to hurt Erich by leading him on. He was more than a perfect Aryan dressed in a Nazi uniform. He was sensitive, thoughtful, warm.

She jerked upright. *Mon Dieu.* It wasn't a game any longer, a way to annoy Guy. She really cared about Erich.

And it was Guy's fault. Why the hell couldn't *he* treat her as everyone else did, with the same mixture of adoration and protectiveness? He'd just told her to cultivate Erich and then he'd left.

She jumped up and paced to the bureau. She was crazy. Just a few months ago she'd yelled at Guy for treating her like a child. She'd always hated being handled as if she were fragile. Now she was complaining because Guy accepted her as an equal. What did she really want?

Michou stalked to the window and pressed her forehead against the cool glass and sighed. Erich stood below in the middle of the vineyard, his back to the château. Could she be falling in love with him, too?

She crossed her arms against her chest and hunched forward. But how could she love a German? And how could any woman love two men at the same time?

30

Crouched in front of the red rosebush, Catherine rocked back on her heels, bracing herself with one hand on the freshly worked dirt behind her. She pushed up her wide-brimmed straw hat and wiped her damp forehead with the back of her other hand. "Damn weather," she mumbled. "Pretty soon there won't be any leaves at all."

Mémé Laure looked over her glasses. "What are you muttering about over there?" she asked, leaning forward in her chair and untangling the ball of yarn at her feet.

Catherine stood up and stretched. "My roses have blackspot and mildew." She snapped a leaf off and held it out. "See? It's the weather. The warm days and cold nights. The only way to keep it from spreading is to pick off every bad leaf."

"Or dust with sulfur." Mémé Laure resumed crocheting. "But Michou says she can't get any even for the vines."

Catherine continued plucking the blighted leaves. "I guess my roses are pretty unimportant, really. Maybe I should just dig the rest of them up and plant more turnips. What do you think?" She turned to Mémé Laure.

Mémé Laure didn't look up. "Why don't you tell me what's really bothering you?"

Shaking her head, Catherine dropped the dead leaves into the bucket at her feet. "How long has it been since we've seen Guy?"

Mémé Laure's fingers paused. "A couple of months?" She shrugged. "Maybe longer?"

Catherine nodded. "Has Michou said anything to you?"

"About Guy? No. I've been wondering what—"

"Happened?" Catherine picked another leaf and crumbled it between her fingers. "I thought she might have talked to you about it. I don't know what's going on, either."

"She hasn't seemed too unhappy." Mémé Laure tugged at the yarn. "She talks quite a lot about that Lieutenant Mueller, how interested he is in the vineyards, how much he helps her."

Catherine grabbed the trowel and moved to the next rosebush. "That's what I mean," she said. "Six months ago she refused to speak to a German. Now Philippe says—" She scraped the trowel through the dirt.

"I know it's pointless to tell you not to worry," Mémé Laure said, "but I'm going to tell you anyway. Don't worry about her. She's learning not to hate."

Catherine sighed. "You're probably right," she said, laying down the trowel. "It's just that she seems so volatile, so happy one day, so miserable the next."

"Now, Catherine, use your head," Mémé Laure said. "Don't you remember when you first met Alexandre?" She closed her eyes and paused, rocking back and forth. When she spoke, her voice sounded thin and far away. "I'll never forget how it was with Patrick. I'd loved him since I was a child. But he was so much older it didn't seem possible. Then I met Robert and married him. I loved him, too. After he died and Patrick started coming around, I was terribly confused."

She opened her eyes and stared at Catherine. "Certainly, you can understand what Michou is feeling, *n'est-ce pas?*" she said.

Catherine's cheeks warmed as she snipped off a spent bloom. Several petals floated to the ground, and she stooped to gather them. "Of course. But he's German. I'm afraid of the trouble she's going to make for herself." She threw the petals into the pail.

Mémé Laure nodded slowly. "That worries me, too. But there's nothing we can do."

"I guess you're right," Catherine said. "I only hope Guy comes back again before it's too late." She bent over the bush and stripped the yellowed leaves from the canes. Her heart ached for her impulsive daughter. It had always been this way—Michou throwing herself into one violent emotion after another, ignoring Catherine's advice to go slowly, to think before she plunged. Finally, Catherine had given up, sent Michou to live with Mère and Père, hoping her mother's sternness would help curb her daughter's fiery temperament.

She tossed the musty-smelling leaves into the bucket. It hadn't worked. Opposition only made Michou more willful, more determined. Alexandre had been right. She should have listened to him. He and Mémé Laure had always understood Michou better than she had. Alain had been the only one of her children like her.

She frowned as she moved to the next bush. This time she'd do what Mémé Laure said. Michou was almost twenty-two, old enough to take care of herself. It would be hard, but she wouldn't interfere. And she'd tell Philippe to leave his sister alone. Not that it would do much good. He didn't listen to her any more than Michou did.

She sighed. If only Alexandre were here—

She slashed at the faded blossoms. Well, he wasn't. She had to handle it by herself. Even if she'd let things go further with Henri, he wouldn't be able to help, either. He had enough problems with his own children.

Grimacing at the irony, Catherine finished grooming the bush, then put the clippers in her pocket. Here she was pledging not to interfere in her children's affairs while they thought they had every right to determine hers. Michou had been silent and withdrawn for weeks after she'd told her about Henri, and Philippe had exploded. She'd ended up telling Henri she didn't want to see him so often, wasn't sure she was ready so soon after Alexandre's death.

Mémé Laure cleared her throat. Catherine looked up, scraping her hand against a thorn.

Henri stood in the doorway. "I hope I'm not interrupting," he said. "I was just checking on Lucien and thought I'd stop by." He coughed. "Don't usually have enough gas to get out here as often as I'd like."

Mémé Laure nodded toward the chair next to her. "It's been a long time, Henri. Sit down," she said.

Catherine pretended to inspect the scratch on her hand. "Yes, do," she echoed. She gripped the bucket handle in her other hand.

"Are you all right, Catherine?" Henri asked. He crossed toward her.

"Yes, I'm fine," she said. The words came out more curtly than she'd intended. She made herself smile up at him. "My favorite pet here just clawed me. She patted the rose-bush. "I take such good care of him, and look how he repays me." She held out her hand.

Henri took her hand and kissed it. "Children and rose-bushes," he said. "Perennial ingrates." His laugh was harsh. "My daughter presents me with an illegitimate grandson, and my son turns Château LeClair-Figeac into a den of iniquity." He shook his head. "The place was a mess. Cigar butts, empty bottles everywhere. Wish I hadn't bothered to stop there." He released her hand. "It was just an excuse for driving out to see you, anyway."

Mémé Laure looked first at Catherine, then at Henri. She crammed her crocheting back into the basket and pushed herself out of the chair. "I'm sorry to take my leave so soon, Henri, but it's time for my nap," she said. She shuffled to the door, winking at Catherine before she disappeared.

Henri took the bucket out of Catherine's hand and set it down. "Come, sit with me," he said.

She rested her hand on his arm. "Do you think this is wise?" she asked.

He pulled her toward the chair. "You can't do this to me," he said. "It isn't fair. Perhaps you're right—it's too soon for what was happening. But you can't deny me your friend-ship—not now, not after all these years."

"I've been lonely," she said. She sat down.

Henri lowered himself into the chair next to hers. "So have I," he said. "We both miss Alexandre."

She raised her head and looked into his blue eyes. "I've missed you, too," she said.

"That's far enough, Daniel," Berthe called. She rose from the park bench, ready to sprint if he didn't turn around and come back. As pleasant as the tree-shaded park was on a warm June day, it was hard for her to feel comfortable there unless Daniel was safely confined to his carriage. The river was too close, a reminder always of her younger brother's death. She sighed when her son waved his arms wildly and fell on his rear.

"He looks like a little windmill," Michou said. She patted the bench. "Sit down and relax. He couldn't possibly make it to the river from here."

Keeping her eyes on Daniel, Berthe slowly lowered herself back onto the hard slats. Michou always seemed to know what she was thinking. Still, what she had to tell her today wasn't going to be easy. Not a bit easy. She'd argued with herself for weeks about it. Would it be better to let her know what everyone was saying about her, or should she just keep it to herself? Finally, she'd decided it was her duty as a friend to tell her.

Berthe glanced sideways at Michou. She was so beautiful, it was no wonder both Lucien and that German lieutenant were in love with her. If only Lucien knew how to treat her. Berthe shook her head. She'd never been able to understand why Lucien antagonized Michou so, when it was obvious how he idolized her. His pretended indifference might fool others, but she'd known better since the day she found the little box in his room while she was putting away his laundry. She hadn't been able to resist the temptation; and when she opened it, inside she found dozens of photographs of Michou, some of her missing letters, a few pale blond hairs, even a pair of lacy underpants. It was like a miniature shrine. Gabrielle had never really had a chance.

Daniel howled, and Michou jumped up. "You rest," she said. "I'll get him this time." She ran to the baby and scooped him up.

Berthe stood. "Put him in the carriage," she said. "He'll be happy as long as we're walking. If we get lucky, he might even fall asleep." She pushed the carriage toward them. Maybe it would be easier to tell her if they were moving, if she didn't have to be worried about Daniel every minute.

Michou set Daniel on top of the blankets and turned to Berthe. "Are you sure?" she said. "I don't want you to tire yourself. You've lost so much weight since Daniel was born, I'm starting to get concerned. Have you been sick again?"

"I'm fine," Berthe said. She pushed the carriage across

the grass toward the path. "It's just the rationing and all the exercise I get running after Daniel."

Michou frowned as she fell into step beside Berthe. "I want you to bring him out to the château for a day as soon as he's weaned. Then go do something by yourself. I'd love to watch him, and you need a chance to rest."

"I couldn't do that," Berthe said. "He'd wear you out in an hour."

"That's what I mean—don't be such a martyr." Her lips turned up in a broad smile. "Besides, after he finishes me off, I can turn him over to Maman."

Berthe sighed. "Maybe," she said as the carriage jolted onto the gravel path running alongside the river. She narrowed her eyes as she saw people coming toward them. She hoped they were strangers, in town for the outdoor market.

The figures grew more distinct as they approached, and when Berthe recognized two of her former schoolmates, she gripped the carriage handle more tightly. Maybe they wouldn't recognize Michou. After all, it had been seven years since Catherine had sent her off to school in Paris. She'd come back a quieter girl, one who preferred to spend most of her time with Marc or at Château Bourdet helping her father.

Berthe's stomach churned, and she pressed her lips together. Why risk it? The path forked ahead. She steered the carriage toward the right.

"Isn't that Sophie up there?" Michou asked. "And Caroline?"

Berthe shrugged. "Can't see that far without my glasses," she said. "I left them at home." She wiped one damp hand on her skirt, then the other.

"If you'd wear them, you wouldn't be forgetting them all the time." Michou laughed.

Berthe swallowed hard as the chattering foursome ahead stopped in the middle of the path and stared at them. Caroline whispered something to Sophie and tugged at her boyfriend's arm. The group moved off the path and cut across the grass, first one, then another glancing back.

Berthe's breath escaped in a huge sigh, and she realized she'd been holding it in. She peeked at Michou. Except for two small grooves between her eyebrows, her face was expressionless. Her smile had disappeared.

"Must have been someone else," Michou said. She grabbed the carriage handle. "Here. Let me push for a while."

Berthe dropped her hands as the carriage surged forward. Now. She should tell her now. "Mich—"

"Look." Michou interrupted, pointing to a tall woman walking awkwardly toward them. "There's Gabrielle. I haven't seen her for so long." She waved. "How far along is she now? Five or six months? She's still so skinny. It hardly shows at all yet."

Berthe squinted. "Are you sure it's her? She's not waving back." Grimacing, she wiped both hands on her skirt. Please, let it be someone else, she prayed. Not Gabrielle. When Gabrielle was angry, she just blurted out whatever she was thinking. And she had been horrid about Michou the last time Berthe had seen her.

"Isn't it funny?" Michou said. She stopped the carriage beside a bench under a large tree. "If everything had turned out the way it was supposed to, we'd both be aunts to Gabrielle's baby. Now neither of us is, not legally anyway." She leaned over and peered inside the carriage. "Daniel's asleep," she said, straightening.

Gabrielle's face finally came into focus, and Berthe sucked in her breath.

Raising her eyebrows, Michou glanced at Berthe before she waved again. "How are you?" she called, smiling. "It's so nice to see you again. I've been wanting to stop by, but I haven't made it into Libourne in ages."

When Gabrielle reached them, she did not return Michou's smile. Her lips tightened into a thin line. She glared at Michou for a second, then nodded at Berthe and kept walking.

Michou's mouth fell open, and her whole body stiffened. She stared at Gabrielle's back for a minute before she turned to Berthe. "What was that all about?" she said.

Berthe sighed. "Let's sit down," she said, slumping onto the bench.

Michou sat down next to her. "Come on, Berthe. You know what's going on. First Sophie and Caroline, then Gabrielle. What are people saying about me? Does it have something to do with Erich?"

Gulping, Berthe nodded. She twisted her hands together and fixed her eyes on the carriage.

Michou grabbed her arm. "Tell me, damn it. I want to hear what they're saying." She tightened her grip, her fingers digging hard.

Tears blurred Berthe's vision, and she sniffed. "Oh Michou," she said, swiveling to face her. "Gabrielle said you were sleeping with a German. I tried to tell her you wouldn't, couldn't, but she wouldn't listen. She said it was as if you were killing Marc all over again, making love to his murderer."

Berthe wiped her eyes with the back of her hand. "She called you a whore, a horizontal collaborator. She said that compared to you, Lucien is a patriot." Berthe squeezed her eyes shut for a second. She was such a fool. Why had she told Michou everything?

She opened her eyes. "I'm sorry," she said.

Michou let go of Berthe's arm and stood up. Her face was white, and her lower lip quivered. She lifted her chin. "She can go to hell," she said. "They can all just go to hell."

31

Michou awoke suddenly. Had the soft tapping been part of her dream? Raising herself up on her elbows, she held her breath and listened.

It came again. A couple of long taps, a short one, a pause, several more short and long taps. It took a minute for her to realize that the taps were Morse code—G-U-Y.

She gasped, her cheeks first burning, then turning cold. It'd been almost four months since the day he'd given her *Les Fleurs du Mal* and then disappeared from her life.

Her teeth chattering even though it was a warm night, she threw her robe on over her naked body as she ran to the door. "Is that you?" she whispered. "Guy?"

"Damn it, open the door!" His voice sounded hoarse and strained.

Something must be wrong. She fumbled with the lock Erich had put in for her after Lucien's attack. *Merde!* Her fingers were sticks. At last the bolt clicked as she ground it into place. She pulled open the door.

Guy stepped into the room. His hair was plastered to his head, and his clothes clung to his body in wet folds. "Get a rag." He pointed to the puddle in front of the door. "Just in case."

She grabbed an old slip from her bureau and mopped up the water. Wet footprints glistened on the steps, and she rubbed at them, too.

When she returned to her room, Guy stood at the window, his back to her. "Lock the door and turn out the light."

Michou did as she was told. Nothing had changed. Guy was still the commanding officer, and she was still the soldier.

She was glad it was dark, so he couldn't see the tears gleaming in her eyes.

Guy eased back the curtain and peered out for several minutes. Finally, sighing, he let it fall back and turned.

She snapped the light back on. "What happened?"

He shrugged. "A little accident. But everything looks all right now." His breath whistled out between his teeth. "Thank God I didn't lead them here."

"You don't want to talk about it." As usual. She spun around and walked to the bed.

"And you know why."

She sat down on the edge of the bed. "What I don't know is why you're here." She couldn't believe he'd really expected someone to follow him. Careless as he was with his own life, he'd never risk anyone else's unless he had no choice.

Guy knelt down in front of her and grasped her hands. "I'm here because I'm selfish and because I almost died tonight. Because I promised myself weeks ago to do this. Because I can't pretend any longer."

Dropping her hands, he stood up, his head bowed. "And because I love you."

She inhaled sharply, staring at him, remaining perfectly still. If she moved, he'd change his mind, disappear again, fade back into her dream.

He raised his eyes to hers. "I love you," he said. "I've loved you for a long time."

Tears glazed her sight. She rose slowly from the bed.

Guy grasped her arms and drew her toward him. "Damn it, say something," he said. "Tell me you love me, tell me you hate me, tell me to get the hell out. Just say something."

Michou gulped and shook her head. "I—I can't," she said. "I can't believe it." She lifted her face, inhaling his warm, sweet breath. Gently, she pushed his wet hair off his forehead.

He pulled her tight against him. "That will do for now," he said. He leaned back and stared at her for a minute before he lowered his head and kissed her.

Entwining her arms around his neck and closing her eyes, Michou clung to him, her whole body shaking. Her lips softened and parted as his tongue flicked and probed and danced inside her mouth.

His hand fumbled with the knot in her sash, and her robe fell open. He stepped back, slid it off her shoulders, and watched it fall to the floor. "Let's leave the light on," he said, his voice a gravelly whisper. "I want to look at you." His eyes riveted on hers, he picked her up and carried her to the bed.

Michou shivered as she watched him strip off his wet clothes. She'd craved him for so long, ached for him until she'd almost given up, given in to her need with another man. Thank God she hadn't. She shuddered violently. Suddenly the confusion was gone. Guy was the only one she wanted.

"Cold?" he asked, sliding into bed beside her.

She shook her head and smiled. "Not a bit," she said.

"Good." He ran his hand up her calf to the inside of her thigh. "Then you must be as scared as I am," he murmured. He brushed his lips against her ear. "I want you so badly."

She turned her head and found his mouth. Looking into his soft eyes, she kissed him, exploring his mouth with her tongue. She slipped her arms around his neck and pulled him on top of her.

"Already?" He raised an eyebrow and smiled down at her.

She nodded, arching her back and rubbing her pelvis against his. Her ears filled with the rasp of his breathing and the thud of her heart.

He closed his eyes, groaning when she slid her fingers around him and guided him slowly inside her. His mouth tightened, relaxed; his nostrils flared; his eyelids flickered; his emotions danced across his face in a hundred small ways.

Finally, she couldn't stand it any longer. She squeezed her eyes shut and pressed her mouth against his and tightened her arms around his neck. She inhaled his warm breath, mingling it with hers and returning it to him. Her head vibrated with a crescendo of breathing and heartbeats and moans; her body pitched and rolled with his. The vibrations turned into thunder, the pitches into a swell. In the distance someone sobbed; gulls cried above the crashing surf.

"Michou?" Guy whispered.

She opened her eyes and tried to smile up at him.

"Are you all right?" He propped himself on one elbow and wiped the tears from her face.

"I-I'm fine." She laughed through the sobs. "I-I don't

know why I'm crying. It was wonderful. W-we were wonderful."

He kissed her cheeks. "I love you," he said.

She held her breath for a few seconds, willing the trembling to stop. "I love you, too," she said. "I love you so
much." Her eyes stung with new tears.

Guy hugged her against him, his body slippery against
hers. "Good," he said. "That's so good." He rolled onto his
side, pulling her with him.

"I'd almost given up," she said. "After what you told me
to do."

He pulled his head back and looked into her eyes.
"About Mueller?"

She nodded.

"I had to," he said. "I wanted you to be safe while I was
gone. I couldn't think of any other way. I knew it was a risk."

Michou frowned. "What were you afraid of?"

"You seemed so bent on getting even with Lucien. I was
worried you'd really do it. I'd rather have you fall for a Nazi
than end up in front of one of their firing squads." His
chuckle sounded forced. "Generous of me, wasn't it?" He
shook his head. "Christ, I've been such a fool."

She kissed the tip of his nose. "Yes," she said. "You
have. I'm glad you've stopped."

His arms tightened around her. "Me, too."

"And you don't need to worry about Lucien. I'm past
the point of stupidity."

This time his laugh sounded natural and relieved. "You
mean you've given up the idea of revenge?"

"No," she said. "But whatever I decide to do, it won't be
dumb."

Guy rolled his eyes. "And here I thought for a minute I
wasn't going to have to worry. You haven't changed at—"

"Don't." She put her finger over his mouth. "You're
doing it again. Treating me as if I'm a hopelessly silly child.
I'm not. I've lived through the deaths of my first love, my
baby, my father. I've run this place by myself for over a year.
I've—"

He pulled her hand away from his mouth. "You've hidden dozens of English soldiers. You've learned Morse code.
You've dangled yourself as bait in front of a Nazi." The smile

disappeared from his eyes. "I've never thought of you as
either silly or a child. You're the bravest person I know."

"I'm not a bit brave," she said. "I'm scared all the time.
I just know what I want."

He arched one eyebrow.

"And put that damn eyebrow back down where it be-
longs," she said, punching him lightly in the chest. "You'd
better be nice to me. I've got some pretty important friends."

"Friends?"

"Well, friend. Erich is in love with me."

"I can understand that."

"Everyone thinks we're lovers."

Guy was silent. Finally, he said, "Good."

"Good?" Her throat tightened and she pulled away from
him. "It's horrible. Marc's sister called me a whore. People
won't talk to me. I hate it." She rolled away from him, onto
her side.

Somehow, her thoughts were clearer when she wasn't
touching him. The lavender-scented sheet felt smooth and
cool against her hot, sticky skin. He was right, of course. She
couldn't suddenly throw Erich over for him. Lucien already
suspected Guy. What if Erich did, too?

She turned back toward him. "I have to keep him dangling, don't I?" she said. "Otherwise, he might—"

"Jealousy makes people do strange things," he said,
propping his elbow on the pillow. "It makes me want to tell
you to get rid of him even though I know it would be dangerous for both of us. The thought of him looking at you
makes my guts ache. I can't even allow myself to think of him
touching you."

"He hasn't," she said.

His eyes searched her face. Then he gathered her against
him. "I hope he never does," he mumbled into her hair.

"Do I have to pretend you mean nothing to me?" she
asked.

"Not for the next few hours, I hope." His laugh was
forced.

Michou poked him in the ribs. "That's not what I
meant."

"I know," he said. "Perhaps it might be easier for both
of us if I didn't come around in the open until the harvest."

"What about the wireless? I've gotten pretty good at code."

Guy pushed himself up on both hands and stared down at her for a minute before swinging his feet over the side of the bed and sitting up, his back to her. "No," he said. "Forget it. I won't put you in that kind of—"

"You forget it," she said. She ran her hands up his back, and he shivered. "I want to help. I've earned the right to help. Remember how brave I am?" She rested her chin on his shoulder and slipped her arms around his waist, pressing her breasts against his back.

"You're right," he said. "I'm doing it again. Old habits and all."

She kissed his ear. "Where is it?"

"In Libourne," he said. "I've rented a new room. I'll bring it next time."

"No," she said, biting his ear. "Now that's too dangerous. And stupid."

"Well, I'm certainly not going to let you—"

"Listen to me," she said. "What if I go visit Berthe for a few days, take my suitcase with me. I can ask Erich to deliver me and pick me up. I can load the suitcase with some heavy books, leave them with Berthe. Erich will never notice the difference."

Guy whistled softly and swung her onto his lap. "You're really something, you know," he said.

She smiled and nuzzled the curly blond hairs on his chest. "And don't you forget it again," she said, running her tongue around his nipples and down his belly, breathing in the mingled smells of sweat and love.

He fell backward onto the bed and pulled her on top of him. "I won't," he said. His fingers tickled her inner thighs, explored her wet, private folds. "You win. I'm the prize. Now, what are you going to do with me?"

Michou grinned. "Exactly what I want," she said.

꙰

32

Why had he ever let Michou talk him into this? Guy folded his newspaper and laid it on top of the tissue-wrapped box beside him. He had to be out of his mind, sitting on a park bench next to an SOE wireless wrapped as a birthday gift. Maybe that captain back at Beaulieu had been right, after all. Love was dangerous; it made agents do stupid things. "If you fall in love, your last dance will quite likely be with the Gestapo," he'd said. "Do whatever you like with your body, but keep your mind clean and clear."

Gus crossed his legs and twisted away from the package. Well, his mind was about as muddy as it had ever been, with as many currents as the river he'd been forced to swim after last week's routine reception of a new agent had turned into a Gestapo convention. Lately, whatever he did turned out wrong. Trying to ignore his love for Michou had distracted him for months. And now that he'd admitted openly to her how he felt, he made up for his natural desire to protect her by letting her become more involved than was safe for either of them. He should have insisted on delivering the wireless himself instead of going along with this crazy scheme of hers.

Slapping at the mosquito buzzing near his ear, he snorted. He was doing it again, exaggerating the dangers just because the task involved Michou. Her plan was solid, made sense. He just didn't want her to risk it.

He glanced at the blood on his hand. Damn mosquito had bitten him. He rubbed his thumb against his fingers, then clenched his hand into a fist. It was one thing for him to take a chance—he was a trained agent. But all Michou had was her stubbornness and courage.

236

Guy shook his head. Logic was the only approach that made any sense. He couldn't pretend Michou would be safe if she didn't help him. Safer, maybe, but not safe. No one in France was safe as long as the Nazis ran things.

He pushed his hat back and wiped the sweat from his forehead, frowning as a German soldier strolled by with a French girl hanging on his arm. He hated every reminder of Mueller, of Michou's unhappiness when she had told him what her friends were saying. Drumming his fingers on the bench, he stared at the couple as they cut across the grass and headed for the path along the riverbank.

Squeaking wheels crunched lightly on the graveled path, and he turned his head. His chest tightened.

Flanked by two Nazis, Michou pushed a large black pram toward him. She smiled up at one of them and shook her head when he tried to grasp the carriage handle. She stopped the carriage, and the soldier shrugged.

Guy picked up his newspaper, unfolded it, and draped it over the package. He bent his head over it and pretended to read. If she decided to keep going, it would be better if the Nazis didn't notice him or the box. He was just another Frenchman enjoying the river breeze and the shade on a hot day.

A baby cried, and he glanced over his shoulder. Michou reached into the pram and swung a squalling child into her arms. She cradled it against her chest and rocked back and forth. The baby kept screaming.

The soldiers looked at each other over her head. One jerked his head toward a smartly dressed young woman sitting on a bench near the river. The other grinned and nodded. The baby screamed again as the Nazis waved at Michou. They strode purposefully away.

Michou nuzzled the crying baby's hair until the soldiers reached their next victim. Gradually, the wails faded into hiccups, and she put the child back into the pram.

Guy's breath exploded through his clenched teeth. He stood as she approached. "What was that all about?" he asked.

"I guess they don't like crying babies," she said, shrugging. "Poor Daniel." She stuck her head under the hood and kissed the baby. "I'm so sorry, little one. I had to do it." She hugged him.

Daniel chortled and waved his arms excitedly.

"He doesn't seem upset now. Convenient he started shrieking like that."

Michou straightened. "Poor child. He hardly ever cries. I had to pinch him. I think he's forgiven me, though."

Guy shook his head. "I don't know why I bother to worry about you."

She smiled. "I don't either." She craned her neck and looked behind him. "Where is it?" she asked.

"Under the newspaper." Guy scanned the park. The two soldiers now sat on either side of the young woman. A lone Frenchman lay on his back under a tree by the riverbank, his cap covering his face. The lovers had disappeared.

Guy refolded the paper, tucked it under his arm, and picked up the package. "Is there room for it in there?" He nodded toward the pram.

"That's why I brought it." She scooped aside a blanket. "Right here," she said.

He set the box behind the child and arranged the blanket over it. The baby immediately twisted around and pulled at the cover.

Guy frowned. "That's not going to work," he said. "What if he rips the wrapping?"

"No, no, Daniel. Don't touch," Michou said. She pulled a small toy from her pocket. "This is for you."

Grinning, Daniel swiped at the toy. Michou put it into his hands, and he laughed.

"You thought of everything," Guy said.

Michou patted her pocket and said, "I've got a few more toys just in case he gets tired of that one before we get back home."

"Good." Guy smiled for the first time that day. Even though the danger was far from over, he felt better now that the actual transfer had been made. And he didn't want his nervousness to infect Michou. She still had to walk back to her friend's house. It was much better if she could do it calmly. He pulled her into his arms, inhaling and savoring her fresh scent of jasmine and vanilla. "Then we have time for a kiss."

She smiled up at him and laced her fingers around his neck. "How did I do?" she whispered.

He lowered his head and kissed her. "You were wonderful," he said, his lips brushing against hers. "A natural."

Daniel gurgled, and Michou pulled away. "I'd better get him home," she said. "I don't have *that* many toys."

"I'll walk you part way," he said. "We can pretend we're a family—mother, father, baby."

"And illegal radio." She released the brake and turned the pram around.

Guy slid his hand next to hers. "Let me help," he said.

She leaned her head against his arm and looked up at him. "Thank you," she said, her voice cracking. Her lower lip suddenly trembled.

Damn. He'd been hoping this wouldn't happen until she was safely back at Berthe's. He pressed his hand over hers on the pram handle. "Just a few more minutes," he whispered. "You're doing fine." He measured his steps to hers. The gravel crunched under the pram's wheels.

At the edge of the park, Michou raised her eyes to his. "I'm better now," she said, her voice still shaky. "You go. It's not far from here."

Guy shook his head and jerked it at the boisterous crowd of German soldiers gathered around a table at the sidewalk café ahead. "As soon as we get past them," he said.

Michou's body stiffened, and her hand clenched the carriage handle tightly. She stared at the soldiers.

One of the Nazis stood and walked inside the café.

"Merde!" she hissed. "That was Erich. I don't know if he saw us." She squeezed her eyes shut and bit her lip. "What do we do now?"

"Leave the motor running," Erich said. "She said she'd be ready at two o'clock."

Corporal Fischer nodded.

Erich jumped out of the car. He licked his lips and cleared his throat before he reached the front door. His stomach had been queasy since yesterday afternoon, when he'd spotted Michou with that wine broker, Guy whatever-his-name-was, the one her eyes used to follow constantly

until he stopped coming around a few months ago. Had he
been her real reason for coming to Libourne?

His stomach churned as he knocked on the door. He
hoped she hadn't seen him. Then he could just pretend everything was exactly the same as it had been when he'd dropped
her off two days ago.

It wasn't, though. Erich let his hand fall back to his side.
He'd watched the two of them as they walked out of the park,
seen the way she looked up at Guy, the way she leaned
against him, the protective, possessive curve of his arm
around her shoulder. He'd dashed inside so suddenly the
others had thought he was sick. They'd been right, but they
didn't know why. By the time he returned, Michou and Guy
had disappeared.

The door opened, and Michou smiled at him. "All
ready," she said. She turned to Berthe and kissed her on both
cheeks. "Thanks so much. Your turn next time." She picked
up the old brown suitcase at her feet.

Erich nodded at Berthe and grabbed the suitcase from
Michou. He shook his head and forced himself to smile at the
women. "I can't believe it," he said. "F-fifty pounds of
clothes for two days? Seems even heavier now than when you
came."

Michou glanced at the floor. "I can never make up my
mind what to take when I go anywhere," she said, "so I pack
everything." She giggled. "I'll carry it if it's too heavy for
you." She reached for the handle, and her hand brushed his.

"I think I can manage." Erich swung the luggage away
from her and trotted down the steps. "Good-bye, Mademoiselle Desroches," he called over his shoulder.

Holding his breath against the diesel fumes, he opened
the trunk and heaved the suitcase inside. He slammed the lid
down and jerked open the back door of the car. He'd
been so pleased when Michou had asked him to take her to
Libourne, so glad she was actually taking a vacation from the
vineyards; and even though she'd been a bit more reserved
than usual on the way in, he'd been looking forward to riding
back with her. Until yesterday.

Michou climbed into the car, and he slid in after her. "All
right, Corporal," he said.

Erich leaned back, staring out the window as the car

moved slowly down the street. So far, he didn't know whether she'd seen him yesterday or not. She had seemed pleased to see him when she opened the door, though.

"You're quiet," she said.

"Sorry," he said, turning back to her. "Just pondering." He met her eyes. "I *am* glad to see you, though. It was quite dull around Château Bourdet with you gone."

She smiled. "Good. That means Philippe didn't do anything stupid. Maybe he's growing up after all."

Relaxing, Erich chuckled. Everything was fine. Perhaps she'd just met up with the wine broker by accident. "I think you're too hard on the boy."

"And I think you're too nice. Especially considering the way he treats you."

"I don't really blame him." Erich shrugged. "In fact, I admire him. He has a lot of courage. He loves his country, and he doesn't back down from what he believes. In his situation I doubt I could behave so honestly, especially if it put my life in jeopardy."

"I may be too hard on Philippe, but you're too hard on yourself," Michou said. "He's always been a noisy rebel. You're just quieter, that's all." She glanced at the back of the corporal's head and lowered her voice. "I can't believe you like this war any better than I do."

Erich grimaced and spoke quickly, to ensure that what he said would be beyond Corporal Fischer's limited understanding of French. "That's the point—I don't. But what have I done about it? What *can* I do about it? I'm an officer in the German army, and I love my country even when I don't approve of her. I have my duty; I obey my orders; and I try not to think about it too much." He shook his head. "If I hadn't met you, I might not have let myself think about it at all."

The car lurched around a corner, and Michou bumped against him. She jerked away quickly, scooting back into her corner.

Erich leaned forward, his stomach knotting again. Had he just imagined her shudder of revulsion? "Take it easy, Corporal," he said in German.

Corporal Fischer glanced over his shoulder and grinned. "Sorry, sir," he said.

Michou cleared her throat, and when she spoke, her voice sounded strained. "I still think I'm right," she said.

Erich stared at the back of the corporal's neck, at the short, stiff blond hairs marching from his cap down to his collar, at the wrinkle creasing the back of his field-gray uniform. "It doesn't really matter, does it?" He sighed and turned back to her. "To you I'll always be a German first, Erich second."

Michou was silent for a long time. Finally, she swallowed hard, looked at his hand on the seat between them, and placed hers gingerly on his. "Be patient," she said, avoiding his eyes. "A few months ago you were only a Nazi and nothing second." She drew her hand away as the car turned into the drive leading to Château Bourdet.

As the car stopped in front of the steps, Erich made himself smile at her. "At least that's some progress," he said. "I can't complain about that." He climbed out of the car and walked around to open her door.

Michou waited beside him while he retrieved her suitcase from the trunk. "Let me take it," she said, snatching it from him.

Erich gripped the handle tightly and frowned. "N-no," he said, heading toward the tower door. "A suitcase full of rocks. Now, that's something I *can* complain about."

33

❧

"The first thing we have to do is encode it," Guy said, handing Michou a folded sheet of paper. "That'll probably take as long as sending it."

Her hands shaking, she carried the paper to her desk and turned on the lamp. She'd mastered Morse code while Guy'd been gone, but there was still so much left to learn before she could send messages on her own. And she wanted to prove she could learn it fast, that he'd been right to let her try.

After she sat down, she unfolded the paper and spread it out on the desk. She glanced at it quickly and turned back to him. "But it's in English," she said.

"Of course."

She set her teeth and peered again at the message. "The only word I recognize is Paris." She frowned. "Are you going to Paris?"

He nodded. "Just got word from London through the newest irregular. He said they wanted me to set up a liaison with the group that started operating there after the collapse of Autogiro. It's not at all standard practice, but—" He shrugged and moved across the bedroom to stand behind her chair. "For now, you don't need to know anything more."

"Don't you trust me?" Raising her eyebrows, she looked up over her shoulder at him.

He rolled his eyes and shook his head. "I trust you with my life, my darling. But in this business, you shouldn't know any more than you need to—for your own safety and everyone else's. When you need to know more, I'll tell you." He draped his arms around her neck and rested his chin on the top of her head.

Michou twisted back to face her desk and the piece of paper covered with his small, neat printing. "Is it going to be dangerous?" she asked. "Or can't you tell me that, either?" Her annoyance had crept into her voice, and she bit her lip. It'd been over a week since she'd last seen him, and she didn't want to argue, didn't want anything to distract her from doing the job right.

Guy nuzzled her hair. "No worse than anything else," he said. "It's dangerous for me to even *be* in France." He kissed her on the top of her head. "Now, stop worrying. Let's get to work on this instead."

She stared at the message as he pulled something from his pocket. He was going to Paris, and it had been months since she'd heard from Rachel. If it wasn't going to be dangerous, maybe she could talk him into taking her with him. July was always the slowest month in the vineyards, and Philippe had actually done some work lately. He could handle everything by himself for a few more days. *If* he wanted to. She grimaced. That was one problem; convincing Guy to take her with him was another.

Guy laid a blank piece of paper on one side of the message and a sheet filled with little squares on the other. "It's a simple code," he said, "but hard to break." He drew a pencil from his pocket and, leaning over her, scribbled on the blank paper.

When he finished, she looked at what he'd written. It was one line in English, with the alphabet scrawled above it. "I can't read this, either," she said.

"You don't need to. All you need to do is match the letters with the ones here." He pointed to his printed message. "In groups of five. Like this." He filled in several squares on the lined paper, his finger moving back and forth from one sheet to the other.

"I see," she said. "You have to know the phrase in order to decode it."

"And I'm the only one who uses this line," he said. "But there's also a security check. I always make a mistake in the seventh word. That way they know it's really from me, not from the Gestapo."

Michou shuddered. "Let me finish," she said.

He handed her the pencil. "Go ahead."

Carefully, slowly, she checked each letter before she

printed it in its square. Her fingers gripped the pencil so tightly that her hand cramped, and the only sound in the room was the scratch of the pencil against the paper. When she finished, she dropped the pencil and rubbed her hand.

Guy leaned over her shoulder, his breath warm against her cheek. "Perfect," he said. "You even remembered the security check. Do you have scissors?"

She rummaged through her desk drawer until she found a pair. "What do you need these for?" she asked.

"Watch." He cut the coded message into strips. "Now you can swallow it if someone comes." He wadded up the original message and the code phrase and carried them to the fireplace. "Always get rid of everything before you start broadcasting," he said, lighting the paper.

Michou stared as the flames blackened the papers and shriveled them to ashes. Wisps of acrid smoke drifted out of the fireplace. There was so much to remember, so much to go wrong if she didn't.

Guy returned to the desk and put his arms around her. "Don't worry," he said. "You're doing fine."

She relaxed, rubbing her cheek against his and inhaling his comforting tobacco-spiced scent. "Aren't you ever going to tell me what I've written?"

"No," he whispered into her ear. "No, no, no."

"All right," she said, sighing. She didn't want to press it, not now, when she had an even more important request. "Can you at least tell me when you're going to Paris?"

"Next week," he said. "Want to come with me?"

She twisted around and stared up at him, her mouth open.

He laughed and kissed her. "I knew that was on your mind. But let's talk about it later." He straightened. "Now, where have you hidden the wireless?"

Michou stood up and walked to the foot of the bed, then stooped. "Under here," she said, pulling back the thick Oriental carpet. "There were some loose stones in the floor, so I took them out and put this in their place." She yanked aside a thin board and pointed to the small case. "I carried the stones out to the pile near the *chai*."

He lifted the wireless onto the desk. "Clever and resourceful," he said. "As usual." He removed the lid and tossed it on the bed.

Michou rested her elbows on the edge of the desk and watched as he set up the radio, repeating each step to herself, imprinting it on her mind.

"First, the crystals," Guy said. He pulled a wadded handkerchief from his pocket, unwrapped it carefully on the desk, and lined up four small pronged objects. "Each one is a different frequency. It's a good idea to change several times during a broadcast. That way if the *gonio* has a fix on you, it has to start over." He inserted one of the crystals.

"But doesn't that confuse London, too?"

"No. Each crystal has a number. You tell them before you switch." He plugged the wireless in and uncoiled a long green wire. "This is the aerial," he said. "The safest place for it is on the roof. Can I get there through that window?" He jerked his head toward the window facing the main section of the château.

She nodded. "It's a bit of a drop, though. Be careful."

The aerial trailing behind him, he climbed onto the bed. "Turn off the light."

She clicked off the lamp and sat motionless at the desk. The curtain swished, and the window creaked. There was a grunt, then a thud as Guy dropped onto the roof, and finally, faint scuffing noises. She held her breath until she heard him back at the window. Thank God the Germans were billeted at the other end of the building and the rest of the third floor was empty.

The window creaked again, and he said, "Done. You can turn the light on."

She fumbled for the switch and blinked as the light stabbed her eyes.

"Can you get up there?" he asked. He stepped down from the bed.

She smiled. "I used to spend a lot of time on the roof." It had been her favorite escaping place even before Maman had let her move into the tower.

"Good," he said. "Because I don't think it's safe to leave the aerial there. You're going to have to string it out every time."

She shrugged. "All right. What's next?"

He checked his watch. "We broadcast at midnight. It's almost time. Are you ready?"

Michou gripped the seat of the chair with both hands

and nodded. Her throat scratched, and she swallowed. *Mon Dieu*, she had to get it right. She raced over the code alphabet in her mind.

Guy stood behind her. "Put these on," he said, pulling a pair of earphones from the case. "Listen for AFG—that's our call sign."

She settled them over her ears as he switched the radio on and twirled the dial. Static filled her head, then faint dots and dashes. She nodded at him and reached for the dial to tune them in.

He glanced at his watch. "Now," he said.

She hesitantly tapped out the call letters.

"Again. Several times," he said.

She continued, her touch growing firmer as she repeated the letters.

"Now wait for the TRS. That means they've received your signal."

She propped her elbows on either side of the radio and cocked her head. In a minute the letters buzzed in her ears. "TRS . . . TRS . . . TRS." She nodded at Guy.

"Go ahead," he mouthed back at her.

Michou took a deep breath and pressed her finger against the key. The slow clackety-clacks of the first word filled her head. By the third line she picked up speed, her finger tapping out each letter almost automatically as her mind registered it. When she finished, she blew her breath out and looked up at Guy. She pulled one side of the earphone away from her head.

"Wait for the TRS again," he said. "That means they got it all down."

She slipped the earphone over her ear and slumped back in the chair, staring at the trembling hands in her lap as if they didn't belong to her. Finally, the earphones crackled: "TRS . TRS."

Grinning, she ripped the earphones from her head. "I did it!" she said. "They got it!" She jumped up and flung her arms around his neck, the earphones still dangling from her hand.

Guy smiled down at her before he kissed her. "I'm not a bit surprised," he said, reaching behind her and taking the earphones. "You made it look easy."

Her cheeks burned. A rivulet of sweat trickled down her

stomach, and she stepped back and pulled her blouse away from her body. Her ears still buzzed with static. "Now what?" she asked.

"I'm going to put it all away while you go get Philippe," he said.

"Now?" She frowned. "But why?"

He unplugged the wireless. "Because I want to talk to him."

She didn't move. "What about?"

"About you and this place. And Paris."

"Good luck." Rolling her eyes, she headed for the door. It might just work, though. Philippe idolized Guy, had asked about him repeatedly the first month he'd been gone. Maybe it *was* time to tell him what was going on. She'd had more than enough of his hostile glares.

Michou let herself out and groped her way down the stairs to the second floor, her bare feet slapping against the cold stone. The door creaked as she opened it, and she sucked in her breath. Mémé Laure was such a light sleeper, and her room was the closest one.

She stepped into the hall and listened. No one stirred, so she quickly padded to Philippe's room at the other end. She slipped inside and scuffed forward until her knees touched his bed.

"Philippe," she whispered, shaking his arm. "Wake up."

His body jerked upright. "What—"

"Shhh," she said. "It's Michou. Come with me."

"What do you want?"

She tugged at his arm. "Come on. Guy wants to talk to you."

"Guy?" He jumped out of bed. "What's he doing here? I thought—"

"He'll explain," she said. She peeked into the hall before she stepped out of his room.

From below her came the sound of a door clicking shut.

Michou froze. *Merde*. The night patrol. Her heart thudded. Guy'd said he was going to bring in the aerial. What if he was still on the roof?

34

🍂

Michou gripped Philippe's hand. Move, she told herself. She couldn't just wait here. Gunshots from the horrible morning when Papa had been arrested echoed inside her head.

Shaking her head, she squeezed her eyes closed. "No," she whispered. She couldn't let herself do this now.

Philippe pulled his hand away. "What's wrong?" he hissed. "It's probably just your boyfriend, and he's out to the *chai* by now. Looking for you, I bet."

Michou clenched her teeth. Her hand twitched, and she doubled it into a fist. *Mon Dieu*, she wanted to hit him.

He laughed softly. "Go," he said, pushing her.

Her feet moved mechanically down the hall. After an eternity, she reached the tower door and eased it open. The cold stones bit her feet, and the slap of Philippe's slippers thundered in her ears as she hurried down the stairs to her bedroom.

Only more blackness met her eyes when she opened the door. "Guy?" she whispered. She felt her way into the room.

The only sound was her own breathing.

"Oh no," she moaned. "He's up there."

"Up where?"

"On the roof."

"Jesus Christ! What's he doing on the roof? There's a full moon tonight. What if that Nazi friend of yours sees him?"

"Shut up," she said. "Just shut up." She gritted her teeth and buried her hot face in her hands.

Scraping noises came from the window. A second later, they heard a grunt and a thud. Guy's voice rasped out of the darkness. "All right," he said.

The light blazed on as Michou ran to him. She threw her arms around his neck and hugged him close. "I was so scared," she said. "Thank God he didn't see you."

Guy brushed his lips against hers. "I just waited," he said. He looked over her head and added, "Hello, Philippe."

Michou twisted in his arms and stared at Philippe. "Well?" she said.

Philippe stood next to the door, his curly brown hair tousled and his pajamas rumpled. "It really *is* you," he said. "I didn't believe her."

Michou put her hands on her hips. "Then why did you come?" she asked.

Philippe shrugged and held out his hand to Guy. "I'm glad you're back. Maybe you can talk some sense into my idiot sister. She won't listen to me."

"See?" Michou said as Guy shook Philippe's hand. "He's impossible."

Philippe glowered. "Me? I'm not the one playing kissing games with—"

Guy held up his hand. "Enough," he said. "I don't want either of you to say anything until I'm through. Understood?"

Michou nodded and fixed her eyes on Philippe.

Ignoring her, he jerked his head.

"Good. Now, sit down, Philippe," Guy said, pointing to the chair in front of the desk. While Philippe obeyed, he scooped the aerial off the bed and handed it to Michou. "Would you please put this away while I talk to your brother?"

"Wh—" Philippe clamped his mouth shut.

As she looped the aerial around her elbow, Michou grinned at Philippe. She was going to enjoy this. No one but Papa had ever been able to make him behave, and since Papa's death, he'd become even more obnoxious.

She lifted the rug and board and tucked the aerial into the hole beside the wireless. Before she replaced the board, she glanced up at Guy. "Is that everything?" she asked. "You put away the crystals?"

"Go ahead," he said. "It's all ready for next time."

She rolled back the rug and sat next to Guy on the bed. He put his arm around her, and she leaned against him.

Guy smiled at her before he turned to Philippe. "I need your help," he said. "Your sister and I are both working against the Nazis."

"But—" Philippe's eyes opened wider, and he squirmed in his chair.

"You don't have any idea what Michou has been doing, do you?" Guy asked.

Philippe shook his head. His lower lip trembled, and he crossed his arms.

Michou raised her chin and looked at him, but he quickly averted his eyes. She smiled and snuggled closer to Guy. She hoped he felt like a fool.

"*I* asked her to get friendly with Mueller," Guy said. "It was one of the hardest things I've had to do in this war, and I've done a few hard things. I also asked her to learn Morse code. Tonight she just sent her first message to London."

"Then that's wh—"

"That's what the green wire was for." Guy pointed toward the floor. "The wireless has been hidden there since she brought it here from Libourne. *Michou* brought it. In the car with Mueller. You probably know what she risked to do it."

Staring at Michou, Philippe nodded. He cleared his throat, then opened his mouth to speak. Nothing came out for a few seconds. "I've been stupid," he said finally. "I'm sorry." He lowered his head. "What do you want me to do?"

"Keep treating her the same way you have been."

Michou frowned at Guy. "But I thought—"

"In public only," Guy continued. "It's important for everyone to keep thinking she's a collaborator—it's protection for both Michou and me."

Philippe raised his head. "Is that all?" His voice cracked with disappointment.

"No." Guy smiled. "We're going to Paris next week. Someone needs to take charge here, see that what is supposed to get done gets done."

"But—"

"It's not exciting, I know," Guy said. "But it's important. If I see you do this right, I'll know I can ask you to do other things later."

"Dangerous things?" Philippe's voice squeaked, and the sparkle came back into his eyes.

Michou rolled her eyes. Nothing quelled his spirit for long.

"Maybe," Guy said. "But first you have to prove I can trust you."

Philippe jumped up. "Oh, you can!" he said. Then his grin faded. "I wish I could go to Paris with you."

"The truth is you'd just be in the way. There are things I have to do by myself. And your sister deserves a rest. Once we're in Paris, we won't be seeing each other. Someone has to run things here." Guy lifted his arm from Michou's shoulder and stood up. "Can I count on you?" he asked, holding out his hand.

Philippe stepped forward and grasped Guy's hand. "Yes," he said earnestly. He turned to Michou. "And I really am sorry about the way I've been treating you. I thought—"

Michou rose and stood next to Guy. Poor Philippe had suffered enough. "Thank you," she said. She put her arms around his neck and pulled his head toward her. "I forgive you. I hated the way you were acting, but I always understood why." She kissed him on both cheeks. "I knew I would probably have behaved the same way."

After she released him, Philippe stared at his feet for a minute. When he looked up, a smile twitched at the corners of his mouth. He put his hands on his hips and glared at her. "How could you disgrace us this way?" he said. "You bitch. How could you?" He turned to Guy. "How was that?"

"Now, don't get carried away," Guy said. "Perhaps it would be best if you just ignored each other in front of other people."

Grinning, Philippe shrugged. "All right. But when do I really get to *do* something?"

Guy rubbed his chin. "Soon enough," he said. "Be patient." He shook Philippe's hand again. "I'll see you when I return. Now, it's time for you to go back to your room." He winked at him. "I need to talk to your sister."

"Sure," Philippe said, returning the wink. "Don't worry about anything. I'll do my best." He waved, then shut the door quietly behind him.

Michou stood on tiptoe and kissed Guy. "I'm amazed," she said. "You handled him even better than Papa used to. He actually agreed to do some work—menial, far-far-beneath-him vineyard labor."

Guy slid his hands under her blouse. "It just takes the right touch," he said, caressing her breasts.

She backed up until her legs touched the bed, then pulled him with her onto the lavender-scented sheets. "And that's something you definitely have," she said.

"I'll be worried while you're gone," Catherine said, resting her hands on the piano keys. "I won't be able to help it. But I think it's the right thing for you to do." She tried to smile at Michou. Even though her concern for Rachel was natural, it was so hard to let her go, especially by herself. But she had to. The child needed a rest from the constant demands of the vineyard, time away from them all to think and, perhaps, see things more clearly, an escape from the whispers.

"I'll be fine." Squatting on her heels, Michou rummaged through the stack of music on the floor next to the piano. "Grandmère and Grandpère will be happy to see me. Compared to Sylvie, I'm a saint. Hah!" Her laugh sounded bitter.

Catherine stroked Michou's soft hair. "People can be vicious," she said. "Perhaps you should make up your own mind about your cousin."

Michou shrugged and selected a book. "Papa always liked Mozart," she said, setting the book in front of Catherine. "Would you play something for me?"

Catherine stood. "Later," she said. "I think we need to talk a little more first." She linked her arm through Michou's and pulled her toward the sofa.

"Is this about Henri?" Michou asked, sitting next to her.

"Actually, I think it's more about me than about Henri," Catherine said. She scanned Michou's face for a reaction, but it was expressionless, carefully blank. "I've started seeing him again. And I mean to keep on seeing him."

"That's your right," Michou said. "You know I've always liked him."

Catherine sighed. "It doesn't bother you?"

"Not too much," Michou said. "I'll admit it was a shock at first. How would you have reacted if Grandmère had told you the same thing?"

"I never thought of it that way." Catherine chuckled. "I still have a hard time picturing Mère falling in love at all. She's never seemed quite human to me."

Michou laughed, softly at first, then so loudly her eyes began to water. "To me, either," she gasped when she could talk. "But you do. At least you did after I started thinking about it. I just needed something to make me realize it." Her smile faded. "After Marc died, I thought I'd never fall in love again. And I know how much you loved Papa. Caring for Henri doesn't mean you never loved Papa. You don't need to feel guilty about it. It was wrong of me to act the way I did."

"That's the nicest thing you could have said to me," Catherine said, her own eyes glazing over with tears. "Thank you." She kissed Michou's cheek. "You're a wonderful daughter. I like the person you're becoming. I know Alexandre would, too."

35

❧

The gate scraped across the cobblestone walk as Michou pushed it open. She frowned at the scraggly weeds among the flowers bordering the walk, *arrivistes* proudly shouldering out the aristocrats. What had happened to Victor, Grandmère and Grandpère's devout old gardener? Sylvie used to claim that if a weed escaped his notice, he'd confess and receive absolution for sloth.

When Michou reached the porch, she set her suitcase down and rubbed her aching arm. Paris had changed so much since then. She'd had to walk from the Métro because there weren't any taxis. And even though it was Bastille Day, the streets were almost as deserted as they'd been the last time she saw Paris, a little over two years ago. A few brave pedestrians, strolling along the Champs-Élysées, arms linked, one in blue, one in red, another in white, a walking tricolor, flouted the German decree—plastered in large posters at every corner—against any demonstration. More of a crowd than she'd seen since she'd gotten off the train at the Gare d'Austerlitz stood in the long lines in front of the *boulangeries, épiceries,* and *charcuteries.*

She knocked on the door and waited. She hoped Grandmère and Grandpère had gotten Maman's letter. The post had been so unreliable since the occupation. What if the letter hadn't arrived? What if they weren't here? The house seemed deserted, blinds pulled over dusty windows.

She closed her eyes and leaned against the door. *Mon Dieu,* what if one of them was sick? If they'd gone to their summer house in Bayonne, they'd certainly have written to Maman.

Slow footsteps sounded from behind the door, and she straightened. Someone was there, even if it was only Aimée, the cook. She'd have a place to stay, at least. She picked up her suitcase.

The door swung open. Grandpère stood on the threshold, his thin, lined face breaking into a smile when he saw her.

She dropped the suitcase and threw her arms around his neck. "I'm so glad you're here," she said. "I was afraid—"

"Of course we're here, little one," he said. "Wouldn't dream of leaving after we received your mother's letter."

She kissed his hollow cheeks. "I thought maybe you hadn't gotten it," she said.

"Is that Michèle, Gaston?" Her grandmother's voice croaked from the family salon. "Bring her in here."

Winking at Michou, Grandpère picked up her suitcase in one hand and linked his free arm through hers. "Mustn't keep her waiting," he said. "She's been so anxious to see you."

Michou raised her eyebrows. Grandmère anxious to see her? That was certainly a change. But everything else had changed—why not Grandmère as well? Grandpère had aged ten years in the last two, his white hair thin and scraggly and his moustache drooping sadly. And in the house, a thin layer of dust clouded the mahogany table tops, and the floors needed sweeping.

Grandpère set her suitcase at the bottom of the stairway and led her into the salon. "Look who's here, Odette," he said with forced cheerfulness. "Our little Michou has finally arrived."

Michou swallowed hard. If Grandpère had aged ten years, Grandmère had aged at least twenty. She sat in a blue wing chair next to the fireplace, her feet propped up on a footstool and her legs covered by an old navy-blue quilt. It was cool inside despite the warm day, and she wore a black sweater draped over her shoulders.

Grandmère held out her arms. "I've been worried to death ever since I received your mother's letter," she said. "Traveling is so dangerous nowadays."

Michou kissed her wrinkled cheeks. The faint scent of old lilac perfume clinging to the black sweater mixed with the

musty odor of the quilt. "It wasn't bad at all," she said. "The
train made several long stops, but nothing happened." Thank
God, she added to herself. Even though Guy claimed his
papers were excellent forgeries, he'd made her sit behind
him; and she'd been able to see by the sudden disappearance
of the furrows in his forehead his relief at reaching Paris
without close scrutiny.

"Nevertheless, I *am* glad you're here, my dear," Grandmère said. She grasped Michou's hand and patted it.

Michou squeezed her grandmother's cold, dry hand.
Grandmère truly did seem pleased to see her. She'd often
wondered if Sylvie had said anything about her miscarriage.
Michou had told Maman about it a few months after Papa's
death, and Maman hadn't been nearly as horrified as she'd
expected. Still, if Grandmère knew, it would be just like her
to wait until some horrible moment to lash her with it. Yet
now her face revealed nothing except pleasure and tenderness.

Michou released Grandmère's hand. For the first time in
her life, she saw the human being under her grandmother's
stern, gray stone façade. Whether it was because Grandmère
had softened or because she herself could see more clearly,
Michou wasn't certain. "Are you feeling all right?" she asked,
frowning.

Grandmère rubbed her hip. "It's just these old bones."

"And two winters without heating fuel and two years
without enough food." Grandpère's voice crackled with bitterness.

Michou reached into her purse. "I brought these for
you," she said, pulling out a handful of ration tickets. "We
grow so much of our own food now, and we trade wine for
extra tickets. I wanted to bring a rabbit, too, but Maman said
it was too dangerous."

She pressed the tickets into Grandpère's hand. Actually,
it'd been Guy who'd refused to let her bring the rabbit, but
he'd made up for it by giving her several more tickets. Although Grandmère had never written about the problem of
getting food, everyone knew how hard it was for Parisians.

"Thank you, little one," Grandpère said. He put the
tickets into his pocket. "Aimée will be most pleased."

"She's still here?" Michou asked. "Then why—"

Grandmère leaned forward. "She has to spend so many

hours in those terrible lines she hasn't any time left to clean. And poor Victor, he can hardly walk, his rheumatism has gotten so bad." She shook her head. "We're just four old people waiting to die."

Michou clenched her fists. "Doesn't Sylvie—"

Grandmère's face stiffened, and she pressed her lips together. "We do not accept help from a German's whore," she said. "It's only because of Gaston that I even allow her in the house." She kicked the quilt off her legs and braced her hands on the arms of the chair.

Grandpère moved quickly to Grandmère's side. "Your mother may have told you that Sylvie lives with a Nazi officer now. We take nothing from her, but she is still our granddaughter." He helped Grandmère stand.   †

Michou nodded and supported Grandmère's other arm. She bit her lip. Perhaps Grandmère hadn't really changed, after all. What if she heard about Erich?

Michou's shoulders sagged as she helped her grandmother to the stairway. All her life she'd put up with Grandmère's disapproval. For a few minutes she'd let herself think everything had changed. Nothing had, really. Grandmère's affection was still based on how well someone met her expectations. If Michou failed—or if Grandmère found out about Erich—*she'd* be "the German's whore" the next time.

She glanced up at Grandpère, and he winked at her. He, at least, loved her no matter what she did. Her lips trembling, she tried to smile at him.

"We've got a surprise for you," he said, stooping to pick up her suitcase at the base of the stairs. He supported Grandmère as she climbed the stairs stiffly, pausing on each step.

Grandmère's hand pressed heavily on Michou's arm until she reached the landing. "I don't come up here often anymore," she said, panting. "I even sleep downstairs now." She lifted her hand and opened the door to Michou's room. "Go on in, my dear."

Michou hesitated, then stepped into the room. Her eyes widened. The ugly dark green coverlet and curtains were gone. Instead, pale rose curtains draped the windows, and a creamy lace spread banded in rose satin covered the bed. She turned back to her grandparents. "But where—"

Grandmère smiled. "Do you like it?" she asked. "These were your mother's things."

"But why—"

"Catherine writes how proud she is of you. We just want you to know we're proud, too," Grandmère said.

Michou stared at her feet. "Thank you," she said finally.

Grandpère chuckled. "The child's exhausted, Odette," he said. "Let's leave her be." He set the suitcase in the room and pulled Grandmère's arm. "Come along."

Michou watched them until they reached the stairs, then closed the door softly. She walked slowly to the large four-poster bed, the bed she'd miscarried in. She ran her hand across the soft coverlet. Tears stung her eyes. It was all so confusing. She just didn't know what to feel.

Guy nodded at the greasy-haired *patron* as he walked across the dingy lobby of the *maison de passe*. The bloody-awful hotel was only one step above a brothel; but at least the owner never asked for identification, and the police and Gestapo never bothered to check on the occupants. Most were there for only an hour or two anyway.

"Au revoir, Monsieur Dubois," the *patron* said with a leer. "I can expect your return?"

"Of course," Guy said. If everything goes well, he added to himself. If not—

Shrugging, he shut the door and stepped onto the sidewalk. If he didn't return, the *patron* wouldn't be the loser—he'd already gotten his money.

Guy headed for the Métro at the end of the block. The street was deserted except for a scruffy white cat that meowed at him from the entry of an apartment building.

Descending the Métro stairs, he lifted his lip at the strong odor of urine tainting the air of the underground station. From below echoed the clatter of wheels and the screech of brakes, and he ran down the remaining steps. He jumped onto the train a few seconds before it pulled out.

He glanced around at the second-class coach's other passengers as he settled himself on a hard pull-down seat near the door. No Germans, anyway. Most of them rode first-class.

The coach ebbed and flowed with people at the various stops. Guy gripped his seat when two Nazi soldiers stumbled into the car, then forced himself to relax. They weren't interested in him. No one in Paris knew what he looked like. Yet.

He fingered the blue handkerchief in his pocket. Coupled with the collaborationist newspaper he had yet to buy, it was the signal to his contact. When he saw their mates and received a casual answer to a casual question, he'd know he had the right man. It seemed easy. He hoped it would be.

Almost by themselves, his fingers moved to the slick scrap of paper wrapped inside the handkerchief. He'd avoided looking at it—in case he was caught and had time to destroy it, he didn't want to have anything left to reveal—but he knew it listed the names of eight surviving members of the Autogiro circuit. It had been passed to London by another member who'd escaped across the Pyrénées, then relayed to Guy by the new agent. Because the new *réseau* in Paris had no wireless yet, it was Guy's job to help it make contact with the remnants of the old circuit.

When the train stopped at the Châtelet station, he got out. After winding through what seemed like miles of subterranean passages, he finally reached the sidewalk. He looked up and down the street for a *café-tabac* until he spotted one at the end of the block. All he had to do now was buy the newspaper and find the little bar on Rue Pernelle by nine o'clock.

He stepped back onto the sidewalk with a copy of *Je Suis Partout* tucked under his arm and directions to Rue Pernelle in his head. Once again he scanned the sidewalk. No one from the train or the station loitered behind him. He doubted anyone was following him, but he made one more stop just to make sure.

He found the bar on a narrow street off the Rue de Rivoli and ducked his head as he passed through the low, open doorway. He paused a moment to let his eyes grow accustomed to the darkness. The place smelled of cigarettes and sweat. A half-dozen customers sipped drinks at the dozen or so scattered tables. Two men resting their elbows on the counter stopped talking and glanced at him.

Guy sat down at the end of the long counter and laid the newspaper down in front of him. From his seat he could see the street; and if he peered carefully into the dusty mirror, he could observe the rest of the small room as well.

Tapping his fingers on the scratched bar, he studied the tariff of *consommations* hanging on the grimy wall. He could use a drink—thank God today was a *jour avec*. The barman, a tiny fellow in a stained, oversized white jacket, approached him and he ordered a cognac.

He checked his watch while he waited for his drink. His contact was due in ten minutes. When the barman brought the cognac, he paid and took a sip, wincing at the bite of the cheap stuff. Frowning, he banged the glass back onto the counter, and the amber liquid sloshed over the sides.

He ignored the sideways look of the workman sitting next to him and pulled the blue handkerchief from his pocket. Slowly, methodically, the handkerchief still folded to conceal its contents, he dabbed at the cognac, then put it under the glass. His signal was ready.

He rested his arm on the counter so he could see his watch without appearing to look at it. Nine o'clock. If the contact didn't show up in the next fifteen minutes, he'd leave, try again tomorrow. But he hoped to hell he didn't have to.

He stared into the mirror and scanned the customers sitting behind him. He inspected each one closely. As far as he could see, none possessed either a blue handkerchief or a newspaper. He shrugged and turned his attention to the window.

A car whirred into the narrow street, its slitted head-lights throwing beams of light and shadow into the room. It stopped in front of the bar, blocking the street. A large dark Citroën. From Bordeaux to Paris, the Gestapo preferred Citroëns. Guy put the handkerchief back in his pocket.

Outlined by the light from the bar windows, two men dressed in suits with big padded shoulders got out of the car. The larger one resettled his light summer hat on his head and nodded at his companion.

The clink of glasses as the barman set them on the shelf was the only sound in the room. Guy glanced around the bar. Every face was riveted on the door. He nudged the news-paper, and it fell to the floor behind the counter with a soft flutter. No one seemed to notice.

He beckoned the barman. It was his only chance. Better to risk it than to sit there. "Where's the toilet?" he asked in a low voice.

The barman nodded toward the back of the room. He ran his fingers through his sparse hair before he turned his attention back to the door.

The two Gestapo agents still chatted in the street. Maybe

they were waiting for more men. "Thanks." Guy nodded, pushed back his chair, and ambled toward the rest room. Behind him, quiet conversation had resumed. He closed the door and locked it with shaky fingers.

He jammed his hand into his pocket and ripped out the handkerchief. Even if they caught him, they wouldn't get the list. He tore the paper into pieces, threw them in the toilet, and flushed it. His mouth so dry he could hardly swallow, he watched the white specks circle the filthy bowl and then disappear. None came back up when the toilet refilled.

Next the handkerchief. If they were looking for him, that meant they'd caught his contact. And if the contact had revealed where they were to meet, he'd probably also revealed their signal. Thank God the poor bastard couldn't possibly have described him. Guy's eyes darted around the small, dirty room. Where the hell could he hide it? It would almost certainly plug the toilet.

But only if he flushed it. Quickly, he lifted the tank lid and dropped the handkerchief into the water. After he replaced the lid, he wiped the sweat from his upper lip with his sleeve. The handkerchief would incriminate only him; if he'd done nothing else, he'd at least saved eight others.

Guy took several deep breaths before he stepped out of the rest room. His eyes sweeping the room and his heart still hammering in his ears, he walked back to the bar. At least the Gestapo agents hadn't come in yet.

He glanced toward the windows. The barman had pulled the shades. The customers at the tables conversed in whispers. The two workmen at the counter stared at the door. No one paid any attention to him.

He sat down and looked at his watch. Only four minutes had passed. Christ. It felt like half an hour since they had driven up. He gulped the cheap cognac, and it seared his dry throat.

Another car turned into the street and stopped. Car doors slammed. Someone gasped. Then silence.

The door flew open, and two men burst in. They stepped to either side of the door while two more strode into the bar and scanned the room. Frowning, the biggest one motioned for the barman.

The barman scrambled over to him and shook his head repeatedly as the German questioned him in a low voice.

Finally, the Nazi turned to the others and shrugged. "He says everyone here is a regular," he said loudly in German. "They've been here all evening."

"Do you believe him?" the thick-necked agent guarding the door asked.

The big German stared at the barman for a few seconds, then inspected each customer carefully.

Guy imitated the drunken slump and blank expression of the workman next to him. The buzzing in his ears stopped, and he forced his mind to go blank.

"*Ja*," the German said, spinning on his heel. He stomped out of the room, and the others followed. A moment later, the doors slammed again and the engines roared to life.

Everyone in the room started talking at once as the cars drove away down the cobblestone street. The barman reached under the bar and brought out a bottle. Grasping it by the neck, he walked toward Guy. "More cognac?" he asked.

Guy nodded, his throat still too dry to speak, and watched as the barman filled his glass with *grande fine* Martell, then poured one for himself. "Thanks," Guy croaked, and cleared his throat. "For everything."

"*De rien*, monsieur." The barman lifted his glass. "To France," he said quietly.

The world never seemed quite real when you walked out of the cinema after a matinee. Jake blinked rapidly until his eyes grew accustomed to the harsh sunlight. Despite the absurdity of Cocteau's latest film, he almost preferred its reality to the one that now confronted him. He stood in the middle of the sidewalk for a moment while Nazi troops paraded down the Champs-Élysées in front of him, and then he headed for the nearest café.

He sat down at the back of the *terrasse* and pulled his chair around so he faced the street. If anyone was watching him, he wanted to know. Yesterday's escape had been much too narrow. If he hadn't spent the night with Françoise—

The white-aproned waiter approached, and Jake ordered a cup of coffee. He knew he shouldn't even be out on the streets, at least not until his new papers were ready, but his new place was disgustingly dirty and the concierge much too inquisitive. Too bad Denis hadn't been able to hold out a little longer. He would have had time to warn more of the others.

Jake glanced away from the street as the waiter returned with the coffee. Only chance—and lust—had saved him from the Gestapo. He paid the waiter, then sipped the filthy-tasting stuff. Actually, he supposed he had more to be thankful for than to complain about. They hadn't caught him.

Two men, obviously Gestapo in their wide-lapeled suits and summer hats, strolled down the sidewalk in front of him. He sucked in his breath and set the cup down carefully, keeping his eyes on their feet. Nobody smart ever looked a Gestapo agent in the eyes—like animals, they regarded a stare as a challenge. The two sets of shiny shoes kept walking. They weren't interested in him.

He let his breath out slowly. At least not this time.

36

🐚

Sylvie yawned and leaned back against the pillow. "It's not fair," she said. "Why do *you* have to leave so early? Can't someone else take care of those silly old Jews?" She pretended to pout, relaxing her lower lip slightly and cocking her head.

"Now, *liebling*," Otto said. Bracing himself against the wall, he pulled on his pants. "You know I wouldn't if I didn't have to. Besides, I'm doing it for you. We must make Paris a pure city." He fastened the fly buttons with a flourish and smiled at her. "Are you going to miss me today?"

"Of course," she said. She tugged at the blue satin coverlet until only the rounded curves of the tops of her breasts peeked out. She smiled down at them. It was his loss, she decided. She had everything she wanted. Well, almost everything. If only she didn't have to put up with him, her life would be perfect. He was such a silly little man.

"Good." He shrugged into his uniform jacket. "I'm going to miss you, too."

Sylvie swung her hair across her face so she wouldn't have to look at him. He was kind, she supposed, but so short. She felt like a giant whenever she stood next to him in heels. Her lips curved in a smile. They were real high heels, anyway—everyone else had those horrible wooden things. But he was so old. At least forty-five, maybe even fifty. She sighed.

"Are you going to be bored without me, *liebling?*" he asked.

Her hair still screening her face, she nodded. If he was going to be gone all day, maybe he'd offer her the car. She still hesitated to ask him directly for favors—it had only been a couple of months since she'd thrown over her handsome lieutenant and moved in with Otto at the Hôtel Majestic. So far she'd only need to hint, and he gave her whatever she wanted. As soon as she had to ask, she'd begin looking for a new officer.

She trailed her fingers across the smooth cover, pressing it down on either side of her so it molded against her waist. Perhaps a major-general next time. Why not? Otto was a colonel. The higher the rank, the better the benefits. "Terribly," she said. "It's so dull around here when you're gone." She tossed her hair back and pouted at him.

His tongue poked out between his teeth for a second before he licked his upper lip. "Isn't there anything you'd like to do, anywhere you'd like to go?" he asked. "A museum, perhaps, or shopping?" He picked up his boots and carried them to the bed.

"Well," she said, "my cousin from Saint-Émilion might be at my grandparents' by now. Grandpère said he was expecting her sometime this week." Wouldn't it be fun to show off the new dress Otto had given her, the darling little white shirtwaist with the sailor collar? Michou would be just pea green with envy.

Otto sat down next to her. "Ah," he said, pulling on his boots. "This cousin, you're quite fond of her?"

"Oh yes," she said. She inspected her shiny red fingernails, frowning at a small chip on her thumb. "We're terribly close. Have been since we were schoolgirls. She used to live with my grandparents, too."

"Perhaps you'd like to take her a little gift, then?" He glanced sideways at her before he stood up and walked stiffly to the gilded commode next to the window.

Sylvie leaned forward, holding the coverlet against her. She'd rather have a present for herself. Of course if it was something she really wanted, she could always just keep it. Otto would never know. And if she didn't like it, she'd bestow it on Michou.

"Would she enjoy silk stockings?" He rummaged through a drawer and held up his hand, several stockings dangling from it. "Perhaps you could share some of yours. You have so many."

She narrowed her eyes. How dare he suggest she give Michou something of hers? Was he joking? She forced a smile and touched a finger to her lips. "She's such a tiny little thing," she said. "Mine would never fit her."

He dropped the stockings back into the drawer and plucked a bottle of perfume from the collection on top of the commmode. "This, then," he said, tossing it on the bed.

She stared at him, her mouth open.

His face was bland, the skin across his plump cheeks smooth and his forehead unwrinkled. He finger-combed his thick dark moustache as he walked back to the bed. "I prefer the perfume you were wearing the night we met," he said, leaning over her. He kissed the top of her head, then jerked the coverlet down and kissed each of her breasts.

She tensed herself against her shudder, forced a giggle, and raised her lips to his face. "Forget my cousin," she said. "Come back to bed."

He pinched her nipples, then thrust his hand between her legs, his stubby fingers poking at her, in her. He brushed his lips across hers. His breath still smelled like the sweet Oriental cigarettes he'd smoked last night after he'd made love to her. "Ah, *liebling,*" he said, withdrawing his hand. "I wish I could. You are so beautiful, and I am such a lucky man." Straightening, he sighed. "But I have my duty."

She pulled his head back down to hers. Running her tongue across his teeth, she worked her hand beneath the waistband of his trousers and massaged his little *quéquette* until it stiffened against her palm.

His breaths turned to gasps, but he pulled her hand away. "You make me wish I could forget my duty," he said. "But today is too important. Still—" He stripped the cover off and stared at her naked body as he groped in his pocket. "I have this for you." He held out a small box.

Sitting up, she laughed and grabbed it from his hand. "You're so good to me, *chéri,*" she said. She opened the box. A large brooch paved with diamonds glittered against the black velvet lining. "It's perfect!" She held it against her pale skin.

"Your beauty deserves nothing less," he said. Smiling at her reflection in the gilded mirror above the fireplace, he picked his cap up off the mantel. He ran his hand across his bald head, then settled the cap on top of it. "After this Jewish business is completed, I will take you to dinner at Maxim's. Perhaps you'd like a new dress to go with the new jewel?"

"Oh, yes," she said, clapping her hands. "A black one."

He turned back toward her, still smiling. "A black one," he said. "Velvet? Satin? Or perhaps silk?"

"You choose," she said. "You have such wonderful taste."

His eyes swept her body. "I do, don't I?" He kissed her. "What time shall I tell my driver?"

She raised her eyebrows.

"You do want the car, don't you?"

She nodded slowly. "Nine o'clock," she said. Sometimes it was uncanny how he guessed what she wanted, almost as if he knew what she was thinking. Thank God that wasn't possible. Smiling, she stretched like a cat, arching her back and thrusting her breasts forward.

He draped the satin coverlet across her shoulders, then crossed the room to the door. He opened it and paused. "Enjoy yourself, *liebling*," he said before he stepped into the hall.

Michou rubbed her eyes and sat up. What time was it? She switched on the lamp next to the bed and grasped the clock, peering at it with sleep-blurred eyes. It was after nine. She hadn't slept so late in years.

She replaced the clock and stretched. What a luxury. How nice of Grandmère to let her sleep—she'd never permitted it before, not even on weekends.

She swung her feet over the side of the bed. The house was so quiet that the ticking clock sounded loud by contrast. She pushed herself up and grabbed her robe from the chair as she walked to the window. She hated blackout shades. The morning sun should creep gradually into a room, not rush in all at once.

Shaking her head, she eased up the shade. Such a petty thing to hate. But it symbolized the unnaturalness of her life—everyone's life—since the occupation. One small indignity piled on another. Everthing rationed, measured out in grams or liters or centimeters. You became so consumed by the little atrocities that the big ones didn't seem so horrible anymore.

The sunlight raked her eyes, and Michou blinked rapidly. The street below was so quiet, so empty, that the single car rounding the corner at the end seemed to be roaring toward her. It stopped in front of her grandparents' gate, and the uniformed driver got out and opened the back door.

A tall woman dressed in white stepped onto the walk. Her hair under the white beret shone red gold in the morning sun, and light flashed from the bracelet on her arm as she waved the Nazi driver away. She turned toward the house.

Sylvie. Michou backed away from the window. Grand-mère was going to be furious. She flung open the wardrobe door and pulled her only good dress off the hanger. Most of the wrinkles had fallen out overnight, but it still looked exactly what it was—two years out of date.

So what? She shrugged, stripped off her nightgown, and tossed it on the bed. Sylvie had paid for her dress in a currency Michou would not, could not, part with. She slipped her arms through the navy shirtwaist and tugged it on.

After she finished combing her hair, she adjusted the little white collar and tightened the belt an additional notch. Two years of rationing had whittled even more from her already slim waist. She stuck her feet into her shoes and clomped down the stairs.

She followed voices to the dining room. When she opened the door, Grandpère stood up. "Good morning, little one," he said. "Did you sleep well?"

Michou nodded and kissed his cheeks. "Hello," she said to Sylvie.

Sylvie grasped her hand. "It's been such a long time," she said. She brushed her lips against Michou's cheek. "You look wonderful. What an adorable dress."

"Thank you," Michou said. She moved back to the place set across from her and slid into the chair, the scent of Sylvie's Chanel No. 5 still following her. "Has Grandmère already eaten?"

"Hours ago," Grandpère said. "She doesn't sleep well. Can't get comfortable. So she gets up early, naps during the afternoon." He filled a cup with coffee and put it on a tray. "I was just taking coffee to her when this young lady arrived."

He smiled at Sylvie before turning back to Michou. "Now that you're here to keep her company, I'd better see to it."

"Tell Grandmère hello for me," Sylvie said.

"I will." The tray balanced on one hand, Grandpère shut the door behind him with the other.

Michou poured the watery-looking coffee into her cup and dipped a hard piece of bread into it. Breakfast at her grandparents' house used to mean hot chocolate and croissants. It seemed like years since she'd tasted either. Now it was chicory-and-acorn-flavored water and old bread. She chewed slowly on the bitter, soggy bread.

"Horrid stuff, isn't it?" Sylvie said. "I've tried to give them things, but they refuse. You know how stubborn they both are."

Trailing another piece of bread through her coffee, Michou was silent for a minute. "Why are you doing this?" she asked finally. "Is it worth it?" She looked up at Sylvie.

"Grow up, darling," Sylvie said. "The Germans are here to stay. You might as well get used to it. And if you're smart, you take advantage of it. That's all I'm doing."

"How can you, though?" Michou pulled her eyebrows together and stared at Sylvie over the top of her cup. "Don't you realize what it's doing to Grandmère and Grandpère?"

Sylvie shrugged. "If they weren't so stubborn, things would be a lot easier for them, too. I've tried to help, but they refuse the least little thing."

"Of course they do!" Michou's words exploded from her lips. She banged the cup down on the table, and coffee sloshed onto the lace tablecloth. "Grandpère was an officer in the last war against the Germans. Or had you forgotten?" She clenched her fists. She shouldn't have lost her temper. Sylvie would enjoy it too much.

"How could I forget?" Sylvie said. She spread her hands out on the table and studied them. "He reminds me every time I come to visit. But they won't have to worry about it much longer. Otto is being transferred to Bordeaux, and I'm going with him. We'll practically be neighbors. I can come to see you at your little farm, and you can visit me in the city. Won't that be nice?" She lifted her hands from the table and held them out in front of her, then turned them toward Michou. "How do you like my manicure?"

"Lovely," Michou said. Shaking her head, she leaned back in her chair. "Grandmère's hands are practically crippled, and you have a perfect manicure." She didn't make any effort to keep the bitterness out of her voice.

"I told you I tried to help," Sylvie whined. "Grandmère just ripped up the tickets I brought her and threw the pieces in my face. Why should I give up what I have just because they can't see the truth?"

"And what is that?"

"Otto says Hitler doesn't want to destroy France, just make it a better place for all of us."

"Oh? How does he propose to do that?" Michou asked. "Starve all the old people? Let them freeze to death?"

Sylvie smoothed her already perfect hair. "You're such an infant. Of course not."

"Well, how?"

"He says the Jews have made France impure. Starting today, they're going to take care of that problem for us."

"How?" Michou gripped the bottom of her chair.

"They're rounding them all up," Sylvie said. "That's why Otto couldn't come with me. I did so want you to meet him."

"What!" Michou shouted. "What are they doing?"

"Taking all the Jews to the Vél d'Hiv. Otto says that when they finish shipping them away, Paris will be a pure city."

Michou jumped up. "Nom de Dieu, Sylvie! Don't you realize what that means? Can't you think about anything besides your nails and your new clothes?"

Sylvie tilted her head and shrugged. "It's not my problem," she said.

Michou's whole body tightened. "You're right," she said, her voice shaking. "Your biggest problem is whether to wear the black or the red." She spun on her heel and stalked to the door. "I suggest black," she said, turning toward Sylvie. "For mourning."

She whirled around and slammed the door behind her. There was no time to waste. She had to warn Rachel.

37

She was almost there. Every breath raking her throat like a claw, Michou forced herself to run even faster. She'd left Sylvie sitting in the dining room, her red mouth open wide in stupid astonishment. She hadn't even stopped to tell Grand-mère or change her shoes, and her blistered feet throbbed and bled.

She gritted her teeth and shoved the pain from her mind. It simply didn't matter, not when Rachel and David were in danger. Only a few more blocks. She had to get there before the police did.

Sweat splashed into her eyes, and she wiped her forehead. French police, not Nazi pigs. How could they? She'd seen them already in some of the Jewish neighborhoods she'd passed through, seen the children screaming and crying as their parents were herded into large wagons and driven away. She'd wanted to scream and cry, too, but she kept running. And praying. Please, God, let her get there in time.

Her chest heaving, she turned onto Rue Gautier. The street was empty. She'd made it before the police. She sucked in a lungful of hot air. Or maybe she was too late. No! She clenched her fists and ran faster. She couldn't be. Just a little bit further.

She gasped and flung open the door to the apartment building, then charged up the stairs to Rachel's apartment. Tears and sweat streaking down her face, she pounded on the door. "Rachel," she cried, banging again. "Rachel! Let me in."

Slow footsteps scuffed to the door, locks clicked, and the door squeaked open. The stench of overcooked cabbage rushed into the hall. Rachel stood in the doorway, thin and gaunt except for her huge belly. Her black hair drooped to her shoulders, and her brown eyes stared dully. "Michou," she whispered, and held out her arms.

Michou threw her arms around Rachel's neck and kissed her cheeks. "Oh my God," she panted. "You didn't tell me you were pregnant."

Rachel reached over her shoulder and pushed the door shut. "I didn't know I was the last time I wrote." She turned away and walked stiffly to the sofa, her hand pressing against her lower back.

"Don't sit down," Michou said, her voice soaring. "Where's David? You're both coming with me."

Rachel swung her body around slowly and faced Michou. She shook her head.

"You have to," Michou said. "The police are arresting Jews all over Paris. Sylvie told me. And I saw them only a few blocks away."

"We were warned. I know." Rachel lowered herself onto the sofa.

"You know! Then why are you still here?"

"Waiting for Joseph," Rachel said. She buried her face in her hands. "He's been gone for two days."

Michou sat next to her. "You can't wait any longer," she said. "They're going to be here soon." She put her arm around Rachel's narrow shoulders.

Rachel shook her head. "I can't leave without him. He was arranging our escape."

"Then he'd want you to come with me," Michou said. "*Nom de Dieu*, Rachel. Think of your children. Joseph can take care of himself." She shook Rachel's shoulders. "Think of David and this little one."

Crossing her arms over her swollen belly, Rachel hunched forward. She rocked back and forth. Tears streamed down her thin face. "I am," she sobbed.

"Then get David. I'm taking you home." Michou stood. "Where is he?"

Rachel nodded toward the brown curtain. "In his room."

Michou stalked to the curtain and pushed it aside. It was

clear Rachel wasn't going to be any help. She would just have to do it all herself.

David sat in the middle of the floor playing with a stack of wooden blocks. He looked up at Michou when she stepped into the room. His face was stiff and serious. "Did you make my maman cry?" he asked. He swung his arm and toppled the blocks to the floor.

"No," Michou said. "I'm trying to make her happy. Do you want to help me?"

David nodded and his straight dark hair flopped into his eyes. He pushed the blocks out of his way and jumped up.

She knelt and held out her arms. "You don't remember me, David," she said. "I'm Michou. Your maman and I have been friends for a long, long time." She hugged him close and kissed his soft hair.

He stood rigidly in her arms for a few seconds, then struggled against her.

Michou released him. "Let's go see your maman," she said, standing.

David ran past her, and she followed him back into the main room. He stopped at the table and stared at his mother.

Rachel still sat on the sofa, looking dazed. When she saw him, she straightened. "Come here, David," she said. "I have something important to tell you." She held out her hands to him.

David walked slowly to his mother. She pulled him up onto her knees, and he rested his head against her breast. She stroked his hair as she stared at Michou over the top of his head. "Michou is my very good friend, David," she said. "And she wants to be your friend, too. Will you promise me to mind her the same way you mind me?"

David turned and looked at Michou, his eyes wide. "Why?" he asked.

"Because I might have to go away for a while," Rachel said, shaking her head at Michou.

Michou opened her mouth, then closed it. Rachel was the only person she'd ever known who was more stubborn than she. If she'd made up her mind to wait for Joseph, nothing would move her to change it. Arguing was pointless. And as long as David was present, it was destructive as well.

Rachel closed her eyes for a few seconds. "Thank you,

mignonne," she whispered when she opened them again. Her smile was wavery. "I know you'll take good care of him."

"But I don't want you to go, Maman," David said, his voice high-pitched and quavering.

"Shhh," Rachel said. She wrapped her arms around him.

The street below filled with the noise of motors, and Michou whirled around. A cold hand gripped her heart as she pulled back the old lace curtains and looked out the window. Several police cars moved slowly down the street, some pulling up to the curb while others continued to the end of the block. Car doors slammed, and uniformed policemen fanned out in front of the apartment buildings that lined the street. A large wagon crept around the corner.

Michou dropped the curtain. "They're here," she croaked. "It's too late."

Rachel kissed David, clinging to him until the hall echoed with the clatter of boots. Holding him to her, she pushed herself off the sofa and carried him to Michou. "Take him," she said as she thrust David into her arms. "There's still a chance for him. The woman next door isn't Jewish, and she hates the Nazis. Tell her who you are. Joseph will know where to find you." She reached into a basket on the table, drew out a yellow star, and pinned it to her blouse.

As she reached into the basket again, the door rattled. "Open up. Police."

Rachel kissed David and set a small packet on the table. "His papers," she said. "He'll be three in ten days." Then she shuffled to the door. She opened it, and two policemen burst into the room.

"Identity cards," the fat one ordered.

Rachel handed him her card while the other policeman moved across the room to Michou. "Your card, mademoiselle," he said.

Michou gasped and tightened her arms around David. Her card was in her purse. And her purse was still in her bedroom at her grandparents' house. "I—I don't have it," she said. "I left it at home."

The moustached policeman looked back at his fat friend and shrugged. "She doesn't look like a Jew," he said. "And she's not wearing a star."

"She's not Jewish," Rachel said. "She was just visiting me."

The fat policeman took a piece of paper from his pocket and unfolded it. He ran his finger down the sheet. "Says on this tenant list you've got a husband living here. Nothing about another female. Where's your husband?"

Rachel shook her head. "I don't know," she said.

The policeman slapped her, and her head thudded against the door. "Where is he?" he said.

"Leave my maman alone!" David shrieked, struggling to escape from Michou's arms.

"Stop it!" Michou screamed. She squeezed David in her arms. "She doesn't know. She really doesn't know. He hasn't been home for two days. Leave her alone. Are you blind? She's pregnant."

"You shut up, Jew lover," the fat policeman said over his shoulder. "Or we'll take you, too."

Michou clenched her teeth until her jaw ached. David's heart beat wildly against her chest. They were going to let her go. For David's sake, she had to obey.

"We can get the husband later," the moustached policeman said. "Let's go."

The fat policeman shoved Rachel out the door.

"Maman!" David flailed at Michou. "Maman! I won't let them take you." He pounded Michou's chest. "Put me down! I want to go with Maman."

Michou clutched David, hot tears washing down her cheeks.

"Stay with Michou, David," Rachel called from the hall. "Be resolute." A loud crack and a scream followed her words.

"Do what she says," the remaining policeman said. He leaned forward and whispered, "Get the boy out of here after we're gone. We're not taking children this time. But tomorrow they might change their minds." He patted David's head. "I've got a son about his age."

David jerked away from him. "I hate you," he yelled. "Where's Maman?"

"Shhh, David," Michou said.

"I'm sorry," the policeman mumbled, staring down at

his feet. He touched his cap. "And don't go anywhere without your papers," he said. Then he strode out the door.

Michou stood up and carried David to the window. She pressed his head against her shoulder, but he twisted in her arms and looked out. "Maman!" he shrieked, pointing. "Don't go away!"

In the street below, the police herded dozens of people into a large van. Sobbing children filled the sidewalk, stretching out small arms and screaming for their mamas and papas. Her face contorted with anguish, Rachel paused and waved before she disappeared into the van.

"No!" David struggled and pounded on Michou with his little fists. "Let me go! I want my maman."

A new wave of tears stung Michou's eyes, and she squeezed them shut and grasped David even more tightly. Be resolute, she told herself. For Rachel. But most of all, for David.

David cradled to her chest, Michou stumbled into the entry of her grandparents' house. The long walk had been an agony of bleeding feet and aching arms, of restrained tears and false reassurances. How did you tell a child of three he might never see his mother again? You didn't. You hoped for a miracle; you reached for a lie.

She put David down and kicked off her shoes. "This is where my grandparents live," she said. "They know your maman, too. They're going to be very happy to meet you."

David looked the room over. "Do you live here, too?" he asked.

"No," she said. "I'm just staying here for a few days. Pretty soon we'll take the train to my house."

"And Maman will come and get me there, right, Misou?" He stared up at her, his big dark eyes still swimming with tears.

"Right." She squeezed his hand. "Now, let's go find Grandmère and Grandpère." She pushed the front door shut.

"Is that you, Michèle?" her grandmother's voice called from the salon.

"Yes," Michou said. She led David toward the salon. Grandmère had never approved of her friendship with

Rachel. No matter how wealthy her parents, Rachel had always been "that Jewish girl" to her, and although Grand-mère had allowed her to bring Rachel to the house, she'd always treated her with a frigid politeness.

"Where have you—" Grandmère stopped when she saw David.

"I went to see Rachel. This is her son, David." Michou pulled him against her legs and crossed her arms over his chest.

"But—"

Michou put her finger to her lips and shook her head. "David's maman had to go away for a while," she said, "So I told her he could stay with me."

Grandmère stared at Michou's feet, then raised her eyes to her face. "I see," she said slowly. She kicked aside her quilt and pushed herself out of her chair. "Are you hungry, David?"

David nodded.

"Then we must tell Aimée to fix something for you to eat." Grandmère held out her hand.

David clung to Michou and shook his head.

"I think it's best if I stay with him until he gets used to it here," Michou said. She picked up David and rested him against her hip. "We'll both go with Grandmère, all right?"

"You're probably right, dear," Grandmère said. She hobbled to the door. "It's been so long since I've been around children. And even then I was never very good with them."

Michou stared at her back. Grandmère's voice sounded so distant, so sad. Had she always loved her children and grandchildren but been unable to show it? What a terrible frustration that must have been for her.

David slipped out of her arms and grabbed her hand. "Misou?" he said.

Michou started, then smiled down at him. She led him into the hall. "I'll bet Grandmère has something wonderful for us in the kitchen," she said. "When I was a little girl, she used to talk Aimée into fixing the best treats in the world. I used to beg my maman to let me visit."

Grandmère looked over her shoulder. "Did you really, my dear?" She smiled.

38

Guy stepped off the train into the crowded Odéon station. What a mess. His contact arrested, the list destroyed, the backup rendezvous spot crawling with Gestapo. Thank God he was meeting Michou tomorrow to arrange their departure. He loved Paris, but it was a diseased city. And definitely not safe for him.

He moved toward the stairs, the herd of people pressing against him, the stench of their sweat, cigarettes, cheap perfumes coating his mouth and his nostrils. At the top of the stairs, a man wearing a black beret paused to read a poster. Guy glanced at him as he walked by, then jerked his head around and stared again.

Jake. Good God, it was Jake. He wanted to go up to him, slap him on the back, shake his hand, but he forced himself to keep walking. Another SOE rule that made sense but was damned hard to obey. Never greet another agent in public, not even if he's your best friend. If the Nazis were watching him, they'd have you, too.

Guy stopped in front of a black and red execution notice and pretended to read it. Well, he wouldn't. He'd follow him, make sure no one else did. He pulled his hat down and turned his back to the Métro exit.

A minute later Jake strode by. Guy waited until he was several paces ahead, then ambled after him, his hands stuffed into his trouser pockets. He paused in front of a bookstore window, staring at his reflection while Jake studied another poster. He raised his eyebrows. Jake obviously suspected he was being followed.

Guy remained at the window until Jake moved on and

turned the corner. He looked up and down the busy sidewalk. He didn't recognize anyone from the Métro station, and no one seemed to pay any attention either to him or to Jake.

He walked quickly to the corner. Jake was right, of course. He *was* being followed. But after several more blocks of stops and backtracks, Guy was convinced he was the only one interested in Jake's progress.

Finally, Jake ducked into a bar. Guy halted again in front of a shop window to see if anyone familiar followed him inside. People pushed by him on the sidewalk, but no one went into the bar.

Guy shoved his hat back off his forehead as he stepped into the small, dimly lit room. Jake sat alone at the long bar, a glass of beer in front of him and both elbows resting on the yellowed oak counter. Guy sat down next to him.

Jake looked at him sideways, a casual inspection of a stranger who chooses to sit too close. His whole body stiffened, and his mouth fell open as he swiveled his head toward Guy. "My God," he whispered.

Guy grinned. "Hello, Jake," he said, shaking his hand. "How are you?"

"Stupefied," Jake said. "Give me a second."

The fat barmaid waddled toward Guy. "You want something?" she asked.

"A beer," Guy said. He waited until she reached the other end of the counter before he turned back to Jake.

"I knew someone was behind me," Jake said. "Made me nervous after what happened a couple of days ago." He ran his hand over his balding head.

The barmaid smacked the beer down in front of Guy, and he paid her. "Let's sit over there," he said, nodding at a table in the corner. He picked up his beer, took a long swallow, and then carried it across the room. He pulled out a chair and sat down, his back to the wall.

Jake eased into the chair next to him. "What the hell are you doing here?" he asked, keeping his voice low.

"Looking for Bluebird," Guy said. "But everything got screwed up."

Jake closed his eyes for a second. "*I* am Bluebird," he said finally.

Guy set his beer down. "You?"

"I got here last month to set this thing up. Nothing has gone right." Jake shook his head. "People arrested, Ian still not here with the—"

"I know," Guy said. "Some of your luck almost rubbed off on me. Your contact man gave me up to the Gestapo."

Jake nodded. "He gave up everyone. Including me. I was out when the Gestapo arrived, and I hid when I returned and saw them in front of my apartment building. Fortunately, I had time to warn some of the others. Now we've all got to set up new identities, find new places to live." He sighed. "At least the poor bastard didn't know anything about our counterfeiter. He's working all day and half the night on our new papers and almost has them finished, but it's still going to take weeks to get everything else straightened out." His hands shook as he lit a cigarette.

Guy drained his glass. "Thank God they got the contact before our meeting. If it had been afterward, they would've had eight more names. And no one could have warned *them* because no one would've known who they were."

Jake exhaled a stream of smoke at the floor. "And each of them might have given up others. That's what happened to Autogiro."

Guy swirled his empty glass around in the pool of condensation on the scarred tabletop, the words of his instructors at Beaulieu echoing through his head. Everyone gives in to the torture sooner or later, they'd said. You can kill yourself first—if you have the courage and they haven't found your poison. Or you can try to hold out for a day or two, give others a chance to hide. You can hold out for a while, but in the end—

"I don't suppose you still have the names," Jake said.

Guy shook his head.

"No matter," Jake said. "My wireless man is due any day. You remember Ian?"

"Of course," Guy said. "Is he still a son of a bitch?"

"Hasn't changed a bit." Jake stubbed out his cigarette. "Must go. Sorry. I was just on my way to pick up my new papers." He stood up and held out his hand. "I have to say, though, I can't think of anyone I'd rather have following me than you." He smiled. "Can we meet again, or are you leaving right away?"

Guy rose and grasped Jake's hand. "Day after tomorrow, probably," he said. "Where can I find you?"

"Seventy Rue Jacob for the next two days. Ask for Dominique Perrel."

"Easy address to remember." Guy walked to the door with Jake. "I'll be by," he said.

"Good," Jake said, smiling. "I'm looking forward to it." He peered up and down the street, then stepped onto the sidewalk without glancing back.

Guy turned back to the bar and seated himself at the counter again. "I'll have another one," he said to the barmaid.

"That's far enough, David," Michou called. "Come back now." She slipped her feet out of her shoes. The dried grass scratched her blisters from yesterday's ordeal, but even that was better than the torture of the stiff, wooden-soled shoes. She leaned over and picked them up, wrinkling her nose at the smell of old leather and dead grass.

"Over here, David," she called. She pointed with the shoes to a bench under a large maple. Gingerly, she walked toward it. What was Guy going to say when he arrived and found her with a three-year-old child? She hoped he didn't tell her she'd have to leave David in Paris. Because she couldn't.

She sat down on the shaded bench. David ran around in circles in front of her, falling down and laughing, then picking himself up and running around again. She smiled at him and waved. He seemed to accept his mother's absence most of the time. But several times he'd stopped in the middle of his play to sit staring at nothing, his eyes glazed with tears, his lower lip trembling, his face a study in misery. Then he'd turn to her and say, "Maman will be back soon, right, Misou?" She'd nod and manage a cheerful reply even though she felt like crying, too, and he'd sigh and go back to his game.

For David's sake, she had to hide her anguish and fear, had to pretend Rachel was going to be fine. She couldn't give in to what was boiling inside her—the sorrow, the terror, the rage. All she could do for Rachel was make sure David was safe and loved. And nothing was going to stop her from doing that.

"May I sit here?"

She jerked her head up. Guy stood in front of her. She hadn't even seen him approach. Had he noticed David? She drew a deep breath and nodded. "Of course."

He sat down next to her. "What's wrong?" he asked. "You look upset."

Michou rubbed at the tears on her cheeks. Her voice stuck in her throat.

He glanced down. "What the hell happened to your feet?"

Swallowing hard, she pointed at David.

"Who's he?"

"Rachel's son. David."

Guy frowned. "Why did you bring him here?"

"I had to." She bit her lip.

He grabbed her hands. "Tell me what's going on," he said.

Michou squeezed Guy's hands and closed her eyes. He had to understand. He had a Jewish friend, and he'd lost his daughter. If he didn't, she'd fallen in love with the wrong man.

She opened her eyes and looked up into his. "The police arrested Rachel yesterday. I was there. They took away all the Jews on her street in a big van. Sylvie told me the Jews were going to be rounded up and sent away." She paused. "We both know they won't come back."

Guy pinched the bridge of his nose. He shook his head slowly as he pulled his pipe and tobacco from his pocket.

"I tried to find his grandparents," she said, "but their house was closed up. And Rachel hadn't seen her husband for a couple of days. I left word for him with a neighbor in case he comes back."

"Can this neighbor be trusted?" Guy asked. He lit the pipe and puffed on it. Smoke drifted up from the bowl.

Michou nodded. "I only gave her my first name." She clenched her jaw and stared down at the bench, remembering the thin woman in the faded dress, a crying baby in her arms. The baby wasn't hers, she'd told Michou. His mother had gone out for something and had never returned. She'd heard the infant screaming for a whole day and night and had finally persuaded the concierge to unlock the door. Two weeks later the police came and asked about the child. His mother was in prison for violating curfew. The woman had tightened her arms around the baby and gritted her teeth. "Two weeks," she'd repeated. "It took them two weeks. The baby would have been dead, and they didn't care."

Guy put his hand under her chin and pulled her face up. "We have to get David out of Paris," he said. "He needs new papers, a new name, and I have a pretty good idea where I can get them." He put his pipe back into his mouth and drew on it, blowing the smoke toward the sky.

Michou let her breath out in a huge sob. How could she have doubted him? Tears spilled down her cheeks.

David ran up to her. He stood close to her legs and glared at Guy. "Who are you?" he asked. He turned to Michou. "What's wrong? Why are you crying?"

Swiping at the tears, Michou smiled at him. "Because I'm happy," she said. "Everything is going to be all right."

The frizzy-haired concierge leaned against her doorway and grinned at him. "Who?" she asked.

"Dominique Perrel," Guy said.

She put her hands on her hips and thrust her huge breasts out. "Sure, he's home." She leaned down and picked up the cat at her feet, and the tops of her breasts jiggled under the thin, low-cut dress. Pressing the cat against her chest, she straightened and smiled at Guy. The cat meowed and squirmed. "Number four," she said, pointing down the narrow hall with her free hand.

"Thanks," he said. As he turned away, he breathed through his mouth to avoid the stench of cat urine permeating the air. He walked quickly to the door the woman had indicated and knocked. "It's Guy," he said.

Jake opened the door and pulled him inside. "Glad you could make it," he said, shaking his hand. "Some wine?" He pointed to a green bottle sitting on top of a spindly wood table.

"Sure," Guy said.

Jake dragged a chair across the room and put it next to the one in front of the table. "Not really set up for entertaining yet," he said. "Only been here for a couple of days." He nodded at the chair. "Have a seat while I find another glass."

Guy sat down and crossed his legs. "Nice place you got here," he said. "Lovely concierge."

Jake sneered as he poured the red wine into two stubby glasses. "I'm a little worried about that one," he said. "She's too interested in everything. Keeps track of my comings and goings. I doubt I'll be here long." He handed Guy a glass and sat down.

Guy raised his glass. *"Chin-chin,"* he said. He took a sip, and his eyebrows pulled together involuntarily.

"Sorry," Jake said. "I should have warned you."

Guy swallowed the sour stuff and shrugged. "I've tasted worse." He drank again. "Is it safe to talk here?"

Jake nodded. "The rooms on either side are vacant. And I haven't caught the concierge with her ear to anyone's door yet."

"Good." Guy leaned forward. "I have a favor to ask. I need a new set of papers. For a little boy. Jewish. Three years old. They took his mother in yesterday's roundup. No one knows where his father is, and I want to get him out of Paris. Can your man make them up for me? First name David, preferably. Religion Catholic."

A muscle in Jake's jaw twitched. "When do you want them?" he asked, his voice tight.

"Tomorrow," Guy said.

39

Michou smoothed back the damp brown tendrils of hair from David's forehead. It hadn't taken long for the monotonous rhythm of the click-clacking rails to put him to sleep. He moaned, and she pulled her hand away. She wanted him to sleep as long as he could before the train reached the demarcation line. He needed the rest, and she needed the time to build her courage, to calm the fear already knotting her stomach, souring her mouth.

She looked over her shoulder at Guy, and he nodded at her, his eyes serious. The white furrows between his eyebrows stood out against his tanned face.

Michou turned back around. Sweat trickled down her belly, and she pulled her blouse away from her body. *Mon Dieu*, it was hot. And smelly. She wrinkled her nose. Sweat, smoke, garlic, cabbage—all mingled with the steamy air inside the car to form an unpleasant cloud that pressed against her skin and coated her mouth.

Nice vacation. She grimaced, remembering her anticipation and excitement, her vision of seeing Paris on Guy's arm, of not having to hide her love for him as she did in Saint-Émilion. The daydreams had persisted despite everything Guy had said about caution and danger, despite her own acceptance of his words.

And it had turned out just as he'd predicted. She hadn't touched him since they'd made their plans. And she couldn't now, when all she wanted was to hold his hand, draw some reassurance from his warm grip. Too dangerous, he'd said again. No one should guess they were together until they crossed the line. Just in case.

She closed her eyes and leaned her head against the back of the hard seat. Just in case. Although her travel permit was fake, she at least had authentic identity papers. Both Guy's and David's were false. Guy had assured her that he never had problems with his, and he claimed the name on David's new baptismal certificate was even entered on a parish registry in Lyon. But still—

Her stomach churned. What if some little thing were wrong, and the *contrôle* at the checkpoint spotted it?

She forced her eyes open. Stop it, she told herself. Her best protection was the appearance of complete innocence. And that was going to be impossible if she didn't stop worrying. And the only way she could stop worrying was to think about something else.

She looked down at her hand resting on David's chest. Stubby nails, callused skin—quite a contrast to Sylvie's perfect manicure. Damn Sylvie. Why couldn't she see how much she was hurting Grandmère and Grandpère? She'd actually come to visit last night, flaunting a new diamond brooch and a black silk dress. On her way to Maxim's, she'd said with a smirk.

Michou sneered. Sylvie wasn't any more in love with her Nazi colonel than—

She sighed. Than Michou was in love with Erich. Yet, for a while, before Guy came back—

Her fingers tightened on David's shirt. Erich was German, and she'd cared for him. She still did. Even so, she'd used him, was still using him. Her motives were more noble than Sylvie's, but her ploy was the same. She frowned, hating the thought that she had anything in common with Sylvie.

David stirred and mumbled. She stroked his hair. "It's all right," she whispered. "Go back to sleep."

His eyes fluttered open, then closed. He stuck his thumb into his mouth, wiggled onto his side, and burrowed his head into her lap.

Where was Rachel now? She ground her teeth. If only she could tell her that David was fine. Her lip trembled. No. She couldn't think about Rachel.

Michou stared out the window. Fields just beginning to turn brown clicked by, accented by green thickets and trees and, although it wasn't wine country, an occasional vineyard.

Vineyards. She wondered if Philippe was doing as he'd promised. He'd certainly been impressed with Guy. It was going to
be almost pleasant going back now that she didn't have to put
up with his animosity any longer.

Not like Lucien's. She rested her head against the vibrating window. If Maman married Henri, Lucien would be her
stepbrother. She shuddered. What a disgusting thought. As
much as she wanted Maman's happiness, she'd never accept
Lucien as a brother. She barely accepted him as a human
being. He was not only responsible for Alain's death but for
Papa's as well.

The train slowed, and she snapped her head back up.
Her bowels cramped. This must be it.

David groaned and opened his eyes. "Are we there?" he
asked, his voice still groggy.

"Not yet," she said. "This is just the border. We have to
show the soldiers our papers." She helped him sit up beside
her.

Brakes squeaked and engines hissed as the train came to
a stop. Everyone around her stood up and pushed into the
aisle. She glanced at Guy, and he nodded. Gripping David's
hand, she rose, too, and forced her way into the crowd leaving
the train.

Suddenly, as she reached the platform, a high-pitched
shriek echoed through the station. Michou pulled David
against her legs and held him there tightly as the scream
turned to hysterical crying and pleading. She swiveled her
head, trying to see, but everyone else was so much taller.

Bodies jostled against her, and someone stepped on her
toe. Finally, she saw what was happening. Three German
soldiers pushed their way through the crowd, thrusting people aside to make room for two officers dragging a sobbing
woman. One slapped her. The station was silent except for
her cries and the harsh commands of the soldiers.

Michou clutched David as the soldiers passed and the
crowd closed back around them. What had the woman done?
Had her papers been forgeries? Was she a Resistance fighter?
Or a Jew? Voices all around her buzzed in the same specula-
tion, and the noise quickly grew to its former level.

David squirmed loose and turned to her. "Who was
that?" he asked. "Why was she crying? Were those men

being mean to her? Was she a bad lady? Are they going to shoot her with their guns?"

Michou shook her head. "I don't know, *mon chou*. But don't let go of my hand. I don't want to lose you." She stood on tiptoe and tried to spot Guy. If she could just see him, she'd feel better. But the crowd pressed against her, and she was forced to move along with it. Gradually, it narrowed until she could see the checkpoint.

She picked up David and settled him against her hip.

"Don't say anything while I'm talking to that man up there," she whispered into his ear. "Do you understand?"

He nodded, his eyes big.

"Good boy." She let him slide back to the floor and looked over her shoulder again. Still no Guy. She swallowed hard and fumbled through her purse for her papers and David's. The man in front of her stepped around the barrier, and she moved forward, David clinging to one hand.

A tall red-haired Nazi soldier, his face set in stiff lines of boredom, stared down at her. He raised his pale eyebrows and held out his hand.

She gave him her papers. Her head throbbed with the poor woman's screams, and her throat ached while he glanced at them.

He poked them back at her and nodded at David. "Now his," he said.

She took a deep breath and put her papers back into her purse. Slowly, calmly, she told herself. She grasped David's papers, her hand trembling only slightly, and held them out.

The soldier snatched them from her and glared at them. "Different name," he said. "He's not your son?"

She shook her head.

"Well?" he said.

She cleared her throat. "He's my nephew," she said. "My sister's little boy."

"Your sister, she married to a Jew?"

She shook her head. Her throat constricted.

He glared at her, then at David. Finally, he shrugged. "Get back on the train," he said, shoving the papers at her.

She snatched them and stuffed them back into her purse. Tugging at David's hand, she headed around the barrier, her chin thrust forward. She would not cry. She would remain calm and walk slowly back to their seats. She bit her lip to keep it from quivering.

David whimpered, and she looked down at him. "What's wrong?" she said.

"You're hurting my hand," he said.

She bent and scooped him up. "I'm so sorry. I didn't mean to. You were a very good boy back there." She carried him onto the train, his legs wrapped around her waist and his arms around her neck.

"Misou," he said, "is my maman your sister?"

"Shhh." She set him down on the seat and put her finger to her lips. "We'll talk about it later. Do you want to sit by the window?"

"All right," he said. He scooted across the seat.

Michou scanned the car before she sat down. She looked out the window over David's head. The platform had emptied. But where was Guy? She clenched her fists.

Just as the train's engines started up again, Guy walked down the aisle and slid into the seat next to her. "Everything went fine," he said.

"Where were you?" She frowned at him. "I looked all over. I was beginning to think—" Her voice cracked, and she sniffed back the tears.

He put his arm around her shoulders and pulled her to him. "God, I've missed you," he said. "I love you."

She laid her head against his chest, and the tightness in her throat eased. "I'm so glad you're here," she said, "not sitting back there anymore."

"This hasn't been much fun for you, has it?" he said. "I should never have suggested it. Seems every time we go to Paris together something awful happens."

"I know." She lifted her head. "But it turned out to be a good thing after all." She glanced at David. "What would have happened if I hadn't been there?"

"You were," Guy said. "Don't even think about it."

She forced a smile, her lower lip trembling. "And what am I going to tell Maman and Mémé Laure?" she asked, nodding toward David.

"The truth," he said.

40

The front door slammed. Catherine pulled her hands off the keys and jumped up from the piano bench. The last note hung in the air, then dissolved. It had to be Michou this time. It had been more than an hour since she'd called from Libourne.

Mémé Laure chuckled. "Relax," she said, looking up from her crocheting. "She's fine."

"I know, but—" Catherine strode to the tall double doors, threw them open, and stepped into the hall.

Michou walked toward her, a dark-haired gamin clinging to her hand, dust clinging to both of them. "Oh, Maman," she said.

"Thank God," Catherine said. "You're home." She pulled Michou to her and hugged her, trying not to wrinkle her nose at the acrid smells of smoke and sweat. Then, raising an eyebrow, she held her at arm's length and stared at her. So this was what Michou'd meant when she said she had something to explain. What had this daughter of hers gotten herself involved in this time? She sighed. She should be used to it by now. She knelt on one knee in front of the child. "What's your name?" she asked.

"David," he said.

"Well, David," she said, rising and holding out her hand. "I'm Michou's mother, and I'm very glad to meet you. Shall we go meet Mémé Laure?"

David looked up at Michou. She smiled and nodded at him, and he took Catherine's hand. "All right," he said.

Catherine led him into the salon. "Mémé Laure, I'd like you to meet Michou's friend David." She glanced back at Michou. "He's come to stay with us for a while."

After she greeted David, Mémé Laure peered over her glasses, first at Catherine, then at Michou. Finally, she dropped her crocheting into the basket at her feet and pushed herself up. "I'll bet you'd like to get cleaned up and have something to eat after that long trip," she said. "Why don't you come with me?"

"Go ahead, David," Michou said. "I'll meet you in the kitchen."

David looked at Michou again before he followed Mémé Laure from the room.

After the doors shut behind them, Catherine put her hands on her hips and faced Michou. "Well?" she said. "Who is he?"

Michou walked to the window. "Rachel's son," she said.

"I thought as much," Catherine said. "He looks like her, doesn't he?" She followed Michou to the window and put her hand on her shoulder. "Come sit by me. Tell me what happened." She linked her arm through Michou's.

Michou turned to her, her violet eyes dark and shimmering with tears. "It was awful," she said. "They took her away because she's Jewish. I couldn't let them take David." She stiffened, inhaling deeply and releasing her breath with a shudder, and dabbed at her eyes. "The bastards," she whispered.

Catherine grasped both of Michou's arms. "You did the right thing. But now we need to decide what to tell everyone, how to explain who he is and why he's here." She pulled Michou onto the sofa beside her. "I suppose you've had some time to think about it?"

Michou nodded. "Plenty."

"Keep in mind that the best lies are closest to the truth."

Michou's eyebrows shot up.

Catherine chuckled without mirth. "If I'd been as strict with you as my mother was with me, you'd have learned that long ago." She paused. "Of course, that was one of the reasons I wasn't. That and the fact that it wouldn't have done much good anyway. If something got in your way, you just butted your head against it until it gave away. I was always afraid that someday you'd smash up against something or someone more stubborn than you. It hasn't happened yet, but—" She paused. "I think it's time you learned to be more cautious, to use your head for something other than a battering ram." She leaned back. "I'm through lecturing now. Tell me your plan."

Michou closed her mouth and stared at her for a minute. "You mean you lied to—"

"Yes," Catherine said.

Michou shook her head slowly. "I'm glad," she said. "I'm really glad you did. I always thought you were—"

"Perfect? Well, I wasn't. I was just a little smarter than you. When people *think* you're perfect, you can get away with a lot more." She tapped her fingernails on the sofa's wood trim. "So?"

Michou twisted her hair around her finger. "He has false papers."

"I won't ask how you got them."

Michou nodded. "They give his name as Jean-David Jourdan."

"I suppose we should call him Jean-David, then."

"Right. I guess I can just tell him since he's a big boy, we've decided to call him by his real name."

"And it is now," Catherine said. "That's as close to the truth as we can get."

"And he's the son of a school friend whose husband died fighting the Germans. And then she died—" Michou paused, tugging at the strand of hair wrapped around her finger. "In childbirth." She bit her lip. "Rachel is seven months pregnant."

"But David, I mean Jean-David, doesn't know yet his maman is dead. He thinks she's gone away on a trip."

"Which she has, of course." Michou stood up. "I think we should tell Mémé Laure. But no one else. Not even Philippe."

"I agree," Catherine said. "One more thing. This friend of yours—what's her name?"

Michou rolled her eyes. "How about Camille Duchamp? She did go to school with us for a while. And she's dark. We can say she married a man named Jourdan, Pierre Jourdan."

Catherine rose. "Do you see what I mean? A lie can get complicated awfully fast. Be prepared, but don't volunteer anything. Answer questions without a pause, but try not to invent any more than you have to. The more you tell, the more there'll be to trip you up."

Michou smiled for the first time. "I don't believe this," she said. "I think you actually enjoy the intrigue."

Catherine shrugged. "I hate the Germans every bit as much as you do, *chérie*. Controlled hatred is far more effective, however."

"That's what Guy—" Reddening, Michou broke off.

Catherine raised her eyebrows. "I always thought he had a lot of sense," she said. "I wonder what happened to him." She stared at Michou.

Michou ducked her head. "I don't know," she mumbled. "Not much reason for him to be around until harvest, I guess."

"You're probably right," Catherine said, a smile twitching at the corner of her mouth. When Michou looked up, she quickly pursed her lips. She wasn't sure what, but something was going on. She just hoped her daughter was better at lying to other people. She put her arm around Michou's shoulder and gave her a quick hug. "Let's go see how Mémé Laure and Jean-David are getting along."

"Famously, I'll bet," Michou said. She opened the door, then turned to Catherine and paused. "Do you think we could give him a birthday party? He'll be three on Sunday."

"I don't see why not," Catherine said. "If we did, it certainly wouldn't appear to anyone that we were hiding his presence." She smiled. "In fact, I think it's an excellent idea. "It's about time we celebrated something around here."

Standing in front of her mirror, Michou tugged the light cotton nightgown over her head. After she smoothed it over her hips, she reached for her brush and sighed. She was so exhausted after a couple of days chasing a three-year-old all over the place, she hadn't had time to worry about Guy or Philippe or the vineyards or anything.

She smiled at herself as she pulled the brush through her frizzy curls. Already she loved David as if he were her own. Jean-David, she automatically corrected herself, frowning. She even had to think of him as Jean-David. His birthday party was in three days, and she couldn't make any mistakes.

A quiet knock sounded at her door, and she whirled around, the brush still in her hand.

Philippe slipped into the room. "Don't hit me with that," he said, grinning and nodding at the brush. "I've just come to say good-bye."

Michou stared at him. "What?" she said. She laid the brush back on the bureau. "You're joking."

"No." He shook his head and held out the bag in his hand. "See? I'm joining the maquis."

"You can't. I need you here. Think about what it'll do to Maman."

He set the bag down. "I know," he said, holding out his hands, palms up. "But look. If I stay much longer, I'm going to get called up for forced labor in Germany, and then I wouldn't be able to help you or anyone else. You know that. Besides—" He grinned lopsidedly. "I've never really been much help. You know that, too."

She sighed. "That's not true. As you've pointed out so many times before, I wouldn't be able to do everything by myself if it hadn't been for you. What am I going to do if one of the pulleys breaks?"

His smile grew even wider. "Ask Erich to fix it. I'm sure he'd be happy to. He stares at you even more since you came back. The man's a goner."

She punched him on the arm. "Stop it," she said. Her lower lip quivered, and she threw her arms around him. "Philippe the Rash. Try not to do anything stupid. It'll break Maman's heart if anything happens to you."

"Nothing's going to. Nothing bad, anyway." He broke away from her. "Tell me how to find Guy."

"Twenty-four Rue Aristide-Briand. Upstairs." She paused, narrowing her eyes. "Is Édouard going, too?"

Philippe nodded.

"Don't both of you go tromping up to Guy's apartment. Leave Édouard at a café. And don't go there tonight. Wait until dawn."

"Yes, *mon général.*" He saluted. "I shall do as you command." He picked up his bag. "Am I dismissed?"

"At ease, soldier," she said, smiling at him. "Not so fast." She kissed both his cheeks. "Papa would be proud of you."

"I know." He opened the door and winked at her. "Give Erich my love," he said, pulling the door shut quickly behind him.

Still smiling, she shook her head and returned to the bureau. *Mon Dieu,* she hoped his high spirits wouldn't get him into too much trouble. Guy couldn't watch out for him all the time—he was just a trainer and a contact man for the maquis in the northern Dordogne. Philippe would be on his own.

Her smile faded as she picked up her brush. As usual, Philippe had left her with the dirty work. She was going to be the one to tell Maman and Mémé Laure. She tilted her head back and brushed furiously at the tangles. And how was she going to explain his absence to everyone else? That was all she needed, now, of all times, when she was still explaining Jean-David's presence.

She slammed the brush back down on the crocheted doily and picked up the silver wine funnel Guy had given her. Closing her eyes, she pressed it against her cheek, the cool metal soothing her flushed face. One thing at a time, she told herself. She'd talk to Maman first thing in the morning. Together they'd devise a story, just as they had for Jean-David.

She opened her eyes and cupped the funnel in one hand, tracing the border with her finger. She missed Guy already, missed his strong, warm hands, his broad shoulders, the dimples that creased his face when he smiled. Was all of this ever going to stop so they could just be together?

She returned the funnel to the little collection on top of the bureau and climbed into bed. The air in the room hung still and hot, and she kicked the coverlet to the foot of the bed before she turned out the light. She missed so many people—Marc and Papa dead, Guy hiding, and now Philippe gone to join the maquis. Their ghosts danced around her like the cats on the funnel.

41

Michou climbed down from the chair and eyed her work. Her heart might be sad, but the dining room, at least, looked festive. Red and blue paper garlands looped across the walls between the tall windows, and yellow streamers decorated both sides of the white fireplace. Vivid bows of green and purple and pink hung from the sparkling chandelier. Jean-David was going to be delighted, she thought as she brushed at the impressions her bare feet had left on the burgundy velvet chair seat.

Cécile bustled into the room as Michou scooted the heavy chair across the Persian carpet and back under the table. Her eyes sparkling, Cécile held out a silver tray on which perched a large cake swirled with chocolate icing and chopped nuts. "*Voilà*," she said. "It is finished." She set it down on the center of the table and put her hands on her hips. "Well?" She turned to Michou.

"It's beautiful," Michou said. "It's been so long since I've eaten cake, I've almost forgotten what it tastes like. And I doubt if Jean-David even knows what chocolate is. He was only a year old when the Germans came." She slid her finger along the tray to clean up a speck of the icing and then licked it. "Mmmm," she said, letting the rich, slightly bitter chocolate dissolve slowly on her tongue. "You're a genius, Cécile. Where in the world did you find chocolate?"

"I have my secrets." Cécile smiled broadly. "Better get back to the kitchen," she said. "Now don't you go picking at that cake anymore." She shook her finger at Michou before she disappeared through the swinging door.

Michou's smile faded. Such a big cake for so few people. Philippe was gone, and of everyone she and Maman had asked, only Berthe and Daniel and Henri had promised to come. The rest had made excuses—no gasoline, other plans, too sick. She'd listened to them all, knowing full well what lay behind their reluctance—the rumors about her and Erich. Gabrielle had made that clear enough, and even her parents had refused. For herself, she didn't care. But it just wasn't fair to Jean-David. And Maman—she'd worked so hard to find the special treats for the birthday dinner.

Footsteps clattered in the hall, followed by a loud giggle. Jean-David burst into the room, followed by Maman. "Misou!" he shouted. "Tante Catherine is getting me!" He ran behind Michou and grabbed her legs.

Maman bent down, her hands shaped like large claws. "I'm a giant lobster," she croaked. "I'm going to catch you and tickle you until you tell me the magic words."

Jean-David shrieked with delight and poked his head between Michou's legs. "Don't let her get me," he gasped between giggles.

Michou stared at Maman, her mouth open. Her dignified, reserved mother crawling after a three-year-old on all fours, her hat askew and her cream-colored dress hiked up around her knees? Papa was the one who had always pretended to be a lobster; Maman had just watched, a slight smile on her face, as if such silliness were beneath her.

Michou laughed, then snarled at the lobster. "Stay away. He's mine!" She formed her hands into claws and whirled around. "Got you!" she said, grabbing Jean-David and hoisting him up. "Now you have to tell *me* the magic words."

"Or you'll tickle me with your claws?" Jean-David said.

Michou nodded. "Or I'll tickle you."

Jean-David put his lips against her ear. "I love you," he whispered.

Michou hugged him against her, tears stinging her eyes. "What nice magic words. Now I don't have to be a lobster anymore," she said, letting him slide back to the floor. "And I love you. But you'd better tell the other lobster the magic words, too, so she can turn back into Tante Catherine."

Jean-David threw his arms around Maman's neck. "I love you," he shouted.

Maman's claws turned back into hands, and she kissed Jean-David's cheek. "Thank you," she said. "It's very hard work being a lobster." She stood up and smiled at Michou. "I'm exhausted."

Jean-David pulled out a chair and climbed onto it. "Look at that!" he said, standing up and pointing at the cake.

"Your cake," Michou said. "You may have as much as you like after dinner."

He sat down in the chair. "I'm ready now," he said.

Maman laughed. "We have to wait for your guests," she said. She glanced at her watch. "They should be here soon, though."

The door clicked open, and Mémé Laure came into the room. "Saw a car pulling into the drive," she said.

"It's probably the Desroches. I'll go." Michou kissed Mémé Laure's cheeks, then strode from the dining room into the hall. Waving, she trotted down the stone steps as Henri's car came to a stop in front of them. Although she was looking forward to seeing Berthe, she still felt awkward around Henri.

Berthe climbed out of the front seat and reached back inside. She straightened, Daniel squirming and kicking in her arms. After she deposited him on the ground, she grinned at Michou. "Welcome to motherhood," she said, kissing Michou's cheeks.

Michou rolled her eyes. "Thanks." She linked arms with Berthe as Henri got out of the car. She stared at him for a moment. What a handsome, distinguished-looking man he was with his gray-streaked black hair and trimmed moustache, much more attractive than Lucien, because his blue eyes held only kindness and warmth. She didn't blame Maman for loving him. She disengaged her arm and offered him her hand. "Hello, Henri," she said.

"Hello." Taking her hand, he raised his eyebrows and smiled slightly, as if he weren't quite sure of what to do next. He glanced back at the car, opened his mouth to speak, then closed it. Finally, he patted her hand and let it drop.

Michou stood on tiptoe and brushed her lips across his cheek. "I'm so glad you could come to Jean-David's party," she said.

The car door slammed, and she jumped.

Lucien walked around the front of the car, smiling crookedly at her. "Didn't think you'd mind if I came, too," he said. "Besides, I wanted to meet the little fellow."

Erich pushed his cap under his arm and swept his hair back with one hand before he opened the dining-room door. Today had been the little boy's birthday party. He'd met the Desroches on their way back to Libourne and no other cars were parked in front of the château, so perhaps the party was over. He didn't want to intrude where he didn't belong, but he did want to find Michou. He'd missed her so much while she'd been away. And even though he'd seen her several times since her return from Paris and she'd smiled warmly at him, he hadn't had a chance to talk to her yet.

He stepped into the room. Michou stood in front of the table, popping something into her mouth. She turned at the thud of the doors. Chewing, she put her finger across her lips. Her incredible iris-blue eyes sparkled at him.

Finally, she swallowed and grinned at him. "Good evening," she said. "You caught me plundering the remains of Jean-David's cake. Would you like some?"

He smiled back at her. "Of course."

"Plates and silverware have already been cleared away." She tilted her head and raised her eyebrows.

"I don't mind," he said, moving next to her.

She broke off a small piece of the cake and held it out to him. He caught her hand, raised it to his mouth, and nibbled the cake from her fingers as he stared down at her. "Wonderful," he said.

Michou giggled. "There's some wine left, too," she said. "A pretty good Sauternes. Henri brought it."

"Are you going to have a glass as well?"

"Why not?"

"All right, then." He put his cap down on a chair.

She crossed to the sideboard and poured two glasses of wine, then carried them back to the table.

He took a glass from her hand and raised it. "To your r-return," he said. He inhaled the honey-scented aroma, then took a sip and let the smooth, rich wine roll over his tongue before swallowing it. Even though the grapes were a different variety, the late-harvest sweetness reminded him of his favor-

ite Johannisberg Trockenbeerenauslese—of the first time
he'd ever gotten deliciously drunk. He smiled at the memory
and at Michou. "How was Paris?"

"Changed," she said. "Actually, it was beautiful. And
quiet. Little traffic, clean streets, clear blue sky, no horrid
smell of exhaust." She shrugged. "Still, I can have all those
things here. I missed the scurry, the noise. It was a sad city."
She drained half her glass and set it down on the table.

"I'm s-sorry," Erich said. *Scheiss Kerl,* he cursed himself. Why the hell had he asked that?

"Not your fault," she said, shrugging again. She dragged
a chair to the wall between one of the pairs of tall windows
and kicked off her shoes before she climbed up on it. She
swayed for a moment, then steadied herself by hanging on to
the burgundy velvet drapes.

Suddenly he realized she was more than a little drunk.
"Why don't you let me do that?" he said, putting his glass
next to hers, and striding to the chair.

"You just stay there and catch me if I fall." She giggled
as she detached the paper festoons from the window trim and
dropped them over his head. Resting her hand on his shoulder, she clambered down from the chair and pulled it between the other pair of windows.

"Be careful," he said as she climbed up again.

She tossed another garland of red and blue paper at him.
"Don't worry about me," she said. "I'm fine."

"You're drunk," he said. "Besides, I always worry about
you." He put his hands around her waist and swung her off
the chair.

She smiled up at him. "You're a nice man," she said.
Sudden tears glittered in her eyes, and then she ducked her
head.

He tightened his arms about her and drew her to him.
She rested her head against his chest, and even though she
didn't seem to mind, he wished he'd changed out of his
uniform first. When it sank in, as it always did, that he was an
enemy, she'd pull away from him again. He nuzzled her soft
hair, breathing in its fresh jasmine scent.

But perhaps this time she wouldn't. Perhaps she'd stay in
his arms, press her body eagerly against his, return his
kisses. Perhaps the wine would help her forget he was a

German, remember only that he was a man, and that he loved her.

Erich lifted her chin and stared into her half-closed eyes. Her lips curved up in a slight smile, and she sagged against him. He lowered his head.

As soon as his lips touched hers, she tensed. But at least she didn't pull away from him as she had that time in the *chai*. If he went slowly enough, kissed her softly enough, held her patiently enough, maybe she'd relax, kiss him back. That was all he wanted, all he hoped for right now. That would be enough for tonight. A beginning.

He moved his lips against hers, probing gently with his tongue. Her mouth remained wooden. He opened his eyes and looked into her face. Wide violet eyes stared back. He pulled her against his chest. She stood like a porcelain doll in his arms.

He let his arms fall to his sides. "I'm sorry again," he mumbled. "I th-thought—" He broke off and stalked to the chair where he'd left his cap. After he snatched it up, he turned back to her. "Please accept my sincere apologies. I took advantage of you. It will not happen again." He spun on his heel and strode out of the room.

Erich ran up the stairs two at a time. What a fool he was. He'd loved her since he met her, protected her, been patient with her. For a while he'd been satisfied just to have won her friendship. But it wasn't enough anymore. Because he wore a German uniform, she denied him the only thing he wanted— her love.

He flung upon his bedroom door, then slammed it behind him. Damn her to hell. He threw his cap on the bed, then turned back to the door and rammed his fist against it. He pulled his hand back and stared at his bleeding knuckles. They were numb. He was numb. If he had any willpower at all, any courage, he'd request a transfer. She'd made it clear that she didn't want him. There was no point in staying. No point at all.

His hand burned and throbbed as he let down the blackout shade. Sighing, he lowered himself to the bed. He was a selfish bastard. He couldn't go now. With Philippe gone (to Paris, Catherine had said, but he doubted it), there was no one left to help Michou, to watch out for that son of a bitch Lucien Desroches.

He shook his head. He couldn't leave her now.

The room spun. Michou edged to the side of the bed and dangled her foot to the floor. Maybe that would make the room hold still. She fumbled for the switch on the bedside lamp. If she could just see—

She finally found the switch and snapped it on. The light stabbed her eyes, and she blinked rapidly. The nightmare came back to her. The same one as always, but this time the water swirled about her, around and around, pulling her under, sucking her down while Lucien laughed from the bank. Then the coffin. Alain, white and still, swirling, whirling, changing into Marc, Papa, Rachel.

She swung her foot back onto the bed and forced herself to sit up. Her stomach roiled. How could she have been so damn dumb? She'd drunk glass after glass of wine during the dinner party, ignoring Maman's raised eyebrows and Mémé Laure's frowns.

She eased herself out of bed, grabbing the bedpost for support. It was all Lucien's fault. She'd been so upset by his presence she'd escaped to the kitchen and downed a glass of wine even before Maman had served the aperitifs. She couldn't have told him to leave with Berthe and Henri standing right there. Maman would have been horrified at her bad manners.

After she reached the commode, she poured a cup of water and rinsed her dry, cottony mouth. She would not have Lucien for a stepbrother. She spat the water back into the basin. She would not. It was her house, too. Maman could have Henri, but she couldn't force her to accept Lucien.

Michou staggered back to her bed. She hoped she hadn't ruined Jean-David's party. She didn't remember much after the dessert. What had happened? Oh, yes. Mémé Laure had taken Jean-David upstairs to bed, and she and Berthe and Henri and Maman and Lucien had moved to the salon for after-dinner drinks. Instead of sipping her cognac, she had swallowed it down in huge, fiery gulps. Lucien kept leering at her, and Daniel fell asleep in Berthe's arms. Maman played the piano, Henri hovering over her.

She lowered herself back onto the bed. What an awful night. She'd been so relieved when Lucien finally left that she'd had another glass of cognac to celebrate his departure before she took down the decorations in the dining room. Still, there was no excuse for the way she'd treated Erich. She'd been shameless, like Sylvie.

She jerked the sheet up to her chin. Poor Erich. It had been her fault he'd kissed her. She'd acted as if she wanted him to, flirting with him like a schoolgirl. She could still see the pain in his eyes when he apologized. He didn't deserve that. She'd been the one to behave badly. She pressed her hands against her hot cheeks. She should have apologized to him.

And that's what she was going to do. She flicked the light off. First thing in the morning.

42

és

"Oh look, Otto." Sylvie pointed out the car window at a vineyard speckled with brightly dressed workers. "Over there. Isn't that wonderfully quaint?"

Otto leaned forward. "Wonderfully quaint, *liebling*," he said, and smiled. "Just as you promised." He patted her knee.

She clapped her hands as the car rounded a curve and the vineyard disappeared from view. "Wait until you see Michou's little farm. It's even prettier. I visited it one other time during harvest, before my mother and father died. I was ten. It was so exciting. I had such a crush on Alain, Michou's older brother. I followed him all over and spied on him every chance I got."

"I'll bet he liked that," Otto said.

"Actually, he was nice about it. For a thirteen-year-old." She sighed. "Two years later he drowned."

"A tragedy."

"It was terrible," she said, her tone flippant. "But I survived the grief. In fact, it made me a better person."

He nodded. "I can see that," he said. He took out a cigarette and lit it.

Even though she hated the way the wind messed up her hair, Sylvie rolled the window down the rest of the way. She detested even more the too-sweet stink of the horrid cigarettes he was always smoking. She didn't know why he bothered giving her all those bottles of Chanel No. 5 when he couldn't possibly smell it. She rested her arm on the sill and stared out the window as her hair whipped across her face and made her eyes water.

"Your cousin sounds like an interesting girl," he said. "Major Stecher certainly gave a fascinating account of her." He snickered and blew the smoke out the window.

She sniffed. "I'm so mad at her. When she was in Paris, she never mentioned a *thing* about her German lieutenant. And Major Stecher went on and on about everything his friend from Libourne had told him about them. All *she* did was go and on about how awful *I* was—"

"I take it she didn't approve of your consorting with the enemy?"

Sylvie brushed her hair out of her face and turned to him. "She's got a lot of gall. Especially after some of the things she's done."

He lifted one eyebrow. "Such as?"

"Well—" Sylvie tilted her chin up and looked down her nose. "She's not as innocent as everyone thinks. She was pregnant when she came to Paris two years ago. She miscarried the day before Paris fell."

His eyebrow arched higher. *"Ach du lieber Himmel.* Not really?"

She nodded vigorously. "And what's more, one of her best friends in school was a Jew."

The twitch at the corner of his mouth disappeared, and his lips pressed together in a firm line. "Now, that's truly interesting," he said. "Tell me more."

Sylvie settled back against the seat and crossed her legs. She smoothed her tight navy skirt against her thighs, folded her hands in her lap, and stared at her shiny red nails for a moment. "One time Michou refused to go to Mass for six months because of something Grandmère said about Jews. I don't even remember now what it was, but I think she said it in front of Michou's Jewish friend. Anyway, Grandmère made her spend every Sunday in her room. She even sent her meals up, wouldn't let her eat with us." She looked sideways at him.

"Then what happened?"

She shrugged. "I don't remember. One of them finally gave in, I guess. Michou said she wouldn't go to Mass again until Grandmère apologized to her friend. Maybe Grandmère did it. Maybe Michou got tired of eating alone. Neither of them ever told me." She laughed. "Maybe I should ask Michou today."

She looked out the window again at the rows of vines zipping by. She *would* ask Michou about Rachel. In front of Otto. It would be fun to watch her squirm, almost as much fun as seeing Michou's jealousy when she saw Sylvie's smart turnout. She'd chosen the navy-blue suit with such care, accenting it with the new strand of pearls Otto had given her last week. She jiggled her foot. Everybody else in France painted on stockings; hers were real silk.

Smiling, she tapped her nails on the sill. But before she mentioned Rachel, she was certainly going to insist on meeting the wonderful Lieutenant Mueller. That was something really worth rubbing in.

Damn Sylvie. Michou narrowed her eyes and stared as the German staff car drove down the drive and out the gates. The whole afternoon had been full of her spiteful tricks, one right after another. Dropping little hints about Rachel, Jean-David, Erich, even Guy. "Oh, my dear," she'd purred, "do you remember that devastatingly handsome man who brought you to Paris two years ago? Guy somebody. English, wasn't he? What do you suppose ever happened to him?" And: "Did you have a nice visit with Rachel while you were in Paris this summer? We didn't get a chance to talk after our breakfast together. I assume that darling little son of hers is still as adorable as ever."

The car turned onto the road, and Michou lowered her hand and ground her teeth. Damn her again. She couldn't possibly know anything about Guy—that had simply been a lucky thrust in what had really been a sly reminder about her miscarriage. And it had been Stecher who had told her about Erich. "That Major Stecher, such a charming man," she'd said. "He speaks so fondly of his time at Château Bourdet. He says he hears you are *quite* taken with Lieutenant Mueller." She'd sniffed and patted her hair. "I am *so* miffed with you. You didn't even *mention* him while you were in Paris."

Michou headed toward the lower vineyard. An involuntary shudder went through her as she thought of Colonel Zeller's interest and amusement throughout the visit. Hands steepled under his chin, he'd watched Sylvie just as a scientist might observe a fascinating new discovery. Michou shook her head. Sylvie was too sure of her power over him and too stupid to realize she had none. He was the user this time, not she.

She picked up a basket and slipped her arm through the handle. Thank God Maman had taken Jean-David to Libourne with her and Henri. Zeller wasn't stupid, and he asked about everything. Did they always harvest in September? Not always. It depended on the weather. Would this be a good year? Still too early to tell. Sylvie said she had a brother. Where was he? In Paris. He'd heard she'd gone to school with a Jewish girl. That was true. Had she heard anything more from her English friend? No. All the time watching her with those shiny dark eyes, stroking his little moustache with his fingertip, a sly smile hovering at the corner of his mouth.

Michou forced herself to smile at the pickers before she squatted in front of a vine and set the basket beside her. Her hands trembled as she snapped off a bunch of grapes and tossed it into the basket. Stecher had talked about Erich— what if he had mentioned Guy? Not that he had any reason to, but he had met him. And what if Sylvie suspected she'd brought Jean-David back with her from Paris? She was just going to have to make sure neither of them was around when Sylvie came to visit.

Several yellow jackets buzzed about her hands as she picked. She tensed but didn't bother to wave them away. "If you don't bother them, they won't bother you," Papa used to tell her every time she complained about getting stung.

One landed on her hand, and she paused and stared at it. Papa's advice was a lot like Guy's. Sometimes it was better to pretend indifference than to show your hostility. Still, she hated it.

Deliberately, she smashed the yellow jacket with her other hand.

Guy shaded his eyes with his hand and scanned the vineyards. He was glad the harvest was early this year. Because wine brokers customarily made the rounds during the vintage, he had an excuse to come openly to Château Bourdet once more. It was going to be nice to be able to see

Michou more than the once or twice a month he'd managed since their return from Paris two months ago.

After he spotted her, he strode toward the lower vineyard. At least there would be plenty of witnesses today to their business dealings. A dozen pickers and carriers worked nearby, and several men operated the grape wagon and the press.

Suddenly, Michou shrieked and jumped up and down. *"Merde!"* she shouted, grasping her hand.

He broke into a run as heads turned toward her. "Are you all right?" he said. "What's wrong?"

"Aïe! A yellow jacket stung me." She shook her hand in the air and hopped from one foot to the other. Finally, she stood still. "It isn't safe for you here!" she whispered.

He nodded and grabbed her sticky hand. "Let me pull out the stinger," he said loudly. "Hold still." He lowered his voice. "Just act as if you expected me."

"I did," she whispered. "But things have changed. You just missed Sylvie by a few minutes." She looked around, then raised her voice. "Hurts like hell," she said. "But it was worth it. He'll never bother me—or anyone else—again."

Guy pinched the tiny stinger between his thumb and forefinger and eased it out. He shook his head. "You hit it while it was on your hand?"

"I don't want to hear what you're going to say next," she said. "I know. It was still worth it."

He shrugged and brushed the stinger onto his trousers. "Fine," he said. "But there are so many of them. What good did it do to kill one? And now your hand is all swollen. I think we should put some bicarbonate of soda on it."

"Good idea," Michou said. She reached for her basket.

"I'll take that." He pulled the basket from her hand and followed her to the wagon at the edge of the vineyard. Hundreds of yellow jackets swarmed about the intensely sweet-smelling grapes heaped in a dull purple-black pile on the wagon. "You stay away," he said, dumping the basket, then tossing it with the others. Sometimes she surprised him by how much she'd grown up since they'd first met; then she did something like this and he wondered again whether he could trust her to use her head. He supposed, though, as long as she stuck to squashing bees there wouldn't be any problems. To her credit Lucien was still alive, and she hated him with a frightening intensity. She never talked about killing him any-more, but her cold glare whenever she mentioned him was indication enough she still thought about it.

"No argument," Michou said. She waited until he caught up and led him toward the kitchen. As soon as she stepped out of sight of the pickers around the corner of the château, she stopped. "Forget my hand. Let's go to my office." She hurried across the garden to the back door.

He followed her into the office, shut the door, and pulled her into his arms and kissed first her lips, then her hand. "Now, what's this about Sylvie?" he said, his arms still around her.

"She was here," Michou said. "With her Nazi lover, the colonel. You probably drove right past them." She leaned back and looked up at him. "She asked me about you. She remembered you were English. And she's met Stecher. Berthe told me Lucien still sees him."

Guy backed up to the large chair and lowered himself into it, pulling her onto his lap. "What a mess," he said, "I guess I'll just have to be much more careful." He stroked her hair. "Is she likely to come back again soon?"

Michou shrugged. "Who knows? She always does ex-actly what she wants. When I told her how busy it was around here during the vintage, she just laughed and said that was why she'd wanted to come." She sniffed and tossed her head. " 'But darling, it's so picturesque. So quaint. I told Otto he just *couldn't* miss it.' "

Guy chuckled. "Sounds just like her."

Michou burrowed into his chest. "I've been looking forward to seeing you more often. And now this."

"Don't worry," he said. "This might be my last daytime visit." He tightened his arms around her. "But there's still the night."

43

❧

Why bother to knock? It would be far more effective to walk in unannounced. Lucien pushed open the door and stepped into the entry. Daniel's laugh and the clanks of silver against china came from the dining room. He paused in front of the large mirror in the hall and, smiling, straightened his black tie. He liked this new uniform: Chasseur Alpin beret, khaki shirt, dark blue pants and jacket, leggings, army shoes. He patted the holster hanging from the wide military belt. Tonight it was padded with paper, but not for long.

He strutted into the dining room, pausing at the doorway to enjoy the reaction. Daniel screamed; Berthe's eyes and mouth opened into little O's; and Father stiffened, his fork in midair and his eyebrows pulled together into a straight dark line across his forehead.

Father put his fork down with a clatter. "It's all right, Daniel. It's just your Uncle Lucien," he said.

Berthe glared at Lucien. "Take off your cap," she said. "You know how scared he gets when someone wears one indoors." She got up and put her arms around Daniel and whispered in his ear. His cries gradually faded into hiccups.

Lucien took off his beret. "See?" he said. "Here I am. Uncle Lucien. Just as Grandpapa said." He raised his eyebrows and stared back at Berthe. When it came to that boy, she was a tigress. He couldn't intimidate her at all anymore. Except for one little thing. He knew she still hadn't told the old man about Kohler. "Better?" he said sarcastically.

"Slightly," she said. She patted Daniel on the shoulder and returned to her seat.

"You mean you don't like my new uniform?" Lucien whined in mock sorrow.

Berthe shook her head. "I don't like collaborators. And the Milice are the worst. They're nothing but a French Gestapo. How could you, Lucien?"

He shrugged. "Just doing my part for France."

"For Germany, you mean," Father said. He pushed back his chair and stood up. "I'd like to talk to you." He stomped out of the dining room.

Lucien grinned at Berthe and shrugged again. He chucked Daniel under the chin. "How would you like a beret just like mine?" he asked, putting it back on his head before he strode into the salon after his father.

Father stood in front of the fireplace, his back to the door. "Sit down," he said without turning around. He tossed a log onto the fire, and black smoke billowed out into the room.

Lucien lowered himself onto the sofa and crossed his legs. So Father actually wanted to talk to him. This was going to be interesting. He waved away the acrid smoke and waited while Father settled himself in his wing chair at the side of the hearth.

Father looked down at his hands, then cleared his throat. He raised his head. "Nothing you can do will ever make me consider you not my son," he said. "I loved your mother, and you know how much she loved you. If she were alive now, she would be—"

"—so disappointed in me. I know," Lucien said. "I've heard this one dozens of times, Father. Why don't you come up with something better, more original? Why don't you tell me how *you* feel?" Not that he really cared, Lucien added to himself. If he pissed the old man off, that was enough.

Father closed his eyes for a few seconds. "Guilty," he said, opening them and staring at Lucien. "For spoiling you after she died. For never correcting you, for always thinking the wildness was from your pain and that you'd gradually get over it. For being so wound up in my own grief that I never made the effort to understand yours. Then later, letting that guilt force me into covering up for your mistakes rather than forcing you to do what was right. When I might have made a difference, I didn't. Now it's too late. I know what you are,

Lucien, and I'm not proud of it. But I don't blame myself
entirely."

Lucien snorted. "Nice speech."

Father frowned and leaned forward. "Why did you come
here tonight?" he asked. "We haven't seen you since Christmas and now you show up wearing this abomination." He
flicked his hand toward Lucien's holster. "You enjoy flaunting the awful things you do, don't you? Why?"

Lucien rubbed the holster. "Maybe I'm just paying you
back. You've always hated me. If you could have traded me
for Alain when he was alive, you'd have done it. You were
always asking why I couldn't be like him." He snickered.
"Then again, maybe I do what I do because I like it."

"I don't hate you," Father said. He sighed and shook his
head. "I've never hated *you*. I've hated some of the things
you've done. I hate what you're doing right now. But I don't
hate you. And even though Alain *was* a good boy, I didn't
want *him* for a son."

Lucien stood up and walked to the fireplace. He
stretched his cold hands out in front of the flames for a few
seconds, then rubbed them together and let them drop to his
sides. Father's reaction wasn't at all what he'd expected. He'd
wanted anger, bitterness, condemnation from him, not sadness and guilt. He turned back to Father. "Fine. You say you
don't hate me. But you don't love me. You haven't since
Daniel died."

"For God's sake, you're my son, Lucien." Father held
out his hands, palms up. "I love you. There are times when I
don't like you, I'll admit. But I never stopped loving you. Not
even when I thought Daniel—" He slapped his hands back
onto his thighs and grimaced.

"Thought what?" Lucien said, his voice tight. He swallowed hard and stared at his father. Had Father known about
the drowning all these years? He clenched his fists at his
sides. No. Father couldn't know. He'd been careful. No one
knew.

Father took a deep breath. A muscle in his jaw twitched.
"Berthe wouldn't tell me who Daniel's father was. I thought it
was you."

Lucien's mouth dropped open. First he snorted, then he
laughed, and finally he howled. He flopped back down on the

sofa. Jesus, what a relief. Tears rolled down his cheeks, and he gasped for air. He pictured himself fucking Berthe and roared with laughter again. "Good God, Father, you didn't really think I—" Another wave of giggles swept over him.

"The boy looks so much like you. And Berthe was so adamant in her refusal. I thought she was protecting you," Father said. "Do you know who Daniel's father is?"

His laughter subsiding, Lucien looked into the fire. If he told Father now, he'd lose the last bit of leverage he had over Berthe. He wasn't ready to give that up yet, not when he might still be able to use it to find out what Michou confided to her. He shook his head. "She wouldn't tell me, either," he said. "But I can assure you that I didn't touch her. On the memory of my mother, I swear it."

"I know," Father said. "Catherine convinced me months ago that I was a fool to think it. But that wasn't my point." He paused. "The point was I loved you even when I suspected the worst thing about you that I could possibly imagine. I love you now even though your collaboration disgusts me. You mock everything I value and believe in, but you are still my son."

Lucien sneered and lifted his shoulders. Even if he believed the old man, it was too late. Years too late. He stood up again. If he stayed much longer, this crap was going to make him sick. "Better watch the company you keep," he said, fingering his holster. "A traitor's widow is always under suspicion. Not even her daughter's German lover can change that."

Sylvie tilted her head and smiled at the handsome dark-haired man staring at her from the other side of the restaurant. Could that possibly be Lucien? If it was, he'd grown into an attractive man since the last time she'd seen him. He'd been a gawky teenager, his face dotted with red spots and spiky little whiskers. Now he looked suave and polished in his black tuxedo, his hair gleaming and his mustache perfectly trimmed.

The man grinned, straightened his tie, and threaded his way gracefully through the crowded room without taking his eyes from her face. Still smiling at her, he extended his hand to Major Stecher after he reached their table. "Sorry I'm late,

Karl," he said, his voice soft and liquid. He didn't offer an explanation.

Major Stecher stood up and shook his hand. "No apologies necessary," he said. "I've been admirably entertained by my other guests." He turned to Otto, who also rose from his chair. "Colonel Zeller, I'd like you to meet my friend Lucien Desroches. Mademoiselle de Bacqueville, Lucien Desroches."

Lucien shook Otto's hand and bowed to Sylvie. "De Bacqueville?" he said. "Have we met before?" His blue eyes glittered at her like pale sapphires as he sat down across the table.

Sylvie nodded. "You probably don't remember, though," she said. "I was a plump little thing of ten. You and Alain used to tease me unmercifully."

His black eyebrows shot up. "Sylvie de Bacqueville—Michou's cousin from Paris. Of course I remember. You followed us everywhere that summer." He glanced at Otto before he continued. "You've certainly changed."

Sylvie laughed lightly. "So have you."

"Both of you for the better, I presume," Otto said. He winked at Sylvie.

"Naturally, darling." She patted his hand and fluttered her eyelashes. "Otherwise it would be rude to notice."

"And that's one of the things I love most about you, *liebling*. Your unfailing sense of politeness. Our waiter appears occupied. Why don't you pour our new friend a glass of champagne?" He smiled at her, his little white teeth glinting in the candlelight, before he resumed his conversation with Major Stecher.

Smiling at Lucien, Sylvie lifted the bottle from the silver ice bucket and splashed what was left into his glass.

"Thanks." Lucien peered at her over the top of his menu. "This is quite a surprise," he said. "I didn't expect to find Michou's cousin as Colonel Zeller's beautiful dinner partner. Are you just visiting Bordeaux?"

Sylvie shook her head. "I moved here a few months ago."

"And you're enjoying the change?" He laid the menu down and took a sip of the champagne.

She shrugged, glancing at Otto. He was completely im-

mersed in whatever Major Stecher was going on about. "I
prefer Paris," she said. "It's livelier. And there are more
black-market restaurants to pick from." She leaned forward
and lowered her voice. "To tell the truth, I've been a bit
bored."

"We'll have to see if we can't change that." Lucien ran
the tip of his tongue across his upper lip and leered at her.
"Perhaps I can find some occupations to amuse you."

Sylvie dropped her eyes. He was charming. If she could
get away with it, she might just take him up on his offer. But
she'd have to be careful. Otto was really quite jealous. He
loved her so much. She looked sideways at Otto, then raised
her chin and smiled into Lucien's eyes. "Anyway, it's been
amusing dropping by Château Bourdet whenever I feel like it.
Michou's reaction is always so droll."

"You've been to see her then?"

"Several times."

"Then the next time you must stop by and see me. I'm
living now at Château LeClair-Figeac. Running it for Father."
He laughed. "Of course, Jacques does most of the work. I've
been pretty busy lately with the Milice. Joined last month."

"Really?" Sylvie picked up her menu and inspected it
again. He'd seemed different at first because he wasn't wearing a uniform, but he was just the same as Otto and the others
after all. She pushed out her lower lip slightly. She was tired
of talk about the war, about the stupid games men played.

"But let's not talk about that," Lucien said, almost as if
he'd read her mind. "I don't want to bore a lovely woman,
and you look ravishing tonight."

Sylvie glanced up from the menu. "Thank you," she
said, stroking the diamond necklace at her throat and smiling
at him. That was better. Maybe he was going to be all right.
Of course, he'd never do for anything but a flirtation. The
Milice. How horrid. Hoodlums, Otto called them. Nasty but
effective. Now the Gestapo could leave the truly dirty work
to the French, he'd said.

She slid her eyes sideways again at Otto. He was still
enthralled with Major Stecher. He hadn't even looked at his
menu yet. She shook her head at the waiter starting across
the room and turned back to Lucien. "Tell me about your
vineyard," she said.

"It's just a small one," Lucien said. "Not nearly as nice as Château Bourdet. I envy Michou that slope above the château. My vineyards are as flat as this tabletop."

"Does that make a difference?" Sylvie asked.

"Better drainage, better sun make better grapes," he said, "and that makes better wine. You've enjoyed your visits with your cousin, then?"

Sylvie giggled and sipped her champagne. "More than she has, I think," she said. "I make her uncomfortable, remind her of her sins."

"Oh?"

"She might act like the Virgin Mary, but I can assure you she's not," she said.

"Now, that's interesting," he said. "Much more intriguing than grapes. Tell me more."

Sylvie set down her glass and leaned forward. "Three years ago she arrived in Paris in the middle of the night of the day before the Germans did. She had a handsome Englishman in tow, Guy something or other. She'd picked him up on the way. And what's more—" She paused dramatically. "She was pregnant."

"No! Not our Michou. I don't believe it."

"Believe it," she said. She picked up her glass and swallowed the rest of the fizzy champagne. Now, why had she told him that? She'd meant to save it. She sighed. Too much champagne again. Made her do stupid things.

Otto patted her hand after she returned the glass to the table. "How are you two getting along?" he asked.

Lucien winked at her and grinned broadly. "Beautifully," he said. "Just beautifully."

44

❧

"The next step is to insert the time pencil into the plastic explosive," Guy said. He stuck the small tube into the smooth, almond-scented mass on the table in front of him. "Are there any questions so far?"

The newest recruit, a tall, thin man with lank blond hair and a scraggly moustache, pushed his way through the small group crowded around the demonstration table under the trees. "Look, Yves. Just how accurate are those things?" he asked. "Wouldn't want it to go off too soon." His Adam's apple jumped up and down in his throat.

"That's not usually the problem," Guy said. "Sometimes when it's cold, they take a bit longer. But usually they're pretty reliable. Just make sure you have the right size—or time zone, I should say—so you have plenty of time to get away."

The man shrugged. "How can I be sure that plastic stuff won't go off by itself?"

"The PE is safe until it's detonated, and that can't happen until after you squeeze the tube. Amazing stuff. Had a friend in training who ate some of it—thought it was chocolate. Didn't even upset his stomach." Guy studied the man. Every time he gave a demonstration, it was the same with him—doubts, fears, even hostility. Where the hell had he come from? Didn't seem like promising material at all for the Resistance.

Several of the dozen maquisards gathered around the table snickered. "What's the matter, Claude?" one of them said. "Scared already?"

"Enough," Guy said. He stared at the men, and they quieted. "Are there any other questions?"

"Yes," Philippe said, stepping forward. "How does it work? The time pencil, I mean."

Guy smiled at him. How typical of Philippe. He always wanted to know why and how. Guy liked that about him. He was turning out to be a good maquisard after all—despite Michou's warnings about his inability to follow orders. Philippe's curiosity and enthusiasm, plus his love for France and hatred for the Nazis, made him one of the easiest men of the group to train for the Resistance's underground army. During the Sten-gun training sessions, he'd been one of the best marksmen in his maquis. And so far, he hadn't slipped up and called Guy by his real name. Not in front of him, anyway. He just hoped Philippe was as careful to hide their previous acquaintance when he wasn't present.

Guy pointed to the tube. "When you squeeze this, it forces out acid, which burns along this little wire until it dissolves it. The length of the wire determines the time of the fuse. When the acid reaches the PE, boom."

Philippe nodded. "Thanks," he said. "I always trust something more when I understand how it works."

Guy surveyed the group. "Anyone else?" He paused. "All right. If it's night and the object you're planning to blow up is dark, I suggest wrapping the entire lump in dark material first. Then the last step is easy. You just put the PE wherever it'll do the most damage, pinch the tube, and get out."

"Still don't trust the damn stuff," Claude muttered.

Guy's jaw tightened. One coward could infect the whole group. "Perhaps it'd be best if you avoided sabotage missions for a while, then," he said. "There are plenty of other things you can do. I'll talk it over with your commander."

Claude glared at him for a few seconds, then spun on his heel and walked back to the large campfire in the center of the clearing.

"Don't mind him," Philippe said. "He's like that all the time lately. Always complaining. And he's not the only one. But it doesn't have anything to do with you."

The other men nodded in agreement. "It's hard being cut off from your family," a short man near the front said. "Stuck out here in the hills, never enough to eat, never comfortable. It gets to you after a while. You start wondering if it's ever going to do any good."

"Just remember this, Roger," Guy said. "Each one of you makes a difference. You may not be able to see it. But it's happening. You have to believe that. Without you, what does France have?"

"The Milice," another maquisard snarled. "The damn Milice."

"And Vichy," Philippe said.

Roger sighed. "You're right, of course." He snorted. "And none of us can claim we weren't warned about this life. As bad as it is, it's better than getting shipped off to work in Germany." He turned to Guy. "Sorry, Yves. We're touchy, all of us, I guess."

"Don't worry about it," Guy said. He removed the time pencil from the plastic explosive and returned each to its container. "That's it for today."

The maquisards stood talking in small groups while Guy put away the materials. Finally, they drifted gradually toward the fire. When the last one was gone, Philippe reached down and picked up one of the containers. "Let me help," he said.

"Thanks," Guy said, tucking a box under each arm. "Put it over there with the rest of the stuff." He jerked his head toward a pile of boxes under a lean-to. "How's it been going?"

Philippe fell into step beside him. "Fine, I guess. Wish there was more fighting and less talking, though. Gets a little boring."

"I'm afraid you'll get your wish soon enough," Guy said. "But for now it's best to lie low, trick the Nazis into thinking everything's under control. Every raid means reprisals, extra guards, more trouble for us the next time." He set his boxes under the lean-to. "You've got to be patient."

Philippe gingerly placed the container next to the others. "Not one of my virtues," he said, smiling slightly. He lowered his voice. "I'm surprised Michou didn't tell you that."

"She did," Guy said. "That's why I mentioned it. She sends her greetings and says not to worry. Everyone misses you, but your absence hasn't caused any extra work for her. She said I should be sure to tell you that." He grinned.

Philippe chuckled. "I miss them all, too. How's the little fellow doing?"

"Adapting well, I think. But I haven't seen the whole family since my visit last fall—I can't, with your cousin Sylvie dropping by all the time. It's been damn awkward." Guy headed back toward the borrowed car he'd parked at the edge of the clearing. "I'll be seeing Michou tonight, though. Any messages?" He rested his hand on the door handle.

"Sure." Philippe beamed. "Tell her she'd better enjoy her German while she can. Now that I'm a soldier, the Nazis' days are limited."

"She's going to love that," Guy said, sliding behind the wheel. "She also told me to tell you not to do anything stupid."

Philippe laughed. "Who? Me?"

A key rattled in the lock, and Michou forced her eyes open and sat up. She groped for the lamp beside the bed and flicked it on. Shivering, she pulled her knees up to her chest and clutched the covers about her. It was going to freeze again, she'd bet. Thank God the vines were late in budding this spring. But if it continued clear and cold into May, she'd be spending her nights huddled over little stoves in the vineyards instead of in her bed waiting for Guy.

He stepped into the room, his shoes dangling from one hand and his key in the other. He set his shoes down, then closed the door quietly and locked it. He smiled at her. "Don't get up," he said. "I'll join you. It's too late to broadcast tonight, anyway." He stripped off his clothes and piled them onto the bench at the foot of the bed.

Michou scooted to the other side of the bed. "I'll even give you my warm spot," she said as he slid in beside her. She wrapped her arms around him and pulled him against her. He smelled like wood smoke and cognac. "You're frozen." She kissed him. "Even your lips are cold."

He ran his hand up and down her back. "You're thawing me out just fine," he said. He nuzzled her ear.

She ran her hand up his leg and stroked him. "Why

wait?" she whispered. "It's been too long already." She rolled to her back and pulled him on top of her. She gasped as he probed her soft folds, then eased slowly inside her. Waves of pleasure radiated through her groin, and she shuddered. Arching her back, she met his thrusts until, with a muffled groan, he buried his face in the pillow beside her.

He pushed himself up on his elbows and looked down at her. "God," he said.

She sighed in answer. "Are you warm now?"

He chuckled as he lifted his body off hers. "You know I am." He put his arm around her shoulders and squeezed.

She laid her head on his shoulder. "I've always thought dessert should come before the main course. Especially if the main course is liver."

"Liver?"

"I hate liver."

"You've got bad news?"

She nodded, and the top of her head brushed against his chin. She wished for once they could just fall asleep together after they made love. But there was always something. At least she didn't have to get up and run the wireless tonight.

"Well?" he said.

"It's the wireless detector," she said. "I think I saw the *gonio* in Saint-Émilion last week. A big van with a round thing on top?"

"Sounds like one," he said. "Best to keep transmissions infrequent and short from now on. Tomorrow night's message shouldn't be a problem, though. It's quite brief. But it does ask for a response."

Michou ran her fingertips lightly across his chest. "Does that mean you'll be here to receive it?"

He sighed. "Afraid not. And if I don't come the night after, I'm going to need you to bring it to me in Libourne. Think you can get away Saturday afternoon?"

"Of course," she said. "But I hope I won't need to." She tilted her head back and looked into his warm brown eyes. No point in telling him that Lucien had been plaguing her lately, asking questions about her trip to Paris, making sneering comments about Jean-David. There wasn't anything Guy could do except worry, and he already had plenty to worry about.

He kissed her. "How about some more dessert?" he said.

Lucien leaned back in his father's large swivel chair and raised his legs slowly to the top of the desk, crossing them at the ankle. He laced his fingers behind his neck and stared at Renet, a skinny weasel lounging against the doorway of Father's office. "Well, Claude," he said. "Any problems?"

Renet shook his head. "Been with the maquis for a couple of months now. Doing fine. Don't much like the bastards, but I don't think they have any complaints about me."

"They trust you?"

"Most of them."

"Not all of them?"

"A couple of them don't trust nobody. A couple don't like me." Renet raised his bony shoulders to his ears. "Nothing I can't handle."

"You know what they're planning to hit next?"

Renet frowned. "The commander plays it pretty close. He don't tell nothing until it's happening. Not to me, anyway. Not so far."

Lucien swung his feet to the floor. What an idiot Renet was. He'd tried to tell the captain it was a mistake to send him to the Corrèze. "It's your job to *make* him trust you. Doesn't do us much good otherwise, now, does it?"

"Why not just wipe them out?" Renet sneered.

Lucien rolled his eyes. "Later," he said. "First we want to find out as much as we can, get the organizers, the big fish. You're supposed to help us do that."

"I know," Renet whined. "But it's not as easy as you think."

"I don't think it's easy. I do think it's possible." Lucien leaned forward, resting his hands on his knees. "Anything else?"

"Had a few run-ins with Yves, the demolitions expert. He told the commander to leave me out of any sabotage missions he had planned." Grimacing, Renet shrugged. "Fine with me. Wouldn't do much good for me to get blown up before I blow the whistle, would it?"

Lucien clenched his teeth. Incompetent bastard. No wonder his commander wouldn't trust him. "You're right," he said sarcastically. "Wouldn't do at all." He waved his hand at Renet. "Get out of here. And be careful."

Renet nodded and slunk out the door.

"Merde!" The word exploded from Lucien's lips. Too bad the captain hadn't chosen him to infiltrate. Give him two months with the maquis and he'd have been second in command.

He sighed and shook his head. Wouldn't work, of course. He was too well known. They were just going to have to put up with Renet.

45

Bubbles rose from the bottom of the glass through the pale amber liquid, then disappeared into the white foam at the top. Erich slowly rotated the glass in his hands before he set it back down on the table. He rested his elbow beside the glass and cupped his chin in his hand. *Mein Gott,* he was tired of everything—the war, himself, the stupid agony of loving Michou. All he wanted to do was go back home. Go back home to what?

He took a book from his pocket and thumbed through it. It had been another world when he'd studied Baudelaire, another life. Then, he'd gotten pleasure from the explication of poems that he now knew he'd never truly understood, from the intellectual exercise of finding meaning in forms, from the close inspection of a diseased soul. Now he sometimes wondered if anything would ever give him pleasure again.

Erich spread the book open on the table next to his beer glass. " 'I think sometimes my blood flows in torrents, with a fountain's pulsating sobs,' " he whispered to himself. " 'I hear it pour out with a long sigh, but I search in vain for the wound.' " He had no blood left; he was transparent, a walking shadow. No wonder Michou seemed hardly to see him anymore.

He slapped the book shut and straightened his shoulders. Enough. No more complaining like an adolescent, no more whining about his lost love. He'd decided to stay because Michou needed his help whether she realized it or not. He'd known how she felt then, known also that in all likelihood nothing would change.

He swallowed a mouthful of the insipid French beer.
He'd been right about that. Nothing *had* changed, at least in
the way she treated him. She was polite, even friendly, but
that was all. And he knew why.

She was in love with Fournier. He'd known it since that
day he'd seen them together in Libourne. Erich drained the
rest of the beer and thudded the glass onto the table. Fournier hadn't been around since the harvest, but he'd seen her
face then, too, soft and bright the same way it was when she
looked at Jean-David.

He beckoned the plump, dark-haired waitress. "Another," he said, handing her the empty glass.

She let her hand brush against his, then smiled and
fluttered her lashes at him before she turned away. She
pranced across the *terrasse,* swiveling her hips as she wove
between the small, round tables. The smell of her sweat
lingered for a few seconds.

Erich stared at her until she disappeared through the
swinging door. He could have her if he wanted her; she'd
made that clear enough in the months he'd been coming to
L'Hostellerie. But he'd never encouraged her, and he still
wasn't interested. Even though she didn't care, no one but
Michou meant anything to him.

The waitress returned with his new beer and an even
larger smile. "Anything else?" she said, setting the glass in
front of him and tossing her head.

"No," he said. "Thank you." He fished in his pocket for
some change and dropped it into her hand, carefully avoiding
touching her.

Her smile faded and she shrugged. She ambled back to
the doorway, pausing and staring down the street for a minute
before she stepped inside.

Erich followed her glance and raised his eyebrows as a
large van cruised slowly toward L'Hostellerie. The *gonio*
again. They were on to something or they'd never bother to
send a detection van to Saint-Émilion so frequently. Every
day now for the last week. They were definitely closing in on
someone.

The van stopped in front of the restaurant, blocking the
narrow street, and two soldiers climbed out and headed

toward the *terrasse*. They saluted Erich before they sat down at a table nearby.

Erich leaned across his table. "You're becoming regulars in Saint-Émilion," he said. "What's going on?"

The larger soldier, a young corporal with serious-looking brown eyes, settled back in his chair and crossed his legs. "Someone around here is operating an illegal transceiver. Haven't been able to locate it yet, sir."

"You think there's a radio in Saint-Émilion?" Erich said.

"Not actually in town, sir," the sergeant said. "Just came here for a beer. We've finished our duty."

"If not in town, where then?" Erich asked. He stared at the copy of *Les Fleurs du Mal* lying in front of him. Michou had given it to him. Vague memories of the day he'd first seen her reading it pushed at him. It had been here, at L'Hostellerie. He'd sat down for a minute with her and Fournier—

"Somewhere between Saint-Émilion and Libourne," the tall corporal said. "One of the châteaux perhaps." He shrugged. "Hard to tell. The operator is smart. Short broadcasts, irregular times."

Erich frowned. He'd opened the book, glanced at a piece of paper that had slipped out, stuck it back inside the book. The paper had been thin, with little dots and lines showing through. *Jesus Maria!* How could he have been so stupid?

"We'll catch him, though, sir. Major Dhose wants him," the corporal continued.

Erich gripped his glass. Major Dhose was head of the Bordeaux Gestapo. Ruthless, efficient, cruel—all the standard adjectives for the Gestapo applied perfectly to him. "I'm sure you will," he mumbled.

The sergeant smiled at him over his beer glass. He set it down and said, "You're billeted nearby, sir?"

Erich nodded. "Château Bourdet," he said.

"Anything funny there?" the sergeant asked.

"Not that I've noticed," Erich said. He ran his fingertip around the top of the glass. "A neighbor—Lucien Desroches—has always seemed a bit odd to me, though."

"Desroches?"

"That's right," Erich said. "He owns Château LeClair-Figeac."

The sergeant finished his beer. "Thanks for the tip," he said, then stood up. The corporal hastily drank down the rest of his beer and jumped up.

Erich forced himself to smile at them. "Glad to help," he said. He watched them climb into the van and drive slowly up the street and around the corner.

Closing his eyes, he took a deep breath and let it out with a slow hiss. He knew where the radio was. It was his duty as a German officer to turn her in. What had he just done? And what the hell was he going to do now?

"This is awfully long." Michou looked up from the message she was encoding and frowned at Guy.

"Sorry," he said. "Couldn't be helped this time. The Scientist circuit is falling apart. More are being arrested every day."

She clutched the pencil tightly and shivered even though it was a warm night.

"Cold?" he asked. "You want something to put on?"

She shook her head. She just wanted all this to be over with. "You're not in danger, are you?" she asked, her voice flat.

He put his hands on her bare shoulders. "No more than usual," he said. "You'd better hurry or we'll miss the signal."

She nodded and resumed the tedious business of coding. At least she didn't have to transmit at exactly the same hour anymore. Since the *gonio* had shown up, Guy had devised a rotating schedule. She liked the three o'clock transmissions the best because they had plenty of time to make love before. Like tonight. She smiled at the memory and transferred the last letters. "Finished," she said, holding up the paper.

"Good." He hooked the aerial to the wireless. "Go ahead."

She inserted the crystal, put on the earphones, and twirled the dial, listening for the call sign. Finally, the faint dots and dashes took the correct form, and she tuned them in clearly. She nodded at Guy and tapped out her call letters. While she waited for London's response, she nuzzled his hand. It still smelled of their lovemaking.

A minute later the go-ahead signal came. Without hesitating, Michou pressed her finger to the key and rapidly clicked out the message. After fifteen minutes she tapped out her code for crystal change, removed the old crystal, and put in a new one. "Halfway there," she said.

Guy squeezed her shoulder. "You're twice as fast as I ever was," he said. "It would have taken me an hour to send this message."

London's coded acknowledgment buzzed in her ear, and Michou continued with the next line of the message. Faster, faster, she told herself. She squinted so hard her eyes blurred, and her hand ached with the tension.

Guy suddenly lifted his hand from her shoulder, and she paused, looking up at him. "What—"

Someone banged on the door.

Michou froze, her finger resting on the key. A long buzz vibrated in her ears, merged with the hard pounding of her heart. She ripped off the earphones and jumped up. Her head still roared.

"It's Erich. Let me in!"

Quickly and silently, Guy unplugged the aerial and grabbed the wireless. He tossed it into the wardrobe next to the desk, then tugged on his pants. He gathered the rest of his clothes and hoisted himself out the window, drawing the aerial after him.

Michou gripped the back of her chair so hard her knuckles turned white. "What do you want?" she said. Her voice sounded tinny.

"For Christ's sake, l-let me in! Hurry!" he hissed.

"Just a second," she said. She pulled some clothes from their hangers and droppped them on top of the wireless, then shut the wardrobe door. She grabbed her peignoir,and stuck her arms into it as she walked to the door.

She opened it, and Erich rushed in and shut the door quietly behind him. His eyes darted past her as he scanned the room. "Where's the radio?" he demanded. His eyes narrowed when she hesitated.

She'd never seen him like this before. Taking a deep breath, she nodded toward the wardrobe.

Erich threw open the door, grabbed the wireless, and stuffed it under her pillow. "Take that off and get in bed," he ordered.

Running feet thudded outside the window. Michou threw

off her robe and shivered under the covers. They felt cold against her bare skin. She bunched them up around her chin.

Erich pulled off his boots and tossed his uniform onto a chair. He threw back the coverlet and lowered his body on top of hers. "I l-love you," he said. His blue eyes gleamed in the light from the bedside lamp.

Hobnails tattooed the stairs. "I know," she whispered. Her mouth was dry and bitter tasting. She put her hands around his neck. She had to make this look real. Guy's life depended on it. And so did hers. The hard edges of the wireless case cut into her shoulder blades as he pressed his body against hers.

There was a pounding at the door, and then it flew open. Two German soldiers pushed into the room.

Erich turned his head toward them. "What is this?"

The taller soldier stared at him. "I recognize you," he said. "Sorry, sir." He looked at his feet. "We picked up some illegal broadcasts from this area."

"Well, they're not coming from here," Erich said, and smiled. "Try the neighbors. Remember? Château LeClair-Figeac."

"Right, sir." Apologizing, the soldiers backed out of her bedroom. Their footsteps echoed from the stone stairs, then crunched in the gravel at the base of the tower.

Erich pushed himself up on one elbow and pulled the wireless from under the pillow. He slid it under the bed without getting off her.

Michou planted her hands against his chest and tensed her arms to push him away, but a thud on the roof stopped her. Guy was still up there.

Erich looked down at her, his eyes sad and his mouth set in a firm line.

Michou let her arms drop. Erich had heard it, too. What if he called the soldiers back? He had no reason to protect Guy and every reason to wish him dead.

She had to do it. She entwined her hands about his neck and pulled his head toward hers. He groaned softly as she brushed her lips against his, arched her back, and rubbed against him.

*   *   *

The small suitcase dangling from his hand, Erich paused at the foot of the stairs leading to the third floor and his room. Except for his own breathing and the nighttime creaks, the hall was silent. He walked slowly up the steps, the refrain in his head starting once again, keeping time with his clamoring heartbeat. How could he?

How could she? He knew the answer to that question. He couldn't blame her. He had been the weak one. She had been strong and brave and loyal. She'd done it for the man she loved—given her body in exchange for his life, given it without thought or hesitation as soon as she realized he'd heard the noise on the roof and knew what it was. And she'd done her best to ensure her lover time to escape.

Erich eased open the door to his room and stepped inside. How could *he*? He had no easy answer for that one. He'd wanted her, but he had since he'd met her. If he'd wanted her that way, he could have forced himself on her dozens of times in the last year. That had never been his plan, his goal.

He locked his door and set the suitcase on the bed. "Bastard," he whispered. He was no better than Lucien. He'd broken his most sacred promise to himself. Michou was to have come to him willingly, with love. Or else not at all.

He sat down on the bed next to the small satchel. She had given him her body tonight. But not her love. He'd watched her face while she moved beneath him. Her eyes had been squeezed shut and her jaw tense. It didn't matter that her body had been open to him, moist, warm, pulsing. Her heart had been closed. It showed when her eyes fluttered wide for a brief second. They'd been glazed, distant, almost surprised to see it was he poised on top of her.

He leaned over and pulled off his boots. And he hadn't cared. All that mattered was his stiff thrusts inside her, his hands caressing her small breasts, his tongue probing her mouth. He'd forgotten everything else—his love, his promises, his ideals.

His chest heaved, and tears rolled down his cheeks. He didn't bother to wipe them off. He'd spoiled the only things he had left to him, betrayed Michou, his duty, and his honor in one act. He hunched forward. *Mein Gott,* how could he? How could he?

Face buried in hands still smelling of her, he rocked back and forth. His throat ached with strangled howls of sorrow, anger. He hated himself, what the war had made him, what it had done to everyone around him. His father dead, no news of his mother in months, his closest friend killed in Russia. Michou had been all there was. Now there was nothing.

Slowly, he straightened and turned to stare at the suitcase. Arms stiff, he pushed himself off the bed and stood in front of the case. He opened the lid. Earphones and tangled wires lay across the dials and knobs. He scooped them to one side.

Taking a deep breath, he doubled his fist. His blood thundered in his ears as, gritting his teeth, he raised his hand. Deliberately, he smashed his fist into the radio.

There was a low crunching sound, and metal pieces jumped about inside the case. He held up his hand and stared at it. Blood poured from his knuckles, but he didn't feel a thing.

46

"It's a shame," Cécile said. "I don't see how I can do it."

Michou looked up from her steaming cup of ersatz coffee. "Don't worry about it," she said. "At least we have plenty of turnips and carrots. And wine. We can just give them lots of wine."

Cécile sniffed. "They'd like that. You'd never get your grapes picked." Muttering to herself, she turned back to the cupboard. "Still say a *soupe des vendanges* without meat is a crime."

Michou shrugged. Every harvest since the occupation, Cécile had complained she couldn't possibly make the traditional grape pickers' soup, and every year she grudgingly had had to admit she was wrong when the pickers contributed their meager portions of meat to the huge pot. "Not quite the same," she'd always say, "but not bad."

Michou wrenched a piece of bread from the small loaf in front of her and dipped it into her coffee. She had at least another week to listen to Cécile's complaints. The grapes weren't quite ready, but if the rain held off for a few more days, it looked as if it might be a good vintage, the best since the invasion.

The swinging door squeaked open, and she raised her head. Erich stepped into the kitchen. When he saw Michou, he hastily looked down at his boots. "S-sorry," he mumbled. "Didn't realize—"

"Good morning," Michou said. "You've taken the bandages off your hand. Is it better? You never did tell me what happened to it."

He put his hand behind his back. "I j-just came in to ask Cécile—" He shrugged, spun on his heel, and pushed back through the door.

Michou frowned at the swinging door. She didn't understand him. It had been more than two weeks now, and he still acted as if he'd been the one to use *his* body to pay a debt. He'd apologized stiffly, formally the next day, and ever since then had taken great care to avoid her. She owed him her life—and Guy's—but he wouldn't even let her thank her. She sighed. Considering what he'd risked, the price she'd paid had been small. He hadn't forced her, after all, and she wasn't a bit sorry for what she'd done. She'd do it again if it meant Guy's safety. If that made her a whore, so be it. She'd been called worse, for less reason. She shook her head at the irony.

"What'd he want?" Cécile asked, her hands on her hips.

"I don't know," Michou said. "He must have changed his mind."

Cécile shook her head. "Doesn't act much like a German, does he?" she said "Always so quiet and polite. Not like Stecher and that awful fat-bellied one that came first—what was his name?"

"Kohler." Michou ripped off another piece of bread and chewed on it.

"That's right." Cécile shuffled to the stove and stirred the bubbling pot vigorously. "Wonder what happened to him."

Michou wrinkled her nose at the garlicky fumes rising from the pot and spreading throughout the kitchen. "He's dead, I hope," she said. The bread halfway to her mouth, she paused for a moment. That's what Erich had meant. "Now you and Berthe can truly be sisters," he'd said after he apologized. At the time she hadn't understood the connection; she'd thought he was referring to Maman and Henri's marriage plans.

She stared at the bread. But he hadn't been talking about that at all. He'd remembered what she'd told him about Kohler attacking Berthe and then disappearing. He'd been comparing himself to a rapist and a deserter.

She laid the bread back down. Poor Erich. He was paying double for saving her life.

*   *   *

Crouched on his heels, Lucien fingered the blue-black grapes. "What do you think, Jacques?" he asked, looking up. "Another week?"

Jacques squinted at the cloudy sky, then peered again at the grapes. He nodded. "Not even that much," he said. "If it doesn't rain."

"If it does, we'll just pick in the rain. Again." Lucien rose and shook out his legs. "Tell Madeleine to provide the usual amenities. Berthe's too busy with that son of hers and Father's wedding to help this year." He headed back toward the drive. When he reached his car, he turned around. "I'll bring supplies in a couple of days."

"Y-yes." Jacques hastily jerked his head up.

The old man had been staring at his pistol, Lucien realized. He smirked as he stroked the handle of the Schmeisser automatic, a gift from Karl. He'd gotten damn good with it in the last few months. Too bad he hadn't had an opportunity to use it yet—since he'd joined the Milice, he'd mostly been involved in interrogation work and in recruiting informants. Still, he enjoyed the reactions he got from wearing it.

The whirr of a car engine drifted up from the road, and Lucien stared out over the vineyards. Mueller's car. The swine. He'd sent the *gonio* around a couple of weeks ago, and when Lucien had accused him yesterday, he'd just admitted it with a shrug and said it was a joke.

Some joke. No one joked with the Gestapo, not even a Milicien. Not even a German lieutenant. Not if he was smart.

The car rounded the curve and disappeared. Mueller wasn't dumb and he wasn't a jokester. That left only one explanation, and Lucien didn't like it.

Jacques cleared his throat. "Anything else?"

Lucien blinked. "No," he said. "Get back to whatever you were doing." He opened the door of the Mercedes and slid into the seat. Tapping his fingers on the wheel, he watched Jacques shuffle back toward the *chai*. Mueller had to have been protecting Michou. And that meant that Michou was even more deeply involved with the Resistance than he'd realized. If she was operating a radio set, someone important had given it to her. And it was damn likely that that someone was a British agent.

Lucien punched the starter and listened for a minute to

the car's smooth idle. A British agent. Of course. What he'd suspected since talking to Sylvie de Bacqueville was absolutely true. Michou's British friend named Guy and Guy Fournier had to be the same. That explained a lot of things. Especially since Berthe had finally given in to his threats and told him Michou was still seeing Fournier.

He smiled as he put the car in gear. The best thing of all was that he didn't have to do a damn thing about Fournier— Renet had told him last week that he'd found out that Yves was a cover name for Guy, and next week they were making the sweep, arresting everyone on the list Renet had compiled. In a week Fournier would be in prison—or, better yet, dead.

Lucien turned sharply onto the main road and spun out on the gravel. If the bastards did their job right, so much for Fournier. He ran his hand through his hair. But what was he going to do about Michou? She was in a lot more trouble than he'd figured. It wouldn't be long before Mueller figured out she was just using him. And when that happened—

He swerved to avoid a rut, then slowed down and lit a Gauloise. Not even Karl could get his cigars for him anymore. He inhaled the pungent smoke and blew it out through his nostrils. Maybe Karl could help, arrange a transfer or something. He had to take care of Mueller soon. He'd put it off too long. He snorted. He had been right about one thing, though. Mueller's presence had been the best insurance he could get for Michou's safety. But once Fournier was out of the way, he wouldn't need it any longer.

His lips twisted around the cigarette. And with both of them gone, she wouldn't have any choice. He'd make sure of that. If he could just get Sylvie to elaborate a little more about Michou's Jewish friend the next time he slept with her, he might be able to get enough information to prove his suspicions about Jean-David. If what he thought was true, Michou would do whatever he asked.

Lucien pressed his foot on the gas pedal as he came to a short straight stretch. Whatever he wanted. And he wanted everything. He pictured her head between his legs. He smiled. Yes, everything. And she was going to give it to him. Whether she liked it or not. He'd already waited too long.

He rounded the curve into Libourne and slammed on the brakes. Sooner or later, though, she was going to like it. Of that he was certain.

Guy paused in front of the window for a minute before he shut it. September still had another week to go and already the leaves were turning and the days were much shorter and cooler. He sighed. Nothing to look forward to but another long, cold winter and worry about Michou. He hadn't seen her since the fiasco three weeks ago. Thank God he'd been right about Mueller. The poor lovesick fool had saved her—and him, too, in the bargain.

He grimaced as he moved back into the makeshift kitchen. He couldn't erase the memory of her standing there naked as he bolted through the window, the aerial in one hand and his clothes in the other. What had happened? He closed his eyes. From the roof he'd seen the two Germans rush into the tower, then reemerge a few minutes later, laughing. They talked for a minute, but he couldn't hear what they said. Finally, they got back into the van and drove away. He had jumped to the roof of the main château and climbed down the ladder at the back. He'd waited behind the tower until it started to get light, but Mueller never came out.

Guy opened his eyes and lifted the lid of the pot on the stove. Of course, that was easy enough to explain—Mueller had just used the second-floor entrance. That was the only explanation he allowed himself to think about.

Yesterday's leftovers bubbling in the pot belched out the combined odors of rancid oil, cabbage, and garlic. He quickly replaced the lid and turned down the burner. When the war was over, he'd never eat cabbage again.

The light tap at the door made him jump. God, he hated unexpected visitors. At the best they brought bad news. At the worst they were the Gestapo.

But the Gestapo didn't knock politely. He swallowed. "Who is it?" he said.

"Philippe."

Guy unlocked the door and pulled Philippe inside. "What the hell," he said. "You young fool. You're supposed to be in the Corrèze. What are you doing in Libourne?"

Philippe's face contorted as if he were about to cry, then he shook himself and stuck his chin out. "I followed Claude here," he said.

"Claude?"

"Claude Renet. The chickenhearted bastard who was afraid of the PE. You remember him?"

Guy nodded. "I wondered a couple of times what had prompted him to become a maquisard."

"Well, I know," Philippe said. "And it had nothing to do with patriotism." He took a deep breath, and his next words came out in a rush. "He went straight to the Desroches warehouse on the quai. I hung around awhile after he left, and Lucien Desroches came out a few minutes later. He was wearing a Milice uniform and grinning." Philippe gulped.

Guy grabbed his arm. "Calm down," he said.

"That son of a bitch Renet is a traitor." Philippe's voice cracked.

Guy nodded. "Looks like it, doesn't it?" he said. He strode to the stove and flicked off the burner. "Lunch will just have to wait." He smiled slightly. "Not that I mind a great deal."

"What are we going to do?" Philippe asked.

"*You* are going to stay out of sight," Guy said.

"But—"

Guy held up his hand. "No arguments." He rummaged in the desk drawer for a pencil and a piece of paper and scribbled the address of his safe house. "Go there," he said, giving Philippe the paper. "Be sure you aren't followed. And don't leave. I'll come for you."

Philippe stared down at the address. "But what about the weapons cache? You can't take care of that by yourself."

"I don't plan to," Guy said. "I need to get word to London first. I have to see if Michou still has the wireless. Then I'll come back for you." He patted Philippe on the shoulder.

"What if something happens?" Philippe cleared his throat. "To you. What if you don't come back?"

"Wait until tomorrow morning," Guy said. "If I haven't come for you by then, go back to the maquis. Tell your commander what you told me. If Renet has been with you for this long, there's a pretty good chance he isn't planning anything soon."

"What if he is? If he has?"

Guy snatched his jacket off the back of the kitchen chair. "Then you're on your own," he said. After he shrugged into his coat, he gave Philippe a quick hug. "Good luck."

47

Michou gasped for breath as she leaned the bicycle against the stone wall. Her throat ached; her heart pounded; her legs quivered. She'd left the pickers at their lunch, ignored Maman's raised eyebrows, and pedaled as hard as she could to Saint-Émilion. Guy was in trouble. Something urgent, he'd said on the phone. Something that couldn't wait until tonight. Something he'd risk seeing her in public for.

Urgent. The word had drummed inside her skull all the way, propelling her legs even faster when they wobbled. Urgent. Guy never exaggerated. So *urgent* meant calamity. Worse than that, maybe. Even her late period seemed unimportant.

Michou braced herself against the wall for a few seconds. She had to appear normal, no matter how scared she was. Hastily, she smoothed her tumbled hair with shaky hands. She forced herself to take several deep breaths until she stopped heaving.

She pushed the bicycle around the corner to the sidewalk in front of L'Hostellerie. Guy sat at a table near the door, his back against the wall. He was the only one sitting on the *terrasse*. He waved when he saw her.

She propped the bicycle against the side of the building and walked slowly toward him. Her legs still shook. Her faced burned—she knew her cheeks were splotched with red. When she reached the table, she slid into the chair next to him.

"That was fast," he said. Smiling, he poured red wine from a bottle into the glass in front of her. "Here. I ordered for you. Hope you don't mind."

"Urgent," she croaked. "You said it was urgent." How could he sit there so calmly, smiling as if they were meeting just for a drink?

"It is." He leaned toward her and clasped her hands in his. "What happened to the wireless?" he whispered as he kissed both her cheeks.

"Erich has it," she said. "He took it with him after—"

"Merde," he hissed. He paused for a moment. "Think you can get it back?"

"I don't know," she said. "He was horribly angry. I guess I could try."

"I buried the aerial at the end of the first row in the upper vineyard. If you don't need it now, be sure to dig it up after the Germans are gone." He squeezed her hands, then let go of them and took a drink of wine. "Because we *are* going to get rid of them."

"I know." She clinked her glass against his and sipped her wine.

"Now, don't forget," he said. "Dig it up. I think it'll be worth your trouble." He put his hand into his jacket pocket and withdrew it, his fist clenched, then covered her hand on the table with his.

She looked up. He licked his lips and nodded. She twisted her hand so it clasped his and palmed the small square of paper.

"There's an infiltrator in one of the maquis in the Corrèze," he whispered. "I know who it is. As soon as I leave here, I'm going to take care of him. But I wanted you and London to know in case I have to disappear for a while. I didn't want you to worry." He paused, his eyes locked on hers. "If you don't hear from me again, listen to *La France Parle aux Français* on the BBC. There'll be a message from the wine merchant if I end up back in London."

Michou curled her fingers around the paper. How could he be so damn calm? He was risking his life just to keep her from worrying. As if his telling her was going to stop her. And her brother was still in the Corrèze. "Philippe," she whispered. "What about Philippe?"

"He's fine. I sent him to a safe house."

"Thank God."

The door banged, and Lucien strode onto the *terrasse*.

He was dressed in his Milice uniform, with a ridiculously large gun riding in the holster at his waist. When he saw Michou, both eyebrows shot high in his forehead.

Michou's fingers cramped as she clutched the slip of paper even more tightly.

Lucien strutted up to the table. "Hello," he said, offering Guy his hand. "Guy Fournier, isn't it? Haven't seen you around much lately." He shook Guy's hand and turned to Michou. He smiled and held out his hand to her. "Hello, *sister.*"

"Not yet." Michou frowned at him and put her hand in her pocket. She wouldn't have shaken his hand even if she didn't have Guy's message in hers.

Lucien shrugged and let his hand drop. "How's the harvest?" he asked. "Surprised to see you here today. Don't you usually direct everything yourself?"

"Maman insisted that I get away," Michou mumbled.

"Nice of her." Lucien smiled crookedly. "But I wouldn't leave her alone too long."

"I don't plan to."

"Good." Lucien nodded at Guy before he crossed to a table on the other side of the *terrasse* and sat down. He leaned both elbows on the table and stared up the street.

Michou gritted her teeth. "I hate him," she said. "God, how I hate him."

"Doesn't seem to bother him much," Guy said.

"It never has. He thinks so much of himself, he can't believe it."

"Wish he hadn't seen us together, though."

"He knows about us. Berthe told him when he threatened to tell Henri who Daniel's father was. Then she told me." Michou shook her head. "She was so upset."

Guy leaned across the table. "Then I might as well kiss you." He brushed his lips against hers. "I have to go," he said. "I love you."

Tears stung her eyes. "I love you, too. Be careful. I'll do my best about the message." Biting her lip, she clung to his hand and stared into his eyes as he rose.

Suddenly a large black car roared up the narrow cobblestone street toward them. Guy squeezed her hand so hard she gasped with pain.

"Gestapo," he hissed, sitting back down. "There's nothing to do but bluff. If we run, they'll shoot. Sit still. Maybe they're after someone inside."

She wriggled her hand out of his clasp and put it into her pocket. She groped for the message with shaking fingers as two men wearing long coats and gray hats climbed out of the car. Finally, she grasped the paper, and her eyes darted toward Lucien.

He rose and smiled smugly at her before he started toward the Gestapo agents. "Just a minute," he said. "I'm Lucien Des—"

They brushed by him and headed straight for her table. Michou's heart thundered. This was it. They were going to arrest her and Guy, torture them both, kill them both. Just as they had Papa. And Lucien had something to do with it. Just as he had with Papa.

One of them grabbed her arm and pulled her roughly to her feet. Her glass shattered at her feet, and red wine splashed against her legs.

"Gestapo." His partner stuck a pistol in Guy's back, then ran his hands quickly along his legs and arms. "Come with us," he ordered in accented French.

Michou jerked away from the Nazi. "I'll come. But don't touch me." Sobbing hysterically, she bent over, covered her face with both hands, and crammed the paper into her mouth. It was too big to swallow. She worked it under her tongue and clamped her jaw shut.

"Enough," a harsh voice commanded.

Something hard poked into the small of her back, and she straightened slowly. The other agent and Guy were standing at the edge of the *terrasse* when another car rounded the corner.

She sucked in her breath. The car stopped in front of the Gestapo car, and Erich got out. His head jerked as he looked from her to Guy to the Gestapo agents to Lucien. He walked toward her, pressing his arm across his middle. His chin jutted out, and the muscles in his jaw twitched. His eyes were narrowed to slits.

Suddenly he pulled out his gun. "Run, Michou!" he shouted.

A huge explosion roared in her ears. She turned around.

A patch of red grew around a black hole in the Gestapo officer's chest, and he slumped to the ground. She twisted back toward Erich.

"Get down!" He knocked the table over and pushed her down behind it. The wine bottle and Guy's glass crashed against the sidewalk.

Michou covered her head with her hands and huddled on the ground. Several more explosions boomed, one right after the other. "Guy! Guy!" She screamed it over and over until her throat was raw with agony.

Something knocked against her shoulder, and she shrieked. Then all was quiet. She jerked her hands away from her eyes.

Erich lay behind her, facedown on the sidewalk.

Michou pushed herself to her hands and knees. Where was Guy? The agent who'd arrested him lay across the black car. Guy was nowhere in sight. She pressed her eyes shut and took a deep breath.

Broken glass cut into her palms, and she brushed them against her pants before she turned back to Erich. "Erich?" she said, grabbing his arm. There was a small dark hole at the base of his head. She gulped, and the soggy piece of paper in her mouth slipped down her throat.

"Leave him alone," Lucien said. "He's dead." He pointed his gun at her. "Get up."

She sat back on her heels and stared up at him, her mouth open. The smell of gunpowder was so strong she could taste it. She shook her head slowly. "No," she said. "No. He can't be."

Lucien swiveled the gun toward Erich and pulled the trigger. Another burst of gunshots shattered the silence.

"Stop it!" Michou screamed. She covered her ears and squeezed her eyes shut. "Stop it!"

More dark spots appeared on Mueller's back. Lucien kicked the limp body. Thoughtful of him to take care of things so nicely. Blood seeped onto the sidewalk. He'd fixed the bastard. "If he wasn't, he is now," he said. "Get up." He grabbed Michou's arm and jerked her to her feet. Jesus, she looked a mess. Damn her, sobbing over a dead German. She'd almost ruined everything. When she got over the shock, she'd be thankful, though—he'd see to that.

"Where's Guy?" she said. Tears made little trails down her dirty face.

The bastard had escaped. If he'd gotten him, too, everything would have been perfect. Too bad he'd shot the Gestapo agent instead. "Ran away. Left you here to take care of yourself." He grinned at her. "Left you here for *me* to take care of." He dug his fingernails into her arm. "Stop crying. Don't worry. I'm going to take *good* care of you."

"Let go of me." She bit his hand. "What are you going to do now? Arrest me yourself? Shoot me, too?"

He rubbed his hand. "Go home," he said. "Get on your bicycle and go home." He narrowed his eyes and glared at her. "You were never here. Do you understand? You weren't here."

"What about her?" Michou waved her hand toward the face peeking out the restaurant door. "Are you going to kill her to keep her quiet?"

Merde, he thought. Just how much had the stupid bitch seen? He sneered as the door clicked shut again. "I have better ways. You'll find out someday." He pushed her. "Go."

"I hate you. I will always hate you." She snarled at him, then limped to her bicycle without looking back. She swung her foot over, pushed off, and wobbled down the street.

Lucien put the Schmeisser back in the holster and patted the handle. The *terrasse* looked like the scene of a battle. One German draped over his car, another in front of the door, and Mueller at his feet. Too bad there wasn't one more body—Fournier's.

Shrugging, Lucien stepped over Mueller's corpse and headed back toward the restaurant. Fournier wouldn't last long out there anyway. Too many people looking for him now.

He pushed open the door. Chantal stood alone behind the bar, her eyes round and her mouth gaping. He was glad the place was empty.

"I'm going to use your phone again," he said. "Got a mess outside that needs cleaning up." He strode behind the bar, lifted the mouthpiece, and jiggled the button. "Get me the Libourne Gestapo," he said loudly after the operator answered.

He held his hand over the receiver and turned to Chantal. "Thought I told you to stay inside," he said.

"I—I did." Her face blanched, and she licked her lips.

"Never mind. I'll take care of you later," he said. He'd make damn sure she never told anyone about Michou—or the Gestapo agent. A word in Karl's ear to keep an eye on her would discredit anything she might say.

The telephone blipped, and he stuck his hand into his pocket and fingered the corkscrew. This was going to be tricky—explaining three dead Germans and no prisoner after he'd called half an hour ago to tip off the Gestapo to Guy's presence. He wasn't really worried, though. Major Dhose was a good friend of Karl's.

48

Michou cracked another egg and dumped it into her hand. She dropped the shell onto the floor, let the slimy egg white slide through her fingers into the wooden bowl between her knees, then tossed the yolk into another bowl beside her for Cécile. She hoped they would pacify Cécile somewhat for the loss of the three dozen eggs she'd been hoarding. Maybe if she could make a custard or something with them, she wouldn't complain so much.

Michou shook her head. Three dozen. Hardly enough to make a decent start on fining—before the occupation. But if she was stingy and limited herself to three eggs per cask, she'd have enough to clarify the dozen casks left of her first wine.

She wiped her hand on the sticky towel next to her and picked up the twig whisk. If it hadn't been for Erich, she wouldn't have even that much left. He'd known how important the 1941 vintage was to her, and he'd managed to fill his quota and leave her some, too.

She missed Erich. During the two weeks since his death, she'd realized just how much she'd really cared for him. If it hadn't been for Guy, she might have fallen in love with him. She frowned and stabbed at the eggs. Be honest, she told herself. If Guy hadn't come back when he did, you would have. He loved you, and he hated the war as much as you did. She whipped the egg whites until they were frothy and her arm ached. It wasn't fair.

But after Marc's death, she'd stopped expecting things to be fair. That was part of growing up, Papa had said. Then the Germans had killed him, too.

A huge sob welled in her chest, and she stood up. It

wasn't for either Marc or Papa, she knew. It was for Erich. She stiffened the muscles in her throat and bit her lip. She couldn't give in to it now. Maybe later, when she was in bed and there was no one who might see. But not now.

Michou removed the bung from the cask and concentrated on pouring in the whites. They'd sink to the bottom and draw the wine's impurities with them. Then, in a month or two, she could rack the wine one last time before she bottled it. This was one wine she was going to bottle herself. Not a drop was going to Desroches et Fils, even if Henri was going to become her stepfather at Christmas.

She banged the stopper back in with her fist. After the shooting, Maman and Henri had decided to postpone their wedding for several months. Henri had been there when she'd wobbled up the drive on her bicycle. She'd taken one look at him and screamed hysterically over and over, "Your son's a murderer!" She hadn't been able to stop. He'd finally carried her, kicking and shrieking and pounding on his chest, into the salon. She'd sobbed in Maman's arms for an hour before she could talk.

After she finally got the story out, Henri had looked at Maman. She'd never seen such anger in his eyes before. The next day, Maman had told her they were putting off the wedding. Henri wanted Michou to have time to get over her grief.

She flopped back on the bench and cracked another egg. But she'd never really get over it, she knew. Even though the heart-tearing part was gone, she still grieved for Marc and Papa; and she hadn't seen them get killed. Erich had died at her feet after he'd saved her life. He'd been murdered by Lucien in front of her eyes. The picture in her head was never going to fade—the explosions; the small, dark holes; the blood; the twisted, limp way Erich had lain sprawled on the sidewalk. Her mind ran through it again and again, the action sometimes slow, sometimes fast. But the final scene was always the same: Erich crumpled on the ground, Lucien standing over him with his gun.

Michou attacked the eggs with the whip, stirring furiously. Sometimes she wondered if it was all worth it. But it had to be. Marc and Papa and Erich were dead—and their deaths were meaningless if she gave up now. She had to keep fighting no matter how tired she was, no matter how sad.

The whites foamed, and she rose to carry them to the last barrel. A sudden wave of dizziness and nausea gripped her, and her vision went black.

An instant later she found herself on the floor, the bowl of egg whites overturned next to her. She pushed herself up slowly onto her elbows. The *chai* reeked of its familiar smells of wood and wine, but she hadn't noticed how unpleasant it was until now. Her stomach churned, and she clamped her jaw to keep from vomiting. *Merde!* What she'd been afraid of for the last month had to be true.

She was pregnant again.

Her period had never come during the harvest, and now this one was more than a week late. She knew it wasn't going to come at all.

What was she going to do?

She pulled herself back up to the bench and sat with her head between her knees. She already knew what she was going to do, had known since she first suspected. This baby gave her one more thing to fight for.

She closed her eyes and rocked back and forth. Her child, Guy's child, was not going to grow up in a France under Nazi rule.

She jerked upright, and her eyes flew open. Guy's child? She counted quickly on her fingers. Erich had come to her room two or three weeks before the harvest. It was during the vintage she'd noticed her period was late. She slumped. *Mon Dieu,* it might just as easily be Erich's. And even if it wasn't, everyone was going to think so.

She straightened her shoulders. Well, she didn't care. So what if people thought her baby was a German bastard? So what if it was? It didn't make any difference, really. Look at Daniel. Berthe hated his father and loved Daniel. If this baby was Erich's, it was almost justice. It didn't mean that she loved Guy any less.

Slowly, Michou pushed herself up. Still, no matter what, this baby was hers. Nothing, no one, was going to hurt it. Her child was the future for Château Bourdet, for France, a future free from the Nazis.

Lucien twirled Sylvie's nipple between his fingers, and it stiffened and pointed at the ceiling of her luxurious suite in the Pavillon. He twisted to his side and sucked it while he stroked between her thighs. Every time she moaned with pleasure, he grew even harder. In a minute or two she was really going to have something to moan about.

He liked screwing Sylvie. He got even with Karl, Otto, and Michou every time he put it to the stupid cow. He betrayed Karl at the same time he made Sylvie betray Otto—that it was in Otto's canopied bed made it even more satisfying. And, somehow, Michou's cousin seemed to bring him a step closer to Michou.

He pulled his mouth off Sylvie's nipple and straddled her. Smiling, he stared down at her. She was an improvement over Gabrielle, at least. The strawberry-blond hair fanned on the pale aqua-cased pillow was much more appealing than Gabrielle's mousy-brown strings, and her slenderness was pleasing where Gabrielle's had been gawky.

Sylvie's eyelashes fluttered, and she opened her eyes. "Now," she groaned. "What are you waiting for?"

"Nothing now," he said. "Roll over."

She shook her head. "Not this time. Please," she whined.

He shrugged. "Fine." Better to keep her happy today. That way she was more likely to tell him what he wanted to know. Next time. There was always next time. He lowered himself on top of her and thrust into her.

She gasped and slid her arms around his neck. "You're so good," she murmured, raising her hips and grinding her pelvis against his.

Lucien closed his eyes and, as he always did, imagined Michou lying beneath him, her platinum curls tousled about her face, her soft, full lips open in wild pleasure, her hips gyrating in perfect rhythm with his strokes. Faster and faster, harder and harder he pumped until he couldn't control the force inside him any longer.

At the last second, he opened his eyes and took a deep breath of Sylvie's perfume. Michou disappeared, the pressure eased. He could go on forever this way if he wanted. It was the secret to his success in bed with women. Each one became Michou for a short while. Too short. Pretty soon he wouldn't have to pretend any longer. If Sylvie gave him what he really wanted.

Sylvie twitched and shuddered beneath him. It was

about time. He squeezed his eyes shut and brought Michou back again, started over again. Clenching his teeth, he rammed deep inside her. Her gasps of pleasure turned to little cries. She loved it. Michou loved it. Michou wanted him. "Please, please," she shrieked as he surged, exploded into her.

He collapsed on top of her. This was the moment he hated. He might as well get it over with. Slowly, he opened his eyes. No platinum curls, no soft, full lips, no Michou. He rolled off the slick body beneath him.

"Oh, Lucien," Sylvie gasped. "Too bad you can't give poor old Otto some lessons."

"I don't think his taste runs in that direction," he said. And it was too bad, he added to himself. A colonel was better than a major anytime. This room made that apparent. It was twice the size of Karl's and lavishly decorated, with a thick Aubusson carpet, rich sea-green drapes, a huge marble mantelpiece, and gilded and brocaded Louis XV furniture.

She giggled. "You're so wicked. That's not what I meant." She pushed herself up and leaned against the satin-covered headboard. "He's even become stingy lately. Says he can't get me silk stockings anymore." She stuck out her lower lip.

Lucien kissed her hand. "I'm sorry I'm not a German general," he said. "You'd have all the silk stockings you wanted."

She smiled at him. "I know." She sighed. "But you aren't, so that's that. I can't leave him."

"Too bad." He eased himself up beside her and nuzzled her neck. "Since I know how to make you so happy."

She rested her head on his shoulder. "Well, I guess I can't complain too much. I haven't had to live without you, after all."

"And you won't. I promise."

She sniffed and tossed her head. "I *would* like to see you more often, though. I thought you'd forgotten me."

"No danger of that. I'd be a fool if I did." And not for the reason she thought, either. He wove his hand through her sleek hair, wrapped it around his finger. "There was just too much going on. I couldn't get away."

"What could be more important than me?"

"Damn little," he said. "But I killed a man."

She raised an eyebrow. "Oh, really? Anyone I know?"

"Not personally. Lieutenant Mueller."

She gasped. "Michou's lieutenant? You killed a German soldier? Does Otto know? How did you get away with it?"

"It turned out to be easier than I'd thought. He was a traitor. He shot two Gestapo agents. And he had a radio set in his trunk. An English radio. I didn't know it when I shot him, but the Gestapo found it later." He laughed. "Jesus, what a relief that was. After they spotted it, they weren't interested in me anymore." He smirked. They'd just taken his word for everything.

"What about Michou?"

He shrugged. He'd never even consider telling her the truth. Sylvie was too stupid to trust with anything important, and she couldn't keep a secret. "She was upset. Father and Catherine postponed their wedding."

"Poor Michou," Sylvie said. "Two dead lovers so far." She yawned and stretched. "She's something of a jinx, it seems. Even her friend Rachel is probably dead. Otto told me most of the Jews rounded up in July were sent to camps in Germany. I've heard talk. They don't survive long."

"Didn't you say one time that Rachel had a son?" He forced himself to sound offhand. "What happened to him? Did he get sent away, too?"

"Ouch," she said, putting her hand over the one he'd entwined in her hair. "Don't pull."

Cursing himself silently, he freed his hand and caressed her cheek. She was dumb like a fox. If she suspected he was interested, she wouldn't tell him a thing. "Too bad about the boy," he said.

"Oh, they didn't take the children that time," she said. "I don't know what happened to David."

"David?" It took an effort to keep his face impassive.

She nodded. "Cute little thing. I saw him when he was about a year old. Dark hair and eyes. Like Rachel."

"Fascinating," he drawled, then yawned. He ran his hand across her breast. God bless you, you stupid bitch, he thought, twirling her nipple between his fingers.

49

Guy peered into the cracked and foggy mirror and ran his thumb across his new moustache. It was coming along nicely. A few more days for it, a new pair of glasses, some black hair dye, new papers—then he'd be ready to return to Saint-Émilion. It was risky, but he had to see Michou. Even though Philippe assured him she was fine, he had to find out for himself.

He splashed water from the basin onto his face and grimaced as he picked up the straight razor. No strop. No soap. He hated shaving without soap. He scraped the dull razor across his face, wincing as it tugged at the whiskers and left his cheeks stinging and raw. And he was sick of this place. After that trigger-happy idiot Desroches had so conveniently gunned down the Gestapo agent instead of him, Guy had done the only thing he could. He'd escaped. It had taken every ounce of self-control he had not to go after Michou, but he'd been afraid Desroches might go crazy and shoot her, too, if he tried. So he'd stolen a car, picked up Philippe at the safe house, and driven both of them to the little apartment he still kept in Bordeaux. He hadn't been out since. Too dangerous. Philippe reported his picture was posted everywhere.

Guy attacked the other side of his face. Thank God for Philippe. Not only had he reported on Michou's safety, but without his help, the whole operation Guy had been working on for months would have been destroyed. Philippe had managed to warn enough members and see to the relocation of enough arms dumps to ensure the continuation of the *réseau*. He'd even arranged the kidnapping of Claude Renet. And the execution.

Guy sighed and put down the razor. There wasn't much left of the boy in Philippe now. He still talked too fast, moved too quickly, but the innocent exuberance had been replaced in the last few weeks with a new grimness. Guy splashed more cold water on his cheeks, then patted them dry with a thin towel. Philippe had killed a man. It was an invisible atrocity of war, a horror he would have to live with the rest of his life—if he survived. Guy knew about that.

He threw the towel down next to the basin and snatched his shirt off the chair. Christ, he wanted out of this hole. Gritting his teeth, he thrust his arms into the sleeves and pulled on the shirt. Patience, he told himself. The instructors at Beaulieu had warned about this. Boredom and inactivity could be an agent's biggest enemy, spur him to do stupid, careless things. He shaved and dressed every day, even when he wasn't going anywhere, just to keep himself from falling into that trap. Thank God he had only a couple more days to go.

On the street below, a car door slammed, then another, then another. Philippe already? He wasn't supposed to come back with the new identity papers until tomorrow. And whom had he brought with him? Frowning, Guy buttoned his shirt as he walked to the apartment's only window.

The car parked below was not the ancient Citroën he'd stolen. It was shiny and black.

Guy sucked in his breath. He grabbed his pants off the bed and pulled them on as he headed for the back door. How had they found him? Philippe was the only one who knew where he was. Philippe—

The back door flew open and two Gestapo agents burst into the room, guns drawn. Behind him, someone pounded at the front door. Guy calmly raised his hands above his head. Even as his eyes darted about the dingy, sparsely furnished room, he knew it was hopeless. But he wasn't afraid, for some reason didn't taste the by-now familiar coppery saliva of fear or hear the roar of blood in his ears. Third time was a charm, he told himself. He just hoped like hell it wasn't for the Gestapo.

The gray-haired agent rammed a gun into Guy's ribs while the younger one unlocked the door. Two more men pushed into the small room, their large Schmeisser automatics pointed at him.

Gray Hair jabbed his gun harder into Guy's ribs. "Search him," he said to his partner.

The baby-faced Gestapo agent stuck his gun into the pocket of his long overcoat, then ran his hands along Guy's pant legs. He shrugged at the older man. "Nothing," he said. He took a pair of handcuffs from his other pocket.

The older agent poked Guy again. "Go," he said.

Guy walked to the door. "It's cold," he said. "All right if I take my jacket?" He nodded toward the dilapidated wardrobe next to the bed.

Gray Hair pointed to the young agent. "Get it," he said.

Baby Face returned the handcuffs to his pocket and strode to the wardrobe. He opened the door and pulled a jacket from a hanger, then inspected the pockets. He pulled out a pipe. "What about this?" he asked.

Gray Hair shrugged. "It's just a pipe. Leave it," he said.

Baby Face returned the pipe to the pocket and tossed the jacket to Guy. "Put it on," he said.

Guy caught the jacket and eased it on, then immediately put his hands back up.

"Go now," the older Gestapo agent barked.

Keeping his hands raised, Guy marched down the stairs surrounded by German agents. They'd forgotten the handcuffs. He stiffened his arms. They'd forgotten the bloody handcuffs. Maybe there was a chance.

When he reached the street, he looked sideways in both directions without turning his head. Nothing, no diversion to distract his captors momentarily. He'd have to wait. And hope.

One of the guards slid behind the wheel of the Citroën while another settled himself in the rear seat behind him. The agent in the back seat pushed open the curbside door.

Guy climbed in and scooted across the dark leather seat. The car smelled of cigarettes and sweat, the bitter, acrid sweat of fear. How many prisoners had it carried to Gestapo headquarters? He pressed his arms tightly to his sides and clasped his hands in his lap.

The young agent, the one with the handcuffs in his

pocket, squeezed in next to Guy while the man with the Schmeisser got into the front. The doors clunked shut, and the gray-haired agent half turned toward the back and pointed his gun at Guy.

Guy nodded at him. Not yet, he told himself. He turned his head slowly to the left and glanced at the agent crammed against him. The man fumbled in his pocket for a match to light the cigarette stuck between his thick lips, then dropped the match on the floor. When he bent to retrieve it, Guy saw what he'd been waiting for.

A chance. A chance in the form of a thin strip of light between the door and the sill.

He looked away as casually as he could, but for the first time his heart began to thud more quickly. He just had to wait, hope no no one else noticed it. But the time wasn't yet. Once the car was moving—

The engine roared, and he tensed himself as the car accelerated. It careened around the corner at the end of the street. The time was—*now*.

He flung himself against the smoking agent. The door flew open, and he landed on top of the agent in the middle of the street. Something crunched beneath him, and brakes squealed.

Guy jumped up and zigzagged toward the maze of narrow streets in front of him. A burst of gunfire exploded behind him, and he hunched his shoulders to his ears and ducked his head as he turned the corner.

He sprinted down a cobblestone alley too narrow for a car, then around another corner, and another. Gasping, he ran until he was sure the Gestapo had given up the chase. When he finally slowed to a walk, every breath of cold air he drew seared his lungs. He didn't care—he was free.

But for how long? What if he got swept up in a *rafle*? He still didn't have his new papers. He felt his jacket pocket. He didn't have any papers. But at least they'd left his pipe. He took it out and unscrewed the base. A tiny compass dropped into his hand. He might just be needing it soon.

He reassembled the pipe and stuck it back in his pocket. Had they arrested Philippe? Or had someone in his apartment building turned him in? Two women had been gossiping in the hall the day he arrived. Had they seen one of the

posters, recognized him? Christ, he wished he knew what
had happened to Philippe. He felt responsible for the boy. If
anything happened to him, Michou would be—

Michou. He stopped in the middle of the deserted lane.
In front of him, a small stone church squatted next to a
rundown cemetery surrounded by an iron fence. He walked
quickly to the gate, pushed it open, and headed for the stone
bench at the side of the church.

He sat down and rested his head against the rough wall.
Now he couldn't risk seeing her at all—it was just too dangerous for both of them. Lucien knew who he was but had
allowed Michou to escape. He was still obsessed with her,
Philippe had said. Had been since she was sixteen. It had
been a family joke, even. If it was a gentle spot in Lucien's
vicious soul that prompted him to protect Michou, good. But
if he harmed her—

Guy's hands doubled into fists. He'd kill the bastard. He
snorted. If she didn't do it first, that was.

Christ, he wanted to go back for her. But he couldn't.
She would never come with him, and he couldn't stay. He had
no choices left.

He had to get out of France.

He shook his head slowly. And there was only one way
out for him now that he'd been cut off from all his contacts.
Through the Pyrénées into Spain.

He stood up. He might as well get started. It was going to
be a long walk.

The man in the black beret edged the wrong way through
the crowd gathered in front of Lucien. There was only one
way out of this street, and it was past him. At the other end, a
dozen Miliciens herded everyone they saw into the narrow
lane.

"You there!" Lucien shouted. "You can't go that way.
Come to the front. And get out your papers." He gritted his
teeth. Nothing was going right lately. First, Fournier had
escaped. He should have just taken care of him himself when
he had the chance instead of waiting for the Gestapo to get
there. But he'd wanted to see him suffer, make sure there
wasn't a chance for him to get away. Then Michou had shown
up and that bastard Mueller had started shooting. And now,

on top of everything else, Sylvie had told him last week that
Otto was acting suspicious, asking lots of questions about
him. Lucien rolled the Gauloise to the other side of his
mouth as he blew the smoke out his nostrils.

The small man turned slowly around and worked his way
back through the crowd. He stuck his package under his arm,
then reached into his jacket pocket. After he pulled a thick
wad from his pocket, he unfolded it and handed it to Lucien.

Lucien thumbed through the pieces of paper: identity
card, draft card, labor card, marriage certificate, baptismal
certificate, ration cards. He shrugged and returned them,
blowing a stream of smoke into the man's face. He didn't
really care about this bastard. It was Fournier he wanted.
"Get out of here," he said.

The man refolded his papers and pocketed them. Clinging tightly to his package, he scooted past the blockade.

"Next," Lucien said. A fat woman with frizzy hair put
her papers into his outstretched hand. He glanced through
them and gave them back. What a bore. This was the fourth
rafle since Fournier's escape a week ago. The son of a bitch
wasn't dumb enough to show up in Libourne. He was probably long gone. Lucien jerked his head at the woman. "Go,"
he said.

She pushed past him, and he stuck his hand out again
without bothering to look up. Someone slapped papers into
his hand, and his eyes skimmed over them. *Michèle*— His
eyes stopped, returned again to the name. *Michèle Patrice
Valette*. His head snapped up, and he spat the cigarette to the
ground.

She stood in front of him, her lips pressed in a thin line
and her eyes narrowed. She straddled her old bicycle to keep
it upright. Her baggy brown pants were tied to her ankles
with a piece of string, and the cuffs of the navy-blue sweater
she wore hung out from under her coat sleeves. Jean-David
sat on the bicycle seat behind her and clutched her shoulders.

Lucien shoved her papers back at her. "Let me see his,"
he said.

"He's just a child," she said.

"Nobody gets past without papers," Lucien said. "Give
them to me." She didn't know how lucky she was. If it

weren't for him, she'd be dead by now. Or worse than dead.
He snapped his fingers. Well, pretty soon she'd know. She'd
know how much she owed him. She'd realize how much he
loved her.

She shoved her cards back into one pocket, then rummaged through the other one. Finally, she produced a small
packet, carefully folded. She dropped it into his hand.

He spread the papers open and inspected the first one, a
baptismal certificate. *Name:* Jean-David Jourdan. *Place of
birth:* Lyon, France. *Date of birth:* 28 December 1938.
Frowning, he read through the rest of the documents. They
all seemed in order. Too bad.

But something picked at his memory, and he went back
to the first one. *Date of birth:* 28 December—

That was it! He grinned at Michou as he returned the
boy's papers. He'd gone to a birthday party for him after he
first arrived. It had been in July, not December. "His birthday's coming up, I see," he said. "You planning to give him
another party?"

Michou clamped her lips shut as she stuffed the papers
back in her pocket. "Are you through?" she asked. "May we
go now?" The hairs at the back of her neck prickled, and she
shuddered. Why was he smiling that way? It wasn't because
of Guy, she was pretty sure. She'd seen Philippe last week,
and he'd told her Guy was safe. He'd been planning to take
him new papers as soon as they were ready so he could get
out of France. Had something gone wrong? Did the sudden
increase of *rafles* in Saint-Émilion and Libourne have something to do with Guy?

"See you at the wedding," Lucien said. He waved her
through, still grinning crookedly. "Next."

Steadying Jean-David on the seat, Michou pushed the
bicyle past the blockade and down the street. As soon as she
turned the corner, she lifted him off and leaned the bicycle
against a building. She took out his papers. It was when
Lucien had been looking at them that his expression had
changed, and the only thing that ever made him happy was
causing other people problems.

She unfolded the papers and studied them. Suddenly
Lucien's comment echoed inside her head: *His birthday's
coming up, I see. You planning to give him another party?*

Her eyes skittered back to the top of the baptismal certificate. *Birthdate: 28 December 1938*.

Her stomach flip-floppped, and she crumpled the papers
in her hand. How could she have been so stupid? She'd never
even looked at the birth date on the false certificate.

"What's wrong?" Jean-David said. He tugged at her
coat. "Is there something wrong?"

She bent down and hugged him against her. Her queasy
stomach churned, and bile flooded her mouth. She swallowed
hard. "Nothing, darling," she said. "We'd better hurry. We're
already late. Aunt Berthe's going to wonder what happened
to us." After she released him, she smoothed out his papers,
refolded them, and put them back into her pocket. "Let's
go." She swung him onto the seat, then eased herself onto
the pedals. "Hang on." His hands clutched at her waist, and
she pushed off.

Lucien knows, the pedals clicked as she pumped the
bicycle down the street. *Lucien knows.*

50

❧

The irony of it. He'd managed to escape the Gestapo twice in the last two months only to end up in a prison cell in Pamplona, Spain. Spain—a professed neutral as blunderingly incompetent as the Nazis were ruthlessly efficient. And because of that incompetence and bureaucratic nonsense, he might just end up still in prison even after the war was over. If he weren't so miserable, he'd have to laugh.

Guy wrapped the thin gray blanket around his shoulders and sat back down on the pallet that served as his bed. It had been five days since he stumped out of the snowy Pyrénées, half frozen and half starved, onto Spanish soil and into the arms of the Spanish police, and he hadn't yet gotten warm. If it hadn't been for the kindness of an old Basque couple, he'd have lost at least three of his toes to frostbite. They'd saved his feet and his life.

His stomach cramped, and he doubled over. The greasy potato soup that was the staple of his prison diet worked its revenge on him again. He'd come down with dysentery his second day in prison, but the prison doctor had declined to do anything for it. Or for his blisters, frostbite, or infected bedbug bites, either. *"Mañana,"* he'd said every day after he glanced at Guy. *Mañana* still hadn't arrived.

The spasm eased, and he straightened. With any sort of luck at all, perhaps he'd be out before it did. He'd told the prison officials to contact both the British and American embassies. Someone had to be doing something for him by now. He supposed it was a matter of identification. He couldn't be released until he had papers, and right now someone at Orchard Court was figuring out something plausible. At least, he hoped so. Otherwise, there wasn't going to be much left of him when they got him back to England, not after the dysentery and the bedbugs.

He ran his hand over his roughly shaven head, another gift from the Spanish government, and grimaced. Still, Spanish prison—bedbugs, bad food, and all—was a hell of a lot better than Gestapo torture. The only thing that really tortured him now was worry—about Michou, about Philippe, about the *réseau* he'd set up with such risk and care. What was happening to them? Was Michou all right? Had Philippe been arrested?

He closed his eyes and ducked his head. If only he'd been able to stay, to make sure. But any protection he might be able to provide was more than outweighed by the danger his presence would cause. And his mission *had* to come first. There'd never been any question about that. All he could do was get out. He knew that, too. It just didn't make him feel any better.

A hand patted his shoulder, and he snapped his head up and opened his eyes.

"Can't sleep, either?" Louis whispered in French-accented English.

Guy shook his head. "Hard enough with the damn bugs biting me," he said slowly. Even though Louis had been an English teacher in France, he had a difficult time with Guy's American inflections. "Then they leave the bloody light on all night." He jerked his head at the naked light bulb in the middle of the ceiling.

Louis sat down next to him. "I asked the trusty," he said, his voice still lowered. "About the missing men. I was right. They were shot. The only ones they are releasing are the young ones, under eighteen."

"Why?" Guy hissed, gripping the blanket. "It's been years since the end of the civil war. Why now?"

Louis shook his head. "Franco doesn't forget," he said. "Or forgive."

"Christ. Where does it all end?"

"When we stop fighting them," Louis said. "Even after we win, we can never stop." One of the other cellmates mumbled in his sleep, and Louis put his finger over his mouth.

Guy nodded. Rubio was the reason he and Louis always spoke in English. Prison rumors had it that he was a Nazi informant. Prison rumors also had it that he wasn't going to last much longer.

As soon as Rubio was quiet, Louis turned back to Guy. "The trusty told me something else," he said, smiling. "You will be released soon. May I offer my congratulations?" He extended his hand.

Guy took a deep breath of the cell's fetid air and shook Louis' hand. "I hope you're right," he said. "I hope like hell you're right."

The open Wehrmacht truck bounced off the Avenue du President-Wilson onto a dirt side road. Jake groaned as the prisoner wedged behind him jostled against his kidneys, still tender from the beating he'd received before his trial.

Trial. *Hah!* A ridiculous formality, no more. Once the Nazis had discovered he was both German and Jewish, everyone had known what the end would be. The only surprise was that he'd been given a trial, hadn't been shipped immediately to a concentration camp. Breathing shallowly to avoid the dust swirling into the truck, he raised his head and stared out the back.

At the end of the road, a hexagon-shaped fortress rose from the top of a wooded hill. So that was Mont Valérian. He'd heard plenty about it during his months in Fresnes prison. At least his stay there wouldn't be for long.

About half an hour, he figured, even though the guards had said nothing when they herded him and the other prisoners into the truck. He glanced around at their faces. Some still held hope, some resignation, some anger. Two of the younger men, boys really, hunched over, their bodies trembling spasmodically from sobs. Not even the wind could blow away the smell of fear, the reek of sour sweat and urine.

The truck lurched and stopped, and guards immediately surrounded the truck. "Out!" one shouted. Slowly, the men at the back of the truck heaved themselves out. When it was his turn, Jake stumbled forward and lowered himself to the ground. A Nazi waved his rifle at him, and Jake clasped his hands behind his neck and followed the others into the courtyard.

The tiny hope that this was merely a transfer dissipated in the cold morning air. A row of Nazi riflemen stood at ease opposite the high courtyard wall.

Jake's bowels cramped. It didn't matter now that he'd spent the two months since his arrest preparing himself for this moment. It didn't matter that everyone he'd ever loved was dead, killed by the same monsters who were going to kill him. It didn't matter that he was a coward, that he'd run away from Germany, that he'd talked during torture, that he deserved to die.

Because now he wanted to live. And it was too late.

Michou removed the little porcelain box from Mémé Laure's bureau and carried it to her bedside table. Every night since Guy's escape, she'd made a ritual of listening to the BBC's *La France Parle aux Français* with Mémé Laure, hoping she'd hear his message letting her know he was safe in London. Every night so far she'd been disappointed. Maybe tonight would be different. She just knew he'd gotten out of France. If he hadn't, Lucien surely would have told her.

Gently, she lifted the lid and set it down on the lace doily. Philippe's miniature radio nestled inside the box, the one he'd built for her after the Germans had confiscated all the others. After Erich had taken her transceiver, she'd sworn there were no more radios in Château Bourdet. She'd been sorry to lie to him, but she'd had to.

She put the box down next to the lid and opened the drawer. Mémé Laure's embroidered and lace-trimmed handkerchiefs covered a small headset and wire plug. She pulled them from the drawer and attached them to the radio.

"It's almost time," Mémé Laure said. A spasm of coughing rattled her chest. She leaned back against her pillow after it subsided.

Frowning, Michou plugged in the radio. She wished there were some way to keep it warmer up here for Mémé Laure, but fuel was even scarcer this winter. In a couple of months there'd be the vine prunings to burn. Since they were green, they made lots of bad-smelling smoke, but they produced some heat at least. All she had now, though, were the briquettes she'd made from squeezing wet paper into little balls and letting them dry. Even though they hardly warmed the room, they made a cheerful-looking fire for a few minutes.

After she sat down in the chair next to the bed, Michou adjusted the headset over her ears, the motions coming automatically after all the months of transmissions to London. As unhappy as she'd been during much of that time, it seemed like a pleasant vacation compared to now. At least she'd known Guy and Philippe were all right, for the moment anyway. Erich had still been alive, and Lucien hadn't yet shown his suspicions about Jean-David.

She took a deep breath. The fumes of Mémé Laure's chest ointment filled her lungs, and her stomach turned. Would she be saying the same thing two months from now, grieving for some new loss? Mémé Laure wasn't at all well, and not knowing was better than finding out that Guy hadn't made it back to London or Philippe had been killed doing something brave and dumb. And what about Jean-David? How much longer would Lucien be content to hint?

She flipped the switch to stop the questions. The earphones vibrated static; then the BBC announcer's tinny voice rasped his nightly greeting. Michou's heart beat faster, as it always did when she first heard him—even if there was no message, it made her feel closer to Guy to know she was listening to someone in London.

She nodded to Mémé Laure and turned the tiny volume knob. *"Romeo embrasse Juliet,"* the announcer droned twice. Then: *"Les baudets habitent dans les boîtes aux lettres"* and *"Les grenouilles mangent les poulets."* The nonsense phrases went on for several minutes. She sighed. They seemed to get longer and sillier every night.

Then she gasped and held her breath as the announcer said, *"Le merchant du vin aime son petit chou."*

She grinned at Mémé Laure and ripped off the headset. "Listen," she said, putting it into her grandmother's outstretched hand. Michou jumped up and twirled around, hugging herself tightly.

Mémé Laure pressed one earphone against her ear. She smiled and nodded. "I think you're right," she said, handing back the headset. She laughed hoarsely. " 'The wine merchant loves his little cabbage.' He's quite the poet, your courageous young man."

Michou laughed, too, as she returned the headset and wire plug to the drawer. "I can't believe it," she said. "He's safe. He's really safe." She replaced the lid on the porcelain box and put it back on the bureau. Her smile faded. "Now, if there would just be some word about Philippe."

Mémé Laure coughed. "Sit with me a few minutes longer tonight, won't you, child?"

"Of course." Michou sat back down. "As long as you want."

Her breath rattling in her chest, Mémé Laure plucked at the coverlet. "I hope you have forgiven me," she said finally.

"Forgiven you? For what?" Michou pulled her eyebrows together.

"Catherine and Henri were going to wait until next summer to get married. I insisted they do it at Christmas." Mémé Laure paused, breathing heavily. "I know I'm a meddling old busybody, but I thought it best for everyone. I love your mother. I want to see her settled and happy before I die." She wagged her finger at Michou and peered over the top of her glasses. "And I love you. Don't take too long to tell me your news."

Michou's mouth fell open. "How did you know?" she asked, her voice soaring high.

"Child, child," Mémé Laure said, shaking her head. "You have every reason in the world to be worried to death, but the strangest little smile keeps popping up on your lips. And the way you keep smoothing your blouse across your belly, as if you're making sure everything is all right." She cleared her throat before she continued. "You turn green every time you walk in here and smell this awful stuff the doctor makes me use, *n'est-ce pas?*"

Michou nodded slowly. "I didn't want to bother you about it," she said. "There's already so much to worry about as it is."

"A baby is a joy, not a worry," Mémé Laure said, pushing her glasses back up on her nose. "Does Guy know?"

"I wasn't even sure myself when he left," Michou said. "Now there's no way to tell him."

"That's sad." Mémé Laure sighed. "I don't suppose your mother knows either?"

"I planned to tell you both after the wedding."

Mémé Laure raised her eyebrows. "For your mother, that's probably best."

Michou patted her hand. "But not for you. I know. It's impossible for me to keep a secret from you. You can still see through walls."

"That's true." Mémé Laure smiled, and her face creased with wrinkles.

"Now, do you forgive *me?*" Michou asked, returning her smile.

"Always, child." Mémé Laure's face suddenly sagged, and the glow left her eyes. "Your father would have, too, you know. He might have ranted for a little while, but he'd have forgiven you. He would have liked your young man."

Tears stung Michou's eyes. "I know," she whispered.

Mémé Laure sighed deeply and closed her eyes for a few seconds. "It's probably better that he's not here, though," she said. "The rumors would have been too much for him." She opened her eyes. "He'd have killed the first person who mentioned a German bastard."

"I know that, too," Michou said.

51

Guy put his hands on his knees and leaned forward. "How long do you think it will be, sir?" he asked. "Two weeks in London, and I'm already itching to be back."

Major Buckmaster stubbed out his cigarette in the ashtray on his desk, then steepled his hands under his chin and looked down his long nose. "Hard to tell. Months, maybe. At this point I have nothing firmer to offer you. You are too well known to the Gestapo for us to send you back in right away. Your presence would jeopardize any network you might come in contact with, and we can't have that."

"No, we can't have that." Guy made no effort to keep the sarcasm from his voice even though he knew what he was doing was stupid. Antagonize Buckmaster and he'd never get back. What was worse was that Buckmaster was absolutely right. He had no business endangering anyone for selfish reasons.

And that was essentially what it boiled down to. Selfish reasons. Oh, he wanted to fight the Nazis, of course. But even more, he wanted to know that Michou was all right. If Buckmaster knew what was going through his mind, he'd never let him return.

Guy stood up, his fist clenched. Knowing he was wrong didn't help much. "Well, I guess that's it, then," he said. "I'll just wait for you to get a hold of me. Sir."

He walked stiffly to the door. He paused, his hand on the knob. He might as well finish what he'd started and make a complete ass of himself.

He turned back to Buckmaster. "Still no word on Jacob Schweiger?"

Buckmaster rose and stepped out from behind his desk. He cleared his throat. "They tell me he has no family left," he said.

Guy nodded. "That's right, but we've been friends since our days at Cambridge."

Buckmaster crossed the room. "I'm damn sorry," he said. "He was a good agent."

"Was?" Guy swallowed as he repeated the word.

"He was arrested in Paris three months ago, executed last month."

"Oh, my God." Guy gripped the doorknob. "What happened?"

Buckmaster shook his head. "Apparently one arrest led to another, then to more after that. By the time the Gestapo finished, they'd wiped out almost the entire circuit. Schweiger was one of the last to get caught."

Guy squeezed his eyes shut and gritted his teeth. He and Jake had both known the risks, but it didn't help much to think about that now. Jake was dead. Tortured by the bloody Gestapo and then executed.

"Let me go back in, sir," he croaked.

"Absolutely not," Buckmaster said. "With your attitude, you wouldn't last three days. You're just going to have to be patient. Let this heal. Then we'll talk about it."

Guy spun on his heel and jerked the door open. Automatically, he scanned the hall to make sure it was empty, then stepped into it and pulled the door shut behind him with a loud bang. His shoes clattered as he strode down the marble-floored hall. Goddamn the Nazis to hell. Goddamn Buckmaster to hell. The butler approached him, and Guy waved him away. Goddamn the butler to hell.

He slammed the door on Orchard Court and headed for the Bond Street tube station. There had to be a way for him to get back to France. He'd sent a message via the BBC to let Michou know he was safe, but there wasn't a way for him to find out about her without going back. Months, Buckmaster had said. Bloody months.

He was still fuming when he emerged from the Green Park station fifteen minutes later. If he couldn't do anything about Michou, he could at least have a drink for Jake. He turned onto Berkeley Street. He'd avoided the Gay Nineties since his return two weeks ago, hadn't even had a drink, in fact. But there was nothing to keep him from getting absolutely pissed if he chose to.

Guy walked into the pub and took a deep breath. The familiar scent of stale beer and cigarette smoke brought memories rushing back to him. It seemed just days ago that he and Jake had sat at the table by the window, so sure of themselves, so pleased to be finally doing something. But it had been almost three years. And now here he was. Alone.

Jake was not coming back. Jake was dead.

Guy stepped up to the counter and ordered a whisky neat. When it arrived, he paid the bartender. "To Jake," he said, and gulped half the drink in one swallow. He was out of practice. The whisky seared his throat and burned his empty stomach. Resting his foot on the brass rail, he drained the rest and ordered another.

Ten minutes and three drinks later, he decided to move to a table. His fourth drink in his hand, he turned slowly away from the long mahogany bar. At the same moment the door swung open and a tall, red-haired man strode into the pub.

Stiffening, Guy stared at him. It was Ian Mapp, Jake's radio man. What the hell was he doing in London? What the bloody hell was he doing alive when Jake was dead? Guy slammed his glass down on the bar.

When Mapp recognized him, he grinned. "Well, hello, mate," he said. "Fancy meeting you here."

"I don't fancy it, you son of a bitch," Guy said. "Not at all. I suppose you know Jake is dead." He advanced a step toward Mapp.

"Almost ended up the same way myself," Mapp said. "Your Jerry friend gave me up to the Gestapo. Didn't even hold out for twenty-four hours."

Guy clenched his teeth and reached behind him for his whisky. "Then what are you doing here?" he asked.

"Got away, mate. They put me in a room on the third floor, and I climbed out the window. Almost broke my goddamn neck, but I got away."

"Too bad you *didn't* break your goddamn neck. Would've saved me the trouble." Guy held up his glass. "But first, let's drink to Jake." He threw the whisky in Mapp's face. "It's on me." He dropped the glass on the floor and swung. His fist smashed into Mapp's chin.

The loud crunch echoed in the sudden silence. Mapp fell backward against a chair and sent it crashing to the floor. He stuck his hand out, grabbed the table next to him, and shook his head. "You bastard!" he roared. "I'm going to kill you." His hands outstretched, he rushed toward Guy.

Guy tossed the chair next to him in front of Mapp. "You'll have to do it yourself, then," he said. "No Gestapo to do your dirty work for you this time."

Mapp kicked the chair aside. "With pleasure, mate," he said. He lunged at Guy.

Guy thrust his foot at Mapp's knees, then, as Mapp fell forward, clasped his hands and pounded the back of his neck. Mapp sprawled at his feet. "Get up!" Guy shouted. "I'm not finished with you yet."

Hands grabbed his arms and pulled him away from Mapp. "Yes, you are, old man," a familiar voice said.

Guy jerked away and turned around, bringing his bleeding fists up again. "What the—"

"Calm down," Charles White said, grinning at him. "Let's get out of here before he gets up or the bobbies nab you."

Guy lowered his fists. "Hello, Charles," he said. "I was just giving the bastard Jake's regards."

Charles nodded. "I heard. I called your father, and he said I might find you here." He put his arm around Guy's shoulders. "Come on," he said. "I'll buy you a drink at my club on St. James'. We've got a lot of talking to do."

Guy stared down at Mapp for a few seconds more before he let Charles steer him out of the pub. Once on the sidewalk, he stopped and pulled a handkerchief from his pocket. Exhaling loudly, he dabbed at the blood on his knuckles. He pocketed the handkerchief and turned to Charles. "Thanks," he said. "I'm ready for that talk."

Michou painted on the last stroke of the sticky reddish-brown liquid, then climbed onto the bench in front of her dressing-table mirror to inspect her legs. She hated the silly stuff, but it was better than nothing. Ordinarily, she wouldn't bother. But today was important to Maman, and she wanted everything to be perfect for her.

She turned each leg slowly. No bare spots. Good. She clambered down and paced the room a couple of times while she waited for it to dry. At least she wouldn't have to worry about runs or snags. She stopped in front of her bed, picked up her slip, and pulled it on over her head. As she snugged it over her hips, she sighed. Thank God it still fit. Except for larger breasts, she wasn't showing much yet.

She stepped into her new maroon wool dress and pulled it up. Maman had had the material since before the occupation, and Berthe had made the dress for her. Just as she finished buttoning the last of the tiny wool-covered buttons, someone knocked at the door. "Who is it?" she called, peering into the mirror and smoothing the lace collar so that it lay flat across her shoulders and chest.

"Berthe."

Michou smiled. "Come in," she said. "It's not locked."

Berthe stepped into the room and held out her arms. "Now we're really going to be sisters," she said. She hugged Michou. "I'm so happy." Her cheeks were flushed, and her blue eyes glowed.

Michou held her at arm's length. "You look wonderful," she said. "Blue is such a good color for you. And I love your dress."

Berthe grinned and twirled. The full skirt flared out from her waist. "Paul does, too. He said a dress like this calls for dancing." She clasped her hands in front of her. "He likes me, Michou. He really likes me."

"Of course he does, silly," Michou said. "He's smart. And nice, too. Papa always said he had the makings of a good *maître de chai*."

"He doesn't even mind about Daniel." Berthe's smile faded. "And I told Father, Michou. I told him about Daniel."

Michou widened her eyes. "What did he say?" she asked.

"That it would have saved him a lot of grief if I'd told him long ago. And he was proud of me for being so strong. And how much he loved me and Daniel and how much he was going to miss seeing us every day while he stayed at Château

Bourdet." Berthe grabbed Michou's hands and squeezed them. "The only thing he was angry about was that I hadn't trusted him. And that made him more sad than angry, he said."

"I'm so glad you told him," Michou said, returning the squeeze, then dropping Berthe's hand and walking to her dressing table. She picked up her brush and turned back around. "Now Lucien can go to hell."

Berthe rolled her eyes. "He's still my brother, and I suppose I'll always love him. But he's mean and sneaky and selfish. I've run out of excuses for him. And I haven't even told him yet that Father knows."

"Why bother? He'll just start looking for something new to threaten you with." Michou tugged the brush through her curls.

"I know," Berthe said. She put out her hand. "Here. Let me do that for you."

"Gladly." Michou handed her the brush. "What made you change your mind? About Lucien, I mean. You never believed anything I ever said about him."

Berthe wrapped a strand of Michou's hair around her hand and eased the brush through it. She raised her eyebrows and sighed. "I don't know what really happed at L'Hostellerie last September. Both Father and Lucien refuse to talk about it to me, but I've heard all sorts of whispers and rumors. And Father has been even shorter than usual with Lucien since then. One time I overheard him say to Lucien it was too bad parents had only the power to give life to their children, that no matter how evil that child turned out to be, a parent was powerless to do anything about it after the child was grown." She dropped the strand and picked up another. "Lucien laughed and asked if that meant Father would like to kill him."

Berthe paused, the brush in midair. "Father said, yes, he would, that Lucien was a traitor and a murderer, and that he was sorry he'd ever been born to cause such grief to good people." She lowered the brush and ducked her head. "Then Father said he knew what had happened at L'Hostellerie, that the German soldier he'd killed had been a better friend to France than he was, and that he and Catherine were postponing their wedding because of it." Her voice was muffled. "Lucien just laughed again and said if they waited long enough, perhaps there'd be a double wedding. Then he left."

Michou took the brush from her hand and put it back on the dressing table. It was about time Berthe realized how awful Lucien was, no matter how painful it was for her. But she needed to know the truth so she could decide for herself, not just accept her father's judgment.

Michou put her arm around Berthe's waist. "Let's sit down," she said, steering her to the bed. "I was there when it happened. Nobody knows that except Lucien, your father, Maman, and Guy—and Chantal, but Lucien probably threatened to kill her if she mentioned it to anyone. Lucien killed Erich when Erich tried to save me from the Gestapo. Guy got away. The rumors about Lucien working for the Resistance aren't true."

Berthe nodded. "I know that," she said. "Otherwise Father wouldn't have been so upset. When Father said that part about Erich, somehow I knew I could tell him about Daniel's father. Not that he was a friend to France. He was like Lucien, a friend to himself. But I hadn't realized Father could be so fair." She sniffed and buried her head in Michou's shoulder. "I've been the unfair one all these years, blaming Father for hurting Lucien."

Michou hugged her. "It'll be all right," she said, smoothing Berthe's hair. "When the war is over, Lucien will be punished. He'll never bother you again."

Wiping the tears from her cheeks, Berthe looked up, her eyes round. "It's not me I'm worried about," she said. "I've suddenly realized what he meant about the double wedding. He meant *you.* He's planning to make *you* marry *him.* Has he been threatening to lead the Gestapo to you?"

Michou patted her hand. "Don't worry. I'll never marry him." She forced herself to chuckle. No point in upsetting Berthe any more than she already was. "I'm perfectly satisfied to be your stepsister. I don't need to be your sister-in-law, too." She stood. "Come on. We'd better get down there. Don't want to be late for our parents' wedding, do we?"

"Of course not." Berthe rose and linked her arm

through Michou's. "Lucien is planning to be here," she said.
"He told Father he wouldn't think of missing it." She took a
deep breath. Her smile wavered for a few seconds, then grew
firm. "I'm ready."

Michou's head buzzed as she walked arm in arm with
Berthe down the tower stairs to the door to the second floor.
She'd known for months that Lucien was building up to
something, but she'd never really expected that he'd have the
audacity to try to force her to marry him. Sleep with him,
maybe. He'd been after that for years. But *marry* him? Even
the thought was disgusting.

When she reached the main staircase, Michou paused at
the top. She swallowed back the bitter acid in her mouth and
made herself return Berthe's smile. This was Maman's day.
Not even Lucien was going to ruin it. She walked down the
stairs slowly, her arm still linked with Berthe's.

Lucien stared up at her from the bottom of the stairs.
"Father wants to see you, Berthe," he said when they
reached the entry hall. "He's in the green salon."

Michou narrowed her eyes. "If you spoil my mother's
wedding, I'll—"

Lucien laughed. "I wouldn't dream of it," he said. He
turned to Berthe and snarled. "Go. Alone. I've got something
to tell Michou about Philippe."

Berthe pulled her arm loose from Michou's. "Will you be
all right?" she asked, frowning.

Michou nodded. Her stomach churned. She hadn't
heard from Philippe in over two months. If Lucien knew
something about him, it had to be bad.

"Such touching concern," Lucien said sarcastically.
"She'll be fine."

Berthe shrugged, then hurried toward the salon. Lucien
waited until she disappeared. "Your precious brother was
arrested in October by the Bordeaux Gestapo. Thought you
might want to know."

Michou stepped back and braced herself against the
wall. "Oh, no," she whispered. "He's still alive?"

"Barely," Lucien said, sneering. "Damn fool refuses to
tell them his name. Wouldn't even tell me when I questioned
him. They practically electrocuted him, but he still wouldn't

tell. Wants to protect his precious family from reprisals the Gestapo inflict on relatives of maquisards. Seems to think I'm going to help him."

"*Mon Dieu,*" she gasped. First Jean-David, then Philippe, and now the rest of her family. Lucien could destroy them—*would* destroy them. "Are you?" The question squeezed out of her throat.

Lucien shrugged. "Depends on you," he said, leering at her. "I think we should get married. Don't you?"

Catherine opened her eyes and smiled up at Henri as he leaned over their bed. "I wish you didn't have to go," she said. She put her arms around his neck, pulled his face down to hers, and kissed him. She hadn't been so happy in a long time, but even this happiness was bittersweet. Their lives were so complicated. Sometimes all she wished for was a normal, quiet day where nothing reminded her of the war.

"I didn't mean to wake you." Henri slipped his arms around her. "I'll be back as soon as I can. If only it weren't for—"

She stopped his words with another kiss. There were too many "if onlys." If only it weren't for the gas rationing; if only Mémé Laure weren't so sick; if only Lucien and Michou could get along; if only the war were over. She didn't like to remember what the list used to include: if only Alexandre were still alive. She knew it was stupid, but both wishing it and not wishing it made her feel guilty.

Henri touched the tip of her nose with his finger, smiled into her eyes, then straightened. He picked his coat up from the chair and shrugged it on. "I'll try to be back before dinner," he said, "but don't wait for me." He slipped out the door, shutting it quietly behind him.

Catherine pushed herself up against the headboard. After more than twenty-five years in the same bedroom, it still felt strange to wake up in a new room. Henri had been so understanding about remaining at Château Bourdet while Mémé Laure was ill, but she couldn't possibly ask him to sleep in the bed she had shared with Alexandre. So she'd spent weeks redecorating one of the guest suites, searching through the attic for interesting pieces and bringing some of Henri's things from his house in Libourne. She was pleased with the result, but she knew both of them would be more comfortable when they lived somewhere without so many associations.

Muted voices from the hall were followed by a soft tap on the door, and she swung her legs over the edge of the bed. "Is that you, Michou?" she said. Usually, no one was up so early. She slipped into her peignoir.

"Yes, Maman."

"Well, come in."

Michou stepped into the room. She looked down at the floor. "I didn't want to bother you," she said, "but I saw Henri in the hall, and he said you were awake, so—"

Catherine put her arm around Michou's shoulders and drew her to the sofa beneath the windows. "Sit down," she said. "You never bother me." She narrowed her eyes and stared at Michou's face. Dark circles shadowed the child's eyes, and her cheeks were thin and pale. How long had she looked like that? Guilt spurted inside Catherine. She'd been so caught up in Henri and the wedding and Mémé Laure she hadn't even noticed that Michou wasn't well. "What's wrong?" she asked.

A funny little smile quivered Michou's lips. "I wanted to wait until after the wedding to tell you," she said. She took a deep breath. "I'm pregnant."

Catherine closed her eyes and leaned back against the sofa. Of course. How stupid of her not to recognize the signs. She sighed and opened her eyes. Another complication, another "if only." It certainly wasn't an opportune time to have a baby, but there wasn't much help for that now. And who was the father? She couldn't ask that. What really counted was Michou's well-being. "How do you feel about it?"

Michou stared at her hands for a moment. "I think I'm happy," she said finally, looking up into Catherine's eyes.

Catherine grasped Michou's hands. "That's all that matters," she said.

52

Michou screamed and sat up with a jerk. Her bedroom was still dark. She rubbed her eyes, flicked on the bedside lamp, and checked her watch. Five-thirty. Too late to go back to sleep even if she wanted to.

And she didn't. She'd just have that awful nightmare again. It had gotten worse since harvest—she never knew who to expect in the coffin anymore. Sometimes it was Alain, other times Marc, but most frequently lately, it had been Erich. And Lucien's face staring down at her through the water grew more menacing each time.

She shivered and wrapped the blankets around herself. *Mon Dieu*, she couldn't possibly marry him. But what was she going to do? She'd asked herself that at least a million times since Maman's wedding, and only one answer kept repeating itself: kill him.

But how? She couldn't just shoot him, no matter how easy it would be. She had her baby to consider, and her family. He had important German friends. They'd make sure she paid. And Maman and Henri—she couldn't do it to them.

She flung off the covers and jumped out of bed. She had to think of something soon. She stripped off her nightgown and threw it on the bed. Poison? Too complicated. She couldn't risk getting caught. Besides, she'd have to wait until after they were married. And that meant—

Even the thought of him touching her made her gag. Revolting. She clutched her stomach and ran to the basin. Vomit flew out of her mouth.

She wiped her lips and straightened. Leaning forward, she stared at herself in the mirror. Could she really be a murderer? Could she really kill someone? Three years ago she could have shot Lucien without thinking about it, but her anger was different now, more controlled.

Huge eyes rimmed by dark circles stared back at her. What would happen if she didn't? That's what she had to think about. If she refused to marry him, the least that could happen would be Philippe's death. *The least*. She couldn't refuse. She knew that, had known it since he'd told her about Philippe. And she knew him well enough to know that he would do what he said. What did their deaths mean to him? Nothing. No more than Daniel's or Alain's or Papa's or Erich's.

She bit her lip. So she couldn't refuse. But she couldn't marry him. She'd never let him touch her. Never. Not now, while she was carrying this baby. Not after it was born. Never.

A tiny drop of blood oozed from her lip, and she licked it off. Even if she married him, she had no guarantee he'd keep his word. He'd always been a liar. If it served his purpose, he'd find a way to get rid of Philippe no matter what he'd promised. She had no choice. She had to kill him. But how? She was right back at the beginning.

She turned away from the mirror, grabbed the work-clothes she'd left on the chair at the foot of the bed, and dressed quickly. After she stopped in the deserted kitchen for a chunk of yesterday's bread, she headed out to the *cuvier*. There were still six barrels of wine left to rack, six big barrels to scrub clean. And eight more casks to empty into the vat, then all those barrels to refill once this year's vintage was equalized. Cramming the last piece of bread into her mouth, she pushed open the door with her shoulder and strode toward the big cement vat. Every day the work got harder for her. She didn't know what she was going to do once the baby came.

She sighed as she fastened the hooks to both ends of the barrel at her feet. Maybe the war would be over by then. Everyone was talking about a big invasion, wondering when it was going to happen and where it was going to be. Of course, the maquis *were* getting bolder lately, executing Gestapo and Miliciens all over France as if they expected support from the Allies any day.

She walked to the crank by the door and turned it, grunting with the effort. Maybe if she just waited, one of them would kill Lucien for her. That would be nice. And tidy. But if it didn't happen soon, it wouldn't do her any good.

The barrel rose slowly from the floor until it was suspended in the air above the ladder leaning on the big vat. She looped a wire around the crank to fix it in place, then moved back again to the vat. A wave of black crashed inside her head, and she steadied herself against the vat until it passed. She couldn't risk climbing that ladder now, not when she was feeling this dizzy. What if she fell?

She hunched over and stumbled back to the *chai*. If she couldn't assemble this year's vintage, she could rack last year's. There was always something to do. As Mémé Laure had said, the grapes kept growing and wine kept fermenting. Even during the worst times of her life.

Lucien shivered and thrust his hands into his pocket. If it weren't for Sylvie, he wouldn't have to walk. He snorted, and a white cloud formed in front of his face. Of course if it hadn't been for Sylvie, he wouldn't have found out so easily about Fournier or the Jew brat living at Château Bourdet. Too bad Otto had walked in on them a couple of weeks ago. At least Lucien had been dressed. Ten minutes earlier and he would really have had something to complain about.

He snickered aloud as he turned onto the main road. He could tell that Otto had been plenty upset at the sight of a rumpled bed and Sylvie in her peignoir, but he hadn't done a damn thing. Not at the time anyway. He'd just shaken his hand, offered him a drink, said how sorry he was that Lucien had to be going so soon.

Lucien curled his lip. Then the swine had told Karl. And that was that—no more gasoline, no more anything. Lucien shrugged. Well, it was bound to happen anyway once Karl found out he was married to Michou. Still, Karl might have understood about that. He'd ranted on and on about loyalty and duty and Nazi brotherhood as if he'd been more angry about the slight to Otto than about any sort of betrayal of himself. Finally, he'd just told Lucien to stay clear—Colonel Zeller was a powerful man and it would be dangerous for Lucien to cross him again. There had actually been tears in

Karl's eyes when he told Lucien not to try to see him again.

Lucien hunched his shoulders and walked faster. He'd gotten used to Karl's little favors—he was going to miss them. But Karl himself—*hah!* The sniveling old maid could rot in hell. Jesus, he hated this weather. The gray fog was so low it suffocated him. He wanted to swing his arms and clear it all out of the way. On either side of the road, grotesquely twisted and bare grapevines crouched snarling at him like an army of trolls.

Lucien clenched his fists and shoved his hands more deeply into his pockets. Once he was married to Michou, everything was going to be all right again. She'd come around after she realized how much he loved her; she had to see that no one else could ever love her the way he did. Then she'd get Father and Berthe off his back. Not that their disgust bothered him much, anyway. Life was just easier when Berthe trembled with fear and Father acted guilty and apologetic.

He kicked a rock, and it bounced into the lower vineyard of Château Bourdet. Soon it would be his vineyard. As much as he wanted Michou, he wanted Château Bourdet more. He'd taken care of Alain—although that had been more luck than anything—and Alexandre. And now that Philippe was dead, there wasn't a thing to stand in his way. Of course, he couldn't tell Michou that Philippe had died during the bathtub torture last week. The son of a bitch had drowned himself on purpose while Lucien watched.

No, he couldn't tell her that until after they were married—even though he still had the little Jew as a backup. Blood was thicker than water, after all. She might just say, Fine, take the boy. He didn't want to risk that.

Lucien pushed open one side of the tall gate that marked the entrance to Château Bourdet and strode up the drive. He'd check the *chai* first—that way he wouldn't have to chance seeing the old man or Catherine. He snickered. Catherine Desroches, his stepmother. What a laugh. And his father living here at Château Bourdet. An even bigger laugh. Just until Madame Valette was well, he'd said. Catherine couldn't leave her now. Just until the old lady kicked off was more like it. Of course, once he and Michou were married, they'd have to leave no matter what shape the ancient one was in. If she was still alive, they could take her with them.

As he cut through the vineyard, he fingered the icy corkscrew in his pocket. Maybe he'd give it back to Michou as a wedding gift. She'd like that, he knew. He still remembered the expression on her face when her father had given it to her. That was why he'd taken it. He'd wanted something she prized. Once he had her, he wouldn't need it—or any of her other things, either.

He opened the *cuvier* door, stepped inside, and pulled it quickly shut behind him. At least it was a little warmer. He rubbed his hands together. The vat room smelled like newly fermented wine. A cask hung overhead, suspended from the pulley in the ceiling. It looked as if Michou was getting ready to assemble the new vintage in the big vat at the back of the room.

He stared up at the ceiling. Philippe might have been obnoxious, but he'd also been damn clever. As small as she was, Michou could do everything by herself with the block-and-tackle system he'd devised for the *cuvier* and *chai*. Of course, once they were married, she wouldn't want to. She'd be too busy taking care of him. Besides, even if she did want to keep making wine, he wouldn't let a wife of his do what everyone knew was a man's job. He was going to be the master of Château Bourdet. And his father and Catherine would not be welcome except as guests.

Lucien wove his way through the maze of barrels until he reached the door to the *chai*. He hoped she was here. He wanted to talk to her alone. He opened it. "Michou?" he called.

Michou stepped out from behind a row of casks, a long-handled brush in her hand. She curled her lip when she saw him. "What do you want?" she said.

"You," he said, narrowing his eyes. "Come out here."

She walked slowly toward him, gripping the brush like a sword.

"I want to know. Right now. And I've got another incentive to encourage you."

"Incentive?" She snorted. "Don't you mean *threat?*"

He shrugged. "Call it what you want. It doesn't matter to me. I have everything I need to expose your little Jean-David for what he is—a Jew. Not Jean-David Jourdan, but David Joseph Chapireau. And then he can join his mother in Jewish heaven, and you can join your brother in German prison." He smiled. "Your choice."

She snarled at him and shook her head. "I hate you, Lucien," she said. "You've never really believed that, have you?"

He shrugged again and stepped closer to her. "Doesn't matter. You'll change your mind. Women always do."

"I won't." She waved the brush at him, her knuckles white and her violet eyes narrowed into angry slits.

"Give me that," he said. He jerked the brush from her hand and laid it on the table across from the vat.

She sneered at him. "I'm pregnant. Still want to marry me?"

His mouth dropped open, and he stared at her for several seconds. "Who's the father?" he said finally.

"None of your business," she said. "If you go through with this, I'll swear it's yours. There will be no more, I'll make sure of that. Château Bourdet will never go to a child of yours."

He tapped his fingernails on the barrel next to him. How could he have missed it? The large breasts, the rounded belly that stuck out beneath the too-big shirts she always wore; even her cheeks were fuller. She was telling the truth, but what did it matter? He didn't want Château Bourdet for his children; he wanted it for himself. He smiled at her. "Maybe you'll miscarry again," he said.

Michou flinched. How could he know? She gritted her teeth. Sylvie. Of course. Now it all made sense. That's how he'd found out about Jean-David, too.

"But even if you don't, I don't care. Gives you another reason to get married, doesn't it? Your German bastard is going to need a father now that his is dead. I want your answer now."

Her eyes darted around the room. What was she going to do? Tell him yes. Buy time. The shadow from the barrel overhead swayed across the table in front of her, and she glanced up. Quickly, she ducked her head, then crossed her arms over her abdomen, over her baby. The barrel.

She stumbled forward, keeping her eyes on the floor. "Yes," she said. "I have it."

"Well?" He grabbed her arms.

"You can go to hell," she said, and she spat in his face.

He backed her to the table and pinned her against it. "I don't think you mean that," he said, wiping his cheek on his shoulder. "I meant what I said."

"I know," she said. "You're a murderer. I believe you. I saw you shoot Erich." Her voice rose. "I saw you push your own brother into the river. I saw you turn and walk away when Alain screamed for help. You knew he'd seen you, but you didn't know I was there."

His fingers dug into her arm. "You're insane," he hissed.

"No," she said. "You are." She gritted her teeth and struggled but he gripped her more tightly. "I tried to save them, but the current was too fast. If Papa hadn't come when he did, I'd have drowned, too. I tried to tell him what you'd done, but he wouldn't believe me. He told me I was never to talk about it again." She beat on his chest with her fists and screamed, "You turned in my father. You killed my brother. Kill me, too. I'll never—"

He slapped her, then grabbed her chin. "Shut up!" Lowering his head, he pressed his lips against hers and thrust his tongue into her mouth. His breath was sour and hot.

Gagging, she groped in back of her with her free hand. Where was the brush? Finally, her fingers touched it and she clutched it. Then with a sudden jerk upward, she smashed her knee into his groin.

He bent forward and grabbed his crotch. *"Merde!"* he yelled.

Michou grasped the long brush in both hands and slammed it down on his head. He sprawled at her feet. "That was for Alain," she said, flinging the brush toward the *cuvier* door. She leaned over and dragged him a couple of feet closer to the vat, then ran to the crank by the door.

"And this is for Papa." She jerked the loop off the handle.

Rope whirred through the pulley. The barrel crashed down on top of him, wood shattering and splintering. Blood and wine spewed against the vat.

53

&

It had been almost four hours since the little Lysander had taken off from the Tangmere airfield near the English coast. Guy stretched his cramped legs into the aisle, flexed them, then pulled them back under him again. At least he hadn't had to share what little space there was with anyone else. Still, he'd have been happy to sit on the wing if that had been the only way to get back to France.

He cracked his knuckles, then folded his arms across his chest. He wasn't nearly as nervous this time as he had been the first. All he wanted to do was get there. Four months without a word of Michou.

He shifted again in his seat. Thank God for Charles White. He'd taken Guy home after the brawl with Mapp, and they'd spent the evening sorting things out between them. Their friendship would never be the same as it had been before Lydia, but at least the antagonism was gone. And if it hadn't been for Charlie's connections, he'd still be sitting on his ass in London.

He ran his hand through his hair. Because Charlie's uncle and Major Buckmaster had gone to school together, Buckmaster had agreed to have lunch with Charlie and a friend of his at the Berkeley. When Buckmaster had arrived, he and Charlie had already been seated. Buckmaster nodded at him politely, then turned to Charlie for an introduction.

Guy chuckled. Buckmaster hadn't recognized him. The dyed hair, clipped mustache, and glasses changed him so much that even his father had done a double take the first time he saw him. Buckmaster's mouth had dropped open when Charles introduced his good friend Guy Chalmers.

It hadn't taken much to convince Buckmaster to send him back to France after that. Guy fingered the gold cuff links Buckmaster had given him as a parting gift. Good thing they suited his new cover as a black-market dealer.

"Start getting ready," the pilot called back to him. "We're almost there. I'm going to circle twice to check things out. As soon as I land, you jump out. I've got four coming on, and I want to be out of there in four minutes flat."

On the ground, three lights in an L-pattern shone in the moonlight and a fourth blinked on and off. Guy pulled his small suitcase from under the seat and tucked it under his arm. This time he carried his uniform with him. With victory in the air, it was an advantage to be a British officer.

He settled back in his seat. It was nice not to have to worry about a broken ankle or hiding a parachute. All he had to do was climb out of the airplane, hop on a bicycle, and make sure he got to the safe house without meeting any German patrols or Gestapo agents or Miliciens on the way. Easy.

Two minutes later, the plane bumped down on the field. It taxied back around, then shook as the brakes screeched on.

The pilot slid back the canopy. "Get out, and good luck," he said with a grin.

Guy jumped down. He nodded at the group waiting to get into the plane and smiled. They were in for a squash. Ducking his head, he ran across the rough ground to the edge of the field, where two more people waited.

A short man stepped forward as Guy approached. "I'm—"

"Roger!" Guy stuck out his hand and grinned. "Glad to see you again," he said. He turned away for a minute to watch the plane take off, then looked back at Roger, his hand still extended.

Roger frowned. "But—"

"Who am I?" Guy laughed. "You don't recognize me. Good. Still like the smell of plastic explosive?"

Roger narrowed his eyes. "Yves?"

Guy nodded. "The same."

Roger shook his hand while his companion sprinted to

the landing field to retrieve the flashlights. "Are you staying here?" he asked.

"Going to Bordeaux tomorrow." Guy paused as the other man returned with the lights. "When did you two start doing reception work?" he said to Roger. "Get tired of blowing things up?"

"You can thank your friend Claude," Roger said. "He scrambled everything. Of course, our young Philippe took care of him." He motioned toward a stand of trees. "Let's get out of here. I hid the bicycles over there."

Guy grabbed Roger's arm as they headed for the trees and pulled him behind his friend. "What happened to Philippe?" he whispered.

"They got him," Roger said. "Word has it that he died in prison while they were questioning him."

An icy stiffness hardened Guy's chest, and he sucked in his breath. "Christ," he muttered. "The poor kid." He walked a few more steps. "Hear anything about his family?" he asked, struggling to keep his voice normal.

"No," Roger said. "Didn't even know his last name."

Guy's breath exploded between his lips. Better nothing than something bad.

"Your bicycle." Roger pointed to a large racer leaning against the tree. "Hope you like it. We went to a lot of trouble to steal a good one."

Guy forced himself to smile. "You won't mind if I take it with me?" he said. He fastened his suitcase to the rear fender and then climbed onto the bicycle.

Roger shrugged. "It's yours." He pushed off. "This way," he said. "And quiet—but I shouldn't need to tell you that."

Guy gripped the handlebars and pedaled after Roger along the bumpy path. Moonlight sliced through the trees, silvering the mist that lay along the ground. The cold March wind smacked against his face.

Guy shivered. Tomorrow was the test. When the train stopped in Libourne, he and his new bicycle were getting off for a little side trip to L'Hostellerie in Saint-Émilion. A couple of comments to get the barmaid started and he'd have his information. He just hoped it would be what he wanted to hear. And that no one recognized him.

The .38 Walther in his inside jacket pocket thumped against his chest as the bicycle jolted over a rock. This time he wasn't going to throw it away. If anything had happened to Michou and Lucien Desroches was still alive, he'd need it.

Michou laid the hoe against the vine support and straightened. Groaning, she pressed both hands against the small of her back. She was so slow now. She was never going to finish. Papa had always plowed with the horses, but the Nazis had taken those long ago. And she was almost seven months pregnant—a poor substitute for a pair of horses.

So many more rows to go. She gazed over the vineyard, and someone bicycling up the road caught her eye. Maybe it was Berthe coming to see her. She waved as the figure bicycled through the gates, then frowned when she realized it couldn't be Berthe.

A tall man with black hair got off the bicycle and waved back at her. He propped the bicycle against the *cuvier* wall and walked toward her.

She shaded her eyes with her hand and squinted. Something about that long, arm-swinging stride looked familiar. But the dark hair, the glasses, the mustache? She shook her head. He walked like Guy. But it couldn't be him.

She gasped as he came closer, and the baby kicked her. It was. It *was*. Tears flooded her eyes. "Guy?" she whispered. She wanted to run to him, but her legs wouldn't move. What was he going to say when he saw her clearly, when he realized she was pregnant? She wrapped her arms across her belly and waited, clenching her teeth to keep them from chattering.

Guy loped to the end of the row, paused, then walked slowly toward her. His eyes moved up and down her body, and a muscle in the side of his face twitched. "My God, Michou," he said, holding out his arms. "I didn't know."

She wiped the tears from her cheek and ran into his arms. Flinging her arms around his neck, she buried her face against his chest. The coarse wool of his jacket scratched her cheek, but she didn't care. Guy was alive. He was in her arms. What she'd been praying for had finally come true.

He pulled her hands gently away from his neck and

stepped back. "Why didn't you tell me?" he asked, squeezing her hands.

"I didn't know for sure," she said. "And I didn't know I wasn't going to see you again for months and months. And by the time you told me you were leaving, the Gestapo was there and you were gone." She sniffed, ducked her head, and pulled one hand away to wipe her nose.

He put his hand under her chin and raised her head. "I love you," he said, staring down at her. He kissed her. "You know that, don't you?"

She nodded. The baby kicked again, and she grabbed Guy's hand and put it on her belly. "Feel it?"

He smiled. "How much longer?"

"June, I think. About two more months. I must have gotten pregnant one of the last times we were together." There—it was out. If he wanted to remember what else had happened their last night, it was his choice. She'd answer any question he asked.

She pulled away from him. "We still have *Boches* billeted here. Let's go into the *cuvier*."

He slipped his arm around her waist and matched his step to hers. "I heard about Erich," he said. "He was a good man even if he was on the other side. If it hadn't been for him, we'd probably both be dead now instead of looking forward to the birth of our first child." He opened the *cuvier* door for her, stepped in after her, and closed it.

There hadn't been a trace of irony in his voice. She glanced up at him. His eyebrows made a dark line over his nose, and his nostrils were pinched. She took a deep breath. If he had any suspicions, they didn't seem to matter to him. "It was awful," she said. "After you got away, Lucien emptied his gun on him." Her voice broke, and she paused before she continued. "He was just lying there." She clung to Guy and closed her eyes.

"Don't blame yourself," he said. "Erich made his own choices."

"But I let him think—"

He put his finger over her lips. "He was an intelligent man. It wasn't your fault." He hugged her against him. "Let's talk about something more pleasant," he said. "Like what happened to Lucien. I heard there was an accident."

"That's what everyone thinks."

He smiled down at her and nodded. "When I heard where it happened, I wondered. So poor Lucien got smashed by a barrel of wine. Was it a good year?"

She shrugged. "Who knows? It was the new vintage."

"And he was all alone when this *accident* occurred?"

"No," she said, shaking her head slowly. "But he was when Jacques came looking for him that afternoon and found him. He and Henri figured the weight of the barrel must have broken the crank." She frowned slightly. "It was odd. I thought his German friends would be upset, but they didn't seem to care. Major Stecher came out, asked me a few questions, then left. That was it. And poor Henri and Berthe—it was as if they'd expected it for a long time. They were more resigned than grief-stricken."

"What made you finally do it?" he asked softly.

She narrowed her eyes. "He told me the Gestapo had Philippe, but that Philippe wouldn't tell them his name because he didn't want anything to happen to us. And he said he knew all about Jean-David. He told me he'd tell the Nazis everything if I didn't marry him."

"So you killed him."

"I had to." Her eyes filled with hot tears, and they streaked down her cheeks. "I wanted to. He drowned Daniel and Alain. He killed Papa and Erich. He threatened my whole family."

Guy wiped her cheeks. "I'm glad you did it," he said. "The son of a bitch wouldn't have lived much longer, anyway. The maquisards are itching to set the Miliciens up like so many empty wine bottles on a fence and shoot them down. They hate them almost more than they hate the Germans."

"I know," she said. "But I couldn't afford to wait." She swallowed. "I still haven't found out anything else about Philippe, but at least Jean-David is safe."

A muscle in his jaw twitched, and he closed his eyes for a second. When he opened them, he pressed her hands between his. "Philippe is dead," he said. "He died in prison."

Michou pulled her hands away and walked toward the large vat at the back of the *cuvier*. "I knew it," she whispered. "They tortured him to death." She stopped and stared down at the red stains in front of the vat. "You bastard," she hissed. "You died too easily."

She stood there until Guy pulled her back into his arms. "I'm so sorry," he said. "I wish I could have done something. I feel so responsible."

"Stop it," she said. "If I've no reason to blame myself for Erich's death, you've none for Philippe's. He made his own choices, too, and he knew the risks."

"Just like us," Guy said. "But I will not risk our child." He turned her face up and pressed his lips against hers. "That's going to have to last us for a long, long time," he said. "Because I'm not coming back until the Germans are gone. I just hope it's before this little one is born."

Michou pulled his head down and kissed him again. "I know you're right," she said. "But it's hard to let you go again so soon."

54

Mémé Laure groaned, and Michou sat up, forcing her eyes open. Sickroom odors surrounded her. "I'm here, Mémé Laure," she said. "Do you want something?"

"Turn—on—the—light," Mémé Laure croaked.

Michou leaned forward and snapped on the bedside lamp.

Mémé Laure's eyes fluttered open, then closed again, as if the effort were more than she could bear. "Is that you, child?" she whispered. "You still haven't had that baby?"

"Not yet," Michou said. "I'm right beside you. May I get you some water?"

"No." Mémé Laure shook her head slightly. "Just talk to me. Tell me what's been happening."

Michou patted her head. It felt light and dry, ready to crumble, like a vine leaf after the harvest. "De Gaulle spoke on the radio last night. The Allies landed in Normandy yesterday."

Mémé Laure's lips turned up slightly at the corners. "Good," she said. "I'm glad I've lived long enough to see the beginning." A hoarse cough shook her body.

"Shhh," Michou said. "Don't try to talk."

Mémé Laure opened her eyes. "Don't shush me, child. I know I haven't got long. There are some things I want to say."

Michou sighed. "You've been saying that for the last three years," she said, adding a lilt of cheerfulness to her voice that she didn't feel. The doctor had said it would be a miracle if she made it through the spring. That miracle had happened. Another might be too much to hope for.

Mémé Laure shook her head. "This time I'm right," she gasped. "Want to see that baby of yours first, though."

"You will," Michou said. "You're even more stubborn than Papa."

"I'm proud of you, child." Mémé Laure paused to catch her breath. "I want you to know that. You've had a harder time of it than I did during the Great War." She hacked and cleared her throat. "But you've held up." She motioned Michou closer. "Help me sit up."

"But—"

Mémé Laure's hand fluttered impatiently against the coverlet.

"All right." Michou stood and leaned over her. She propped another pillow against the headboard, then put her hands under Mémé Laure's arms and pulled until her head rested against it.

"Good," Mémé Laure said. "I wanted to see you better." She patted the bed. "Sit here, child, the way you used to."

Michou sank back down on the bed and clasped Mémé Laure's hand between both of hers. "Is this better?"

Mémé Laure nodded. "You've grown up a lot since your father's death," she said, peering intently at Michou. "The bitterness is gone. But that determination is still there. And *you* talk about stubbornness." Her chuckle turned into a wheeze, and she fought to regain control of her breath. Her head sank back against the pillow, and she turned her face away. "Have you decided on a name for your baby?" she mumbled.

Michou bit her lip and squeezed her eyes shut to keep back the sudden tears. Mémé Laure asked her that same question every day and never remembered the answer. "I want to name it after Papa," Michou said. "And you."

"That pleases me, child," Mémé Laure said, slumping down in the bed again.

Michou waited until Mémé Laure's breathing quieted to soft wheezes, then removed the extra pillow from behind her and settled back into her chair. It was going to be another long night. She prayed that Mémé Laure would live through it, prayed she would live to see her great-grandchild.

*   *   *

Michou pushed herself up on her elbows again to get a better look. She couldn't stop looking at her. The baby lay wrapped in a little white blanket, only her red face and her fuzzy blond hair showing. Her nose was still a bit crooked and one ear had a funny crease, but she was the most beautiful child in the world. Alexandra Laure Valette. Someday, perhaps, Chalmers.

Michou lay back down and ran her hands over her pudding-soft belly. Now that everything was over, it was hard to believe that only a few hours ago it had been taut and hard and she'd been grunting and screaming with the worst pain she'd ever felt in her whole life. The cramps still came, but they were nothing now. She had her baby, and that was all that mattered.

The door creaked, and Maman poked her head in. "So you're awake," she said. "I thought you were going to get some sleep."

Michou smiled. "I tried," she said, "but I can't. I'm too excited. Did you tell Mémé Laure yet? What did she say?"

Maman stepped into the room and closed the door. "She couldn't talk," she said. "But she smiled. I'm sure she understood."

Michou took a deep breath as another cramp knotted her abdomen. "I'm so glad," she said.

The baby mewed. Maman gave the cradle a little push, and she quieted almost immediately. "Alexandra's tired, too," she said. "Both of you worked hard." She leaned over Michou and brushed her curls off her forehead. "Try to sleep," she said. "It's going to be a while before this little one knows the difference between night and day. You're going to need your strength."

Michou obediently closed her eyes, then popped them open again when a tap sounded at the door. "Come in," she said.

Berthe opened the door. "Cécile said you were in your old room. Are you feeling up to visitors?" she said. "Father called, and the boys and I hopped on our bicycles. I can hardly wait to see her."

Maman sighed and shrugged. "I give up," she said with a smile. "I'll leave you two alone. But"—she wagged her finger at Berthe—"don't you stay too long. And don't wake up that baby to look at her eyes. They're blue, just like all babies'."

Berthe laughed and held up her hand. "I promise." She crossed the room and peered into the cradle as Maman let herself out. "She's so beautiful," she said. "She's absolutely perfect." She turned back to Michou. "And you look wonderful. How do you feel?"

"You want the truth? As if I just gave birth to a full-grown tiger that clawed its way out. I hurt like hell." She grinned. "But I don't care a bit."

"I know," Berthe said. She tilted her head and stared at the cradle for a minute before she walked to the other side of the bed and sat down in the chair. A smile twitched at the corners of her lips. "I'm ready to do it again."

Michou pulled herself up. "Has Paul—"

"Proposed?" Berthe nodded and beamed. "But we're going to wait until we're liberated."

Michou held out her arms, and Berthe leaned forward and hugged her. "Congratulations," Michou said, kissing her cheeks. "I'm so happy. What a perfect day."

Berthe sat back down. "Father is going to give us Château LeClair-Figeac as a wedding present."

Michou clapped her hands. "And we'll be neighbors for the rest of our lives, and our children will be best friends—"

"Just like us." Berthe stood up and kissed Michou's cheek. "But I promised your mother not to tire you, and Jean-David is probably beside himself by now. I made the boys wait downstairs until I was sure you were all right. Do you want to see him?"

"Of course," Michou said. "He was excited?"

Berthe turned at the door, her hand on the knob. "He jumped up and down and wouldn't stop yelling for ten minutes after Father called. All the way out here he kept bragging to Daniel about his little sister until Daniel finally informed me he *had* to have one, too, just like Jean-David." She laughed. "I told him he was going to have to wait for a little while yet. I'll be right back." She closed the door softly.

Michou closed her eyes and laid her head back against the pillow. Everything was so wonderful. Except—

But she couldn't start that, couldn't spoil her happiness by wishing Papa and Philippe and Rachel could be here to share it with her. And Guy. If only he could be with her now. She'd gotten a note from him yesterday, so she knew he was all right, but she missed him. She wanted him here, to share her joy, to see their baby daughter.

Alexandra squalled, and Michou hefted herself forward and scooped her out of the cradle. She pulled the blanket away from her face and stared down at her. "Who are you going to look like, little one?" she whispered, rocking the baby in her arms. Guy? Or Erich?

The baby gazed back at her, then wrinkled her face and cried again.

"You don't care, do you?" Michou said. "Well, I don't either. You are the most important thing in the world to me, and all you want is something to eat." She pulled down the shoulder of her nightgown and brought the baby's open mouth to her nipple. "And you know just what to do about it."

The baby sucked, and Michou smiled down at her. Her first baby had died during a time of defeat. Alexandra had come into a world on the brink of triumph.

55

꧁

Sylvie wrapped the two pieces of jewelry Otto hadn't taken with him—the diamond earrings and brooch she'd been wearing at the time—in a black silk camisole and stuffed it into the side of the leather suitcase. She slammed down the lid and fastened the latches and buckles. She still couldn't believe he'd left her here. Alone. He'd loved her, believed what she'd said about Lucien, and never brought it up again except to tell her that Lucien had been killed in an accident at Château Bourdet. But one day last week, before the Allies liberated Bordeaux, she'd come back to their room in the Pavillon and all of his things and most of hers had been gone.

At least he hadn't taken her mink jacket. She picked it up off the bed and slung it over her shoulder. Hot as it was, she had no choice. It wouldn't fit in the suitcase, and she wouldn't leave it. She'd worked too hard for the damn thing, and now it was about all she had left. The measly little bit of money he'd left her was almost gone, and the Pavillon cost a fortune.

Sylvie crossed the room and looked out the window. Below, a mob filled the street, yelling as it drove a half-dressed man along in front of it. Perhaps if she hurried across the lobby, out the door, and squeezed in among all those people, she could get away without paying the rest of the bill. The clerk would never find her once she was out on the sidewalk.

Squaring her shoulders, she heaved the suitcase off the bed. Maybe it had been a mistake to take everything. The damn thing was going to pull her arm out of the socket before she'd gone two blocks. She set her teeth. No. She would not leave a thing. It was all hers.

The suitcase bumping her legs, she hobbled down the two flights of stairs in her high heels. When she reached the lobby, she hurried across the huge marble expanse to the front door. The clerk yelled at her, but she ignored him and slipped out to the front steps. In front of her, a horde of people screamed and pushed and waved little tricolors. She paused at the top of the stairs. This hadn't been such a good idea after all. She was going to get crushed.

Suddenly a voice in the crowd below shrieked, "German whore!" Another voice added, "Get her!"

Sylvie's mouth dropped open. She squeezed the suitcase handle even more tightly and backed up. Her fur slipped off her shoulder. She clutched at it with her other hand, then turned and pushed at the door with her hip.

But she was too late. Hands grabbed her, fingers poked and pinched her. Someone ripped the fur jacket from her hands, and it went flying into the mob. Another man wrenched the suitcase from her and kicked it down the stairs. It burst open at the bottom, and a crowd of women jerked her clothes out and danced around, holding her beautiful dresses up against themselves.

"I want her hat," a woman's voice screeched from the street.

"It's yours." The fat, smelly man who'd taken her jacket pulled the little white hat from her head and sailed it out over the crowd.

The mob cheered. "Her dress! Her dress! We want her dress!"

"No!" Sylvie clutched at herself. "You can't." Tears trickled down her cheeks. "Leave me alone!" she screamed.

The fat man slapped her. "Shut up, whore," he said. "You weren't ashamed to share your body with the *Boches*. Now you get to share it with us." He grasped the neck of her pink and white silk dress with both hands and jerked. The dress ripped down the back, and he threw it to the crowd.

Sylvie shuddered and crossed her arms in front of herself. What were they going to do to her now? Damn Otto. It was all his fault for not taking her with him.

A short man with wolflike blue eyes and a black beret

gripped her arm. "Come on, you," he said. "We're not through with you yet."

"Wait," the fat man said. He tore off her lacy underslip, then took a knife from his pocket.

"No!" Sylvie screamed. "Don't kill me. I'll do what you say. Don't kill me!"

"Shut up," Fatty said. He leered at her.

Sylvie sobbed. "Don't kill me," she whispered, clutching at him.

Fatty shook her hands off. "Hold her," he ordered the smaller man.

Wolf Eyes nodded and pinned her hands behind her back while Fatty sliced through her bra straps and panties. The crowd shrieked and applauded as her pink underclothes dropped to the ground and Fatty kicked them off the stairs.

"Now," Fatty shouted. "Now we're ready. Let's take her to the platform." The crowd roared its approval and divided to form a narrow pathway.

Sylvie pulled her arms away from Wolf Eyes and buried her face in her hands. If she ever found Otto again, she'd kill him. This was his fault. He never should have left her. She'd kill him for it.

Hands pushed her, and she stumbled down the stairs. They'd stripped her of everything but her high heels. The horrid smell of sweat and the hot August air pressed against her. She took her hands away from her face and lifted her chin as the crowd surged toward her. Let them look. She'd kick the first one who touched her.

They made room for her, shouting, "German whore! German whore!" She followed Fatty around the corner to a rickety platform in the middle of the street. On a chair in the center of it sat a naked woman with a baby in her arms. Her head was shaved bald, and long clumps of dark brown hair lay strewn about the platform. A man in a long white coat with a razor and a mirror in his hand stood in front of her.

Sylvie gasped. "Oh, no!" she whispered. Her hands flew to her hair, and she clutched it against her neck. Not her hair. Not her beautiful, soft hair. They couldn't. They *wouldn't*.

The barber jerked the woman to her feet and pointed to the ladder. As she descended with the baby in her arms, Sylvie swallowed back the bile flooding her mouth.

Wolf Eyes slapped her derrière. He winked at her. "You're next, mademoiselle." He pushed her toward the ladder leaning against the edge of the platform. "Up you go. We mustn't keep your hairdresser waiting."

Sylvie cringed away from the ladder. All around her, hundreds of faces leered and grinned. "Shave the whore!" someone shouted, and the rest of the crowd took up the chant. "Shave the whore!"

"If you don't go up by yourself, I'll drag you up," Wolf Eyes hissed in her ear. He gripped her arm and jerked her toward the ladder.

"Don't touch me!" Sylvie scrambled up the ladder, her heels slipping on the rungs. When she stepped on the platform and straightened, a loud whistle rang out from the back of the mob. Everyone laughed, and a shrill voice called, "Enjoy it now, dearie. No one is going to whistle at you for a long time to come."

The barber pushed her down onto the hard chair. He reached into his coat pocket and took out a tube of lipstick. While he drew a large, red swastika across her bare breasts, he grinned at her. "No extra charge for makeup today," he said. He put the lipstick back into his pocket and picked up the mirror and razor from the platform. "Would mademoiselle like to watch?" he said, handing her the mirror.

Sylvie dashed the mirror at his feet, then hunched forward, crossing her legs and arms.

He bent down and retrieved it. "Mademoiselle *will* watch," he said with a smirk. He put the mirror in her hand and brandished the razor. The crowd cheered again.

The razor scraped against her scalp, and long strands of golden-red hair brushed softly against her back and chest and fell to her feet. Sylvie clenched her jaw and stared at her beautiful hair lying on the platform. She would not cry. And she would *not* look in the mirror.

Finally, the awful rasping of the razor stopped. The barber shoved the mirror in front of her face. "Satisfied?" he said. "Good. Next customer." He pulled her out of the chair.

Hair stuck to the sweat on her back, and she tried to brush it off. Tears filled her eyes and coursed down her cheeks. "I hate you," she hissed at the barber. She scooted down the ladder.

He shrugged, then bowed. "Good day, mademoiselle," he said. "So glad to have been of service."

Fatty caught her arm as she stepped off the ladder. "You're not through yet," he said. "Time for the parade."

Sylvie ran her hand across her prickly scalp and sobbed openly now, unable to stop.

Shaking his head, Guy stood on the steps of the bank. It had been going on all morning, ever since the tricolor was hoisted over the Hôtel de Ville. Male collaborators without their pants or shoes and women stripped naked or clad only in their slips paraded through the streets of Bordeaux while the jeering crowds yelled insults at them. Guy had had more than enough, but it wasn't worth it to fight his way back to his room now. It was just easier to wait it out.

He lifted his peaked cap and swept his hair back with his other hand. God, it was hot. He settled the cap back on his head. The uniform he'd brought with him wasn't meant to be worn on a sweltering August day. Still, he was glad to have it; it accorded him some respect from the boisterous mob.

He raised his eyebrows as the crowd's next victim trudged around the corner. Even shaved bald, she was beautiful. Long, trim legs, high breasts streaked with a bright red swastika, a fuzzy triangle of reddish-blond hair between her legs. He squinted and frowned. Something about her looked familiar. He stared at her as the mob marched her past him.

Suddenly a joker in the crowd shouted, "Tell us your name, German cunt." The woman raised her head and looked around. "Yes, you, whore," someone else shouted. The fat man at the woman's side grabbed her arm and twisted it behind her back, and she mumbled something. "Louder," a man's voice roared. "Sylvie," she screamed as the fat man jerked her arm higher. "Sylvie de Bacqueville."

Guy slapped his hand against his forehead. Of course. Michou's cousin. He hadn't seen her since 1940, but he'd heard plenty about her. She'd been living in Bordeaux with a Nazi colonel. No wonder they'd stripped and shaved her. Why hadn't the little fool gotten out before?

"Don't you mean *de Vacheville,* stupid cow?" another voice taunted her. The crowd howled with laughter.

She probably deserved everything she got, but— Guy sighed and elbowed his way through the crowd. At the sight of his uniform, people made way for him. The group surrounding Sylvie quieted as he approached them.

"I'm Captain Guy Chalmers of the British army," he said. "I know this woman. I would like you to give her up to me." He held out his hand.

The fat man shrugged and pushed Sylvie at him. "She's yours," he said, leering. "Use the whore well."

Sylvie stared at him, her eyes huge. "Michou's friend," she whispered. She tried to smile, but her lips trembled and a deluge of tears, apparently not the first, streaked down her dirty face. "Oh, thank you."

Guy took off his jacket and put it over her heaving shoulders. "Come on," he said, grabbing her hand. "Let's get out of here."

The crowd parted, and he dragged her after him to the sidewalk, then edged along the buildings until he reached the corner. "This way," he shouted. "My room is about ten blocks from here. Do you think you can make it in those things?" He nodded at her ridiculous heels.

She wiped the tears from her face with his coat sleeve. "Of course." She sniffed. "Just don't let them get me again," she whined.

The crowd thinned as he hurried her down side streets to his rooming house. He didn't speak to her again until he'd escorted her safely past the bug-eyed concierge and into his room. He pulled a dingy sheet from his bed and handed it to her. "Wrap yourself in this," he said, turning his back.

A few seconds later she threw his jacket on the bed. "You can look now," she said.

He turned around. She'd draped the sheet so that it covered her head but exposed a generous amount of cleavage and one whole leg from her waist to her toes. "Bathroom's down the hall," he said. "I'll be back in an hour or so." He picked up his jacket and put it on.

"Where are you going?" she whined. "Please don't leave me alone after what I've been through."

"I've got to find you some clothes and a bicycle," he said. "I'm taking you to Château Bourdet."

"A bicycle?" She pouted. "I hate bicycles."

He rolled his eyes. "Maybe you'd prefer walking there?"

"Why can't I stay here with you?" she asked. The sheet slipped a little lower across her breasts.

"Because I'm not staying here," he said. "Although if you'd prefer, I'd be glad to let you use this room. Rent isn't up for another two weeks. I would suggest, though, that you not go out too often. Not unless you're ready for a repeat of today."

Sylvie flung herself on the bed. "I'll go with you," she said, glaring up at him.

He opened the door and stepped into the hall. "I thought you might," he said.

56

❧

"It's just around the next corner," Guy said. "You can make it that far." He took one hand from the handlebar and pointed toward the iron gates. "See?"

"Thank God," Sylvie gasped. "My legs are killing me. I hate this nasty old bicycle."

Guy put on his brakes, then rested both his feet on the ground while he waited for her to catch up. First her feet, then her back, and now her legs. She'd had something to complain about the whole way.

"I wish you hadn't bothered," Sylvie said, panting. "It might have been just as easy to stay in Bordeaux. Michou's just going to laugh and say, 'I told you so,' when she sees me. As if she's never had anything to do with a Nazi. I can hardly wait to see her German brat." She pulled up next to him, got off her bicycle, and let it crash to the ground. "I can't ride that thing any further."

His jaw set, Guy stared at her. Even now, the only person she could think about was herself. She'd hated the clothes he'd gotten for her, sent him out again for a piece of material so she could make a turban to cover her head, complained about his uncomfortable bed after he'd given it up to her and slept on the floor, refused to wear anything but her high heels. It had taken him twenty minutes to get her out of bed this morning; then all she could talk about for the next twenty was the ungodly hour.

"Fine," he said. "Walk, then." He pushed off. After what she'd said about Michou, he didn't give a damn what she did. She could walk all the way back to Bordeaux for all he cared.

"Wait!" she shrieked. "I'm coming with you. I can't go back. The sun's already going down."

Guy kept pedaling until he reached the gate. He'd already accepted that the baby might not be his, but either way, it was no one else's business. He was going to make that clear. Michou had suffered enough for him already. And although this little girl would never be able to take Tessie's place, she meant a new life to him. Nothing was going to tarnish that. Sylvie caught up with him as he opened the gate. "Why did you do that?" she whined.

"Look," he said, turning toward her. "I'm the father of Michou's baby. And we're getting married as soon as this war is over. That is, if she wants to." And if he came back, he added to himself. That was why he hadn't asked her yet and, he supposed, why she hadn't brought it up. She'd already lost one fiancé, and he'd seen what it had done to her. Even though she was a woman now and strong, he wanted to save her whatever pain and worry he could.

"You?" Sylvie's mouth dropped open. "But how—"

"It was dangerous, and we were careful," Guy said. "Not many people knew." He straddled the bicycle and pedaled down the drive without looking back.

When he reached the château, he leaned his bicycle against the tower and raced up the stairs. Michou had told him that she and the baby had moved back to her room. With any luck, she'd be there now. He wanted to see her alone.

He banged on her door. "Michou!" he called. "Are you in there?"

The door flew open, and she threw her arms around his neck. "It's about time," she said, kissing his cheeks, his lips, his neck. "We've been liberated for two whole days."

He laughed and scooped her off the ground and into his arms. "I love you," he said. He cradled her against his chest, then kissed her before he carried her to the bed. He laid her down and looked around the room. "Where's our daughter?" he said.

"With Maman." She pulled him down on top of her. "Do you want to go get her right now, or shall we wait for a little while?" She slid her hands under his shirt and ran her fingertips over his back.

He smiled down at her. "Let's wait a few minutes," he said. "I don't think she'll mind, do you?"

Michou bit her lip and glanced sideways at Guy. He rocked back and forth in the chair next to her, Alexandra in his arms. Only three days, and he had to leave already. The war wasn't over yet for him, he'd explained, and she understood, but she hated it anyway. Still, there was no point in making him feel any worse, and that's all that would happen if she made a fuss. He hadn't mentioned anything about marriage, but she had a pretty good idea why.

She stood up and walked to the piano. Well, it didn't matter. Married or not, engaged or not, her feelings for him were the same, and if he were killed, her grief wouldn't be any different. It was what made *him* feel best that counted. All she wanted was for him to come back to her. Her fingers drifted over the keys, and she picked out the sad little lullaby Maman had taught her years ago.

Alexandra turned her head toward the piano. "She likes it," Guy said. "She's going to be a great musician." He rose and carried the baby to her. "She keeps nuzzling my chest. Do you think she's hungry again?"

Michou held out her arms, and he gingerly placed the baby into them. Alexandra immediately butted her head against Michou's breast. "Looks like it," she said. She sat back down on the sofa and lifted her blouse.

The baby latched on to her nipple and sucked, and Michou made herself smile up at Guy. "We'll be all right," she said. "We'll miss you, but we'll be fine."

He lowered himself onto the sofa next to her and put his arm around her shoulder. "I know," he said. "My brave French lover. You've survived everything so far."

She leaned her head against his chest and stared down at Alexandra. There had been so much death at Château Bourdet. Her heart still ached from the horror of Philippe's murder. She'd had to fight violence with violence, and she'd cared for her enemy. Mémé Laure had been right about the bitterness: it didn't help. It wouldn't bring back Philippe or Papa or Marc or Erich. But at least her sorrow over Mémé Laure's death was pure. No one had been to blame, and she'd lived long enough to hold Alexandra Laure in her arms.

She sighed and looked up at Guy. He didn't want to leave any more than she wanted him to. "Don't you think it's—"

Sylvie rushed into the salon, her face white and her lip trembling. "They're here," she shouted. "Do something." Tears bubbled out of her eyes. "Don't let them get me again." She ran to the window overlooking the drive.

Guy got up. "What are you talking about?" he asked, frowning. He rolled his eyes at Michou.

Sylvie pointed out the window. "Look!"

He strode to the window and looked out. "I don't think it's you they want this time," he said. "I doubt they even know you're here. You stay inside." He turned back to Michou. "Come on. We're going to take care of this now."

After she pulled the baby off her nipple, she handed her up to Guy. She tucked in her blouse and put her arm through his. Her heart thudded, but she kept her voice calm. Ever since she'd heard about what Sylvie had gone through, she'd been expecting this. "I'm ready," she said.

By the time she stepped out the front door with Guy and the baby, the mob had reached the gates. "German whore! German bastard!" her neighbors shouted as they marched up the drive.

Guy moved to the step below her and stared at them. The chant broke down to a confused murmur. "She's a collabo," a man at the back shouted. "Give her to us. Her child is a German bastard."

"Do you mean this child?" Guy held out the baby.

"If it's hers, it's the one," the man yelled.

"This *is* her child," Guy said. "This is also *my* child."

The crowd murmured, and several people at the front edged backward.

"Some of you may know me as Guy Fournier," he said. "That was my cover identity. My name is Guy Chalmers, and I'm a captain in the British army. You might take a moment to notice the uniform I'm wearing." He pointed back at Michou. "This woman you accuse of collaboration has been more than my lover. She has risked her life to hide Allied airmen, send wireless messages to London, and act as my courier. How many of you have done as much?"

Michou stepped down beside him. "Go home," she said. "There's been enough hatred. You're my neighbors and my friends. I forgive you all."

Silently, the crowd turned around and trudged back down the drive. Only one woman remained in front of the stairs. "Berthe told me I was being stupid," Gabrielle said. "I didn't listen to her. I'm so sorry, Michou." Her eyes glittered with tears.

Michou looked up at Guy, then ran down the steps. She hugged Gabrielle. "It's over," she said. "We'll never talk about it again."

Gabrielle sniffled and nodded, then turned away and stumbled after the rest.

Michou stared at her as she caught up with the mob. Then she climbed the steps and stood beside Guy.

He handed Alexandra back to her. "I doubt you'll have any more problems with them." He shaded his eyes with his hand, watching the last of them file out through the gate.

Michou kissed the baby on her fat cheeks and smoothed back the thatch of unruly hair. She didn't want to look at him.

"Michou?"

Her face buried in the baby's soft hair, she inhaled her sweet milky aroma. Why didn't he just go now? It would be easier for both of them.

"I love you."

She squeezed Alexandra, who squeaked in protest and flailed her arms wildly.

He laughed. "Here," he said, and held out his arms. "Give me that baby again before you smother her."

"She's all right," Michou said, but she placed the baby in his outstretched arms. She liked seeing him hold Alexandra, but it was hard. What if he didn't come back? The war wasn't over yet, even though Bordeaux was free. What if he never held her or the baby again? She'd already lost so much—what if she lost him, too?

He rocked the little girl back and forth, and her yowls gradually faded. "I love you, too," he said to the baby. "I love you, little Alexandra Laure Chalmers."

Alexandra swiped at his nose, and Michou made herself laugh.

"You're just like your mother—beautiful and feisty," he

told the baby. "I hope this war is over before you're too old to sit on your papa's lap."

The door clicked behind them. "What are you two doing to my grandchild? I could hear her squawking from my studio." Maman stepped between them and, smiling at Guy, lifted Alexandra from his arms. "Let me take her in and give her a bath."

He kissed Maman on both cheeks. "Good-bye," he said, opening the door for her. "Take care of them for me."

"Thank you," Maman said. "For everything. I saw what you just did. Be careful and come back." The door swung shut behind her.

Michou stiffened her arms and clenched her fists. She would not cry, could not send Guy off with a memory of his brave French lover in tears. She wanted him, but if he didn't come back, she'd survive.

He pulled her into his arms and kissed the top of her head. *"Au revoir,"* he said, forcing her chin up and looking into her eyes. He covered her mouth with his and tightened his arms around her.

Blinking back the tears stinging her eyes, Michou returned his kiss. *"Au revoir,"* she said, and then he was walking away, mounting his bicycle, riding through the gate. She stood motionless at the top of the stairs until he was a tiny brown speck against the brilliant green of the vines.

The vines. She pulled back her shoulders and walked slowly down the steps. Despite everything, the grapes were thriving. Maybe *this* vintage would be a great one.

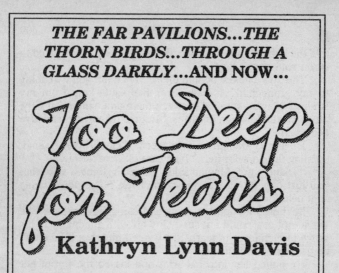